BOZEMAN PAYMASTER

BOZEMAN PAYMASTER

A TALE OF THE FETTERMAN MASSACRE

ROBERT LEE MURPHY

FIVE STAR
A part of Gale, a Cengage Company

LIBRARY OF CONGRESS CATALOGING-IN-PUBLICATION DATA

Names: Murphy, Robert Lee, author, cartographer. | Mignard,
    Phyllis, cartographer.
Title: Bozeman paymaster : a tale of the Fetterman Massacre /
    Robert Lee Murphy ; [Maps: Robert Lee Murphy, Phyllis Mig-
    nard].
Description: First edition. Regular print. | Waterville, Maine :
    Five Star, a part of Gale, a Cengage Company, [2022] | Identi-
    fiers: LCCN 2021056234 | ISBN 9781432892999 (hardcover)
Classification: LCC PS3613.U7543 B69 2022 | DDC 813/.6—dc23
LC record available at https://lccn.loc.gov/2021056234

First Edition. First Printing: June 2022
Find us on Facebook—https://www.facebook.com/FiveStarCengage
Visit our website—http://www.gale.cengage.com/fivestar
Contact Five Star Publishing at FiveStar@cengage.com

Printed in Mexico
Print Number: 01   Print Year: 2022

For Barbara Murphy

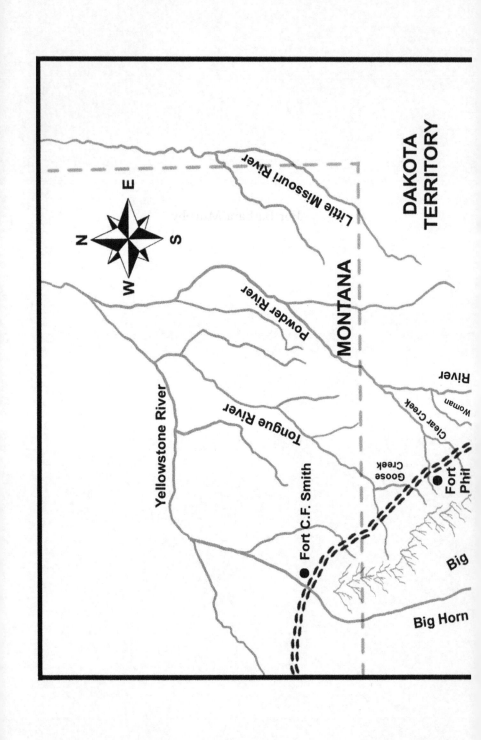

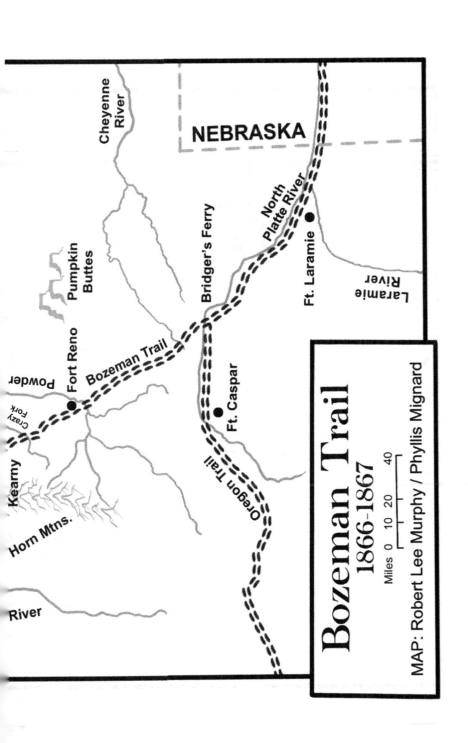

Cheyenne River

NEBRASKA

Pumpkin Buttes

Bridger's Ferry

North Platte River

Ft. Laramie

Laramie River

Fort Reno

Bozeman Trail

Powder

Crazy Fork

Kearny

Ft. Caspar

Oregon Trail

Horn Mtns.

River

Bozeman Trail
1866-1867

Miles 0 10 20 40

MAP: Robert Lee Murphy / Phyllis Mignard

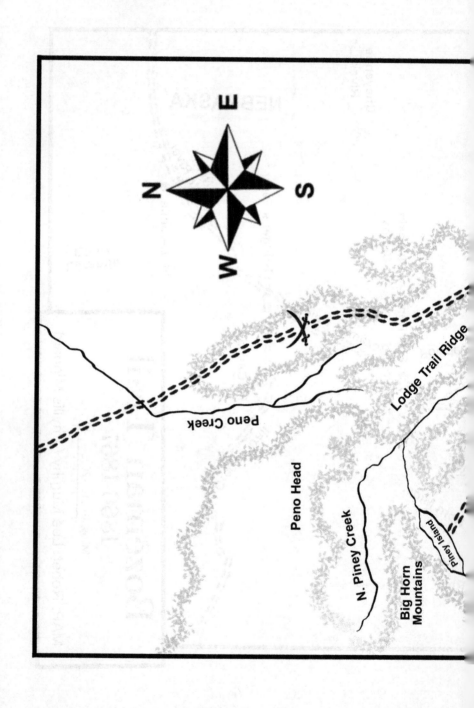

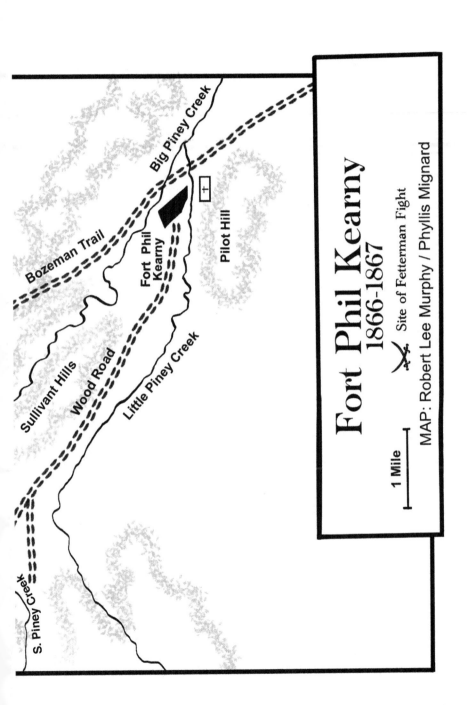

Bozeman Trail

Big Piney Creek

Sullivant Hills

Wood Road

Fort Phil Kearny

Little Piney Creek

Pilot Hill

S. Piney Creek

Fort Phil Kearny
1866-1867

Site of Fetterman Fight

1 Mile

MAP: Robert Lee Murphy / Phyllis Mignard

ACKNOWLEDGEMENTS

Thomas B. Hamilton, U.S. Army Garrison West Point, answered questions about the service requirements of officers following the Civil War. Bob McConnell, Curator, U.S. Army Finance Corps Museum, provided information about difficulties faced by paymasters during the Indian Wars. The late Sandra Lowry, Librarian, Fort Laramie National Historic Site, conducted research of Fort Laramie's records concerning Major Henry Almstedt and other paymasters who served along the Bozeman Trail. Thomas M. Baker, Superintendent, Fort Laramie National Historic Site, answered questions about life and service at forts along the Bozeman Trail. Jeff Wilson, Fort Phil Kearny State Historic Site, provided back issues of *Lookout,* the newsletter of the Fort Phil Kearny/Bozeman Trail Association. Misty Stoll, Superintendent, Fort Phil Kearny State Historic Site, advised me on traveling the unpaved roads that follow the old Bozeman Trail. When I got stuck in a mudhole at Fort Reno, local rancher Joe towed me out. Dr. Thomas Peters confirmed a frozen body smells bad and answered questions about wounds created by arrows. Dr. Kurt Samlaska explained what happens when an arrowhead breaks a clavicle. Dr. Allen Rhodes, a Wyoming native, recommended sites for me to visit along the Bozeman Trail. Michael Zimmer, fellow Western Writers of America member, advised me on loading a Colt .44-caliber army revolver. The Henderson Public Libraries obtained obscure reference texts through the inter-library loan program.

Acknowledgements

Members of Anthem Authors critiqued this work as I wrote it. I extend special appreciation to Phyllis Mignard, my mapmaker. Hazel Rumney, evaluation and developmental coordinator for Five Star Publishing, did her usual excellent job in cleaning up the manuscript to prepare it for publication. Thanks to Erin Bealmear and Cathy Kulka for providing the copy editing. I thank my wife, Barbara, for her understanding.

INTRODUCTION

The Fetterman Massacre occurred on December 21, 1866, on a desolate stretch of the Bozeman Trail, near Fort Phil Kearny, in what is now Wyoming. That day, the United States Army suffered its worst defeat at the hands of American Indians until Custer's Last Stand a decade later. No soldiers survived to describe the battle.

This account of Red Cloud's War is presented through the eyes of a young white man who was impacted significantly by the events. This novel does not apologize for wrongs now recognized as having been done to Native Americans during the years of westward expansion in the nineteenth century. This story presents the conflict as perceived by those people who struggled to survive while striving to achieve the objectives of Manifest Destiny.

Apart from the fictional involvement of the Knights of the Golden Circle, the events in this book happened as described. The historical personages presented performed their roles as written.

The following are fictional characters:

Zachary Taylor Wakefield, paymaster's clerk
Duggan Maguire, former Confederate soldier
Kathleen Muriel O'Toole, schoolteacher
Katy's family members

Brandon Hollister, Katy's fiancé
Megan Hollister, Katy's friend
Megan's family members
Sergeant Marley
Private Franz Stroebel
Arapaho Chief Running Bear
Major Armond MacFadden Bonnet, paymaster

Although Major Bonnet is fictional, he is based upon a real paymaster, Major Henry Almstedt. I mean no disrespect to Major Almstedt, but I needed the paymaster to be places and do things I could not substantiate as factual. The method and timing of paying troops along the Bozeman Trail is accurate.

Several unnamed fictional characters appear, most notably the former Confederate member of the Knights of the Golden Circle, an associate of Duggan Maguire.

The names of Zach's mules and the paymaster's horse are fictional. All other animals' names are historical.

CHAPTER 1

"Red Cloud's mad!" I leaned over the railing to get a better look at the throng of Indians gathered below on Fort Laramie's barren parade ground.

"He may have good reason, Zach." Major Bonnet, the paymaster, stood beside me on the second-floor balcony of Old Bedlam. The building served as the fort's headquarters and bachelor officer quarters.

Red Cloud had jumped up from where he had been squatting on the ground among his companions. He shook a fist in the air and shouted at the peace commissioners concealed from my view beneath a bower of cottonwood saplings. The temporary shelter sat in the southwest corner of the parade ground to shade the officers and civilians of the commission from the blazing sun.

"Great Father sends presents and wants new road," Red Cloud exclaimed, "but White Eagle goes with soldiers to steal road before Indian says yes or no!" The Indian's English, while not perfect, was certainly understandable.

The "White Eagle" to whom Red Cloud referred was Colonel Henry B. Carrington, commanding officer of the Eighteenth Infantry. The spread-eagle emblem on his shoulder boards provided the name. The colonel had arrived yesterday with seven hundred soldiers now camped four miles from the fort. Carrington was headed north with two hundred and sixty men of the Second Battalion of his regiment to build forts along the

15

Bozeman Trail to protect immigrants flooding up the new road to the Montana goldfields. The other two battalions of the Eighteenth would be spread out along the Oregon Trail across Dakota Territory and into Utah, with some units stationed in Colorado Territory.

"For not being a chief," I said, "Red Cloud certainly dominates the others."

"He's getting them stirred up," the paymaster said.

With his outburst, the fierce war leader of the Oglala band generated a chorus of grunts from the Indian crowd. What started as low-level grumbling soon escalated into a roar of discontent. Red Cloud turned away from the bower and berated fellow Indian leaders arrayed beside him.

"What's he saying, Major?" My boss understood the Sioux language.

"He's lecturing them to stand with him in defending Absaraka from the encroachment of the white man. He says he would rather die than give up their hunting grounds."

Absaraka was a Crow Indian word for the Powder River country adjacent to the Big Horn Mountains. The land was home to the largest buffalo herd in the northern plains.

The commissioners emerged from the bower, the meeting adjourning for the afternoon. The first to appear on the dirt road in front of Old Bedlam was Colonel Carrington. He trailed a finger down an aquiline nose, then tugged on his dark, Vandyke beard. With his other hand he returned his broad-brimmed campaign hat to his head, concealing his sloping forehead and shoulder-length black hair. He strode through the dust toward a mule-drawn, Rucker-pattern ambulance parked below us in what little shade existed at one corner of the building.

"Henry!" A woman's shrill voice called from the front seat of the ambulance. Her bonneted head thrust forward from the shadow of the canvas cover, and a warning finger pointed beyond the colonel. I recognized Mrs. Margaret Carrington. I had met the Carringtons earlier at Fort Kearny, Nebraska, on my trip west with Major Bonnet.

Colonel Carrington glanced over his shoulder, bringing a hand to rest on the butt of a pistol in a flapped holster on his hip. He did not slow his pace.

Red Cloud rapidly closed the distance from the parade ground to where Carrington approached the ambulance. The war leader clutched a large knife tucked into a belt around his waist.

Carrington reached the ambulance and took the reins of a thoroughbred saddle horse from an orderly. The colonel and Red Cloud glared at each other as the latter stalked past.

"Henry," Mrs. Carrington said, "I thought he was going to assault you."

Standing on the balcony above the ambulance, Major Bonnet and I were close enough to overhear the colonel reassure his wife everything was fine. He told her the peace commissioners assured him a treaty would be signed the next day.

"Come, Zach," Major Bonnet said, "I need to speak to the colonel. This may be my best chance."

The major walked ahead of me along the wooden-floored balcony to a flight of steps descending to the ground. With each step, he swung the wooden portion of his left leg forward with a purposeful jerk of his hip. He moved surprisingly quickly for wearing an artificial limb.

The side curtains of the ambulance were rolled up, and I saw two other women sitting in the rear.

"Colonel Carrington." Major Bonnet came to attention and saluted. "A word, if I might, sir?"

Carrington had lifted a foot into a stirrup in preparation for mounting but removed it and stood beside his horse. "Certainly,

17

Major." He returned the salute.

"Sir, you remember my clerk, Zachary Wakefield?"

The major motioned to where I stood nearby. No longer a soldier, I didn't salute, but I did stand at attention.

"Yes," the colonel said, "we've met."

"Sir," Major Bonnet said, "the payroll cash is not here. I'm not sure when it will arrive. I receive conflicting telegrams from headquarters. One day I'm told the pay chests are departing Omaha, the next day I'm told they are not."

"It's been four months since the troops were paid, Major. Why this delay?"

"I don't know, sir. When I left headquarters in March, General Cooke assured me the payroll would be sent out immediately. I'm sorry, sir."

Brigadier General Philip St. George Cooke commanded the Department of the Platte with headquarters in Omaha, Nebraska. That was where I had responded to a newspaper advertisement for a paymaster clerk. Major Armond Bonnet hired me because I had worked for my father handling money in his hardware store. Another factor had also weighed in my favor. During the recent war, I drove a Rucker ambulance, the vehicle assigned to a paymaster.

"No need to apologize about confusing instructions from headquarters, Major," Carrington said. "I receive them myself. I asked permission to stay here until the peace commission concludes. Omaha orders, however, direct me to proceed north no later than June seventeenth, eighteen sixty-six—tomorrow. It would be nice to wait for the arrival of the payroll and, more importantly, the arrival of ammunition and food. General Cooke informed me there was adequate ammunition here, but when I requisitioned ten thousand rounds this morning, I was issued one thousand. They claimed even that cut Fort Laramie's supply short. The food provided is hardly worth taking. The bacon is rancid, the flour moldy, and the hardtack infested with weevils."

"I'll follow you north as soon as I receive the pay chests, Colonel," Major Bonnet said. "I have to pay the troops at Fort Reno. Maybe I can catch up with you there."

"Good. Now, if you'll excuse me, Major, I must get back to my encampment."

"Have a safe journey north, Colonel," Major Bonnet said.

"After the peace treaty is signed tomorrow," the colonel said, "I don't anticipate any problems. General Sherman is of the opinion we will encounter no difficulties. Otherwise, why would he have encouraged us to bring our wives along?"

CHAPTER 2

Wednesday morning, June 20, Major Bonnet came out of his quarters, located on the second floor of Old Bedlam, and joined me on the balcony overlooking the parade ground. Streaks of white added highlights to the brown of his neatly trimmed beard and short-cut hair. He'd not told me his age, and I would never ask. I guessed him to be about forty. He settled a gold-braided, black slouch hat on his head and buttoned his blue uniform frock coat over a gray, collarless shirt. The gold leaves on the jacket's green shoulder boards identified him as a major in the Pay Department. Gold cord along the seams of his sky-blue trousers also marked him as an officer.

My trousers were the same color, more faded to be sure, and they bore no gold cord. My pants were left over from my service as a private a year ago. They were wearing thin in the seat and the knees, but they were still serviceable. I didn't want to waste money on a new pair. I had spent two dollars in Omaha for two checkered, red and black, wool shirts. They were too hot for comfort in this weather, but they were all I had.

Major Bonnet packed a briar pipe with tobacco, then returned the leather pouch to a jacket pocket. He struck a lucifer match against the porch railing and coaxed a trickle of smoke from the bowl. He used the blackened tip of the little finger on his left hand to fiddle the dollop in the pipe's bowl.

A telegram from Fort Sedgwick, a hundred sixty miles south of Fort Laramie, had informed the major that the pay chests had arrived there from Omaha. The message advised the chests would be sent forward with the next wagon train.

We were watching such a wagon train approach the fort along the dirt road that ran along the west bank of the Laramie River. A foot bridge crossed the river next to the fort and provided access for the Indians who camped on the east bank, but no wagon bridge existed here. The Oregon Trail crossed the Laramie River where it flowed into the North Platte River a mile north. At that point, this side road led south to the fort.

Since no stockade enclosed Fort Laramie, our view of the train's approach was unobstructed. This military facility that sprawled for a half mile along the river's western bank resembled a ramshackle village more than a fort.

In the train, I counted eight blue army supply wagons, each pulled by six mules. Following them, four horses pulled a lightweight, canvas-covered farm wagon. A single horseman led the procession. Muleskinners' curses could be heard faintly at this distance. The freight wagons would be destined for the quartermaster warehouse, which was blocked from our view by the intervening roof of the infantry barracks at the north end of the parade ground.

The lone horseman rode back down the line of wagons to the trailing farm wagon. He tipped his hat to a couple sitting on the wagon's seat and pointed in our direction. He swung his horse around, and the driver of the wagon pulled his rig out of line to follow the rider. They came toward us down the road that led to the center of the fort.

After passing in front of the barracks, the rider and wagon turned north. When they made the turn, two young ladies came into view on the tailgate of the wagon. One of them cradled a baby in her arms. The rider and the wagon continued a short distance until they reached the sutler's store, where they halted.

The rider rode back in our direction. When he passed the

21

wagon's tailgate, he paused to speak to the young ladies before continuing. He did not retake the turn to the east in front of the barracks but came straight on toward Old Bedlam.

A squad of infantry performed close order drill on the parade ground. A sergeant shouted commands. The only sound from the marching column came from the stomping of the men's brogans, which stirred up the dust on the hard-packed ground. If grass had ever grown there, it had long ago been tromped away.

A few cottonwoods lined the edge of the roadway directly in front of Old Bedlam. These scraggly trees provided the only green color except for a few weeds that grew in the shade of their trunks. Fort Laramie had evolved from a trading post erected in 1834 near the confluence of the Laramie and North Platte Rivers. In the intervening years, trappers, soldiers, and immigrants had chopped down every tree. Now, the army sent a detail to Laramie Peak, fifty miles away, to find firewood.

The clopping sound of the rider's approaching horse added to the shuffling sounds of the troopers' feet. No breeze fluttered the tree leaves. Nothing abated the heat emanating from the morning sun climbing into a cloudless sky.

The clean-shaven rider halted at the hitching rail in front of our two-story, wooden structure. He made a quick survey of the porches stretching along both floors of the building before stepping out of his saddle. He lifted a pair of saddlebags off the horse's rump.

"This headquarters?" he called up to us.

"No," Major Bonnet answered. "This is Old Bedlam."

"Unusual name," the man said.

"The young buck officers who've lived here over the years have been known to throw an occasional wild party. Thus, the name."

"I see." The man lifted his hat to reveal thick, shoulder-length black hair. He slapped the hat against his leg, releasing a spray of dust. His sun-bronzed face revealed high cheekbones. "You the commanding officer? I was informed a major was in command here."

"No, I'm the paymaster. Major Armond Bonnet. You the captain of the wagon train that just arrived?"

"That I am. Duggan Maguire's the name."

"Irishman, eh," the major said. "Don't hear much Emerald Isle in your accent."

Maguire smirked. "Don't speak Gaelic. My pap came from the old country, but I was born and raised in Indian Territory. I'm half Cherokee. English was taught in my school. I'm occasionally accused of repeating an Irish phrase I heard my pap use when I was growing up."

"Don't suppose you brought the pay chests?" the major asked.

"Pay chests?"

"Well, I didn't think so, or you'd have a military escort. Plus, you would've set a record for bringing a train from Fort Sedgwick."

"Well, sir, I didn't bring any pay chests. I did bring dispatches for the commanding officer." Maguire lifted his saddlebags.

"Adjutant's office is over there." Major Bonnet pointed the stem of his pipe toward the southeast corner of the parade ground. "You'll find Major James Van Voast there."

"Thank you, Major."

"Don't mention it, Captain Maguire."

"Call me Duggan. My time as a wagon train captain will end as soon as I drop off these dispatches. I only signed on to bring this train of supplies to Colonel Carrington's Eighteenth Infantry. Figured that'd get me closer to the Montana goldfields."

"You missed Colonel Carrington. He led the Second Battalion of the Eighteenth out of here three days ago."

23

"Oh, no," the wagon master said. "Looks like my days as a captain may not be over."

Bonnet knocked his pipe against the butt of his hand, dislodging the dottle, allowing it to fall into the dirt a few feet from the wagon master. "If you'll excuse me, Captain, I'm out of tobacco and need to head over to the sutler's store."

"I plan to stop there myself. See you later." He waved a hand, remounted, and trotted down the road.

Major Bonnet headed toward the stairs leading down from the second floor. "Coming, Zach?"

I didn't have any money to spend in the sutler's store, or anyplace else for that matter. I'd foolishly shot dice recently with some old sergeants, and they'd cleaned out what cash I had, plus they now held my markers for most of the money I had coming on payday.

"Yes, sir. I'm coming."

CHAPTER 3

I walked with Major Bonnet to the sutler's store, where a half-dozen scruffy Indian males loitered in the shade of the building. Two old squaws stood gesticulating to the tailgate of the farm wagon Maguire had escorted there earlier.

A female, probably one of the two I'd seen earlier sitting on the rear of the wagon, stood there holding an outstretched blanket to block the Indians' view into the wagon's bed. Wisps of blonde hair escaped the edges of a blue bonnet, but with her back to me, her face was hidden.

When the major and I drew abreast of the tailgate, I saw what she tried to shield. A young woman sat on a rocking chair inside the wagon nursing a baby.

The major stopped beside the tailgate. He made hand signs and spoke a couple of phrases in Sioux to the two old squaws. They sidled over to join their male companions.

"Ladies," the major said to the two white women, "you are creating quite a stir here with these old squaws."

"How?" the female holding the blanket asked without turning around. "What could interest them about a mother nursing her baby?"

"These squaws want to buy the baby," the major said.

"What?" The blanket holder exclaimed without moving. "Oh, goodness."

"I suggest," the major said, "you go inside the store."

"Lyndon is cutting teeth, sir," the one nursing the baby said.

"I'm afraid his crying will disturb the patrons."

"Ma'am," the major replied, "you can't disturb *these* patrons. They're so loud, they'll never notice."

"All right." She eased the baby off her breast and closed the front of her dress. "We'll go inside."

The major touched the brim of his hat with a finger and took a step toward the store's front door. When he realized I hadn't moved, he grabbed my arm and pushed me through the door ahead of him.

Inside, it took a moment for my eyes to adjust from the bright outdoor sunlight. An assortment of people crowded against the counter that extended around the opposite three walls. Soldiers wearing faded, blue blouses rubbed elbows with civilian teamsters in multicolored wool shirts. Indian men, bare to the waist, stood silently behind buckskin-dressed squaws. The Indian women, with papooses snuggled into backboard cradles, gestured energetically to desired items on the shelves. Brown-skinned toddlers crawled naked on the dirt floor gathering up crumbs of hardtack dropped by their elders. English served as the predominant bartering language, but smatterings of Sioux could be heard.

"Morning, Mr. Bullock," the major said.

The slender, middle-aged sutler, with a neatly trimmed,white beard, replied, "Good morning to you, Major Bonnet. Did the pay chests arrive?"

"No. They did not."

"When are you going to pay the past-due bills the army owes us?" Bullock asked. "Not to mention the soldiers who are piling up IOUs you wouldn't believe."

"It's been four months since the troops have been paid. They're in worse shape, I imagine, than you or Mr. Ward." The major pointed to the diamond stickpin in Bullock's cravat. "They don't have your wherewithal to fall back on."

"You'll be following after Colonel Carrington to pay his men?"

"Yes," the major said. "Hopefully, nobody will have to wait much longer. Fort Sedgwick telegraphed the pay chests will be with the next train. Adding that train to the one that came in this morning, we'll have enough wagons and men to comply with regulations so we can head north."

"Well," the sutler said, "I assume you didn't come in here to discuss pay problems."

"I need pipe tobacco."

Bullock reached to a shelf behind him and slapped a paper packet of Minne-Ha-Ha! Cavendish tobacco on the counter.

Major Bonnet paid for the tobacco with a twenty-five-cent paper note—coins being rare on the frontier. He shoved the packet into his coat pocket and headed toward an adjacent room where soldiers were engaged in beer drinking and card playing.

I remained standing inside the doorway. Mr. Bullock cocked an eyebrow at me. "You buying something, son?"

"No, sir. Just waiting for the major."

"Well, wait over there out of the way of paying customers." Bullock pointed at two old Indian men occupying a bench against the wall, smacking their lips around peppermint candy canes. He shouted at them in Sioux, and they vacated the seat.

No sooner had I sat down than the door opened, and the two young ladies and the baby came in.

"Ladies?" Bullock reached over the counter to shove an Indian aside. "Can I help you?" He motioned them forward.

They occupied the place he'd cleared. "Thank you, sir," the young mother said.

"I'm William Bullock. Welcome to Bullock & Ward's. My partner, Seth Ward, is waiting on that couple at that other counter." Bullock pointed to a man with a full-flowing, white beard.

"Oh, he's helping my father, Reverend Garrick Hollister, and my mother. I'm Mrs. Megan Hollister Sawyer, and this is my son, Lyndon."

Bullock's gaze shifted from Megan to the girl standing beside her.

"I'm Miss Kathleen O'Toole," she said.

Traces of pale blonde hair were visible around the edges of her bonnet, but I still could not see her face.

"Pleased to meet you both. What suits your fancy?" Bullock waved a hand at the shelves loaded with cans and boxes of food stuffs, stacks of clothing, and an assortment of hardware. "Sweets, perhaps?"

"You handle the mail for Fort Laramie, sir?" the girl who'd said her name was Kathleen asked.

"This store houses the post office for Fort Laramie, yes."

"Would you have any letters from Mister Brandon Hollister? My fiancé would have written from Montana and probably addressed his letter to me in Pennsylvania."

"I don't personally handle the mail. The postmaster is Ordnance Sergeant Schnyder. He's sorting the mail your wagon train brought in. I'll get him."

Bullock came around the counter and entered an area set aside for the post office between the store and the adjacent barroom. He returned, followed by a sergeant.

"You have a question, miss?" the sergeant asked.

The blonde repeated her question about looking for a letter from her fiancé.

"Miss, I am holding no letter for you. It would be improper for me to hold mail addressed to Pennsylvania. I would have forwarded it. I've been the postmaster here for seven years, I have a good memory, and I do not recall ever seeing a letter addressed to your name."

"Thank you, sir."

"You're welcome." The ordnance sergeant left.

"How can I help you, ma'am?" Bullock addressed Megan.

"Do you have something for a baby's toothache?" The baby fidgeted and fussed in his mother's arms.

"I have clove oil," Bullock said. "I understand it helps, but you shouldn't use too much of it. It could harm a young one."

"How do I use it?" Megan asked.

"The officers' ladies rub a little on the youngster's gums with a finger."

"I'll try it."

"Very well. Shall I include it with your parents' purchases?"

"You can add the item to the family bill, but if you will, give me the oil now."

"Certainly."

Bullock stepped farther down the counter, then returned with a small bottle. "Here you are. You ladies can sit on that bench over there until your folks have finished. I'm sure that young gentleman will make room for you."

As the two approached, I stood, stepped aside, and removed my hat. When I saw the blonde's face, my mouth dropped open. I'd gone to school with nice-looking girls and had seen many beauties in New York City, but I'd never encountered one that absolutely mesmerized me.

"Oh, don't leave, sir," Megan said. "There's room for all of us."

The ladies settled on the bench, with Megan sitting closest to the door. I resumed my seat on the opposite end of the bench, next to the blonde. I crushed my hat in my lap and glanced sideways at the two ladies.

"Can you take out the cork?" Megan handed the small bottle to her companion.

The blonde struggled with the cork stopper. She turned to me. A delicate cleft graced her chin. "Sir, could you . . . ?" She extended the bottle with a smile. Dimples indented her cheeks at the corners of her lips and accentuated the slight indentation below her nose. Deep-blue eyes gleamed beneath dark lashes. Arched eyebrows matched the pale-blonde curls framing her face.

"Sir?" she repeated.

"Oh . . . oh, yes." My hands let go of my hat, and it fell to the floor at my feet.

When she passed me the bottle, the tips of my fingers burned where they touched her cool, slender ones. Her slight shift on the bench brought her hip in contact with mine. I let out an inadvertent grunt as she released the bottle into my hand.

I grasped the cork with the nails of a thumb and two fingers and drew it out. The pleasant fragrance of the spice wafted from the bottle. I passed it back, wishing I'd taken time that morning to scrape the dirt from under my nails with my pocketknife.

Megan placed an index finger over the opening of the bottle, and her friend tipped it. Megan transferred the drop of liquid to her son's mouth and gently massaged his gums. The baby murmured contentedly.

I still held the cork, which the blonde beauty now took from me—her cool fingers once again searing mine. "Thank you, sir."

Could she hear my heart thumping? I reached down to retrieve my hat. After I straightened up, I managed to stammer, "You're . . . you're welcome."

She held the bottle to her nose and sniffed. "Maybe we should sprinkle a little of this in the air." Her laughter tinkled.

"I doubt it would help," I said.

I had grown immune to the overpowering odor of animal grease emanating from the half-clothed natives. Mingled with the stench of soldiers' and teamsters' sweat-soaked, wool clothing, the atmosphere probably proved repugnant to her delicate sense of smell. Pungent pipe and cigar smoke also permeated the crowded store. The sour smell of beer floated in the air from the far end of the room where the boisterous laughter of card players frequently drowned out the nearby shouted bargaining for supplies and sundries.

"I'm Kathleen O'Toole," she said. "Most people call me Katy. This is Megan Hollister, my sister-in-law to be."

"I know," I said.

"How did you know she is to be my sister-in-law?"

"Oh, I didn't mean that. I meant, I know your names. I overheard you tell the sutler."

"I see. And you are?"

"Zachary Taylor Wakefield." I blurted out my full name.

"Named for the president?"

I nodded. "My father served under him in the Mexican War."

Out of the corner of my eye, I saw Major Bonnet returning from the barroom. That momentarily drew my attention away from Katy.

When the major passed the Hollisters, the reverend stopped him. The minister was a couple inches shorter than Major Bonnet, who stood two inches shorter than my six feet. A beard that would have made Moses proud completely covered the front of the preacher's frock coat. Had he been standing by himself, he would have appeared taller with his regal bearing.

"Major," Reverend Hollister said, "did I hear you say a wagon train was heading up the Bozeman to Montana?"

"No, that's not what I said."

"Aren't you the commanding officer?" Hollister asked.

"No, sir. I'm the paymaster."

"Well, I can't wait around here forever. I have a mission to fulfill. I'm Reverend Garrick Hollister, an ordained minister of

31

the Methodist Episcopal faith. The Lord has called me to go to Montana to preach the good word to the heathens. I must be on my way . . . now."

"Reverend, I suggest you take the matter up with the post commander. He determines when travelers can proceed up the Bozeman Trail. You will find Major Van Voast at his headquarters in the adjutant's office, at the far end of the parade ground."

The major excused himself with a bow. He had taken only a couple of steps when he abruptly stopped in front of me.

What had I done wrong? It took a moment to realize he wasn't looking at me.

Just as I had done, the major stared at Kathleen with an open mouth. He reached into an inside coat pocket and extracted his pocket watch. I'd seen the major check his watch frequently, but I'd never paid much attention to the action. He continued to look at Kathleen as he flipped open the cover and faced it toward her. A miniature painting filled the inside of the watch's lid.

My mouth dropped open again as I looked from the picture to Kathleen. The portrait was of her.

Major Bonnet snapped the lid closed and slipped the watch into his pocket. He removed his hat. "My apologies, ladies." He nodded to Kathleen and Megan. "I'm Major Armond Bonnet, and I must admit, I was taken aback."

"I can understand why," Megan said. "There is a striking resemblance between my friend and the painting."

"How did you obtain a miniature resembling me?" Katy asked.

"It's of my wife. God rest her soul. She gave me this watch on our honeymoon. She is no longer of this earth. She and my daughter were murdered by Bloody Bill Anderson's guerrillas during the last year of the war."

"I'm sorry, sir," Katy said. "I do understand that in this world

32

there occasionally appears a person who resembles another. I hope my appearance does not offend you."

"Oh, no, my dear. It pleases me immensely that the good Lord sees fit to continue my wife's beauty in yours."

When the major made this last comment, Katy responded with a grin. Her dimples matched those in the watch's portrait.

The door to the sutler's store banged open, and Duggan Maguire barged in. He halted and touched the brim of his hat but did not remove it. "Ah, Major Bonnet . . . ladies." He didn't address me. "Why the solemn look on everybody's face?"

"I was telling this young lady . . ." Major Bonnet paused. "I'm sorry, I don't know your name, Miss."

"Kathleen O'Toole."

"I was telling Miss O'Toole that she resembles my deceased wife," Major Bonnet said.

"I see." Maguire spoke slowly. The wagon train captain stared at the major, who continued to look admiringly at Katy.

Major Bonnet missed the frown on Maguire's ruddy features. Nor did the major see Maguire extract a small gold shamrock from a pants pocket and caress it with his thumb and fingers.

CHAPTER 4

On Thursday, June 21, as I did every morning, I rose early and went to the teamsters' mess for breakfast. Major Bonnet had arranged for me to board there and had advanced funds against my future wages for my meals. Following the forthcoming payday, after I reimbursed the major and reclaimed my markers from my gambling losses, there wouldn't be much money left. The major had admonished me only once for my sin.

After breakfast, I went to the officers' stables behind Old Bedlam where I watered, fed, and groomed the major's saddle horse, Hector, and the four mules we used to pull the paymaster's ambulance. In Omaha, when the major had asked me to select mules, I didn't have a clue how to do it. An old muleskinner guided me in selecting four geldings. He advised against females. When they went into heat, he said, the Mollies caused a real ruckus among the Jacks.

I checked the ambulance, which was parked behind the stables, to make sure some thieving Indian hadn't made off with the canvas cover to use as a teepee.

An hour later, I reported to Major Bonnet in his second-floor accommodation. The door stood open, but I knocked anyway. He called for me to enter. I stepped into the room, which doubled as bedroom and office.

"Major."

"Yes, Zach, what is it?"

"The duty sergeant caught me coming up the stairs and said

34

you were to report to the commanding officer right away."

The major sat on the edge of his bed with the left leg of his trousers pulled up above his knee. That leg had been amputated below the knee, and I watched as he pulled a stocking over the stump. Then, he guided the stump through a tangle of harness attached to a wooden leg and nestled the appendage's hollowed-out top into place. He buckled leather straps above the knee and pulled the material of his pants leg down over the artificial limb. A Wellington calf-high boot was permanently attached to the wooden leg. He slipped his good right foot into a matching boot.

He stood and shrugged into his frock coat. "All right," he said, "let's go."

"The sergeant didn't say anything about me."

"Well, I'm giving you an order." He grinned and slapped me on the shoulder. "Come along."

When we entered the adjutant's office, the duty sergeant looked up from his desk. "Major Bonnet, go right in. Major Van Voast is expecting you."

I hesitated, but the major grabbed my elbow and pulled me after him.

The sergeant rose from his chair.

"Don't fret, Sergeant. Whatever orders Major Van Voast gives me will apply to my clerk, as well."

The sergeant shrugged and sat.

Major Bonnet knocked once on the closed door leading to the commander's inner office and opened it.

"You asked to see me, Major?" the paymaster asked.

"Come in, Armand," Major Van Voast said. "Morning, Mr. Wakefield."

Since the commanding officer didn't tell me to leave, it appeared my boss's assumption about mutually applicable orders was correct.

"Sit down, gentlemen." Van Voast indicated two straight-backed chairs in front of his desk. "As you are aware, Major, the pay chests are arriving from Fort Sedgwick tomorrow . . . I'm guessing late afternoon."

Major Bonnet nodded.

"I want the men paid Saturday. I realize that doesn't give you much time to prepare, but I'm making this decision for two reasons. First, the men haven't been paid for four months. They're getting restless. Second, you can get on the way to Fort Reno on Sunday, the twenty-fourth, to catch up with Colonel Carrington. Any objection?"

"No, sir," the paymaster said.

"Fine," Major Van Voast said.

A knock sounded on the office door. The door swung open, and the duty sergeant entered. "Captain Maguire is here, sir."

"Send him in, please."

Duggan Maguire stepped past the sergeant into the office. "Sorry if I'm late, Major. I just got word you wanted to see me."

"You're right on time, Captain. Come in."

There were only two chairs in front of the desk, so I rose and offered my seat to Maguire. He sat without saying thank you.

"A wagon train will arrive from Fort Sedgwick tomorrow afternoon with the pay chests," Van Voast said. "The paymaster has agreed payday here can be Saturday. Then, he'll depart for Fort Reno on Sunday. I'm anxious to push the supplies and the payroll forward to Colonel Carrington."

Maguire glanced at Major Bonnet, then to Major Van Voast. "What does that have to do with me?" Maguire asked.

"I'm placing you in charge of the wagon train," Van Voast said. "We'll combine your wagons with the arriving ones. The captain of the new train is not familiar to me or any of my officers. You weren't either until a few days ago, but I've observed

36

that you conduct yourself as if you had been in the army."

"I was," Maguire said, "but not yours."

"That's behind us. I like the way you control your teamsters. I expect you can easily assimilate the newcomers. Therefore, the expanded train, the paymaster's ambulance, and an escort squad of infantry will depart here on Sunday to head for Fort Reno. Understood?"

"Yes, sir," Maguire said.

The door to the office banged opened. Reverend Garrick Hollister stormed in dragging the duty sergeant with him.

"Sorry, sir," the sergeant said. "He refused to wait to be announced."

Major Van Voast held up a hand. "Sir, it is customary for visitors to the commanding officer to be announced first, but since you're here . . ."

The reverend jerked his arm away from the sergeant, who returned to the outer office.

"What can I do for your, sir?" Major Van Voast asked.

The preacher stomped up to the side of the major's desk and shook a finger at the officer. "I'm Reverend Garrick Hollister and generally a patient man, but I have been repeatedly told I have to wait here for an escort before I can proceed up the Bozeman Trail."

"That's correct," Major Van Voast said. "Regulations require thirty armed men before a train can proceed from Fort Laramie."

"Why?" Hollister asked. "I thought the army signed a peace treaty with the Indians less than a week ago."

"We did."

"Then what's the problem?" Hollister continued. "Everything around here looks peaceful. Hundreds of Indians camp along the river and wander freely through this fort day and night."

"The Laramie Loafers seldom cause trouble," Major Van

Voast said. "This is not the Bozeman Trail."

"Well, this requirement for thirty men is ridiculous! I see single soldiers riding in and out of here every day. They're obviously traveling up and down the Bozeman."

"Those are experienced, armed couriers who know how to defend themselves. Wagon trains contain unarmed women and children. Even some of the men who pass through here are without arms."

"I'm unarmed," Hollister said. "I'm a man of the cloth, ordained by God to be a minister of peace and love. I've been directed by the Methodist Episcopal Church to establish a mission in Montana. I intend to proceed there expeditiously to undertake my assignment."

"You will wait," Van Voast said, "until the army says it is safe for you to travel up the Bozeman Trail. I am sitting here with these gentlemen right now making preparations for a train to depart on Sunday. I'm sorry if, as a religious man, you have objections to traveling on that day, but you and your family will travel with that train. That's an order!"

"I'm not in the army, Major. I don't take orders from you or anybody else in the army."

"According to the regulations applicable to Dakota Territory, you do."

The room grew silent. Reverend Hollister stood back from the desk. He glared briefly at Major Bonnet, Captain Maguire, and me before facing Major Van Voast again.

"We'll see," Hollister said. The reverend marched across the room, jerked open the door, and tromped out.

CHAPTER 5

Early Friday morning, June 22, after tending to the animals and checking the ambulance, I reported to Major Bonnet. He handed me a requisition for ammunition and directed me to proceed to Ordnance Sergeant Schnyder's magazine to draw it. In Omaha, I'd been issued a muzzle-loading Springfield rifle-musket, firing a .58-caliber Minié ball, the standard weapon for infantrymen. I was expected to double as a guard when driving the ambulance. The major decided we needed twice the amount of ammunition we had to travel up the Bozeman Trail. After I took care of this chore, the major said I was free until the wagon train arrived in the afternoon with the pay chests.

Several minutes later, I walked out of Fort Laramie's magazine with five packets of .44-caliber army revolver ammunition for the major and four packets of rifle ammunition for me. A paper packet of revolver ammunition contained six combustible envelope cartridges, providing the major thirty additional rounds to what he already had. A packet of rifle ammunition held ten cartridges. That added forty rounds for me. I also picked up two tins of percussion caps—one for each weapon. While trying to balance the assorted containers, I wasn't paying attention to where I was going and bumped into a fellow pushing a handcart.

"Heads up!" he shouted.

"Sorry," I said. "Didn't mean to run into you."

"No harm done." A grin crossed the clean-shaven face of a

young man with pale-blond hair. "Where are you going with all that ammunition?" he asked.

"I'm the paymaster's clerk. We're heading up the Bozeman Trail, and we might encounter hostiles."

"Don't believe in guns, myself. Don't own one. Raised a Quaker. Prefer to shoot my subjects with a camera." He lowered his two-wheeled cart onto its rear legs.

"That's a camera?"

"That's my perambulator dark tent. The camera's inside."

"Perambulator? Looks like a canvas-covered dog cart."

He laughed. "Pretty much the same thing. It contains everything I need to take photographs . . . camera, chemicals, wet plates. Also functions as a portable darkroom."

"Forgive me," I said. "I haven't introduced myself. I'm Zach Wakefield." I shrugged and lifted my arms, which were filled with the ammunition. "Sorry I can't shake your hand."

"I'm Ridgway Glover, photographer for *Frank Leslie's Illustrated*. The Smithsonian Institution is sponsoring my efforts to photograph the natives. You mentioned traveling up the Bozeman. I intend to head that way myself. In fact, Colonel Carrington wanted me to travel with him, but I wasn't ready then."

"Maybe you can travel with us," I said. "We'll be leaving Sunday. I'll speak to Major Bonnet about it if you like."

"That's probably too soon. I'm awaiting a shipment of developing chemicals. I'm running low."

"There's a wagon train arriving tomorrow with the pay chests," I said. "Maybe your chemicals will be with it."

"I doubt it. I just telegraphed my order to Omaha two weeks ago. I hadn't anticipated using so many chemicals, but the Indians are demanding I take their photographs. It didn't start out that way. At first, they were afraid they would die if I captured their image. One old fellow rolled on the ground and encased himself in his blanket, he was so frightened. But now they like the Ferrotypes I make. I put a little brass frame around the picture, and they treasure it."

He grasped the handles and lifted the cart. "Must get to work."

He pushed the large-wheeled perambulator ahead, and I fell in beside him.

"Aren't you going the wrong direction?" I asked. "The Indians are camped on the other side of the river."

"Today I plan to photograph the Indian maiden Wheat Flower's burial scaffold. Up at the post cemetery."

"You want some company?" I asked. "I've not been to the cemetery, but an Indian burial scaffold sounds interesting."

"You're welcome to come along. You can help push this rig up the hill."

"Is it heavy?"

"Weighs a hundred pounds when it's fully loaded with chemicals. It's a little lighter now. Lay your ammunition on the top there."

I placed the packets on the canvas cover and slid the small tins of caps into a pants pocket. I took one handle and he the other. We easily pushed the perambulator up the hill toward the cemetery, which lay on elevated ground at the northwest corner of the rectangular-shaped fort.

"Why do you want to photograph a burial scaffold?" I asked.

"Spotted Tail is a chief of the Brulés. They're one of the bands that live here on government subsidies. You've probably heard them called the Laramie Loafers. It seems Chief Spotted Tail's eighteen-year-old daughter, Wheat Flower, became enamored with the white man's ways and adopted the Christian belief. Some say she was in love with a lieutenant. When she learned she was dying of tuberculosis, her father promised to bury her among the whites. She died earlier this year, and the army donated a coffin and allowed her to be buried in the cemetery. Everybody attended the ceremony, from what I've been told. The fort's band led the procession, and the chaplain said prayers."

Fifteen minutes later, we reached our destination. A plain, pine coffin rested on a platform higher than my head. Four corner posts provided support. Pony skulls were nailed to two of the posts, and white pony tails dangled from the other two. Ridgway and I stood for a moment awed by this strange apparition.

"It appears to be true," Ridgway said. "They said Spotted Tail slew Wheat Flower's two favorite ponies to decorate the scaffold. This will make an interesting photograph."

I helped him remove the contents of the cart and arrange them on the ground. He set up a tripod on which he affixed a large Roettger camera. He busied himself with wet plates and chemicals, then ducked beneath a black hood attached to the camera to focus the lens on the burial platform. After taking his shot, he transferred a glass plate from the camera to the interior of the perambulator darkroom and dropped the canvas cover over his head.

He'd removed his hat while he worked and his shoulder-length, corn-silk hair streamed freely in the steady breeze. Some warrior would love to decorate his war lance with Ridgway's scalp.

Since I couldn't help him, I wandered through the graveyard. The last time I'd visited a cemetery had been before departing Albany to join the army. I'd gone to pay my respects to my father, who'd been killed at the First Battle of Bull Run. I probably should have returned home after my discharge a year ago to visit his and now my mother's graves, but I hadn't.

No granite monuments here at Fort Laramie. A few wooden crosses mingled with assorted slabs of wood on which had been carved or painted names and dates. Many markers were so weathered the writing was difficult to decipher. I reset one cross that'd toppled over. No manicured lawn surrounded these graves. A lone cactus bloomed at the foot of one mound—the only flower in the cemetery. Who were these people? Why had they come west? Could this be my fate?

Ridgway completed photographing the scaffold, and I helped him reload his perambulator. By now, the noon hour approached, and my stomach growled. Rather than heading directly to the teamsters' mess, however, I decided to make a detour around the north end of the fort before going for my dinner. I hadn't been able to stop thinking about the dimples of a certain blonde-haired young lady. Perhaps I could manage another glimpse.

"Ridgway," I said, gathering up my ammunition bundles. "If you can make it down the hill by yourself, I'm going to leave you and head over to the river. I want to visit the Hollister campsite."

"Oh, I can handle the perambulator. But the Hollisters aren't down by the river any more."

"They aren't? Where are they?"

"I imagine several miles down the Oregon Trail. They left last night."

Chapter 6

I dragged myself out of bed before dawn that Sunday morning, June 24, and joined a few teamsters for a breakfast of hardtack, fried bacon, and coffee. The teamsters, unlike me, would have the day off. The cook, whom the teamsters and I collectively paid to fix the daily meals, had arrived only shortly before we hungry fellows descended on the dining area. The frying bacon smelled better than it tasted. I grabbed a piece out of the skillet before it was crisp. The coffee, thick enough for my spoon to stand upright in my tin cup, soaked the unleavened hardtack cracker so I could chew it without breaking a tooth. I didn't complain. This would be the last breakfast someone else would prepare for me for awhile. One of my jobs on the trail included cooking for the paymaster and me. My mother, God rest her soul, would never believe that possible.

Yesterday had been a long day—exceedingly long. I was tired, and Major Bonnet was probably just as tired. Paying four months' pay to the twelve companies of troops stationed at Fort Laramie had consumed all the daylight hours. None of the companies was at a full strength of seventy soldiers. Still, we paid almost eight hundred men. Afterward, the major and I sat by lantern light in his office-living quarters and completed entries in the myriad muster rosters. Midnight approached before we finished, and I trudged off to grab some sleep.

The sky in the east showed tinges of pink when I went to the officers' stable. I fed all five animals before harnessing the mules and saddling the horse. My mules had come from a new army purchase, and the task of naming them fell to me. The names I chose weren't very original—Matt, Mark, Luke, and John. The old muleskinner in Omaha had said "Matthew" was too long. I called them my Gospel mules.

I drove the ambulance, with Hector tied behind, to the front of Old Bedlam. Major Bonnet stood on the lower porch awaiting my arrival.

"Good morning, Zach," he said. "Right on time. I like that."

"Good morning, Major." In the east, the tip of the sun poked above the horizon, spreading red and yellow flares along the bottoms of the low-lying clouds.

The garrison's bugler blew reveille, and I stepped down from the driver's seat. I stood at attention beside the major, and he saluted while the garrison flag was hoisted up the parade ground's flagpole. When the banner with its thirty-six stars and thirteen stripes unfurled in the light breeze, I took a deep breath. I always did. When the flag reached the pole's apex, the salute cannon fired.

I made three trips up the stairs to the major's quarters. I returned first with his traveling chest, then followed with his portable desk. Finally, I brought down a folding worktable and two camp stools that we used to pay the troops. I stored the items in the bed of the ambulance close behind the driver's seat.

I drove south around the perimeter of the parade ground to reach the adjutant's office at the southeast corner. The major walked alongside. Once there, he entered the building.

A minute later, two privates staggered out carrying an iron pay chest between them. The chest, the size of a small steamer trunk, weighed a hundred and fifty pounds when loaded with paper money.

The major followed the privates carrying two lanyards holding keys for the locks that secured the lids of three chests. The locking mechanism required two keys to open it, like a bank's safety deposit boxes. Normally, the paymaster kept one set of keys and another officer the second. There would be no other officer traveling with us, so the major entrusted me with one lanyard. I hung it around my neck and dropped the keys inside the front of my shirt.

I had collapsed the two lower side benches of the ambulance flat on the floor. The upper-level benches remained raised and secured to the inside of the frame. When used as a medical ambulance, the Rucker could transport four wounded soldiers. I had also rolled the canvas sides down to limit visibility into the bed of the vehicle.

The privates positioned the first chest next to the items I had already placed behind the driver's seat. Two more trips completed the movement of all three chests. The ambulance was filled to its tailgate.

The officer of the day came out onto the stoop. "Major, we'll keep the empty chests here until you return, then we'll ship all of them back to Omaha. Hopefully, we'll get a fast refilling and not wait four months before the next payday."

The lieutenant was referring to the chests we'd emptied yesterday to pay the Fort Laramie troops.

"Thanks for your help, Lieutenant," the major said. "Give my regards to Major Van Voast when he comes in this morning."

"I'll do that, sir." The two officers exchanged salutes.

Major Bonnet untied Hector and approached the animal from the right side. He placed his good, right foot, into the stirrup. With a grunt, he heaved himself up, swung the dead weight of his wooden leg awkwardly over the horse's rump, and landed in the saddle. It had taken special training to get an army horse used to being mounted from the right side. Since officers and cavalrymen wore a saber on their left hip, they always mounted from the left to avoid sitting on the dangling weapon. Major Bonnet didn't wear a saber, only a sidearm.

The major reached down and guided the boot attached to his wooden leg into the left stirrup. He sat up and cleared his throat. "Well, Zach. You going with me?"

"Yes, sir." I'd been so engrossed in watching him mount the horse I hadn't moved from the rear of the ambulance. I hurriedly climbed onto the driver's bench. A horsehair-filled, leather pad lay atop the wooden seat. Its limited cushioning would do little to lessen the abuse my bottom would suffer for the next several days.

With the major leading the way, I drove the ambulance down the east road beside the parade ground. We rolled past the infantry barracks where troops had assembled for morning inspection. Beyond the barracks, next to the quartermaster warehouse, twenty heavy army freight wagons waited side by side. The blue paint on the wagons' boxes was faded, and the red wheels were tarnished to a rust color. These wagons had seen service in the war. Mules fidgeted and snorted in their harness. Six mules were hitched to each wagon. A teamster, a jerk line in one hand and a whip in the other, sat mounted on a saddle on each near-wheel mule. The wagons, loaded with food for soldiers and fodder for animals, were destined for Colonel Carrington's Eighteenth Infantry. The item the colonel wanted most was missing—ammunition.

Counting the paymaster's ambulance, our train contained one vehicle more than regulations required for the Bozeman Trail.

Major Bonnet guided his mount up to where Duggan Maguire waited on his horse. "Morning, Captain Maguire," the major said.

"Morning, Major."

"I see the wagons are ready. Where's the escort?"

Duggan pointed behind the major. "Coming now."

A squad of infantry, with rifle-muskets at right shoulder arms, marched around the corner of the barracks and came toward us. A minute later, a sergeant ordered, "Detail, *Halt*. Right, *Face*. Order, *Arms.*"

The sergeant faced the major and saluted. "Sergeant Marley reporting with the paymaster's escort, sir."

"Very good, Sergeant. Take the lead with your escort. I will follow with the ambulance. Captain Duggan Maguire will swing his wagons in behind."

"Sir!" The sergeant saluted, executed an about-face, and addressed the ten privates and a corporal who comprised the escort squad. "Shoulder, *Arms*. Left, *Face*. Forward, *March.*"

Our compliment of muleskinners, wagon master, infantry escort, paymaster, and me totaled thirty-five—five more than the required minimum.

I clucked to the team, snapped the reins, and the Gospel mules pulled the ambulance in behind the marching men. I looked back through the open rear and watched the wagons move into line one after another. Muleskinners' shouted curses and cracking whips got their teams moving. Leather harness creaked as the mules leaned into their loads. Iron tires crunched on the gravel road. Once we were sorted out, our entourage stretched for a quarter mile.

Maguire joined Major Bonnet, and they rode in front of the ambulance as we passed beyond the outskirts of the fort and down the road that took us north to intersect the Oregon Trail a mile away.

"As I said the other day, Major," Maguire said, "I have not been up the Bozeman Trail before, and neither have any of these muleskinners."

"I've been as far as Fort Reno," the major said. "The route is easy enough to follow. Three days from now we'll reach

Bridger's Ferry, where we'll cross the North Platte. The Oregon Trail continues along the south bank to Fort Caspar. On the north bank of the Platte, we'll follow the Mormon Trail until we come to Sage Creek. The Bozeman Trail heads northwest from there."

"The muleskinners will stay with us long enough to reach Colonel Carrington's command," Duggan said. "Like me, most of them took the job just to get closer to Montana's goldfields."

"That's fine," the major said. "Once you turn your wagons over to Colonel Carrington's quartermaster, you're all free to go wherever you want."

"How long 'til we reach Fort Reno?" Maguire asked.

"Ten, maybe eleven days. Colonel Carrington has orders to relieve the garrison there and fortify the place before moving on. He'll be there a few days."

I wondered if Katy O'Toole and Reverend Hollister's family had caught up to the Eighteenth Infantry.

CHAPTER 7

About midmorning on Sunday, June 24, several hours after making the turn onto the Oregon Trail, we rolled past Nine-Mile Ranche. Two of the resident ladies of the night stood in the openings to their cribs and tried to entice the soldiers of the escort into paying them a visit.

"Eyes, *Front!*" Sergeant Marley commanded. "There's nothing for you boys there, today."

Nine-Mile Ranche provided the closest female entertainment to Fort Laramie. Since payday had occurred yesterday, there were probably some of last night's carousers hiding in the bar or sleeping it off in the cribs. Even though it was a day off, the enlisted men would not want to be seen by an officer.

Ten miles west of Nine-Mile Ranche, the road curved sharply to the right, and we entered a canyon of the North Platte that reminded me of the Palisades of the Hudson River in New York. Turbulent water roared and tumbled through this narrow defile for three hundred yards. At the end of the passage, the road abruptly curved to the left, and we found ourselves once more plodding beside the wider, rapidly flowing river.

Except for the brief period when the wagons had to pass single file through the short canyon, the freight wagons traveled two by two. A few miles beyond the canyon brought us to Bitter Cottonwood Creek. Because the Oregon Trail was well worn, we made good progress that first day, traveling twenty-one miles. We would spend our first night at this location named for the trees that used to line this small creek that dumped into the North Platte. Emigrants had long ago chopped down all the cottonwoods for fuel.

Duggan Maguire pulled his horse up beside Major Bonnet, who rode next to the ambulance. "Major," he said. "Halt your ambulance in the center of that clearing yonder. I'll circle the wagons around it to form a corral."

"All right, Captain." The major pointed ahead. "Pull up there, Zach."

I halted where the major indicated and watched the teamsters circle us with their wagons. The two lead wagons initially swung wide apart on either side of the ambulance, then curved back toward each other several yards ahead. The right wagon's teamster guided his six mules to the inside of the body of the left wagon. As soon as the mule teams of the right wagon cleared the tailgate of the left wagon, the drivers of both wagons halted. Each succeeding wagon tucked in behind the one in front of it. The wagons gradually expanded the circle to its widest point on either side of me. When half of the wagons had created the front half of the circle, the remainder diminished the difference in circumference. The final two wagons closed the circle except for a ten-foot gap they left between them to serve as a gateway into the corral of wagons. When not in use, the gateway was closed with ropes.

With the circling completed, drivers unhitched their teams and led their mules to the creek for water. I took my four mules and the major's horse along and did the same. We returned our animals through the gateway, removed their harnesses, and turned them loose inside the circle of wagons. We would repeat this dance every night until the end of our journey.

On June 25, we proceeded eighteen miles to Horseshoe Creek telegraph station. Little more than a shack with an adjacent corral, this was the first military installation we encountered after Fort Laramie.

Major Bonnet and Duggan Maguire were greeted by a civilian, a sergeant, and a half-dozen soldiers. I leaned down from my seat and spoke to one of the privates. "Who's the civilian?"

"John Friend. Telegrapher. Our job is to protect him and restring the line after the savages tear it down."

I sat back and listened to the conversation.

"We're mighty glad to see you, Major," the sergeant said. "We'll be relieved here in another week and rejoin the rest of our company at Bridger's Ferry. You'll be leaving our pay with the captain, there?"

"Yes," Major Bonnet said. "If you're on his muster list, I'll entrust your pay to him for you to collect later."

"Pay won't do us no good here, Major. Nothing to buy. Not much to buy at Bridger's Ferry either. But the company will soon rotate back to Fort Laramie. There the boys can squander their money at the sutler's. The braver ones might make a run on Nine-Mile Ranche."

"Sergeant, is it necessary to corral here?" Duggan Maguire asked.

"I recommend it. The hostiles hit every few days. We only got two horses now . . . not much left for them to steal. The savages tear down the telegraph wire regular like."

"They've gotten smarter," John Friend volunteered. "When I first came here, they just cut the wire. They figured out we could splice it together. Now, they rip two or three hundred yards off the poles and ride away with it. Takes time for the boys to restring it."

We spent a quiet night at Horseshoe Station. In the morning, we led our mules up onto the slope behind the station so they could graze. From this high ground, Laramie Peak loomed on the horizon twenty-five miles to the south. At over ten thousand feet, this snow-capped mountain could be seen by travelers from a hundred miles away.

After consuming our breakfast and harnessing the teams, we unwound the corral and headed west. A short day of nine miles brought us to Bridger's Ferry, and we corralled on the south bank of the North Platte River.

It was nearly sundown before the ferryman, Benjamin Mills, came across to coordinate operations. The major, Duggan, and I sat around a campfire and shared our coffee with Mills. Although still known as Bridger's Ferry, the old mountain man had sold the business to Mills. In 1860, Mills had married Sally No Fat, a member of Red Cloud's Oglala band. The couple had three young children. The teamsters referred to Mills as a "squaw man."

"Sorry I couldn't get here sooner," Mills said. "I been busy trying to recover my horses. The Sioux stole my herd the night before Colonel Carrington arrived with his circus. I ain't never had no trouble afore. I figured being married to one of 'em would protect me. But this business of sending the army up the Bozeman to build forts has the Indians riled. Nobody's safe now."

"You have a company of soldiers posted at your place, don't you?" Major Bonnet asked.

"Yep. Didn't do no good. That night my herd was grazing about a mile away, and the Sioux got them before the troops could roll out of their blankets. I sent my helpers out to get the horses back. They're Brulé, part of the bunch what signed the peace treaty. They ain't part of Red Cloud's troublemakers. My boys brought most of my animals back today."

"What's the charge for using the ferry, Mr. Mills?" Duggan asked.

"Normal like, its three dollars for each team and wagon, but since you're an army train, ain't no charge. That's the agreement I made with Fort Laramie to get soldiers stationed here. Lot of good that done me the other night."

"Looks like your ferry can take only one wagon at a time," Duggan said.

"Yep. Old Jim Bridger measured her right smart to hold one wagon and a team of six."

"How long will it take to get my twenty wagons across?"

"Well, the way the current's flowing, we can make a round trip in about eleven minutes. I'd say four hours total."

"Captain Maguire," the major said, "I'll go across tonight. I can be paying the troops in the morning while you're crossing. That way, we'll be ready to press on for a few miles in the afternoon."

"Fine, Major," Duggan said. "We can start crossing about seven o'clock tomorrow. That suit you, Mr. Mills?"

"Yep. Works for me."

"Zach," Major Bonnet said, "get the ambulance on the ferry."

"Yes, sir."

It took me a few minutes to harness my mules and hitch them to the rig. I tied the major's horse to the rear of the ambulance, climbed aboard, and signaled the major I was ready.

"Sergeant Marley," the major called. "Get your escort on the ferry. We're going across tonight. The train will cross in the morning."

"Sir!" The sergeant, who'd been standing close to the fire, snapped to attention and saluted.

Mr. Mills had grounded his ferry against the south bank and had flipped a wooden ramp down from the stern to provide access to the craft. As I approached the ramp, Mr. Mills grasped the bridle of the near-lead mule and coaxed him onto the ferry. Hector came up the ramp behind us. Once we were aboard, the ferryman shoved chocks beneath all four wheels to keep the ambulance from shifting.

Sergeant Marley marched his troops on board with one file lining the starboard side of the ferry and the other file occupying the port side.

Mr. Mills heaved the ramp up and secured it to the ferry with chain. He released a brake that blocked a line leading from a pulley on the deck to another pulley that traveled along a heavy line above the vessel. This heavy line stretched from one bank of the river to the other. The force of the river's current immediately dragged the ferry away from the bank. The flow of the water against the side of the boat, working with the action of the pulleys and the lines, caused the craft to slide across the river.

"You soldier boys keep your eyes open," Mr. Mills called out. "It's getting dark, and you can't see what might be heading toward you until it's on top of you. All kinds of snags and logs come rushing downstream."

I stayed on the ambulance, while Major Bonnet joined Mr. Mills at the front of the ferry. A light rope passing through stanchions affixed to the raft's sides provided the only barrier between the standing soldiers and the water.

"Look out!" Mr. Mills shouted. "Tree coming!"

A loud bang accompanied a shudder that rippled through the ferry when the tree crashed into the aft end. The large cottonwood rolled over as it dragged along the rear of the ferry. One of its limbs whipped upward, sprayed us with cold water, and entrapped the rearmost soldier as it swept past.

I heard a scream, then a splash. "Man overboard!"

CHAPTER 8

The night before, Sergeant Marley and two of his men had searched the north bank of the river for the soldier who'd been swept off the ferry. Major Bonnet had shouted across to Duggan Maguire, and he'd sent men down the south bank. All the searchers returned after the light had faded. They'd found nothing.

On the warm morning of June 27, Major Bonnet and I set up the pay table in the center of the tents housing the company assigned to protect Bridger's Ferry and quickly paid this small contingent. The major entrusted the company commander with the pay for the soldiers assigned to Horseshoe Station and three other telegraph stations farther west.

While we conducted payday, Sergeant Marley borrowed the major's horse and rode several miles downstream. He returned without finding his missing infantryman.

By eleven o'clock, the final freight wagon ferried across the river. We consumed an early dinner of hardtack and coffee. We planned to press on westward until sundown, which occurred at a late hour this time of year.

A wagon road known as Child's Cutoff ran along the north side of the river. Wagons traveling the Mormon Trail continued west without fording the North Platte at Fort Laramie to join the Oregon Trail, which proceeded on the south side of the river to Fort Caspar. At the fort, a bridge took the Oregon Trail over the North Platte and intersected Child's Cutoff. The rejoined parts of the Emigrant Road continued west over South Pass and on to Salt Lake City.

It was a hot, dry sixteen miles we traveled that afternoon before reaching water at La Vinta Creek. In addition to good water, we had ample grass for grazing, and adequate firewood from the cottonwoods along this small stream. Child's Cutoff was not heavily traveled, and all the trees had not been chopped down.

Major Bonnet directed Sergeant Marley to post sentries outside the corralled wagons that night. We were now in Sioux country. The sentries disturbed my sleep from time to time with calls challenging what was probably some animal or shadow, but no shots were fired.

The next day, June 28, fifteen miles traveling brought us to Sage Creek, where we turned north on the Bozeman Trail.

At the turning, we found a makeshift road ranche. Unlike Nine-Mile Ranche, it was more like a portable sutler's store. Planks of various widths and lengths had been cobbled together to create a lean-to shelter. Beneath a flimsy roof, wooden pieces lay atop crude sawhorses to form tables. Unlike the shelter itself, the goods covering these shelves were impressive—canned fruit, tobacco, cutlery, crackers, cheese, hard candy, even bottles of liquor.

"Bonjour!" A middle-aged man with a ragged, gray beard greeted Major Bonnet and me when we stooped to enter the open-sided store.

"Bonjour," the major answered. " 'French Pete,' this is my clerk, Zachary Wakefield. Zach, meet Monsieur Pierre Gazeau, the proprietor of this establishment."

"*Bonjour*," I said.

"Ah, *bienvenue*, Monsieur Wakefield. *Comment allez-vous?*"

"*Bien, merci.*" I had studied French in grammar school, but if

57

French Pete spoke anything complex, I would be lost.

"Welcome." He shifted to English, occasionally punctuated with a French phrase.

"The paymaster, he is chasing the new colonel, *n'est-ce pas?*"

"Yes," the major said. "They passed through here recently?"

"*Mais, oui.* Five days ago."

"If I'd been able to pay the soldiers earlier, they would've bought you out."

"Ah, 'tis my misfortune. Had it been so, you would not be shopping here today. I would have retired and taken my lovely wife and beautiful children to live far away in a chateau."

French Pete laughed heartily and waved a hand to the opposite end of the lean-to where a plump, round-faced, Indian squaw stood. Five brown-skinned children, who couldn't have been separated in age by more than a year, clutched her skirt. The smallest sucked a thumb.

After reclaiming my gambling markers and reimbursing the major for the advance funds for my room and board, I had a few fractional currency notes left. I dug two twenty-five-cent ones out of my pants pocket and placed them on the counter. "French Pete," I asked, "may I buy some candy for your children?"

"*Mais certainement.* Mary, help Monsieur Wakefield, *s'il vous plaît.*"

When I pointed to a jar of hard candy and then to her children, the woman's stoic expression cracked. Her broad smile revealed a mouthful of crooked teeth. She waddled over, dragging her youngsters with her.

She plunked the candy jar in front of me and removed the lid. "You like?" she asked.

I nodded. "I like, yes."

"Mary is Sioux," French Pete said. "Her Indian name means 'Goes Slow.' "

I reached into the jar and selected five pieces. I spread them out on the countertop and motioned the children to help themselves. The candy promptly disappeared.

Goes Slow Mary scooped up one of my bills, raised her eyebrows, and looked down at the candy jar, as if to ask me if I wanted more.

I nodded, took a handful of the hard candy, and stuffed the pieces into my pants pocket. Mary scraped up the remaining note.

I walked to the other end of the shed, where the major was paying French Pete for a bag of pipe tobacco.

"I will soon follow you up the road, Major," French Pete said.

"How's that?"

"With all those soldiers going to build forts, there will be many wagon trains to follow, *n'est-ce pas?*"

"Perhaps."

"Travelers need supplies, *oui?*"

"Yes. What's your point?" the major asked.

"I, Pierre Gazeau, and my partner, Henry Arrison, will open a new road ranche between here and the Yellowstone River. When the travelers reach our ranche, they will be in great need of things. They will have to buy from French Pete, *n'est-ce pas?*"

Major Bonnet laughed. He had filled his pipe with his newly purchased tobacco while French Pete explained his grand plans.

"I will double . . . no, *peut être* triple my prices. Then, *certainement*, I will be rich."

"You're more than likely to find yourself scalped if you try to set up shop in the Powder River country," the major said. He dragged a lucifer match across the countertop and lit his pipe.

"No, the soldiers will protect me from the Indians. Besides, I am married to one." French Pete placed an arm around Goes Slow Mary, who had moved up beside him.

59

"That didn't do Ben Mills any good." The major shook the stem of his pipe at French Pete. "He still lost his horse herd. You better rethink your plan, my friend."

"*Merde!*" the trader said. "Sioux never scare me. Not Cheyenne or Arapaho either. Henry and me, we have three helpers—Donaldson, Dowaire, and Moss. We five are better armed than the soldier boys with their old Springfields. We not fear a bunch of savages, *pour sûr.*"

"Well," the major said, "good luck." He touched his slouch hat in a salute to the French trader, then looked at me. "Ready, Zach?"

"I want to ask French Pete a question. Then, I'll be along."

Major Bonnet stooped beneath the low hanging roof and headed toward our corralled wagon train.

"Did a wagon with a preacher and his wife, and two young ladies and a baby, pass by here?" I asked.

"*Mais, oui.* Yes. Two days ago. They buy a few things, then go on."

"They were traveling alone?"

"*Oui.* I asked how that is possible. The preacher said the army at Bridger's Ferry tried to make him wait for a wagon train. He says the Lord will protect him because he takes the good word to the heathen."

"And the two young ladies? You saw them?"

"Oh, *mais certainment.* The blonde *très belle.* Very pretty. Any warrior would like that scalp tied to his lance . . . or maybe share his buffalo robe."

CHAPTER 9

The Bozeman Trail was just that—a trail. The Oregon Trail could be called a road—in places. So many wagons had traveled the main route west over the past twenty years, it was well defined. In most places, this new cutoff for the Montana goldfields could only be identified by the ruts of wagons that had mashed the vegetation flat.

Since early Friday morning, June 29, after leaving French Pete's shack behind, we'd meandered back and forth across the dry bed of Sage Creek. At times, we followed the left bank. At other times, the trace paralleled the right bank. Most of the time we plowed straight up the middle of the creek bed. Not a drop of water flowed on the surface. Occasionally, a wagon wheel broke through the sandy surface and a muddy puddle filled the resultant hole. When we stopped for a break every hour, we used shovels to dig into the creek's bottom so enough moisture could accumulate to water the mules and horses. The animals frequently turned up their muzzles at the brackish swill. We humans were fortunate to have barrels of drinking water strapped against the sides of the wagons.

The afternoon sun beat down from a sky devoid of clouds. The heat reminded me of my tour through the coastal Carolinas after the war, but without the humidity. Far to the northwest, thunderheads towered into the sky. They would be forming above the Big Horn Mountains, not yet in view. Any moisture those clouds might bring our direction would dissipate as virga before it hit the ground.

Duggan Maguire pulled his horse close to the ambulance. Major Bonnet had tied his horse to the tailgate and joined me on the ambulance seat. The canvas cover provided a hint of shade—if we leaned back far enough.

Maguire lifted his hat and swiped his brow with the sleeve of his shirt. "I swear, Major," Duggan said, "I'm about to think I'm in Texas with this heat."

Major Bonnet chuckled. "Wait a few months. You'll think you're in Alaska."

"How hot is it?" Duggan asked.

The major reached behind him and pulled a thermometer forward from where it hung on a string tied to the second bow to keep it out of direct sunlight. "One oh nine, in the shade."

Duggan glanced up at the sky. "The sun's just beyond the zenith. It'll get hotter before the day's over."

"How far have we come today?" the major asked.

"When we stopped a half hour ago, we'd made a little over six miles. Probably pushing seven, by now."

The train's roadometer was mounted to the rear wheel of one of the freight wagons. The wheel made three hundred sixty revolutions per mile, and the device tracked each ten miles before it started over. One of the wagon master's jobs was to record the distance in a logbook.

"Well," the major said, "we're making good time, considering how the sandy bed of this creek grabs the wheels. It's fourteen miles from where we started this morning to the head of this creek. We'll camp there for the night."

Stubby sagebrush and a dozen varieties of cacti lined the edges of the creek competing for the scarce water. Not a single cottonwood, nor any other specie of tree, could be seen.

Maguire called a halt for the noon meal break. Sergeant Marley spread his men along the upper banks of the creek on

62

each side of the wagons so we didn't have to go into corral. Before any of us bit into our ration of hardtack, we manned shovels and scraped out holes in the creek bed to allow water to accumulate for the animals. When we again got underway, we moved single file up the narrow creek bed.

Maguire had been right. It grew hotter as the day wore on. Around five o'clock, I checked the thermometer. One hundred thirteen degrees Fahrenheit. I quickly dropped the hot glass tube.

We reached the head of Sage Creek before sunset. A few scrawny bushes struggled to survive here. They would provide some sustenance for the mules if they were hungry enough.

Above the creek's head, the ground reached a barren apex that sloped away in all directions, signifying a change in the watershed. Sage Creek's dry bed extended to the southeast. Other dry stream beds radiated in other directions. I halted the ambulance at the highest point, and the wagons swung into corral around us at a slightly lower elevation.

Major Bonnet dismounted, and Duggan Maguire joined him. The major pointed down the north side of the ridge on which we were camping. "Tomorrow we'll drop down and pick up the South Fork of the Dry Fork of the Cheyenne River," he said. "It's as dry as Sage Creek for the first couple miles. There we might pick up some water flow."

The teamsters and I led our teams down to Sage Creek and dug holes to reach water. After we returned to the corral, the mules commenced munching on sagebrush and tufts of buffalo grass growing around cactus plants. The ground on which we camped had been compacted by previous wagon trains. With no trees for firewood, we gathered buffalo chips from lower down the slope.

The chips produced a surprisingly hot fire that I coaxed into a flame within a circle of small stones I'd piled up. I balanced my skillet on stones close to the meager blaze and soon had the bacon sizzling. I broke up hardtack and dropped the crumbled biscuit pieces into the bacon grease. Next to the skillet, I set a battered metal pot filled with water and crushed coffee beans I'd roasted prior to our departure from Fort Laramie. After the major and I finished our simple supper, he lit his pipe and leaned against one of the ambulance wheels.

"Another cup of coffee, Major?" I grasped the hot coffee pot with a driving glove.

"Thanks." He held out his tin cup, and I topped it up with the thick black liquid.

After scrubbing the skillet, the plates, and the utensils with sand, I filled my own cup and sat down near the major. I'd just taken my first sip when a distant rumbling sound grew louder. Were those cumulus clouds bringing a storm our way?

"Buffalo," the major said.

"Buffalo?"

"That's a herd moving in our direction at a pretty good clip."

Duggan Maguire appeared opposite our dying fire. "Thunder?" he asked, looking to the north.

"No," the major answered. "Buffalo stampede."

"Buffalo stampede," Maguire said. "Do we need to do anything?"

"We should be safe here on this summit. I witnessed a stampede on my last trip to Fort Reno. We were at a lower elevation, and the herd pressed in quite close to our wagons. They'll probably just flow around us."

"Sergeant Marley put his sentries out already. Should we call them back?"

"Yes," the major said. "I'll give him the order to relieve his watch for now."

The major handed me his cup, knocked the tobacco remnants

out of his pipe, and using the rungs of the wheel, got himself to his feet.

The rumbling noise grew louder, and the ground trembled beneath me. Contrary to a thunderstorm, which would have been intermittent, this sound continued unabated. I tossed sand onto the remaining fire and returned the cooking utensils to a storage box in the ambulance.

The soldiers came in to the corral one by one, followed by the sergeant, who reported to Major Bonnet that all had safely returned.

I climbed onto the ambulance footboard to get a view over the circled wagons. A dust cloud approached from the north. The noise became so loud I hardly heard the shouted question from the major, even though he stood right beside the ambulance.

"What do you see, Zach?" he yelled.

"A cloud of dust." I squinted to see better. The twilight provided little illumination, but I finally made out the form of approaching buffalo. "Now I see them."

"Are they coming up our slope?"

"I don't think so." I turned and cupped my hands around my mouth to magnify my reply. "Looks like they should pass below us."

A shot rang out from the north side of our corral. It was followed by another shot, then another. Teamsters and soldiers were firing into the passing herd.

The roar of pounding hooves reached a crescendo that continued for several minutes before gradually diminishing. The shouts and cheers of the men grew louder. Ten minutes later, the only sounds coming from outside our corral were the screams and moans of wounded animals.

"All right," Captain Maguire called out. "Get out there and shoot those poor animals you wounded."

Soon, scattered shots ended the cries of the wounded buffalo. I climbed down from the ambulance and watched men return to the corral with slabs of meat.

Sergeant Marley approached with a private whose extended hands held a piece of something dripping blood. "Major?" the sergeant asked. "Would you like a tongue? It's the tastiest part of a buffalo."

"That it is, Sergeant," the major said. "Give it to Zack. He'll fix it for our breakfast."

The private slapped the blood-red hunk of meat into my hands. The tongue felt slimy and scratchy. "Thanks," I said.

"You're welcome," the private answered.

I went to the rear of the ambulance and retrieved the skillet from the cook box. By curling the tongue in a semicircle, it barely fit the pan. I covered the meat with a tin plate to keep flies off. I'd have to cook it in the morning, or it would spoil in tomorrow's heat.

Soldiers and teamsters loudly congratulated each other on what good shooting they'd done. I thought it was blind luck. So many tightly packed buffalo ran past the wagons, all a shooter had to do was point a gun in the general direction and pull the trigger. No one bothered to aim. That's probably why there were so many wounded animals.

The camp settled down, and Sergeant Marley reposted his sentries.

The temperature dropped somewhat, but it remained a warm night. We had been sleeping in the ambulance, but tonight the major gathered up his blanket and announced he was sleeping under the stars. I decided to do the same.

About midnight I had to pee. I crawled out of my blanket and slipped between two of the wagons to find a suitable place outside the corral. It was only two days past full moon, so there was plenty of light to see where I was going. Since the knoll on which we were corralled dropped away steeply in all directions, the sentries would not have been posted far from the circled wagons. Didn't want to surprise a skittish soldier and get shot.

"Whoops!" I'd tripped over something soft.

A grunt informed me I'd stumbled over a sentry.

"What? Who goes there?"

A rifle hammer clicked loudly as it was cocked.

"Don't shoot! It's Zach Wakefield, the paymaster's clerk."

"Oh, sorry," the sentry replied. He scrambled to his feet.

The moonlight revealed the private who'd given me the buffalo tongue.

"You fell asleep on guard duty," I said.

He didn't reply.

"If this were wartime, you could be shot," I said. "You're lucky it wasn't the sergeant who tripped over you."

I heard him exhale sharply.

"I won't say anything," I said, "but you'd best stay awake for the rest of your watch."

"I will. Thanks."

I took a few steps away, relieved myself, then returned to my blanket.

CHAPTER 10

I simmered the buffalo tongue in bacon fat. The major turned his nose up at my attempt.

"You can't eat the skin of the tongue, Zach," he said. "The Indians boil it all day, then they slough off the skin and eat the tender inner meat. They use the skin for a hairbrush."

"Sorry, Major. I didn't know how to cook it."

"Never mind. I'll go share breakfast with Sergeant Marley. His men kept their fire burning all night to boil the tongue." He handed me his tin plate.

I dumped the contents of the skillet on the ground. I soaked a hardtack biscuit in my coffee for my own meager breakfast.

The muleskinners finished breakfast and found their mules from among the dozens of animals within our circled wagons. I located the Gospel mules and the major's horse and joined the teamsters in watering and feeding the animals. My mules were used to their places along the wagon tongue, and after I harnessed them, they sidled up to their individual singletrees ready for hitching.

"Time to go!" Duggan Maguire shouted from on his horse in the center of the wagon circle. "Move out!"

The first two wagons separated enough for me to drive the ambulance through and take up my position at the head of the column. We had been doing this enough that we quickly settled into our assigned locations. Sergeant Marley spread his men along either side of our column.

Maguire and Major Bonnet rode in front of my ambulance. We descended from the knoll and continued on the trail beside the South Fork of the Dry Fork of the Cheyenne River. Like Sage Creek, no surface water existed. The morning of June 30 was already warm and promised to turn into another blistering day.

We were strung out single file along the trail that followed the south bank of the creek. Sand grasped the iron tires as the ambulance's wheels sank deeply.

A piercing yell overshadowed the groaning of the wagons and the curses of the muleskinners as they struggled like me to drive through the sand.

"Indians!" Duggan Maguire shouted. "Circle!" He turned his horse back to the ambulance. "Get on the high ground there, Zach. We'll circle around you."

"Now, Matt!" I slapped the reins hard against the animals' backs. "Get up there!" I pulled hard on the right rein to steer us out of the sandy trail and up a steep, rocky bank. When I cleared the top of the embankment onto higher ground, I hauled hard on both reins and slammed my foot against the brake lever. "Whoa!" The mules stopped but continued to prance in place.

The major had followed me up the bank and struggled to get out of the saddle. He stumbled when his wooden leg hit the ground, but he grasped a stirrup and kept himself upright. "Grab your rifle and get down from there, Zach!" He pulled his revolver from its flapped holster.

The wagons rumbled into their encompassing circle. It had not closed completely when the Indians swept around us on their ponies. Rifle shots zinged overhead, and arrows whizzed through the air. An arrow ripped through the ambulance's canvas cover behind me and exited through the opposite side with no pause. It was my first experience with the power of an arrow.

The soldiers scrambled inside the protection of the circled wagons. The teamsters left their mules hitched in harness.

"Come on, Zach." In spite of his wooden leg, the major hobbled quickly toward one of the wagons.

I followed him as he crawled beneath a wagon bed. We lay prone and faced outward from our circle.

Few of our attackers had firearms. The warriors suspended themselves off to the far side of their ponies with one foot hooked over the animal's spine and shot arrows rapidly from beneath the necks of their racing mounts.

There were at least two dozen in the attacking party. After racing around our wagon circle, they pulled back to higher ground. The Indians assembled around a leader mounted on a large, black pony. He alone wore a war bonnet. Its feathers pointed straight up from the headband. He held a lance with feather adornments along the shaft. When he pointed it in our direction, the savages screamed and raced toward us again.

"Make your shots count, men." Duggan Maguire's command carried over the rattle of musketry and the shrieks of the circling warriors.

"Is that thing loaded, Zach?" the major asked. He methodically cocked and fired his pistol.

"Yes, sir."

"Well, shoot the damned thing! Kill those sons of bitches."

I aimed along the sights, remembering to lead the rider, and pulled the trigger. The loud bang of my rifle almost deafened me. White smoke billowed from the barrel and obscured my vision.

"You got one," the major said.

"What?"

"You shot that one."

"I killed a man? I've never done that before."

"I thought you were in the army," the major said. "When I

interviewed you, you said you'd been with the Hundred and Eighty-eighth New York."

The major now lay on his back reloading his revolver one cylinder at a time with paper cartridges.

"I served with the Hundred and Eighty-eighth," I said. "I never fought with them. I spent most of my service in a hospital recovering from dysentery. I rejoined the regiment just before Appomattox and was assigned to drive an ambulance. The war was almost over. I never shot at a Reb, and no Reb ever shot at me."

Whap! An arrow zipped between me and the major and buried itself in his left calf. He didn't flinch.

"Major! You've been shot."

He yanked the arrow out. "It doesn't hurt in a wooden leg. Put a hole in a good pair of trousers, though."

The major commenced shooting at Indians again.

"Are you going to reload?" he asked.

"Oh, yes." I lifted the forty-inch-long weapon, but the barrel banged against the underside of the wagon. "I can't do it under here."

"Get out from under, then."

I scooted out from beneath the wagon and stood between it and the mules, who were still hitched to the wagon behind. I fished a paper cartridge out of my belt pouch, bit off the end, and winced at the bitter taste of the gunpowder. I poured the black powder down the barrel and followed it first with the lead Minié ball and then the paper wadding. I extracted the ramrod from beneath the barrel and inserted it into the muzzle. I shoved the ramrod down hard, tamped it twice, and pulled it up.

Whish. An arrow sliced through the canvas cover of the wagon beside my head. I ducked. When I did, the partially extracted ramrod slammed against the side of the wagon and bent. I couldn't pull it out.

71

"What's taking so long?" the major called out. "Can't you load it?"

"It's loaded, but the ramrod's stuck in the barrel."

"What?"

"I can't get the ramrod out. It's bent."

"Look around. Someone's probably been shot. Get his rifle."

Across the circle, a soldier lay motionless on the ground. I dropped my rifle, slipped between the mules, and scurried across the opening. The soldier lay on his back, the front of his blue blouse soaked in blood. His open eyes stared at me. He was the sentry I'd found sleeping last night.

I picked up his rifle and dashed back to rejoin the major beneath the wagon. He was once again reloading his revolver. The rifle I'd picked up was apparently loaded, because a percussion cap sat atop the nipple beneath the hammer.

I stretched out and cocked the hammer. Coming into view raced the chief wearing the war bonnet. I led his pony with my sights and squeezed the trigger. I missed.

The Indians harassed us for another fifteen minutes. Then they gathered up the bodies of three fallen comrades, including the one I had killed, and rode away.

A few minutes later, I crawled out from beneath the wagon and returned to the ambulance to check on my mules. They were unhurt, even though I had left them standing where they could have been struck by flying arrows. Other mules had been struck, and they brayed their protest as teamsters worked to extract arrows.

Duggan Maguire, Sergeant Marley, and Major Bonnet gathered near where I was standing. "Sergeant," the major said, "you have the most experience out here. Can you identify those Indians? The one wearing the war bonnet was at the Fort Laramie treaty gathering."

"Yes, he was, sir," Marley replied. "He's Arapaho chief Running Bear."

Other than the one soldier who had been killed, two more soldiers and one teamster had been wounded. The three wounded men were soon bandaged and able to return to their assigned duties.

Sergeant Marley ordered his men to dig a shallow grave within the circled wagons. An army blanket served as a shroud for the dead private. We gathered around his grave while the major read a short passage from his Bible.

We unwound the circled wagons and returned to the trail. At the creek, we halted and unharnessed the teams. We scratched at the sandy bed with shovels to coax muddy water into holes for the mules and horses.

A half hour later, we resumed our march and soon reached the South Fork of the Cheyenne River. Here, we found scattered cottonwoods for firewood and clumps of buffalo grass for grazing. Intermittent stretches of water appeared in the sandy river bed, but we still had to dig holes.

After a quick meal break, we left the Cheyenne River behind. We climbed a low divide that would take us to the next water course at Sand Creek. From the crest of this divide, we spotted a thin column of black smoke rising into the air some distance away. It was too far to determine the source.

Maguire pulled up beside Major Bonnet. "That's not an Indian fire," Duggan said.

"No," the major replied, "but Indians probably set the fire. There aren't any buildings out here that I recall."

As we drew closer, the smoke diminished until only a trickle teased the sky. Finally, I made out what had burned.

"It's a wagon, Major," I said.

CHAPTER 11

We approached the smoldering wagon. The iron tires that had collapsed into the wreckage revealed it to be a smaller wagon than our large ones.

Sergeant Marley spread his soldiers out in a skirmish line ahead of us as we approached the scene. The sergeant halted the line a short distance from the wagon's ruins. At his feet in the dry grass lay the body of a man in a black suit. Another body clothed in a green calico dress lay a few paces farther away.

Major Bonnet and Duggan Maguire rode up beside the sergeant and stepped from their saddles. Maguire looked in my direction and circled his arm above his head, signaling to the teamsters and me to go into corral.

I halted the ambulance, so the wagons could form around it. I climbed down and walked over to join the group gathered near the two bodies. Arrows protruded from each victim. Even though he'd been scalped, I recognized Reverend Garrick Hollister. Even his long beard had been stripped from his face.

Mrs. Hollister lay on her back, her mouth open. The shafts of five arrows protruded from her chest. Dried blood darkened the bodice of her dress. Ribbons of congealed blood radiating down her face had flowed from her forehead, the skin of which lay sloughed down in wrinkles above drooping eyebrows. Black-red liquid pooled in each eye socket.

I moved around and saw the top of her head. I wished I

hadn't. During my short service as a wartime ambulance driver, I'd seen men shot through the face and the gut and some who no longer had an arm or a leg, but I'd never seen anything like this. A deep gash stretched from her forehead, across the crown of her head, and down to her neck in back. The light breeze fluttered tufts of gray hair above each ear. The skull bone shone white among streaks of red. The savages had probably scalped her while she lived.

My stomach lurched. I clasped a hand over my mouth and dashed around the rear of the wagon's remains. I spewed vomit five feet ahead of me and dropped to my knees. The bitter taste of bile filled my mouth, and I retched with dry heaves. I sucked air into my lungs and wiped the slimy mess off my lips.

That's when I heard the whimper—barely above a whisper.

"Help."

I would not have heard it except the wagons had completed their corralling, and the noise from creaking wheels and jingling harness had ceased. I followed the faint sound of the plaintive cry to a bank that rose three feet above the dry bed of Sand Creek. Standing on the bank, I decided the call came from a dense clump of sagebrush below and to my right.

I slid down into the bed of the creek. There I paused to listen.

"Help."

The moaning came from the bushes. I moved slowly along the pebbly edge of the creek, peering into the thicket. A splash of blue color jumped out from among olive-drab green leaves.

"Who's there?" I asked.

A louder moan responded. "Katy."

"Katy O'Toole?" I stared into the gloom of the encompassing brush. A pair of blue eyes looked back at me. "Come on out. It's all right."

"Can't."

"What do you mean? It's all right. The Indians are gone."

75

"Dammit, I'm stuck," she hissed.

Such language I'd not expected. "Here, I'll give you a hand."

"No, it will hurt."

"What will hurt?"

"The arrow in my shoulder."

The point of an arrowhead barely protruded through the front of her dress. She was kneeling among the intertwined branches of a cluster of five-foot-high sagebrush that concealed a cave-like depression extending several feet into the bank of the creek.

"It's caught in the branches behind me," she said. "I can't reach it to untangle it. Oh, God! When I move, it really hurts."

I turned and cupped my hands around my mouth. "Major Bonnet!"

When the major looked in my direction, I waved a hand. "Down here!" I shouted. "Katy O'Toole's down here!"

"Katy O'Toole?" he responded.

"Bring bayonets!" I yelled. "We have to cut her out."

Duggan Maguire, Sergeant Marley, and two privates joined me in the creek bed. Major Bonnet remained atop the bank. With his wooden leg, he would've had difficulty getting down the slope.

I knelt and reached in to grasp Katy's hands. I steadied her while the two soldiers used their bayonets to cut away the brush behind her. She cried out whenever the branch that entrapped the arrow moved.

She looked at me. "I remember you. We met in the sutler's store."

"Zach Wakefield."

"She's free now," one of the privates said.

"All right, Miss O'Toole," I said. "Come on out."

"I can't get up, damn it. I'm kneeling on my skirt."

"Wait. I'll help you."

While I held her forearms to steady her, she raised one knee at a time until she had her feet under her. Loud groaning accompanied each movement. I let go with one hand and pulled the material of her skirt from beneath her bare feet as she raised one then the other foot.

"I think I can get up now," she said.

I placed my hands under her elbows and helped her stand. Once clear of the entanglement, she collapsed against me. The tip of the arrowhead poked me in the chest. I grunted, and she moaned. Her head dropped against my chest, and I could see the arrow's shaft extending two feet behind her left shoulder. A few inches lower and it would have penetrated her heart. The material of her dress around the shaft revealed a widespread wet stain.

"Let's get her to the ambulance, Zach," Major Bonnet called down.

I took one arm, and Duggan took the other.

"Oh, damn!" She cried out when we struggled to help her up the bank. "Go slower," she said. "I'm not wearing shoes."

Katy did not take her eyes off the bodies as we led her beyond the remnants of the Hollisters' wagon. We guided her through a gap in the encircling wagons to the rear of the ambulance. Major Bonnet dumped out the contents of my kitchen box, turned it upside down, and had Katy sit on the makeshift stool.

"We have to get that arrow out, Miss O'Toole," the major said.

Katy nodded. "Reverend and Mrs. Hollister are dead," she muttered. "Have you found Megan and the baby?"

"No," Major Bonnet said, "we haven't."

"How are we going to do this?" Duggan asked.

"From the way her shoulder droops," the major said, "I suspect her collarbone is broken. If I try to pull the arrow out the barbs on the arrowhead will tear muscle and blood vessels.

77

I'll have to shove the shaft forward and cut the arrowhead off. Then pull out the shaft."

"Oh, no," Katy groaned.

"Duggan," the major said, "you have whiskey in your saddlebags, I believe."

"Rye," Duggan answered.

"Fetch it, please. We'll use it as anesthesia. It's all we have."

While Duggan went to his horse, the major went to the rear of the ambulance and returned with my sharp butcher knife. He also brought the arrow that'd been shot into his wooden leg. He compared his arrow with the one protruding from Katy's back.

"The markings on the shafts are the same. We'll take them to Fort Reno. If Jim Bridger's there, he'll be able to confirm they're Arapaho."

Duggan handed a half-empty bottle of whiskey to the major, who extracted the cork and extended the bottle to Katy.

"Drink some of this, Miss O'Toole," the major said. "I'm sorry there's no doctor here with chloroform to perform proper surgery. But we can't leave that arrow in you."

"I don't think I can hold the bottle, Major," she said.

"Here, Zach." The major handed me the bottle.

I knelt beside her and tipped the open bottle to her lips.

She took a gulp, coughed, and choked. "Ho!" she whooped. "That's strong stuff."

"Now, Miss O'Toole," the major said, "I've got to cut your dress away. I don't want to drag more material into the wound."

Katy nodded.

"Keep drinking." The major walked around behind Katy.

I tipped the bottle to Katy's lips again. She took a long swig and smacked her lips.

"Thish ish good." She slurred her words.

I noticed Duggan, standing out of view of the major, reach into his pocket and pull out the gold shamrock I'd seen him fondle in the sutler's store. He rubbed it a couple of times and shoved it back into his pocket.

Katy's cotton dress buttoned from her neck halfway to her waist. The major unfastened the top four buttons, then ran the knife blade beneath the seam above her shoulder and slit open the top of her dress. He trimmed portions of material away from the arrow shaft, front and back. "I have to cut the upper part of your chemise, as well," he said.

While the major worked, I held the bottle to Katy's lips. She hummed between sips, looked at me, and smiled, causing her cheeks to dimple.

The major cut the shoulders of the chemise away from the arrow. The swell of Katy's breasts held up what remained of her clothes. Even though it wasn't proper, I couldn't take my eyes off the pale, white skin that lay exposed.

"Now," the major said, "I want you to bite on this." He placed the shaft of his arrow between Katy's teeth. "Zach, you and Duggan each take an arm. Put one of your hands under her upper arm and grasp her wrist with the other. Hold her arms down at a forty-five-degree angle. Don't let her lift her arms. That will create more pain."

"Ow!" She shrieked as I took her right arm, and Duggan took her left.

The major stood behind Katy and clasped one hand over the top of her left shoulder. He wrapped the fingers of his other hand around the arrow's shaft.

Katy whimpered.

"Ready, Katy?" the major asked.

Katy nodded.

"Bite down hard," he said. "Now!"

The major shoved the arrow forward.

"Ah!" Katy screamed, and her head slumped forward.

Duggan and I struggled to hold her upright.

With Katy passed out, the major cut off the arrowhead and withdrew the shaft. Blood streamed down her breast and her back. Duggan and I lifted her up long enough for the major to draw the remnants of her dress and chemise down and off her legs. He cut the finer chemise material into strips and formed two makeshift bandages. The first he ran beneath her armpit and over her shoulder to cover the entrance and exit wounds. The second he wrapped around her upper torso across the top of her breasts to hold the first bandage in place. He then cut a large swath of material from the skirt of her dress and fashioned a sling. He eased it under her elbow and forearm and dropped one end over her head.

The major supported Katy on the makeshift stool while Duggan and I dragged the money chests out of the ambulance. I raised the lower stretchers into their bench configuration. The major wrapped a blanket around her, and we laid her on her right side with her back pressed against the sideboard. We wanted to keep pressure off her injured left shoulder.

After we'd gotten Katy settled, the major and Maguire went to check on the digging of the grave for the Hollisters. I stayed to watch the patient. I was sitting on the bench opposite her when she groaned and showed signs of coming awake.

"Wait," I said. "I'll help you sit up."

I dropped to my knees in front of her bench, slipped a hand under her side, and lifted her into a sitting position. The blanket slid down, and I pulled it up to re-cover her.

"Ow!" She let out such a wail, I felt she might pass out again.

She raised her right hand to her head. "I don't know what hurts more," she said. "My head or my shoulder? I've never drunk whiskey before."

"Would you like some coffee?" I asked.

"Do you have tea?"

"*Tea?* No."

"I prefer tea," she said. "Oh, well. Maybe I can drink coffee with lots of sugar."

I slipped out of the ambulance and waved toward the site where men were digging the grave. "She's awake!" I shouted.

Major Bonnet raised a hand to indicate he'd heard me, and he and Duggan headed in my direction.

At the cook fire, I prepared the sweet coffee, then returned to the ambulance. When she took the tin cup from me, the fingers of my hand tingled where she touched them.

She took a sip of the coffee and drew the blanket more closely around her. "Where's my dress?"

"The major had to cut it off."

"What? Did you see . . . ?"

"Well . . . a little."

"You took my clothes off?"

"Except your drawers. There are replacement uniforms in one of the wagons, so the major got these for you." I held up a dark-blue army fatigue jacket and a light-blue pair of trousers. "Also, a pair of army brogans." I indicated the shoes on the bench beside me.

"The major has been married, I know. I don't know whether Mr. Maguire is or has been married. I don't think you're married . . . are you?"

"No."

"It's not proper for a man," she said, "especially an unmarried one, to see a woman like that." She took another sip of the coffee and glared at me over the cup's rim.

"Like what?"

"Wearing only her pantalettes."

"Well, we didn't have much choice. It was either that or let you bleed to death."

"Humph!"

I decided to try a little lie. "I looked away . . . most of the time."

"I'll bet you did."

Major Bonnet and Duggan Maguire arrived at the rear of the ambulance.

"The patient is awake," the major said. "It appears you will survive."

"Mr. Wakefield told me what happened while I was passed out," she said. "Thank you."

That wasn't the attitude she'd expressed to me. "Women, huh." I uttered the comment before I realized it.

She lifted her left elbow slightly, accompanied by a groan. "Why the sling?" she asked.

"I'm pretty sure the arrow broke your collarbone," Major Bonnet said. "It will be a rough ride for you until we reach Fort Reno. I hope the sling will stabilize your shoulder until a doctor can fix it properly."

She nodded.

"What were you doing here?" the major asked. "You left Fort Laramie eight days ago. You should be almost to Fort Reno by now."

"Our horses played out," she said, "The reverend was not good with them. He hadn't brought along proper feed, and he didn't stop to water them often enough. They just couldn't pull the wagon any farther. We were waiting here for the horses to regain strength."

"When did the Indians attack?" Duggan asked.

"Noon. The sun was directly overhead. They didn't really attack. They just rode up. Maybe twenty of them. The leader—I assume he was the chief, because he was the only one wearing a war bonnet—he rode a big, black pony and carried a spear decorated with feathers."

Major Bonnet, Duggan, and I looked at one another. It was

the same band that had attacked us earlier in the day.

"The chief spoke a few words of English," Katy continued. "He asked Reverend Hollister for food. The reverend told him we didn't have any to spare. The Indian asked for tobacco. The reverend said he didn't smoke. The chief asked for whiskey. The reverend said he didn't drink. The reverend told the chief he'd come in peace to preach to the Indians. The chief pointed his lance at the reverend, shouted something, and several warriors shot arrows into him."

Katy paused, and a low sob trembled on her lips. "When Mrs. Hollister ran to her husband, one of the Indians grabbed her by the hair and scalped her. Then others shot her with arrows, too."

"The young lady and her baby?" Duggan asked.

"Megan was tending our cook fire, and Lyndon was sleeping on a blanket near her. The chief shouted something else and pointed his spear toward the south. He seemed to be indicating a dust cloud that must have been caused by your approach. He apparently decided they needed to leave. A couple of the Indians took our horses and led them away. The chief pointed his lance at Megan, uttered another command, and one of the warriors grabbed her and dragged her up onto his pony. Another one picked up Lyndon and shoved him into Megan's hands."

"Where were you?" I asked. "How'd you manage to survive?"

"I was inside the wagon when the Indians came. I had to change shoes and stockings because I'd stepped in a mudhole while fetching water from the creek. I watched everything through a gap in the canvas top."

"How'd you get shot?" Duggan asked.

"After they grabbed Megan, they tossed firebrands into the front of the wagon. It burst into flames, and I jumped out the rear and raced toward the creek. That's when I was shot. The force of the arrow striking my back drove me over the bank. I crawled on hands and knees into that brush tangle and hid. One of the Indians rode his pony along the creek bank looking for me. It was all I could do to keep from crying out from the pain. He would've found my hiding place soon if the chief hadn't shouted something that caused him to ride away. The baby screamed then. His screams didn't stop until they faded away along with the sounds of the ponies' hoofbeats. I don't remember much else until Mr. Wakefield found me."

"It's getting late," the major said. "We can't make Antelope Creek before nightfall, and there's no water between here and there, so we'll camp here for the night. We'll finish burying the Hollisters, fix an early supper, and get some rest. We're still two days from Fort Reno."

"Major," Katy said, "I'll need help putting on this uniform. It's not proper for Mr. Maguire or Mr. Wakefield to do that. Will you help me?"

"Certainly," he replied. "You two step around to the side of the ambulance."

I made sure I stood between Duggan and the ambulance.

CHAPTER 12

Sergeant Marley, who had been supervising the digging of the Hollisters' grave, appeared at the rear of the ambulance. "Major, we're ready."

"All right, Sergeant. I'll get my Bible and say a few words over them."

"I want to go," Katy said.

"Are you sure you're up to it?" the major asked.

"I'll lean on Mr. Wakefield, if he doesn't mind." She grinned at me.

Would I mind? I couldn't think of anything I'd rather do. I nodded.

"Duggan," the major said, "you and Zach help Katy down. I'll be right behind you."

"Right, Major," Duggan said.

I helped Katy slide off the bench, so she could sit on the tailgate. With me holding her right arm, and Duggan steadying her left side, she scooted off the tailgate until her feet touched the ground. Duggan Maguire placed his hand too close beneath her breast to my liking, but Katy didn't say anything.

Katy linked her right arm through my left while we walked toward the gravesite. When we approached the rear of the burned-out wagon, she pulled back.

"Wait," she said. "I want to fetch my bonnet."

"I thought you said all your clothes were burned?"

"My bonnet got ripped off by a tree branch when I tumbled

down to the creek bed. It should still be there."

Why hadn't I seen her bonnet earlier? When she led me to the creek bank, I understood. I had descended farther from her final hiding place and had not gone down the bank at the spot where she had. She pointed to a scrap of blue material caught in the branches of a small willow tree.

When I pulled her bonnet off the branch, a clump of willow bark fell at my feet. I remembered willow had medicinal qualities, so I picked up the scrap and stuffed it into my pants pocket.

"Can you put the bonnet on for me?" Katy asked.

I settled the poke bonnet on the crown of her head and tied the strings beneath her chin.

"Do I look like a lady again?" She cocked her head to the side and smiled.

I forced myself to take my eyes off her mesmerizing dimples and scanned down her army uniform. Only the bonnet and her beguiling smile looked much like a lady. I returned her grin. "Almost," I said.

She shoved her arm beneath mine and clasped my forearm. "Well, can't be helped. Escort me to the funeral, sir."

The soldiers and muleskinners who'd dug the grave stood several feet away from the site. Major Bonnet, Sergeant Marley, and Duggan Maguire stood at the foot of the open grave.

"Stop," Katy said. "I want some flowers for Mrs. Hollister." She pointed at a clump of sagebrush covered with purple blossoms.

I raked a hand across the top of a bush and swept off a handful of the colorful flowers.

We stood at the open side of the grave while Major Bonnet read a passage from his Bible. I didn't really listen to the words. I was too distracted by Katy leaning against me.

"Ashes to ashes," the major said, "and dust to dust." He reached down, picked up a handful of dirt, and tossed it onto the two bodies that lay side by side in the shallow hole. The men had tied army blankets around the bodies so only their protruding shoes identified them.

Katy took the flowers from me, kissed the makeshift bouquet, and scattered the petals over Mrs. Hollister's body. Katy held my arm and reached down to pick up a good-sized rock. She threw it hard into the grave. The stone struck the reverend's body with a muffled thump.

"You got you and your wife killed," Katy exclaimed, "and lost your daughter and grandson. I hope you're happy wherever you've gone!"

The major, Duggan, and Sergeant Marley heard her exclamation and looked at her with disbelief on their faces.

Then, she whispered words heard by nobody but me. "You son of a bitch."

The next morning, July 1, Katy refused to ride in the rear. I usually sat in the center of the seat—to balance the load. Since it was her left arm in the sling, it worked fine for me to sit on the right, so I didn't bump her injury. It was also easy for me to reach the brake lever mounted on that side of the ambulance.

She bit off a snippet of the willow bark I'd given her. The dimples that appeared as she chewed mesmerized me.

"Does that help?" I asked.

"The willow?" she answered. "Yes, I think it does."

"Don't you think you'd be more comfortable lying down in the back?"

"I would not. I know what riding in the back of a wagon is like, and it's not fun. Besides, I would be bored. I expect you to entertain me."

"Entertain you? I can't sing, and I don't dance. Even though I had to memorize lines in school, I don't remember any poetry. I might be able to recite a nursery rhyme or two."

"Tell me about yourself. Where are you from? Who are your family? Do they know where you are? Where are you going? Why? That sort of thing."

She sure asked a lot of questions. I flicked the reins over the mules to encourage them to increase their pace. We had crossed Sand Creek shortly after first light and were on our way north toward Antelope Creek. Sergeant Marley and two of his men led the way fifty yards ahead of our column. The other infantrymen were spread out down the length of the wagons that snaked along the trail single file. The Montana Road here was simply two grooves worn deeply into hard-packed earth bordered by cacti and scrub grass.

"Well." Katy prodded me with her elbow. "Start entertaining."

"I came west with the intention of heading to the Montana goldfields . . . like you, I guess. I ran out of money when I reached Omaha, so I took this clerking job with the paymaster."

"What made you want to go to the goldfields?"

"When my unit was mustered out in July last year, I wandered around the southern states for a few weeks to see what they had been fighting to defend. Most every place was in ruins. I imagine it looked a lot nicer before the war."

"Why didn't you go home after the war? And where is home?"

"I grew up in Albany, New York. My father owned a hardware store. As a boy I helped with the clerking. That's one of the reasons why the paymaster hired me. When the war started, my father enlisted. He was an abolitionist and thought it his duty to fight to free the slaves. I was only fifteen, too young to enlist."

I paused, and she poked me to continue. "What happened after your father left home?"

"I helped my mother run the store. I'm the oldest of six children . . . the only boy. Pa had borrowed a lot of money from the bank the year before to expand the business. The economy had been good, but after a couple of years of war things got tight. Most months it was hard to sell enough hardware to pay the mortgage." The memory of that difficulty caused me to stop talking again.

"Go on."

"I was torn between the need to help my mother run the store and my desire to join the army. My oldest sister, Florence . . . she's two years younger than me, stayed home to take care of our sisters so mother could work. Still, the strain of being at the store all day took its toll on Mother."

The ambulance lurched sideways when the right wheels sank into a soft spot. Katy bounced against me.

"Oops," she said. "Sorry. This darn sling makes it hard to stay upright with only one hand to grab onto something."

"You can lean against me if it helps." *Please* lean against me is what I really wanted to say.

She scooted closer on the seat. When we hit the next bump, her right hand shot out and landed on my thigh to brace herself. I reflexively gripped the reins tighter and inadvertently hauled back on them. The mules abruptly slowed.

"You don't have to slow down, Zach. I'm doing fine now." She patted my leg. "Please continue with your story."

She might be doing fine, but I had to cough to clear the burrs out of my throat before I could continue. "In May 1864, a week after I turned eighteen, word came Pa had been killed at the Battle of the Wilderness in Virginia. I was tormented about what to do. My mother would cry every time I suggested I should enlist. Finally, in early September, I left home without telling Mother and went to New York City. They were forming a new regiment, the Hundred and Eighty-eighth New York Volunteer Infantry. I enlisted, and a few days later I was on a train headed south."

"Did you see a lot of action?"

I didn't answer her right away.

"Well?" she asked.

"No, not much. I came down with dysentery and was confined to hospital in Washington City for months. I recovered . . . a lot of my comrades didn't. I rejoined the regiment on April sixth, three days before General Lee surrendered at Appomattox. Since I was emaciated, the colonel assigned me to drive the regiment's ambulance. The Battle of Saylor's Creek was my introduction to fighting. I transported dead bodies and wounded soldiers to the field hospital. I never shot at a Rebel, and no Reb ever shot at me."

"You were safe, then, and free to go home." She looked at me and smiled. From beneath the wings of her bonnet a few strands of golden curls framed the gorgeous dimples of her cheeks.

"No," I said, "I didn't want to go home. Maybe I should have, but I didn't."

"Why?"

"While I was in the hospital, I received a letter from Florence informing me Mother had died. Florence wrote that in order to keep the store going to provide for herself and my sisters, she gave up her true love and married the banker's son. He took over running the business, and she no longer had to worry about a mortgage. It's her business now, not mine. I won't take that away from her."

We had been traveling for several miles across the undulating prairie. In the distance, a line of cottonwood trees appeared on the horizon. We were approaching a water course—Antelope Creek.

I was on the verge of asking Katy to tell me about her life when we were interrupted by a shout from Sergeant Marley to halt the column.

"Whoa!" I pulled on the reins and stepped against the brake lever.

The sergeant came running to where Major Bonnet and Duggan Maguire had been sauntering along on horseback ahead of the ambulance.

"I don't think you should bring the ambulance any farther just yet, Major." Sergeant Marley looked toward Katy and me. "Up yonder under a tree along the creek bed, we've found a young woman who's dying."

CHAPTER 13

"I heard the sergeant's words, Zach," Katy said. "It's Megan, I know. She will need me. Don't try to keep me away."

I hated the thought of Katy seeing her friend injured and dying. On the other hand, I imagined I would feel the same way if she were my friend.

"Zach," Major Bonnet shouted from where he rode in front of the ambulance. "Stay there until I check this out."

"She wants to go, Major," I yelled. "She's certain it's her friend."

The major shook his head, obviously not agreeing, but he motioned us forward anyway.

I flicked the reins, and the mules pulled the ambulance down the gradual slope to the level of the trees lining Antelope Creek. Two infantrymen knelt beside a woman wearing a rumpled yellow dress and lying slumped against a large cottonwood.

The major, Duggan Maguire, and Sergeant Marley reached the scene before us.

Katy, in a hurry to get down by herself, bumped her injured arm against the sideboard. "Ow! Help, Zach, I can't do it alone."

I jumped down and hurried around to Katy's side of the ambulance. I held up my hands, and she eased forward into my grasp while I lifted her off the seat and set her feet on the ground.

Her wounded shoulder bumped against my chest, and she groaned again. She blew out a long breath and linked her good

92

arm with mine.

Katy and I walked over to where Megan Sawyer lay with her head propped at an awkward angle against the tree trunk. Her face was turned away from us. A wide strip of hair was missing down the center of her skull. The shaft of an arrow had penetrated deeply into her lower back. The dress material was soaked with blood. A putrid smell hung over her. I helped Katy step around Megan. The front of Megan's dress was covered in blood and feces where the arrowhead protruded through her abdomen.

"Oh, Megan," Katy whispered. "Megan, dear Megan." Tears glistened in Katy's eyes.

Megan slowly lifted her head away from the tree and looked at Katy. When she did so, blood oozed down her forehead from where her scalp had been stripped off.

I helped Katy kneel beside the wounded girl. Katy picked up one of her friend's hands and kissed it. "Oh, Megan," she sobbed.

Major Bonnet walked up and stood behind Megan. He looked across the injured girl and spoke to Katy. "We can't do anything for her, Miss O'Toole. She's been gut shot."

"Megan?" Katy asked. "Where is Lyndon? Where is the baby?"

Megan struggled to raise her eyes from beneath drooping eyebrows. "I . . ." She smacked her dried, cracked lips and ran her tongue over them.

"Water," the major said. "Who's got a canteen?"

One of the privates handed over his canvas-covered canteen. Major Bonnet pulled the cork and passed it down to Katy, who tipped the spout against Megan's lips. Most of the water ran down the side of her face.

Megan licked her lips again. "He cried . . . toothache. No clove oil."

"Oh, my," Katy said. "The clove oil was in the wagon."

"He cried . . . wouldn't stop." Megan exhaled sharply and went silent.

"What happened then, Mrs. Sawyer?" Major Bonnet asked.

"Chief yelled. Took him from me."

"They took him?" Katy questioned.

Megan barely nodded.

"I jumped from horse. Reached for Lyndon."

"Then what happened?" Katy asked.

"Chief kicked me. I fell. Arrow hurt first . . . then, knife hurt." She whimpered, and her head dropped back against the tree. "They left me. Crying continued . . . grew fainter." Megan sputtered and spat blood. "Then scream."

Tears trickled down Katy's cheeks, and she pressed her lips against Megan's fingers.

Sergeant Marley had been searching the nearby area and returned to the cottonwood. "She crawled to the tree from over there." He pointed to the roadway several feet away. "You can see where she dragged herself through the dirt. Lots of pony tracks circling in the road."

"Mrs. Sawyer," the major asked, "did you crawl here right after you were shot?"

Megan nodded.

"The Indians probably continued north," Major Bonnet said. "If they'd traveled south, we'd have seen them as we approached."

"I agree," Sergeant Marley said.

"Sergeant," Major Bonnet said, "take your men and search on the other side of the creek. Whatever you might find, I suspect it won't be far from here."

"Yes, sir."

"I'll go with them," I said. I ran to the ambulance and got my rifle-musket.

After we waded across the shallow creek, Sergeant Marley spread us out in a skirmish line on either side of the road.

We'd only gone a hundred yards when broken clumps of sagebrush caught my eye. "Sergeant Marley," I said, "look. I think they left the road here and headed west. These breaks could have been made by ponies."

Searching near the damaged brush, I found pony hoofprints in the sandy soil. I also spotted prints made by horseshoes. "This has to be their trail," I said. "The shod prints would be the reverend's horses."

Sergeant Marley pulled his men into a closer formation, and we followed the hoof impressions and disturbed vegetation to the west, away from the Bozeman Trail.

One of the privates abruptly stopped and held out his musket, pointing to his front.

"Oh, no," I said. A splash of yellow cloth along with an expanse of white skin lay sprawled across the top of a four-foot-tall yucca plant. Sword-like leaves speared upward through the tiny body. Baby Lyndon's eyes stared unblinking, lips lay open in an unfinished scream.

"Fire a shot," Sergeant Marley told one of his men.

Shortly after the discharge of the rifle, Duggan Maguire trotted up on his horse. "Spanish dagger," he said when he reined in beside us.

"Spanish dagger?" I asked.

"That's what we called this type of yucca down in Texas. Wonder why they did this? Indians usually kidnap white children to raise as their own."

"They must really not have liked his crying," I said.

"How're we going to get him out of there?" Sergeant Marley asked.

"We have pitchforks in one of the wagons," Maguire said. "I'll fetch one."

A short time later, Duggan returned with a pitchfork, which he handed to me. I passed my rifle to one of the privates. Duggan tossed a wool army blanket to Sergeant Marley.

I stepped as close to the trunk of the yucca as I could without skewering myself. I eased the tines of the pitchfork through the fronds and guided them beneath the baby. With the pitchfork extended far in front of me, tiny though he was, I had to strain to lift the boy. A dozen yucca spears pierced the little corpse and did not want to yield up their prisoner. Beneath the body, dark blood stains discolored the penetrating fronds.

"Don't drop him, Wakefield," Duggan Maguire said.

I did not look at the wagon master when he challenged me, but a growl reverberated in my throat. I adjusted my grasp of the end of the wooden handle and heaved the load upward. The body jerked away from its prison, and I held it momentarily suspended above the treacherous blades. I stepped backward, swung sideways, and transferred the awkward burden to the blanket held out by Sergeant Marley. He folded the dark-blue material around the little body and handed the package up to Maguire.

The soldiers and I fell in behind Maguire's horse and followed him to where Major Bonnet, Katy, and the teamsters had remained at Antelope Creek. Megan's body lay stretched out beneath the cottonwood tree.

"Oh!" Katy cried out when we approached. "You found the baby."

Major Bonnet took the blanket-covered body from Duggan.

"Thank you, Mr. Maguire," Katy said, "for bringing Lyndon to be buried with his mother."

So much for my effort.

Katy lifted the edge of the blanket. Her tears splashed on the baby's stark-white cheeks. She placed a kiss on the pale forehead. "I'm glad Megan did not have to see this."

The soldiers and the muleskinners dug another grave, and we buried the mother with the baby lying on her chest. The major read from his Bible, and Katy sprinkled sage blossoms on the bodies.

CHAPTER 14

We pulled out of our campsite at Antelope Creek before sunup on July 2 to start on a long, dry stretch of the Montana Road. The temperature already approached ninety, and it grew hotter with each passing hour as we climbed the divide separating Antelope Creek from the Dry Fork Powder River.

"Hyah! Up Matt. Pull Mark. Get a move on Luke. Come on John."

"Hmm?" Katy mumbled. She'd been leaning against me and dozing.

"Sorry," I said. "We were bogging down in the loose sand. Had to encourage the boys into a little more effort. Didn't mean to wake you."

"It's time I woke up anyway."

Except for the creaking of harness and the crunching of soil beneath the iron tires, the only sounds were muleskinners shouting to their teams.

"I'm sorry about your friend, Megan," I said, "and the baby."

Katy sighed. "Thank you for your condolences."

"You said Megan was your best friend. How'd that come about?"

"We went to college together."

"College? You have a college degree?"

"Aye. Megan and I earned our Mistress of English Literature degrees from Irving Female College in Mechanicsburg, Pennsylvania."

"What kind of degree is that?"

"Qualifies me to be a schoolteacher."

"You're a schoolteacher?"

"Yes. I taught for a year after graduating . . . before coming west."

"But you're not even eighteen."

"What difference does that make? How old are you? Do you have to be a certain age to be a paymaster's clerk?"

"I turned twenty on April thirtieth. And, no, there's no age requirement for being a paymaster clerk."

"None for being a schoolteacher either," she said. "As long as you have the required education, you can teach."

"You met Megan in college?"

"Aye. I lived in Mechanicsburg. Megan was from Harrisburg. She boarded with us."

"Did she teach, too?" I asked.

"No. She married right after graduation."

"At Fort Laramie you called her your future sister-in-law."

"I'm engaged to her brother, Brandon Hollister."

"How did you meet him?"

"Well," she huffed, "I don't see as how that's your business."

"Sorry. Didn't mean to pry."

We rode in silence for a few minutes, then she spoke. "I'm sorry I snapped at you, Zach. I know you're not prying."

"It's all right."

"I met Brandon after the Battle of Gettysburg," Katy said. "Word came to the Hollisters their son had been wounded and was recuperating near the battlefield. Megan went there to tend to her brother, and I went along. At the hospital, we were put to work helping other wounded, too. It was not a pretty sight. Fortunately, Brandon was not severely injured. Megan met Brandon's friend, Dennis Sawyer, there. The two men were in adjacent cots. Megan fell in love with Dennis, and I fell for Brandon."

She stopped talking and left me hanging. I finally screwed up my courage. "If Megan got married, why haven't you?"

"I was not yet fifteen when we went to Gettysburg. Megan was sixteen. She and Dennis married as soon as the war was over. She was eighteen then. Brandon and I wanted to get married, but my parents wouldn't have it. They'd seen too many unhappy young marriages in Ireland. They made me promise to wait until I turned eighteen. So, I'm going to Montana to get married on the day I turn eighteen."

"When's that?"

"October tenth."

"Is your fiancé a miner?"

"Aye, he and Dennis got the gold bug and went to Montana together. They wrote to Reverend Hollister suggesting he become the minister of a new Methodist church in Virginia City. The reverend was enamored with the idea of converting the Indians and agreed to go. Brandon asked his folks to bring me with them. I could be a schoolteacher for the miners' children. The Hollisters promised my folks they wouldn't let me get married until I turned eighteen. I guess there's no one left out here to hold me to that promise."

"You still going on to Montana?"

"I don't know. Everything I had went up in flames in that wagon. Not sure how I'll get there."

"Maybe you should go back to Pennsylvania."

"I've thought of that. But, since I don't have any money, how would I pay to get there? Brandon's the only Hollister left. He'll need my moral support now, as well as my love. With Megan and the baby gone, Dennis Sawyer will need comforting, too. Those are strong reasons to go on to Montana."

"You're injured. You can't travel alone."

"I'll find a way."

We continued pulling up the gradual slope of the divide. About noon, the trail leveled out. "I think we've reached the top," I said. "We'll probably take a break here."

True to my prediction, Duggan Maguire called a halt, and we swung into corral. I dropped down from my side of the seat and went around to help Katy dismount.

"Wow!" Katy said. "Look at that." She stood in the driver's box and pointed to the northwest.

I followed her gesture. A long line of snow-capped mountains stretched across the horizon. "The Big Horns," I said. "Looks more inviting than this blasted hot country."

"And look there." She pointed the opposite direction.

"The Pumpkin Buttes. Major Bonnet said we'd see them when we got close to Fort Reno."

Four flat-topped mesas dominated the northeastern horizon about forty miles away. I compared the distance to the Big Horns. The mountains were twice as far from us as the buttes.

Katy sat in the footwell with her legs extended in my direction. It was easier for her to descend from that position than from a standing one. Since she wore army trousers, there was no danger of her embarrassing herself. She slid into my grasp. I always wanted that moment to last longer than it did.

I transferred water from our barrel with a bucket to my mules. The teamsters did the same for their strings. While I held the bucket beneath a mule's muzzle, I gnawed on a piece of jerky. We didn't plan to stay on this shade-deprived ridge long enough to prepare a regular noon meal.

We'd been underway about an hour, heading down slope on the northern side of the divide, when Katy unfastened the top two buttons of her shell jacket. My mouth fell open as I watched her do it.

"Keep your eyes on the road, Mr. Wakefield."

I turned my head straight ahead, but my eyes kept shifting to my left.

"How can soldiers stand these heavy wool coats in this heat. Why do they keep them buttoned up to their necks?"

"Regulations," I answered.

"Pooh on regulations," she said. "I'd take this off if I wore anything under it. How hot is it anyway?"

"When I checked the thermometer on the ridge top it was one hundred six." No breeze rendered relief from the heat. Sweat trickled off the tip of my nose. Perspiration blanketed the coats of the mules.

Late in the day, the ragged tree line of the Dry Fork Powder River appeared ahead of us. Major Bonnet said even though its name evinced a foreboding destination, we could find brackish water by digging. Hopefully, it wouldn't be so foul the mules would refuse to drink it. The water in our barrels was running low.

Duggan Maguire suddenly pulled away from the head of the column and raced after an antelope, chasing it into a ravine. I heard a shot. Not long after, he rode out of the ravine with an antelope carcass draped across his horse's rump.

"You would think he's an Indian, the way he rides," Katy said. "I hadn't really paid attention to his pronounced cheekbones until he brought back Lyndon's body yesterday. I could have sworn I was looking into the face of a handsome Indian. What do you think, Zach?"

"He said his mother was Cherokee."

"That Indian blood may explain why he exudes such a commanding manner," she continued. "I've been impressed with him ever since he allowed the Hollisters to join his wagon train in Julesburg."

Maguire came abreast of us and tipped his hat to Katy. "Miss O'Toole," he said. "Good afternoon."

Katy leaned forward. "Good afternoon, Mr. Maguire."

Maguire's eyes focused on the unbuttoned shell jacket. I reached over and pulled on Katy's good shoulder. She shot me a fierce glance, then turned back to Maguire.

"You ever eat antelope, Miss O'Toole?" Maguire asked.

"No, Mr. Maguire, I haven't."

"Well, after the boys butcher this, I'll bring some steaks over and invite myself to join you for supper. It'll be the tastiest meat you ever ate . . . if Zach doesn't burn it." Maguire rode back to the freight wagons.

"Have you eaten antelope, Zach?" Katy asked.

"Yes. He's right about it being tasty meat. Maybe you should be the cook tonight, so I don't burn it."

"You're doing fine as the cook, Zach. And since I'm injured, I might be the one to make a mistake with the frying pan." She laid her good hand over her sling and mimicked a look of pain. Then she laughed, emphasizing the gorgeous dimples at the corners of her mouth.

That evening, we went into camp at the Dry Fork Powder River. We were sixteen miles from Fort Reno. After caring for the animals, I fried the antelope steaks in bacon grease . . . without burning them. The major, Duggan, Katy, and I enjoyed the best meal we'd had since leaving Fort Laramie. Around our fire that night, it irritated me that Katy only had eyes for *Mister* Maguire.

CHAPTER 15

For three miles beyond the point where the Dry Fork joined the Powder River, the Bozeman Trail paralleled the south side of this largest stream we'd encountered since leaving the North Platte. Good-sized cottonwoods lined the river. The mules and horses drank uncomplainingly from the water flowing in the Powder River, but the alkaline taste didn't suit me.

We got our first look at Fort Reno with the sun directly overhead. The opposite bank of the river rose fifty feet above the stream at this point, and the fort lay on a flat plain atop that northern bank. Three civilian emigrant wagon trains were circled in the river bottom along the south bank. At stream level along the opposite bank, a herd of cavalry horses grazed on plentiful grass under the watchful eyes of a dozen soldiers.

Duggan Maguire circled our wagons in the valley to the west of the other wagon trains. Major Bonnet directed me to cross the river where the trail approached a ford. The major, on horseback, led the way through the knee-deep water. Sergeant Marley and his detachment followed my ambulance and waded across the stream. Splashing out of the river on the north side, the trail climbed the steep embankment up to the fort.

The Eighteenth's two hundred blue freight wagons were arranged in a huge square that stretched along the bench of land south of the fort. Inside this giant corral, hundreds of mules intermingled with a herd of cattle. Army wagons moved in and out of the gate of a small stockade that encircled a ramshackle

104

quartermaster warehouse and a rundown commissary store-house. To the north of this enclosure, barracks, officers' quarters, shops, a small hospital, and a sutler's store sprawled in the open across the dusty flat. Fort Reno looked even less like an army post than Fort Laramie. Between the scattered build-ings and the square wagon corral, dozens of tents were lined up in company rows. The neat appearance of the tent village made the fort's buildings appear even more squalid.

Major Bonnet stopped at the large headquarters tent, in front of which flapped an American flag. A sentry ducked inside, and Colonel Carrington stepped out to greet us. Even in this remote location, the colonel wore a crisp uniform.

The two officers exchanged salutes.

"Major Bonnet, reporting with the payroll, sir."

"Welcome, Major. The men will be glad you're here. Not much for them to spend money on, except the sutler's store."

Colonel Carrington called into the tent's open flap, "Captain Phisterer."

A slender officer who came out wearing a kepi and sword had been addressed as "captain," but his epaulettes were those of a second lieutenant—reflecting a fate forced on most regular officers following the war. Addressed by the highest rank previ-ously held, he now served at a lower rank.

"Notify company commanders that, since tomorrow is the Fourth of July, we will suspend work for the day. Have the men turn out for dress parade inspection and pay call at eight o'clock tomorrow morning."

"Ja, sir." The adjutant spoke with a German accent.

"Colonel," Major Bonnet said, "we have an injured young lady, Miss Kathleen O'Toole, who should be seen by a surgeon." The major relayed how Katy came to be traveling with us.

The colonel addressed the nearby sentry. "Private, convey my respects to Major Horton and ask him to join me."

"Sir!" The private saluted, shouldered his rifle, and headed down the row of tents at quick time.

"Come in, Major Bonnet," Carrington said. "It's not much cooler in the tent than out here, but at least it shields our balding pates from the sun. Bring Miss O'Toole with you."

I helped Katy descend from the ambulance and escorted her into the tent following the colonel and the major.

Colonel Carrington motioned to a camp stool in front of a folding field desk. "Miss O'Toole, please sit."

Katy sat and folded her hands in her lap. "Forgive my appearance, Colonel." She had the blouse buttoned all the way up. "I'll return your uniform as soon as I can obtain more suitable clothing."

The colonel laughed and stroked his fingers down his Van Dyke chin whiskers. "I never saw a uniform worn more beautifully. I'll ask my wife to help you, however. Excuse me for a moment. Our quarters are in the next tent."

The colonel left but soon returned. "Miss O'Toole, allow me to present Mrs. Carrington."

The colonel's wife nodded to me in recognition, then approached Katy.

"Miss O'Toole." The colonel's wife held out her hands. Katy stood and extended her good hand, which Mrs. Carrington clasped. "I'm Margaret Carrington. My husband has explained your circumstances. I'm sorry for your losses . . . and for your injury."

Mrs. Carrington stood the same height as Katy. Her dark hair streaked with gray was drawn into a tight bun. Her pleasant smile reminded me of my mother in her younger years.

"Thank you, ma'am," Katy said. "Please forgive my appearance. Major Bonnet did the best he good to provide my attire."

"Oh, the other ladies and I will remedy your clothing requirements," Mrs. Carrington said. "If what we have doesn't suit you, Mr. Leighton, the sutler, has materials in his store. We can make something that will work."

"Thank you, Mrs. Carrington," Katy said.

"Please, call me Margaret." She turned aside and coughed lightly into a lace handkerchief. Before she could return it to her sleeve, I noticed a spot of red on the material.

Another major and a woman entered the headquarters tent. His black shoulder boards indicated an officer of the Medical Department.

"Major Horton reporting as requested, Colonel. I've asked Mrs. Horton to be present while I inspect the young lady's injury."

"Doctor," Colonel Carrington said, "this is Miss Kathleen O'Toole. Tell the surgeon about your wound."

Katy related her story.

"Miss O'Toole," the surgeon said, "I need to examine the wound. My wife, Sallie, will stay with me while I do. Everyone else step outside a moment, please. Mrs. Carrington, you may stay if you like."

Those of us invited to leave did so. While we stood outside, Colonel Carrington explained to Major Bonnet that he was retaining Fort Reno as a stopping point for future wagon trains. His original orders had been to relocate the fort farther north, but when he discovered there were more supplies stored at Fort Reno than he had wagons to transport, he decided to leave the installation in place. His men were at work transferring the goods he needed to take north with him from the warehouses to his wagons.

The colonel pointed to the river. "I've ordered those civilian wagon trains to wait until I proceed north to provide them protection. I have insisted they comply with the regulation requiring thirty armed men. Some of those folks don't have weapons of any kind."

"Reverend Hollister," Major Bonnet said, "found himself in the same predicament when he faced a band of Indians. He was unarmed."

"Major, did you bring any ammunition with you?" the colonel asked.

"No, sir, we didn't. We have canned and dry food, a few tools, animal fodder, an assortment of uniforms, and blankets. Our wagon master is corralled down on the flat to await your distribution orders."

"I'll have Captain Brown, my quartermaster, check the inventory and decide what to do with the items."

A loud screech emanated from the interior of the tent.

A moment later, the surgeon came out. "The arrow cracked the collarbone. I've seen worse. I'll need to clean the wound and align the bone. The ends will grow together, but the shoulder may be contracted somewhat. You did a good job stabilizing the injury, Major Bonnet, but bouncing and shaking in the ambulance probably aggravated the break. That couldn't be helped, I know. The young lady will be uncomfortable for several weeks while the healing takes place."

"When will you do the surgery, Doctor?" Colonel Carrington asked.

"Tomorrow. I want Miss O'Toole to have a little rest tonight because the surgery will sap her strength. Mrs. Carrington and my wife will assist me."

At eight o'clock on the Fourth of July, eight companies of the Eighteenth Infantry, its band, and the rag-tag two-company Fifth U.S. Volunteers assembled in formation on a parade ground laid out in front of Carrington's headquarters tent. The Eighteenth totaled almost seven hundred men. The band mustered twenty-five. The "galvanized Yankees," the former Confederate prisoners who served in the Fifth, added less than a hundred. Altogether, about eight hundred soldiers would receive four-months' pay.

The men turned out in full-dress uniform wearing white gloves but carrying no rifles. Plumes streamed in the breeze from the officers' dress helmets. Tassels on the ends of red waist sashes twirled in the breeze against polished saber scabbards. Bright morning sun reflected off brass shoulder epaulettes. The enlisted men had kept the laundresses working late last night to press fresh creases into their jackets and trousers. Brogans and boots shone from fresh blacking.

Crowds of emigrants arrived on foot from the wagon trains below to jockey for good viewing spots around the parade ground. The brass band entertained with waltzes and marches until Adjutant Phisterer stepped to the front and raised his saber in salute.

"Sound Adjutant's Call!" Captain Phisterer ordered.

The trumpets blared out the traditional call signaling the commencement of a parade.

"Pass in Review!" Phisterer ordered.

The band played Pay Day March, and the companies stepped off in close column march. As each company passed the reviewing area the troops executed "eyes right," and the company commander raised his saber to his nose to salute Colonel Carrington.

After the troops returned to their original formation, the entire battalion was ordered to parade rest. Colonel Carrington lectured the assemblage on patriotism for several minutes before turning the command over to the paymaster.

Each company commander came forward to present his muster roster to Major Bonnet, who sat at our folding field table next to the money chests. The roster listed each soldier alphabetically in descending rank order. Each soldier stepped in front of the paymaster and removed the glove from his right hand. I quickly scrutinized the entries on the roster for that man and advised the major how much money to give him. A private was entitled to sixteen dollars per month, but deductions were always made. It was compulsory to withhold one dollar per month from each soldier to pay the company's laundress. There were also stoppages for lost or damaged uniforms and equipment. A missing rifle easily consumed most of a soldier's pay. Everybody was paid in greenbacks. Fractional currency, in five-, ten-, twenty-five-, and fifty-cent denominations, took the place of coins. The soldiers called these small bits of paper money "shinplasters." A soldier affixed his signature to the muster roster, then accepted the cash from the paymaster with his ungloved right hand while strangely saluting with the gloved left one.

I was folding up the field table and camp stools after we'd paid all the troops and the laundresses and reimbursed the quartermaster when a scruffy-looking farmer approached.

"Bon jour, monsieur Bo-nay." The man used the French pronunciation for the major's name. The six-foot tall fellow doffed his slouch hat to reveal a full head of auburn hair streaked with gray. A pronounced goiter protruded above his shirt collar.

"Major Bridger," Major Bonnet responded. *"Comment allez-vous?"*

"Oh, can't complain, for an old-timer, I reckon."

"Zach," the major said. "Meet James Bridger, guide and mountain man extraordinaire."

I stuck out my hand and felt it crushed in the older man's grip.

"Zachary Wakefield is my clerk, Jim."

"Nice to meet ya," he said.

"Old Gabe knew my father," Major Bonnet continued. "They were both part of William Ashley's Rocky Mountain Fur

Company in the twenties."

"I knew that old Frenchie before he anglicized his name when he married that MacFadden girl."

"My mother was the daughter of a Scotch/Irish keelboat operator," the major said, "and he didn't like the idea of his little girl marrying a Frenchman, so he pronounced the family name like a lady's bonnet. Since my mother always spoke English at home, *bonnet* stuck."

"You have pay for me?" Bridger asked.

"No. You're an employee of the quartermaster. Captain Brown will pay you."

"Fair enough. Long's I get paid. That old codger Phillip St. George Cooke, loafing in Omaha headquarters, thinks I'm not worth the money the army pays me."

"Well, are you earning your pay?" the major asked with a teasing grin.

"I reckon Colonel Carrington thinks so. He refused to obey General Cooke's order to fire me."

"Oh, almost forgot," Major Bonnet said. "I want to show you something."

The major went to the rear of the ambulance and returned carrying the arrows.

"We think they're Arapaho." The major handed them to Bridger.

"Sure are. Where'd you get 'em."

Major Bonnet described the incidents that had yielded the shafts.

"Like I been telling the colonel," Bridger said, "and all these paper-collar officers riding with him. That treaty signed down to Fort Laramie don't mean a thing to Red Cloud and his warriors. The day after we got here to Fort Reno, a band ran off the sutler's horse herd, and he hadn't had Injun trouble in the two years he's been out here. A detachment of soldiers chased after them savages for two days, all the way to Pumpkin Buttes. They came back with one Injun pony."

He raised a finger and shook it to emphasize *one*.

"Know what was on that pony?" he asked. "Trade goods, including a keg of black powder, handed out at the Fort Laramie treaty meeting. Them Injuns rode away from Laramie with no intention of honoring any treaty. The colonel's gonna have to fight every Injun in the Powder River country to protect this road."

"There's not a West Point graduate in the battalion," the major said. "I don't think."

"That wouldn't make a whit of difference," Bridger responded. "The whole bunch believes they can line up like they did against the Rebs and blast away with volley fire. No Injun's gonna play that game. These boys are in for a big surprise."

Bridger excused himself saying he had to give Colonel Carrington his latest scouting information.

With the pay chests empty, Major Bonnet and I could lift them into the ambulance for the return journey to Fort Laramie. Colonel Carrington had invited the major to join him and his wife for an early supper, so I was on my own.

The mules had stood harnessed to the ambulance just off the parade ground area while we'd conducted pay call. Now, I needed to park the ambulance in a secure location and water and feed the mules. I returned to where Duggan Maguire had corralled the wagons at the Powder River.

After unhitching and watering the mules, I turned them loose among the teamsters' animals where they could help themselves to piles of hay scattered inside the wagon corral.

Since I did not see Duggan, I asked one of the muleskinners where he was. He told me Captain Maguire had gone to the hospital to check on Miss O'Toole.

CHAPTER 16

It was late in the day, but I didn't want to take time to prepare a hot meal. I grabbed a hardtack cracker and headed to the river. Not relishing walking around in wet boots, I removed them as well as my stockings. I tried to bite the end off the cracker, but it seemed more likely a tooth would break before the hardtack. As I waded across the river, I dragged the cracker in the water. By the time I reached the far bank the hardtack had softened enough I could munch on it. It left a gummy residue stuck to the roof of my mouth, which I pried out with a finger. I put my boots on and headed for the hospital.

A wooden slab door secured with leather hinges served as the entrance to the hewn-log building. A knotted piece of rope lifted the door latch. I entered and pulled the door closed behind me. Except for one end of the room, which was partitioned off, a single large bay served as a ward. A glance convinced me Katy did not occupy any of the dozen cots.

Having been confined for weeks in a hospital ward in Washington City, I had become accustomed to seeing cleanliness in medical facilities. Here, a dirt floor and sod roof must have made maintaining good sanitation a challenge. I was impressed with how neat the place appeared.

"Can I help you?" A hospital steward held a bed pan beside one of the cots.

"I came to see Miss O'Toole."

His eyebrows raised at my comment for a moment, then he

113

said, "Oh, of course. I recognize you from this morning. You're the paymaster's clerk."

"Yes, and I drive his ambulance, which we used to bring Miss O'Toole here."

"She's resting back there." He motioned to a curtained doorway in the partitioned wall. "It is a little more private for the young lady. You can visit her if you like."

"Thank you."

I pushed the curtain aside and stepped into the hospital's dispensary. Katy lay on a cot against the wall beneath a single window covered with glazed paper. The filtered sunlight did little to brighten the room.

"Zach," she whispered. "Thank you for coming." She slurred her words.

Seeing no chair or stool, I squatted beside the cot. She grinned, and the beautiful dimples appeared.

"How do you feel?" I asked.

"Tired."

The hospital steward came through the curtained doorway. "She was given chloroform and ether while the doctor performed surgery," he said. "The anesthetic has a lingering, lethargic effect, but it will wear off overnight."

"Captain Maguire came to see me." Katy spoke slowly, licking her lips and making an extra effort to enunciate clearly. "He's such a nice man. Don't you think?"

"Yes, I suppose." I wished I knew what they'd talked about.

Katy wore a red and green gingham dress. Her left arm rested across her chest restrained in a standard army sling. It would provide better support than the makeshift one the major had fashioned.

"I see you turned your uniform in." I smiled.

"Lady came with Mrs. Carrington," Katy said. "Gave me the

114

dress. Can't remember her name." Katy looked at the hospital steward.

"Mrs. Bisbee," he said, "wife of Adjutant Bisbee."

"I thought Lieutenant Phisterer was the adjutant," I said.

"Lieutenant Phisterer is regimental adjutant," the steward said. "Captain Bisbee is the second battalion's adjutant, as well as commander of Company E."

I remembered Captain Bisbee had been at the head of his unit during payday.

"I didn't get your name," the steward said to me.

"Wakefield. Zachary Wakefield."

"Well, Mr. Wakefield, I believe Miss O'Toole needs to rest now."

"Of course." I reached for Katy's free hand. "I'm glad you are receiving good medical attention. I'll come see you tomorrow."

When she squeezed my fingers, my heart beat faster.

Later that evening, while cleaning the dishes after I'd prepared myself a modest supper, I watched a soldier of the Fifth U.S. Volunteers come into our corral and approach Duggan Maguire. They stood face to face and exchanged an unusual handshake—intertwining and twisting fingers. Following that, they sat on a log next to a small campfire. The light from the reflected flames allowed me to see the two men rather well. Maguire shared the contents of a whiskey bottle with his guest.

The soldier removed his well-worn blouse and sat dressed only in a tattered collarless gray shirt. Because the sleeves of the garment ended at his elbows, I got repeated glimpses of a tattoo on his right forearm when he extended his cup for Duggan to refill it. Beneath skull and crossbones, three block capital letters were visible. By squinting, I could make out *K.G.C.*

Duggan pulled the golden shamrock out of his pants pocket

and held it up. Both men broke into peals of laughter. Duggan passed it to the soldier, who touched it to his lips before giving it back.

I had been dragging out the task of washing my dishes, but some drunken teamster staggering around inside the corral might stumble across me and reveal my presence. Duggan Maguire might not appreciate that. I climbed into the ambulance and lay down on one of the stretcher benches.

The noise of carousers went on late into the night. The teamsters within our corral were noisy enough, but frequently I heard the commotion created by the eight hundred soldiers on the far side of the river. They obviously were having a good time with four months' pay to spend and nothing but the sutler's cheap whiskey to buy.

Shortly before sunrise on July 5, I hitched up the mules. The major had kept his personal gear with him overnight where he'd slept in a tent with some officers of the Eighteenth. He would want to re-stow his belongings in the ambulance.

Reveille sounded as I drove across the river. The troops assembling on the parade ground bore little resemblance to their spit-and-polish turnout of the preceding day.

Approaching the headquarters tent, I came across evidence of the overindulgence from the night before. A soldier lay face down in the dirt, his arms and legs spread wide apart and tied to stakes driven into the ground. Flies swarmed over his naked back. I had seen the spread-eagle punishment meted out during the war. This poor fellow probably wouldn't remember the transgression that earned him this dubious reward.

Major Bonnet was chatting with Colonel Carrington when I pulled up short of the headquarters tent. I stayed parked until the colonel and the major exchanged salutes, and the colonel went into the tent. The major motioned me to come forward.

"Morning, Zach," he said. "Did you sleep any last night, or were you among the carousers that disturbed everybody else who was trying to sleep?"

"I got some sleep. Our corral was noisy, but it died out not long after midnight. I did witness one thing though that puzzled me."

I described the handshake greeting between Duggan Maguire and the "galvanized Yankee." When I described the soldier's tattoo, Major Bonnet said, "Knights of the Golden Circle."

"What?" I asked.

"*K.G.C.* are the initials of the Knights of the Golden Circle. That soldier is a member of the secret order trying to reestablish the Confederacy. We know Maguire was in the Southern army. If what you observed was a secret handshake known only to members, then Duggan Maguire may be one."

While we were talking, a lieutenant had gone into the headquarters tent. Now, Colonel Carrington and this lieutenant came back outside.

"Major Bonnet," Carrington said, "you met Lieutenant Daniel Dana yesterday at pay call. He's been commanding officer here at Fort Reno. As the senior officer of the Fifth U.S. Volunteers, he's taking his two companies to Nebraska for discharge. He will escort you to Fort Laramie."

The colonel, the major, and the lieutenant spoke among themselves for a few moments and agreed departure would be at first light tomorrow. The colonel said he'd keep all of Duggan Maguire's wagons as he moved farther north. He realized many of the muleskinners would eventually desert for the goldfields, but in the meantime, they could drive the wagons to move supplies.

Lieutenant Dana saluted and took his leave. Colonel Carrington ducked inside his headquarters tent. I accompanied Major Bonnet to retrieve his kit. Once we had his gear stowed, he directed me to go to the hospital.

We found Katy sitting on her cot finishing a light breakfast of bread, cheese, and tea. She'd finally gotten her tea.

"Miss O'Toole," the major said, "we'll be leaving in the morning to return to Fort Laramie. Can you be ready early?"

"I'm not going," she said. She spoke alertly, no longer affected by the anesthetic.

"You're not going?" the major asked. "How can you go to Montana with your injury?"

"Oh, I won't go to Montana right away," she answered. "I've talked with Mrs. Carrington and Mrs. Horton, and they have agreed I can remain with them until I'm well.

"I thought you didn't have any money," the major said. "How will you survive? I think you should return to your family in Pennsylvania. Your fiancé can come for you after you've recovered . . . after this threat of an Indian war is passed."

"Thank you for your concern, Major Bonnet, but my mind is made up. Doctor Horton has offered me a position as a hospital matron. Perhaps you are unaware, but I tended wounded men following the Battle of Gettysburg. I am not without some experience."

"I disagree with your decision," the major said, "but it has to be yours. All right, Zach, let's get organized for the return trip."

"I'm not going," I said. "I'm signing on with the quartermaster as a muleskinner."

The major looked at me, glanced at Katy, then again at me. A grin spread across his lips. "I see," he said. "Well, I suppose Sergeant Marley won't complain too much about driving the ambulance. Beats walking all the way to Fort Laramie."

CHAPTER 17

Early on the morning of July 6, Major Bonnet waved goodbye and rode his horse ahead of the ambulance, now driven by Sergeant Marley, down to the Powder River ford. Falling in behind the ambulance, the two small companies of the Fifth U.S. Volunteers stepped out with more liveliness from them than I had witnessed since arriving at Fort Reno. A year after the war was over, these former Confederate prisoners were finally going home to be discharged.

"Get to work, Mr. Wakefield!" The command came from Captain Frederick Brown, my new boss. "No more easy job driving an ambulance. You're assigned to the firewood detail this morning."

"Yes, sir."

I grasped the short-handled splitting axe I'd been issued and climbed into a wagon with seven other quartermaster employees. The rear ranks of the "galvanized Yankees" marched past as I settled onto the sideboard for the ride to the chopping area. I saw the man who'd shared drinks with Duggan Maguire last night, and it reminded me I'd forgotten to tell Major Bonnet about the shamrock episode.

I felt rather than saw someone jump into the wagon bed.

"All right. Let's move out." My head jerked around at the familiar voice. Duggan Maguire sat on the wagon's opposite sideboard.

The wagon lurched forward, and I stared across the wagon.

"What are you doing here?" I asked.

"I'm the foreman of this detail. You work for me now. You will call me *Mister* Maguire."

We crossed the river along with a half-dozen other wagons occupied by soldiers in their undress uniform of blouses, shirts, trousers, and kepis. They were armed with double-bit, long-handled chopping axes in addition to rifles. We drove through the trampled area where our wagon train had camped, but those wagons had now been moved across the river and integrated into the larger train of the Eighteenth Infantry. For a mile in both directions along the banks of the Powder the large trees had been chopped down. It took half an hour to reach a stand of cottonwoods that was our destination.

"Pay attention," Maguire said to the men in our wagon. "Those soldier boys are going to down trees to be used in the building of a new stockade around Fort Reno. Colonel Carrington has ordered Captain Proctor to enclose all the buildings within a stockade. After they fell a tree and trim off the branches, you step in and chop those branches into useable firewood. When we get this wagon full, we'll return to the fort and distribute the wood to the company cooks."

The soldiers laid their blouses aside and set to work in their gray collarless shirts. The big cottonwoods began to crash to the ground. Cottonwood is not dense. An axe makes quick work of felling and trimming one.

"Each of you pick a tree," Maguire ordered. "Chop the larger branches into sixteen-inch lengths . . . that's about the size of your forearm with your fingers extended. Use the stump the soldier left where he felled the tree as your chopping block. Then, load your wood into the wagon. I expect each of you to produce half a rick. Now, get with it."

I'd left my jacket on the sideboard of the wagon, and sweat soon dampened my wool shirt. My back and biceps ached. I hadn't done physical labor for months.

We stopped for a few minutes at noon to munch on hardtack and cold bacon. We took turns using a dipper to scoop drinking water out of a barrel lashed to the wagon's side.

By midafternoon we had the wagon loaded with firewood. Each half-rick stood two feet high and spanned the four-foot width of the wagon. Each of the seven infantry company messes plus the teamsters' mess would receive half a rick. The mule-skinner re-harnessed his team, and we all scrambled to find a place atop the wood for the ride to the fort. There, we paused long enough beside each mess tent to unload firewood.

Since I was now a civilian employee of the quartermaster department, I would take my meals with the teamsters' mess. Each of the fifty quartermaster employees contributed a dollar a month to fund a cook. This fellow made three times as much as the soldiers who had to rotate their own cooking duties. As a new employee of the department, I would receive thirty-five dollars a month, twice what a private made. Such discrepancies in pay led to hard feelings at times. Soldiers could be ordered to do their assignment. Civilians had to be enticed with money to stay on the job. The lure of the Montana goldfields always beckoned.

Duggan dismissed us from duty an hour before mess call. I hadn't had a bath since I'd left Fort Laramie. I decided I'd feel better if I cleaned up. I grabbed a fragment of bar soap from my kit and headed to the river.

Several wagons and men moved along the road. I blended in with the crowd, so I passed the group of ladies and children without them noticing me. Mrs. Carrington, Mrs. Bisbee, Mrs. Horton, and Katy were strolling along the edge of the north bank not far from the road. The officer's wives shielded themselves from the sun with parasols.

Nine-year-old Harry Carrington rode his pony, Calico,

behind the ladies, while his six-year-old brother, Jimmy, skipped alongside. I had seen the boys taking turns riding. Mrs. Bisbee held the hand of her two-year-old son, Gene, who laughed heartily each time Mrs. Horton's pet antelope, Star, butted him. French Pete had given the surgeon's wife the little fawn when the Eighteenth had passed by his ranche at the mouth of Sage Creek.

I followed the steep road down to the river. There were not any full-sized cottonwood trees standing along this portion of the Powder River. A few saplings struggled to get a foothold. I found a shaded spot under the north bank that would mitigate the hundred-degree heat. I hung my jacket on a branch and removed my brogans, shirt, and trousers.

The water came up to my knees when I waded out wearing only my drawers. I sat down on the bottom of the river and proceeded to scrub my shirt and my hair with the soap. Even though I couldn't see my legs through the muddy water, I felt cleaner, and my shirt smelled better. After a few minutes, I rose, using my shirt to swipe the water from my hair and bare torso before returning to the bank. When I drew my damp shirt over my head, my eyes came to rest on a figure standing on the bank fifty feet above me.

The red and green gingham dress and the blonde hair unmistakably identified Katy O'Toole as the watcher. Mrs. Carrington suddenly appeared beside her.

"Come away from there, Katy," Mrs. Carrington said. She looked down toward me. "I recognize you. You're the paymaster's former clerk."

I nodded. Water still dripped from my hair.

"You get your clothes on, young man, and get away from here."

"Yes, ma'am." I scooped up my clothes and brogans and

scurried along the bank to the skimpy concealment provided by a sapling.

Chapter 18

I worked on the firewood detail one more day, then word passed that Colonel Carrington planned to push north on Monday, July 9. On Sunday we were allowed a partial day of rest to observe the Sabbath. We couldn't take a whole day off because we had to pack for an early departure the next morning.

I looked forward to my first day as a muleskinner. I had practiced driving one of the rigs to the wood-chopping area. The old timer who normally drove the wagon walked beside me and coached me on how to handle the jerk line. I didn't make many mistakes, and I felt comfortable I could do the job with my first assigned rig.

Before supper time, I stuffed my spare shirt and toilet articles into my saddlebags. All I would have to do in the morning was dress, roll up my bedding, and deposit my items into the wagon assigned for transporting muleskinners' personal belongings.

"Mr. Wakefield."

The summons came from outside my tent, so I lifted the flap. Captain Brown stood there.

"Mr. Wakefield, you have a change of assignment."

I stepped outside and faced the quartermaster. Captain Brown removed his forage cap and wiped his balding head with a kerchief. It had been another hot day, and the temperature still hovered above one hundred. This was the first time I'd seen the captain without a hat. It was apparent why the men privately called him Baldy Brown. His heavy beard contained more hair than his receding hairline.

"You're to drive Mrs. Carrington's ambulance tomorrow," the captain said. "Find it and move it over to her tent."

"But, I—"

"No questions. The decision came down from the colonel himself. You drove the paymaster's ambulance and safely delivered Miss O'Toole without ruining her shoulder. He allows as how you can be careful with his wife and sons, too."

I sighed. "Yes, sir."

"You'll be under the colonel's orders until he releases you back to the quartermaster department. Understand?"

"Yes, sir."

"Get a move on, then." He walked away but stopped and turned around after two steps. "Mrs. Carrington will expect you to load her belongings into the ambulance."

I found the colonel's ambulance parked with three others inside the wagon square. Each married officer was entitled to an ambulance. There were three such officers in the command— Colonel Carrington, Major Horton, and Lieutenant Bisbee. The fourth ambulance served its originally intended purpose. How one ambulance could transport the number of sick who might occur among six companies of infantry baffled me.

When Sergeant Marley had departed with Major Bonnet's ambulance, I'd convinced him to let me keep Matt, Mark, Luke, and John. I rounded up my familiar Gospel team and hitched them to the colonel's ambulance. The fact that the mules and I knew each other should help with my new assignment, but pleasing the commanding officer's wife might not be as easy as satisfying the paymaster.

A few minutes later I pulled up in front of the wall tent occupied by the Carringtons. The first person to greet me was Katy O'Toole.

"Oh, good," she said. "I see the colonel took my suggestion."

Her blonde hair was not concealed beneath the folds of a bonnet. Yellow curls spread across her shoulders and fluttered around her face in the evening breeze, accentuating the dimples in her cheeks.

"What's that?" I asked.

"I told Colonel Carrington you weren't a bad ambulance driver. I thought his family might appreciate your touch with the mules. I see you were smart enough to keep your team together." She reached out and patted Luke.

"I don't believe this." I shook my head, my mouth open.

"Believe it. Get down. You've got loading to do." She turned and went into the tent.

George, the Carringtons' black cook, helped me load Mrs. Carrington's personal belongings into the ambulance. By the time we finished, the supper meal at the teamsters' mess had ended. After feeding and watering the mules, I made do with hardtack and cold sow belly the mess cook grudgingly scrounged up for me. I would have done better to beg some leftovers from George.

The night turned out to be shorter than usual. The bugler blew reveille at four in the morning. The sun had yet to peek over the horizon. I found my mules and soon had the ambulance back in front of Mrs. Carrington's tent.

The colonel's wife escorted her boys out and helped them climb into the rear of the ambulance using a small trunk for a stepping stool. She settled them onto the benches, and they dropped to sleep. Even though it would make for a warmer interior, I'd rolled the side curtains down to provide privacy.

A squad of soldiers marched up, surrounded the Carringtons' wall tent, and knocked it down in a matter of minutes. They packed it and the beds, chairs, and tables into a supply wagon that also contained Colonel Carrington's office tent and equipment.

While all this was going on, Mrs. Carrington and Katy stood to one side chatting. Colonel Carrington rode up mounted on his thoroughbred, Gray Eagle.

"We're all set, Margaret," he said. "It's going to be hot today. There's no water other than what we are carrying for the next twenty-six miles. That's why I've ordered an early start. We need to reach Crazy Woman's Fork before nightfall. That's the next water."

"Very well, Henry," Mrs. Carrington said. "We will do fine. Mr. Wakefield will take care of us."

The colonel looked to where I stood at the rear of the ambulance. "See that you do, Mr. Wakefield. Please keep a sharp eye out for Indians. Major Bridger assures me they're watching our every move."

"Yes, sir."

"Do you have a weapon?"

"Yes, sir. Captain Brown issued me a rifle-musket."

He waved a casual salute in my direction and rode away.

"Help me up, please," Mrs. Carrington said.

I held her hand while she stepped on the trunk and into the ambulance. I offered my hand to Katy, but she shook her head.

"I'm riding up front with you."

I placed the trunk in the bed of the ambulance. "Come on," I said to Katy.

Once we were settled on the driver's seat, it seemed almost as if the last week had not occurred. We sat side by side once again.

The colonel and his mounted staff officers took up position ahead of us. Mrs. Carrington's conveyance would be the first wheeled vehicle in line. Colonel Carrington raised a gloved hand and signaled forward. The colonel exchanged salutes with

127

Captain Proctor when he rode past the old captain. The men of Company B, being left behind to occupy Fort Reno under the command of Carrington's cousin, First Lieutenant Thaddeus Kirtland, brought their muskets to present arms.

I flicked the reins and clicked my tongue to get the mules into motion. George walked beside the ambulance leading Calico. George never attempted to ride the boys' pony or to climb into the ambulance, and Mrs. Carrington offered no opportunity for him to do so.

The other three ambulances rolled into line behind mine. Mrs. Horton's antelope fawn, Star, was tied behind her ambulance. A little black cow trailed Mrs. Bisbee's ambulance. Six infantry companies, marching four men abreast, extended two hundred yards behind the ambulances. The mounted infantry of the seventh company spaced themselves along either side of the column and rode as flankers. One 12-pounder field howitzer and three 12-pounder mountain howitzers, each pulled by four-mule teams, rolled behind the marching soldiers. Then came two hundred freight wagons, each pulled by six mules. With only fifty employees in the quartermaster department, one hundred fifty soldiers had been assigned to drive three-fourths of the wagons. Colonel Carrington wasn't happy about the loss of armed men from the companies. Following the wagons, herders struggled to keep a thousand cattle on the trail. Farther back were the three civilian wagon trains that had been held at Fort Reno awaiting military escort.

A half-dozen miles west of Fort Reno the trail crossed the dry bed of a nondescript water course appropriately named Dry Creek. From there, we climbed to a long ridge along the top of which the Montana Road stretched ahead of us to the northwest. At one point during this climb the road curved around a swale, and the entourage spread out behind me. It extended for over four miles. The cattle herd and the civilian wagon trains were barely visible through the cloud of dust the freight wagons kicked up. The soldiers called the parade Carrington's Overland Circus.

We plodded steadily ahead all day, stopping to rest the marching men and the animals every hour. Doctor Horton, as required of army surgeons, had the extra duty of maintaining a weather log. Midafternoon, he reported the temperature in the medical ambulance registered one hundred thirteen degrees, the hottest day of the year, so far. The one ambulance dedicated to medical duty soon became overwhelmed with bedraggled soldiers suffering from heat stroke and blisters.

At each rest stop, Mrs. Carrington opened a leather-bound journal and wrote in it.

"General Sherman himself suggested each lady keep a diary of her experiences," Katy said.

"Are you writing one?" I asked.

"Me? How can I write with this arm in a sling? How would I hold a journal?"

"Perhaps at night," I replied, "when you can lay it on something."

"Excuse me," Mrs. Carrington said. "I couldn't help but hear what Mr. Wakefield suggested, Katy. You know how to write, I believe. Didn't you say you planned to teach when you got to Montana?"

"Yes, ma'am. I have a Mistress of English Literature degree from Irving Female College."

"For heavens sakes," Mrs. Carrington said. "Irving Female College. What an interesting coincidence. That school was named for Mr. Washington Irving."

"Yes, it was," Katy said.

"Did you know that Colonel Carrington was Mr. Irving's secretary before we were married?"

"The famous author, Washington Irving?" I asked.

129

"The same." Mrs. Carrington held a hand over her mouth to cover a small cough before continuing. "We have a book of his essays and short stories with us. My sons like them."

"I really like *The Legend of Sleepy Hollow*," I said.

"So do my sons. They could listen to the 'Headless Horseman' over and over."

We reached Crazy Woman's Fork of the Powder River late in the day. The freight wagons formed a large box corral on a shelf of land above the south bank. The four ambulances, as well as the mules, horses, and cattle, sheltered within the corral's expansive protective shield. The surrounding ground cover had recently burned, so no grazing existed inside the corral for the animals. The water flowing in the shallow creek was more alkaline than the river water at Fort Reno. The extremely hot weather made for a miserable camp site.

Jim Bridger came by later in the evening to report to Colonel Carrington, who had joined his wife and sons around a small fire for the supper prepared by George. Mrs. Carrington poured a cup of coffee for Bridger, and he sat on the ground beside the family. Katy, George, and I remained off to the side within hearing distance.

"Colonel," Bridger said, "I came across a band of Oglala Sioux a few hours ago. They claimed to be heading over the mountains to fight the Shoshoni."

"Those may have been the Indians we noticed trailing along beside us on a parallel ridge," the colonel said.

"I reckon so. I don't believe their story one bit. I think they were sent by Red Cloud to scout your column. They're counting your soldiers to determine just how strong you are."

The colonel and the major fell silent and concentrated on sipping their coffee.

"Major Bridger," Mrs. Carrington said, "Crazy Woman is an unusual name for a creek. Where does it come from?"

"Well, now," the guide said. "There's two stories about that. One is an old squaw who lived alone here in a tepee became demented, and died. The other story says a white family camped here, and when the husband was killed by Indians his wife went crazy. Don't know whether either story is true."

The following morning, Colonel Carrington's officers reported half of the wagons had suffered severely on the trail from Fort Reno and were not suitable for onward travel. Iron tires had separated from wheel rims, because there had not been enough water to keep the wooden spokes wet. With the terrible heat, the wood had dried and split. Blacksmiths would require timber to be cut so they could produce charcoal to fuel their forges.

Two days later, it became evident repairs would take some time. What vegetation around Crazy Woman's Fork that hadn't burned had succumbed to the hot, dry weather and was not suitable to support a large herd of livestock.

On Thursday, July 12, Colonel Carrington left Captain Henry Haymond, his most senior officer, at the Crazy Woman camp with four companies of infantry to complete the repair work. We crossed the ford of the shallow stream and proceeded northwest with the half of the wagons that were still serviceable, three companies of infantry, the band, the cattle herd, and the civilian wagon trains. The sagebrush and cactus we'd grown used to as ground cover since leaving the North Platte River gave way to deep green grasses. Verdant forests were visible on the slopes of the hills that lay at the foot of the snow-capped Big Horn Mountains. The temperature dropped dramatically.

After traveling nine hours, we reached Clear Fork, a mountain-fed stream of water in which swimming fish were visible against a pebbly bottom. Colonel Carrington called a halt midafternoon. He announced this was a good place to replenish water barrels, allow animals to graze, and provide a break for the hot, dusty soldiers and family members.

Mrs. Carrington, Mrs. Horton, and Mrs. Bisbee took folding camp chairs to the creek's edge to enjoy the cooler weather and watch the sun set over the Big Horn Mountains. Katy and I helped George build a fire and set a folding table for the Carringtons' evening meal.

"Zach!" Katy yelled. "Look!" She pointed to where the three wives relaxed by the stream.

Beneath one of the folding chairs, a rattlesnake lay coiled.

Before I could find something to fend off the snake, Duggan Maguire strolled up to the ladies with an axe and proceeded to chop the viper to death.

"Oh," Katy said, "isn't Mr. Maguire wonderful? He saved them from great harm."

"Humph!" I grunted.

CHAPTER 19

Early the next morning, Friday, July 13, we forded Clear Creek and moved closer to the mountain range. Tall, straight pines crowded the slopes of the foothills. Riding as flankers away from the well-traveled road, the mounted infantry struggled to urge their horses through chest-deep grass too thick to allow a trot.

About midmorning, we reached Rock Creek, another clear-flowing mountain stream. As Colonel Carrington and his leading party descended the slope leading to the ford, Jim Bridger signaled them to halt. He dismounted and retrieved two pieces of wood that were leaning against a large rock. He handed them to the colonel. Mrs. Carrington and her sons stood in the bed of the ambulance behind where Katy and I sat on the driver's seat. We were close enough to overhear the conversation ahead of us.

"Gentlemen." The colonel addressed the other officers riding with him. "The pencil notes on these slabs tell about recent Indian attacks on two wagon trains. One a week ago Tuesday, and the other last Friday. No mention of death or injury, but the Indians made off with some stock."

"You're deep in Absaraka country now, Colonel," Bridger said. "The Injuns are gonna put up stiff resistance. They don't want you soldiers here."

"Well, Major Bridger," Colonel Carrington said, "my orders are to stay. So, stay we will."

The colonel handed the cracker box pieces back to Bridger, who returned them to their site so others following could read the warnings.

The colonel rode back to our ambulance. He spoke to his wife as if Katy and I weren't sitting between them.

"Margaret," he said, "don't be alarmed. Those wagon trains came through here before I issued the order at Fort Reno. They probably didn't have the requisite arms to defend themselves. We're a large body of troops and have little to fear. Don't be concerned."

"I understand, Henry. Do not be worried about the boys and me." She shooed the youngsters back into the interior of the ambulance.

The colonel wheeled his horse away. I couldn't help but admire how he handled Gray Eagle. The only other officer who had horses of comparable breeding was Captain Tenodor Ten Eyck. The captain with the Dutch heritage possessed a couple of fast race horses and loved to bet on them.

"Colonel Carrington has such fine bearing," Katy said. She massaged her aching shoulder cradled in its sling. "Have you noticed how he is always 'spit and polish'?"

The colonel stood two inches shorter than I, but you would never know it unless we stood side by side. He rode his horse erectly in his immaculate uniform. Mrs. Carrington made stitching repairs to his clothing each evening by their campfire. She made sure he looked "spit and polish." The other officers, who'd been through years of fighting during the war, often looked like they'd wallowed in a mudhole the night before. Of course, I had to give them credit—they'd fought battles, the colonel hadn't. The resentment in the regiment had become evident, not only from the officers, but also from the dozens of long-serving corporals and sergeants who'd seen action at Stones River, Chickamauga, Atlanta, and other battlefields.

"Why do you suppose he was given this command?" Katy asked.

"Shh," I said, jabbing a thumb over my shoulder toward the interior of the ambulance. "We'll talk about that later."

Carrington had been a brigadier general during the war, but he'd always been on recruiting duty and never served on the front lines. His officers and men did not address him with the courtesy rank of "general." He was always *Colonel* Carrington.

We remained at the creek's bank long enough to water the animals. I led Matt, Mark, Luke, and John into the stream and let them drink, then re-hitched them. I flicked the reins and drove the ambulance into the ford. It rocked and bounced over the uneven surface submerged beneath the swiftly flowing water.

"Ouch!" Katy said. "Zach, you've hit every bump in the road. I don't know why I told the colonel you were a good driver."

"I can't help it, Katy. This isn't some macadamized road in Pennsylvania."

She reached into the pocket of the hospital matron apron she wore over her dress and brought out a small bottle. Doctor Horton had given her laudanum. She pulled the cork and took a swallow. I'd witnessed soldiers in the hospital become addicted to the medicine. I knew it eased the pain, but the long-term effects had been devastating to some of my fellow patients. I wanted to caution her but didn't know how.

The column pressed on along the Montana Road until eleven o'clock, when we passed Lake De Smet, a large body of water visible a couple miles off to our right. Jim Bridger informed us that even though the lake looked inviting with its blue surface shimmering in the sun, its water was salty.

At noon we stopped for lunch, then continued to the northwest another five miles. Far to our left the mountains reared up in succeeding levels to Cloud Peak, the highest snow-covered summit of the Big Horns. The cool weather provided a wonderful change to what we'd experienced over the last several weeks.

After an easy crossing of Little Piney Creek, the colonel kept pointing to a flat-topped knoll to our left. He finally signaled a halt and called to Bridger to join him.

"Major Bridger," the colonel said, "I'd like to check out that plateau as a possible site for our fort."

"Colonel," Bridger said, "I think you'd do better to go on to Goose Creek or Tongue River. Sites there are a heap better."

The colonel shook his head and pointed toward the mountains. "There's tall timber to be had in those foothills. Look at those magnificent trees. And the grass in the bottom land surrounding that rise is deep and thick . . . make for good grazing. That plateau appears to be the right size to accommodate the fort I've planned."

"Look at them hills on both sides, Colonel." Bridger threw his arms out and pointed simultaneously to higher ground north and south of the plateau. "Injuns can sit on them hills and look down into your fort, and they'd be out of your gunshot range."

"If they're out of our gunshot range, we'd certainly be out of range for their arrows. Those hills don't worry me."

Bridger lifted his slouch hat, ran a hand through his graying hair, and shook his head. He realized he couldn't win this argument.

Colonel Carrington signaled for the column to resume its march. In another couple miles, we halted where the Bozeman Trail crossed Big Piney Creek. Here, the water tumbled over rocks in a stream twice as wide as Little Piney Creek. Instead of running through grassy meadows, this creek flowed among a thick stand of trees.

"Gentlemen," the colonel said, "I want to explore this location a little more. Captain Brown, circle our wagons here. The civilian trains can proceed north on their own from here."

The quartermaster, who'd been one of the officers accompanying the commander, saluted and rode toward the freight wagons. "Wakefield," he said as he rode past, "halt your ambulance here. Guide the others up next to you. We'll circle the wagons around all of you."

"Yes, sir." I wrapped the reins around the brake lever and dropped from the seat to the ground. I went to the following three ambulances in turn and instructed them to pull into line to the left of mine. The corral would form near the creek and provide easy access to water.

Captain Brown returned riding at the head of the lead wagon. He pointed to where he wanted it to start the circle, then gave instructions to the succeeding wagons. The circle was almost complete when Colonel Carrington rode up.

"Captain," the colonel said, "that's not good enough." His gloved hand waved indiscriminately at the wagons. "Do it again. More compact."

"Yes, *sir.*" Brown's curt response went unnoticed by the colonel.

Colonel Carrington joined Captain Ten Eyck, whom he'd appointed acting battalion commander now that Major Hammond remained at Crazy Woman's Fork performing wheel repairs.

"Captain Ten Eyck," the colonel said, "as soon as Captain Brown gets the wagons properly corralled unpack the tents and set up camp next to the circle. I'm going to take a few men and ride over to the foothills to check on the timber there. While I'm gone, check out the dimensions of that plateau and confirm that our planned layout of the fort will fit."

"Yes, sir," Captain Ten Eyck replied.

Captain Ten Eyck had been a surveyor and lumberman before the war, and Carrington had designated him to be the officer in charge of building the new fort. Ten Eyck was older than any of the officers except for Captain Proctor, who'd been left in com-

mand of Fort Reno. Ten Eyck had been captured at Chickamauga and confined in Libby Prison in Richmond for almost
two years. He was paroled late in the war after he came down
with dysentery. I knew how debilitating that was, so I sympa-
thized. He had a habit of removing then replacing and fiddling
with a pair of wire-rimmed glasses, which he probably wore to
conceal his wandering left eye and his drooping right one. He
usually gave the impression of being half asleep. I'd seen him
stagger from the sutler's bar to his tent at Fort Reno, after
imbibing heavily. Many soldiers commented about his craving
for alcohol.

Unlike the other single officers, Ten Eyck had a black female
servant travelling with him. Susan Fitzgerald, whom the men
called "Black Susan," occasionally visited George following the
Carringtons' evening meal. I was never able to overhear their
conversation.

I remained with Mrs. Carrington and her ambulance while
the wagons reformed the corral. I commenced unharnessing my
mules.

"No, no!" Colonel Carrington rode over from the small
cluster of officers with whom he'd been conversing and
confronted Brown.

"That won't do at all, Captain," Carrington said. "Look at
the gaps between the wagons. Tighter. Make the circle tighter.
Start over."

Color rose in Captain Brown's cheeks. He executed a sloppy
half salute, said not a word, and jerked his horse away. The
wagons unwound and reformed in a tighter corral. The shouting from the unhappy muleskinners rose loudly above the creaking of wagons and the bellowing of mules.

Captain Brown reined his horse in next to Captain Ten
Eyck's. "Goddamned desk-bound imbecile," Brown mumbled.
"He's not fit to command a latrine detail."

Ten Eyck shook his head, laid a finger against his lips, then pointed toward Mrs. Carrington's ambulance. Fortunately, she was occupied with her boys in the interior and probably hadn't heard Brown's derogatory comment.

With the help of Duggan Maguire, Captain Brown finally formed the corral to Colonel Carrington's satisfaction. The colonel took an escort of half a dozen men and rode toward the foothills. While his detail inspected the potential for timber for a stockade, the rest of us set up camp along Big Piney Creek.

The colonel returned shortly before sunset. The band played, and the soldiers marched into formation on the plateau. I witnessed the first of a tradition that would occur every evening to signal the end of the workday. After the company commanders made their reports to the adjutant, a howitzer fired a powder blast at sundown. A bugler sounded retreat, and the colors were lowered from a makeshift flagpole. The Eighteenth Infantry had arrived to make its mark on the Powder River country.

CHAPTER 20

The next morning, July 14, I waited by Mrs. Carrington's ambulance. The preceding evening, following his return from his ride, I'd overheard Colonel Carrington tell Jim Bridger he favored building his fort where we now camped. The colonel agreed with the guide, however, to look farther north before making a final decision.

This morning, the colonel came out of the family's tent, settled his hat on his head, and straightened his saber. His wife followed him out.

"Margaret," the colonel said, "I plan to be back by nightfall."

"Do be careful, Henry. Major Bridger cautions we are in the midst of Indian country. He's sure they plan you harm."

"I am aware of that, dear. I'm taking an escort with me. We will be careful."

Captain Ten Eyck, Captain Brown, Lieutenant Phisterer, and twenty enlisted men stood a few yards away holding the reins of their horses. Two guides, Jim Brannon and Jack Stead, also stood with them.

Colonel Carrington joined the cluster of men and returned the salutes of the junior officers. He accepted his horse's reins from an orderly. "Ready, gentlemen?"

Simple nods indicated they were.

"Mount," the colonel said. He swung into his saddle, as did the others. Carrington motioned for the two guides to approach. "You're both familiar with where we are going?" he asked.

140

"Yes, Colonel," Stead answered.

Jack Stead, dressed in buckskin, rode a horse equipped with a blanket saddle instead of the McClellan saddle of a soldier. The guide's lengthy, black hair partially concealed black eyes set deeply into a swarthy face. He could easily pass for an Indian. To the contrary, he was an Englishman who'd been shipwrecked on the Oregon coast. A young man then, he'd traded his seafaring ways for that of a trapper. He'd lived among the Pawnees for several years, joining that tribe in their eternal wars with the Sioux. Now married to a Cheyenne, Stead spoke several Indian dialects, and Carrington relied upon him as an interpreter.

"Lead off," the colonel ordered. "Let's stay close to the foothills. I want to see if there is any better place than here for a fort. Such site would have to be close to timber."

The small contingent swung away from the circle of wagons and rode north, staying well to the west of the Bozeman Trail.

They hadn't been gone long before a commotion near the guard tent caught my attention. Lieutenant John Adair, officer of the day, was shouting orders to a handful of men who were in the process of saddling their horses. Adair, a nervous little officer, wore multiple hats, as did all the officers assigned to the Eighteenth. Although Adair commanded Company C, the mounted infantry company, he also served as the regimental adjutant and the acting adjutant general for the Mountain District.

The sergeant of the guard stood before Lieutenant Adair explaining nine men had deserted during the night.

"Which way would they have gone?" Adair demanded.

"I don't rightly know, Lieutenant," the sergeant answered. "But some of their mates say they were talking about the goldfields. They took their rifles with them. Not only are they deserters, they've stolen government property."

"Corporal," Adair addressed the senior member of the assembled detail who were climbing into their saddles. "The deserters are on foot. They'll probably use the Montana Road for speedier travel. Get after them."

The corporal saluted, led his detail across Big Piney Creek, and picked up the Bozeman Trail heading north.

Katy and Mrs. Carrington joined me beside the ambulance, where I worked repairing harness. Harry and Jimmy crowded close beside their mother.

"What was that all about, Mr. Wakefield?" Mrs. Carrington asked.

"A detail is riding after some deserters. Lieutenant Adair thinks they may be heading for the goldfields."

"Oh," Katy said, "I wish I'd known."

I looked at her, then at Mrs. Carrington, who stared at Katy.

"Why?" Mrs. Carrington asked. "Did you plan to go with them?"

"No, but they could have taken my letters."

"Letters?" I asked.

"Yes, I've written a letter to my fiancé and one to Megan's husband. I want them to know what happened and to inform them it'll be a while before I get to Montana."

"I doubt your letters would make it to Montana with those deserters," I said. "They're on foot in hostile Indian territory. Why didn't you send your letters with the civilian trains that kept going yesterday?"

"I just wrote them last night," Katy replied.

"There will be other wagon trains coming through," Mrs. Carrington said. "We'll get one of them to carry your letters."

Katy shrugged.

"Come along, boys," Mrs. Carrington said. "It's time for your morning lessons."

"Ah, Ma," grumbled the older boy. "Do we have to? Jimmy and I want to ride Calico."

"You can ride the pony later, Harry. Now go find your books."

Mrs. Carrington shooed her young sons into the tent. Katy stayed with me.

"This certainly is a pleasant place, Zach," she said. She swept her arm toward the forested area surrounding the gurgling creek. "Much as I should probably get to Montana, I wouldn't mind staying here a while."

"We just might," I said. "However, the man with the strongest wish we locate elsewhere is right over there." I pointed to Jim Bridger. He stood a few yards away talking with James Beckwourth, another guide who'd been left behind this morning by Colonel Carrington.

Beckwourth had an even darker complexion than Jack Stead. Beckwourth was the son of a slave mother and a white father. He stood the same height as Bridger, and both men's ill-trimmed beards were streaked with gray. When Beckwourth removed his hat, a full head of kinky black hair sprang up. Bridger's snow-white hair always lay plastered to his skull. Both were powerfully built and at least sixty years old—an age when most men in the States would seek retirement beside a warm hearth.

Katy slipped her bottle of laudanum from her apron pocket, turned away, and took a sip. She dropped the bottle into her pocket and pretended to be adjusting the position of her sling before looking at me. "What?" she demanded.

"I'm concerned about the laudanum."

"You needn't be. As soon as my shoulder is healed, I'll stop using it."

"I hope so."

Katy snorted, sauntered back to the Carringtons' tent, and went inside. I returned to forcing the heavy needle through the leather strap I was working on.

Shortly before noon, the detail sent out to pursue the deserters returned. They didn't have any of the missing soldiers with them, but they did have a rough-looking civilian in tow. I wanted to learn more, so I set my harness mending aside and got as close to the guard tent as I thought appropriate.

"Well?" Lieutenant Adair asked the corporal of the detail.

"Sir, we were stopped by a band of Indians who ordered us to turn back."

"*Ordered* you?"

"Yes, sir. There were a lot more of them than us. One of them spoke fair English. He told us to bring this man along to deliver a message to the colonel."

"You look familiar," Lieutenant Adair said to the civilian.

"Name's Donaldson. Joe Donaldson. Used to work as a teamster for Captain Brown."

Adair nodded that his recognition had been confirmed.

"I quit the quartermaster department a few weeks ago," Donaldson said, "and joined up with French Pete."

"Pierre Gazeau?" Adair asked. "The French trader down on Sage Creek?"

"He relocated north of here on the Montana Road. Plans to sell wares to passing wagon trains."

"I see," Adair continued. "What're you doing here?"

"The Cheyennes knew I'd worked for the army. So, Chief Black Horse picked me to deliver his message."

"And?" Adair asked.

"Chief said, and these are his words: 'Ask the Little White Chief, does he want peace or war? Tell him to come with black white man to talk.' "

" 'Little White Chief'?" Adair asked. " 'Black white man'?"

"Little White Chief is Colonel Carrington. That's what the Indians call him. Black white man is Jack Stead. They trust his translation since he's married to one of them."

"Why should I believe you?"

"Makes no never mind to me." Donaldson shrugged. "I delivered the message . . . now I'm leaving."

"No, you're not," Adair said. "Sergeant of the guard! Arrest this man. He may be a spy."

"Inside," the sergeant ordered, waving his rifle in the direction of the guard tent. When Donaldson took a step backward, the sergeant cocked the weapon.

Colonel Carrington and his reconnaissance party returned at six o'clock in the evening. The sun's rays sprayed heavenward from behind Cloud Peak. I was helping George lay his cooking fire when the colonel separated from the other members of the group and rode toward his family's tent.

Walking beside the commanding officer's horse, Jim Bridger shook his head and stroked his goiter with a finger.

Mrs. Carrington appeared in the open tent flap. "Henry, I'm glad you returned safely. Did you encounter any savages?"

"No, we didn't see a one."

"Have you decided on a location?" she asked.

The colonel dismounted, and since no orderly was present, he handed the reins to me. "Yes," he said. "I was just explaining to Major Bridger that this is the best place for a fort."

Mrs. Carrington glanced at Bridger, who shook his head, then she returned her gaze to her husband. "I sense the major does not share your conviction."

"The country we explored is rich in game and wild fruits. Vast fields of tall grass abound. There is good water at both Goose Creek and the Tongue River, as the major claimed, but good timber to build a stockade is three times the distance from any suitable location. No, with the timber only five miles distant, this is the best choice."

Lieutenant Adair came hustling over from the guard tent. "Colonel Carrington, sir!" The officer of the day halted at attention and saluted. "Something important happened earlier today, sir."

The colonel returned the salute. "Yes, what is it?"

Lieutenant Adair told the colonel about Joe Donaldson and the message from Chief Black Horse. "Another thing, sir," the lieutenant continued. "A Cheyenne approached our picket line after I arrested Donaldson. The Indian told me in broken English he'd accompanied Donaldson to bring Black Horse's message. He demanded I release Donaldson, and when I refused, he slipped away. That confirms my suspicion they were sent to spy on us."

"Let me talk with the man," the colonel said. He touched his wife's arm. "I may be late for supper, dear."

He walked toward the guard tent with Lieutenant Adair, leaving me holding the horse. I looked at Bridger, who shrugged and motioned for me to join him. We followed the colonel.

Colonel Carrington stopped at the entrance to the guard tent and turned to Bridger. "A spy, Major?" he asked.

"I don't think so," Bridger replied. "I know old Chief Black Horse. He's peaceable. I suspect he's been put up to this by Red Cloud."

"Should I go meet with Black Horse?"

"No, Colonel. Invite him to come here. You can impress him with the size of your force and your weaponry. He will tell Red Cloud. Might make the hostiles think twice about challenging you."

"In this matter, Jim," the colonel said, "I accept your advice. Will you take my invitation to Black Horse?"

"Be better to send Jack Stead. They asked for the 'black white man.'"

"All right." Colonel Carrington ducked into the guard tent.

I led Gray Eagle to where the officers' horses were picketed and turned the thoroughbred over to an orderly. Then, I returned to the Carringtons' tent and helped George with his meal preparations.

Mrs. Carrington went ahead with supper for herself and her boys, not waiting for the colonel to join them. Katy ate with Mrs. Carrington in the tent, while I shared a spot by the fire with George. After he and I cleaned the dishes, I took the mules down to the creek for a final watering, then returned them to the side of the ambulance.

I was brushing down Luke when the colonel came out of the guard tent. It was after dusk, but twilight enabled me to identify him, Joe Donaldson, and Jack Stead. Lieutenant Adair stood off to one side with a guard who held his rifle at the ready. I wondered what the lieutenant thought of Colonel Carrington releasing the "spy."

An orderly led two horses up, and Donaldson and Stead mounted. When they rode away into the night, the colonel called after them, "Godspeed."

The next morning, I was sure I was the first one awake. Dawn provided enough light for me to see that no other person stirred nearby. I must have done a lot of thrashing during the night, because I no longer lay wrapped in my blanket. I shivered when I pulled on my boots. As I came fully awake, I remembered my nightmare in which Katy had not survived her arrow wound. I shivered again, but not from the cold morning air.

I pushed my hair back and settled my slouch hat to hold the unruly locks in place. I grasped the spokes of the ambulance's rear wheel to pull myself up. When I was on my feet, I stood next to my mules, who were tied to the ambulance. The discarded blanket lay beneath them. In my restlessness, they hadn't stepped on me.

"Come on, boys." I unhitched the mules and led them down to Big Piney Creek. The babbling of water tumbling over its rocky base drowned out the gulping sounds my animals made. While they drank, I looked toward the encampment and discovered I wasn't the only human stirring early this morning. On the plateau, above and beyond the circled wagons, two silhouettes stretched a line between themselves, then walked back together. After conversing with a third individual, the two separated and again stretched out their measuring tape.

The sun broke the horizon, and the snow atop Cloud Peak burst into a brilliant white gleam. Light crept steadily down the forested mountain slopes, turning the black mass into differing shades of green. The plateau destined to become the site of the new fort was soon illuminated. Captain Ten Eyck and his survey team must have awakened long before me.

A bugler sounded reveille. I led the mules back to the ambulance as soldiers and teamsters stumbled out of their tents. The hum of voices grew to a crescendo of strident noise. Shouted commands mingled with the neighing of horses and braying of mules.

"Morning, Zach." Major Bridger came around the rear of the ambulance while I was retying the mules.

"Good morning, Major. Looks like Captain Ten Eyck is off to an early start." I nodded in the direction of the plateau.

Bridger followed my gaze. "He's measuring off the ground for the new fort. I 'spect everybody'll be hustling up there to get to work right soon."

Bridger's prediction came true right after I finished helping George prepare the morning meal for Mrs. Carrington, her boys, and Katy. I was in the process of scrubbing the dishes when I was loudly addressed.

"Wakefield!" Duggan Maguire stood with arms akimbo looking down at where I knelt scouring a skillet clean with sand.

"What?" I demanded.

"Don't talk smart to me, Wakefield. You work for me . . .

148

remember?"

"If you say so, *Mister* Maguire."

"You can no longer get away doing the easy life of driving the colonel's ambulance. Every civilian employee of the quartermaster has real work to do."

I stood and faced Duggan.

"The soldiers," he continued, "have been assigned other duties. They'll not be driving wagons. I need every teamster driving rigs."

"So, what do you want me to do?"

"Are these mules of yours trained for the jerk line?"

"I doubt it. They've never worked one while I've had them."

"Well, you'll have to teach them. We'll eventually need every mule we've got capable of jerk-line work. You see that last freight wagon over there?"

"Yes."

"That's your rig for the day. Leave your ambulance mules here for now. I'll assign someone to help you train them later. The colonel wants all the wagons up on the plateau now. Get to it!"

While Maguire had been issuing me orders, Katy had come out of Mrs. Carrington's tent. Duggan tipped his hat to her and stalked off, shouting orders to other teamsters who were busy harnessing their teams.

"Oh," Katy said, "listen to how Mr. Maguire directs the workers."

"Humph!" I handed the partially cleaned skillet to George and left.

The soldier who'd driven the rig from Fort Reno helped me harness the six mules, then he left me with the team and the wagon. Duggan, mounted on a horse, was directing the freight wagons out of the circle and up the slope onto the plateau.

He rode up to where I sat on the near-wheel mule. "Follow

that wagon up the hill and keep following him once you're on top." He indicated the wagon exiting the circle ahead of me.

I had only driven a six-mule, jerk-line rig once before when the old timer had coached me at Fort Reno. I had even less practice with a bullwhip. I hadn't needed one with my Gospel team.

The army's freight wagons weren't equipped with a driver's seat. The teamster rode the near-wheel mule and used a jerk line to control the teams. In muleskinner's terminology, near meant "left" and off meant "right" when facing forward. The jerk line was fastened to the left side of the near-lead mule's bit, ran back through rings on the near-swing mule's harness, and wound up in the left hand of the muleskinner sitting astride the near-wheel mule. The teamster's right hand remained free for the bullwhip.

To get this big freight rig moving I tried to snap the bullwhip above the mules. My feeble effort produced no sound. So, I shouted, "Get up!" I snapped the line I held in my left hand, like I would do with reins, and the near-lead mule's head lurched to the right. This forced the jockey pole leading from the hame of his collar to the bit in the off-lead mule's mouth and forced that mule to turn right, too.

"No! Wrong way. Whoa!" The mules had taken two steps, but they stopped. I wanted to turn left. Jerking on the line had told the lead mule to turn right. "Get up," I said again. Now, I pulled steadily on the jerk line, and the head of the near-lead mule turned left. The jockey pole pulled the off-lead mule to follow.

As the lead mules moved into the left turn, the near-swing mule jumped the chain that extended from the end of the wagon tongue, between the two swing mules, and up to the lead mule's doubletree. I had to train my Gospel mules in this jumping maneuver. Otherwise, on a turn, the chain would cut their legs out from under them. The wagon tongue separated the wheel

mules, which meant they didn't have to jump anything. Muleskinners hooked the two strongest mules to the tongue, because
they pulled most of the weight.

The line of wagons ahead straightened out, and as my turning ceased, the near-swing mule jumped back across the chain.
The ease with which this was done reminded me that old-time
skinners considered mules to be smarter than horses.

My wagon lumbered up onto the plateau, and, when we
reached the top, I saw that stakes bearing small red flags
outlined a square four hundred feet on a side. All the wagons
spent the rest of the morning driving around that square creating a roadway through the deep grass. While we did this, a
mowing machine cut the grass in the center of the square to
create a parade-ground lawn. Another mowing machine cut the
grass around the outside edges of the road to create space to
erect tents. Soldiers raked the cut grass and hauled it away to
use as fodder.

By noon, the layout for the new fort had taken shape. After a
short lunch break, soldiers and teamsters dismantled the tents
beside Big Piney Creek and hauled them to the plateau. A well-
organized tent city soon surrounded the new parade ground.

Colonel Carrington stood in front of a large wall tent survey-
ing the accomplishment. His headquarters tent occupied a
central spot on the outside of the road on the east side of the
quadrant. To the south of this tent stood the guard tent, and on
the north side was a tent for the sutler and beyond it a tent for
the band. Opposite, on the west side of the square, stood a line
of tents to house officers and families, as well as a large tent to
serve as the hospital. Tents housing enlisted men lined the
outsides of the northern and southern roads. The howitzers
were prominently displayed in the center of the newly created
parade ground.

Late in the afternoon, Maguire directed the drivers to park

their wagons several yards south of the area we'd carved out to serve as the main fort. This space would become the quartermaster yard for storing supplies and corralling mules.

Duggan reined in beside me. "Wakefield, get down to the creek right away and bring Mrs. Carrington's ambulance to her tent. The colonel has assigned a squad of soldiers to unload her belongings."

After pulling the ambulance up to the Carringtons' tent, the soldiers emptied its contents in minutes. I'd remained in the driver's seat, but before I could snap the reins to move the ambulance to the wagon park, a dense cloud obscured the sun. Instead of pattering raindrops, the whirring of thousands of wings engulfed me. A swarm of locusts descended on tents, wagons, animals, and people. I swatted them with my hat. Mrs. Carrington had brought along a half-dozen cages of turkeys and chickens, and she released them to feed on the bugs. There were too many of these short-horned grasshoppers for the domestic fowl to make any difference. Then, as quickly as they'd arrived, a cool breeze descended from the mountains and carried our attackers off to the east. The only significant damage was the shredded stalks of grass in the piles of accumulated fodder.

I now had ten mules to water and feed. The other teamsters had finished their husbandry work by the time I got the ambulance parked, so I was alone in the makeshift quartermaster yard. With so many mules, I had to make two trips down to Little Piney Creek. It was dark by the time I stumbled into the teamsters' mess tent. There wasn't much food left, and it didn't compare to George's cooking.

CHAPTER 21

On the morning of July 16, my status changed again. I'd finished breakfast in the teamsters' mess and gone out to round up my mules for watering when Duggan Maguire cornered me.

"Wakefield, you're to report to Captain Brown, promptly."

"Why? What'd I do?"

"You're no longer a teamster," Maguire responded.

"You mean I'm fired?"

"No, you're now the quartermaster clerk."

"What? I didn't volunteer for that."

"I volunteered you. You were the paymaster clerk, right? And you worked in your father's hardware store, right?"

"So?"

"So, you're better qualified than anybody else here to serve as the quartermaster clerk. You know how to post figures in a ledger, and you're familiar with hardware. Captain Brown needs help sorting out the cargo." He swept his hand in the direction of the dozens of blue army wagons lined up in what was to become the quartermaster yard.

"What if I refuse?"

"The job pays the same as a paymaster clerk, one hundred twenty-five dollars a month. That's ninety dollars more than a teamster makes and twice what I get paid as a wagon master. If I had your skills, I'd take the job myself. I thought you were trying to earn money to go to the goldfields. Stop complaining. I'm doing you a favor."

I shrugged. What the hell. I could use the money.

I reported to Captain Brown, who handed me a ledger book and a pencil. "There's a page for each wagon," he said. "The wagon's number and its contents are listed on the page. Verify the contents as each wagon is unloaded. Yesterday, we erected this row of wall tents to serve as temporary warehouses." He indicated a dozen tents in front of which a squad of soldiers stood at ease. "These troops will move the supplies into the tents and place them where I tell them. We need to get the transfer done quickly so the wagon bodies can be separated from the running gears. Timber for the stockade will be tied to the running gears to move the logs from the pinery to the fort. The colonel expects logging to start tomorrow."

One after another a teamster drove his wagon up to the warehouse tents, and the soldiers dragged the contents out of the beds. Captain Brown directed the men into which tent to take the boxes and crates.

"Captain," I called out. "They're unloading faster than I can check the items off."

"Work faster! We have to finish the unloading this morning. This afternoon, we've got to play nursemaids to a bunch of damned Indians."

Captain Brown kept shouting at the soldiers to hurry. They mainly ignored him, hauling items into the tents at their own pace.

I begrudgingly admitted that Duggan Maguire had his part of the operation well in hand. After a wagon was unloaded, it was driven to a spot west of the quartermaster yard. Here, teamsters unbolted the wagon bed from its wooden running gear, and two mules were hitched to the wagon's tongue. A dozen men lifted the unbolted, empty bed, and the team pulled the running gear out from under it. The bed was lowered to the ground, and the running gear was arrayed in an adjacent row several yards away. This exercise was repeated all morning until a row of blue wagon beds, and a separate row of running gears, extended the length of the planned quartermaster yard.

"Are you keeping track of things, Wakefield?" Captain Brown peered over my shoulder while I checked off items in the ledger.

"I'm trying, sir."

The eclectic inventory consisted of pre-made window sashes, crates of horseshoes, kegs of nails, cans of paint, barrels of pickles, sacks of grain, and a thousand other items. The colonel had been quite thorough in planning for the myriad items required to build a fort.

At noon, the bugler blew Officers' Call. Captain Brown called a halt to work, and we headed to the teamsters' mess for lunch—such as it was. Word spread through the mess tent that the expected Indians were approaching.

Jack Stead had returned the night before with word that Chief Black Horse had accepted Colonel Carrington's invitation. During the morning hours, a detail of soldiers erected the roof of a spare hospital tent in the center of the parade ground to serve as an open-air meeting place. An American flag covered a folding table, behind which were folding chairs for the senior officers. Other chairs had been arranged in front of the tent for the visitors.

I joined the muleskinners along the south edge of the parade ground. No one was permitted to walk on the grass without permission, so we stood in the center of the newly created roadway.

The Indians crested the top of the high ridge to the north that Colonel Carrington had named Sullivant Hills, to honor his wife's maiden name. One of the warriors waved a white flag.

On the parade ground, the infantry companies were drawn up in formation. Bandmaster Samuel Curry marched and counter-marched the band in front of the assembled troops.

Each of his twenty-five musicians strained to outdo the others in blasting out martial tunes. Colonel Carrington led his staff out of the headquarters tent and across the road to the hospitality canopy. The officers were more resplendent in their full-dress uniforms than they had been on payday at Fort Reno. Shoulder scales replaced shoulder boards. Plumes streamed in the breeze from dress helmets. Saber scabbards sparkled in the sunlight where they dangled from belted red sashes. White gloves concealed dirty fingernails.

Jack Stead led the Cheyennes down to the site of the fort from the Sullivant Hills. Forty mounted warriors headed the procession. Three squaws rode at the rear on ponies pulling travois. Papooses were probably concealed in the cargo of the travois. When the Indians reached the hospitality tent roof, Colonel Carrington stepped out to greet them.

Stead translated loud enough for the assembled soldiers and us to hear. Some Indians wore feathered war bonnets, and one bare-chested fellow held a gaudy umbrella aloft. Black Horse was introduced as the senior chief, but Stead indicated others were important also—Two Moons, Dull Knife, The Wolf That Lies Down, The Rabbit That Jumps, Bob Tail, The Man That Stands Alone On The Ground, and more.

Some of the chiefs wore large silver medallions suspended around their necks on ribbons. A teamster who'd worked out west before the war claimed they probably bore the likenesses of Jefferson, Madison, or Jackson. Either these chiefs or their fathers had received the awards during visits to Washington City.

Colonel Carrington raised a hand, and the quiet was shattered by a loud explosion. One of the mountain howitzers had fired a shot at the Sullivant Hills.

At the same time the spherical case shot exploded in a cloud of smoke over the hilltop, I felt a stab in my ribs. I turned with

156

fists raised to confront whoever thought it was funny to surprise me that way.

"Thought you'd been shot, eh Zach?" Katy giggled.

"I thought one of the Indians had shot me with an arrow." I grinned.

"Oh, you'd know if you'd been shot with an arrow." Her dimples accentuated her smile as she rubbed her wounded shoulder beneath the sling.

Jack Stead translated Chief Black Horse's startled reaction to the cannon firing. "The shooting wagon shoots twice. White Chief shoots first, then Great Spirit shoots again."

"Where'd you come from?" I asked Katy.

She jabbed a thumb over her shoulder. "The hospital tent is over there. Since there aren't any patients, I thought it was safe to leave for awhile."

I nodded toward the assembled Indians. "Recognize any of them?"

"No, they aren't the ones that attacked us. I hear these are Cheyennes, not Arapahos."

"That's what I understand."

Chief Black Horse produced a red-sandstone pipe, filled it with tobacco, and lit it from a tinder handed to him by an associate. The chief puffed on the pipe, then passed it to Colonel Carrington. The colonel drew a puff and coughed. He wasn't a smoker. The other officers took a turn with the pipe, then the Indian chiefs and warriors did likewise.

Katy poked me in the ribs again. "We're not the only spectators." I followed her gaze. Mrs. Carrington, Mrs. Bisbee, and Mrs. Horton sat on chairs beneath the raised side of the headquarters tent observing the proceedings on the parade ground.

Chief Black Horse retrieved his pipe from the final smoker, returned it to a carrying pouch, and stood. Even though it was a warm day, he drew his blanket about his shoulders.

"Little White Man brings soldiers to take all from us." Stead translated Black Horse's opening remark.

Colonel Carrington drew up straighter in his chair. A collective murmur arose from the officers surrounding the colonel. A smirk creased Captain Brown's lips.

Black Horse spoke again, and Stead translated a more diplomatic form of address. "Two Spread Eagles brings soldiers to take all." The chief had decided to name the colonel after the eagle emblems adorning his shoulder scales.

Each chief took a turn speaking. Stead translated, since none of them spoke intelligible English. All of them expressed a warning to Colonel Carrington that the great Sioux chief Red Cloud would not tolerate building another fort in the Powder River country. They advised if the colonel withdrew to Fort Reno, the Indians would no longer object. The colonel repeatedly responded those were not his orders.

We stood there for three hours listening to the laborious translations back and forth between the colonel and the chiefs. Stead paused occasionally to sip from a flask. Whether he used water or something stronger to soothe his dry throat, I couldn't tell.

Jim Bridger sat at one end of the flag-draped table, cradling his goiter in one hand as he leaned his elbows on his knees. Bridger did not speak, but he nodded his head during Stead's translations, indicating he agreed with the "black white man's" efforts at conveying the chiefs' messages to the commanding officer.

A groan beside me drew my attention to Katy. She rubbed her wounded shoulder, then slipped a hand into the pocket of her apron. She brought out the vial of laudanum and tipped it to her mouth. She licked her lips, savoring each drop.

"Why don't you go to the hospital and rest?" I asked. "This

is going to drag on all afternoon."

"I'll be fine now." She slipped her good arm through mine and leaned against me.

I tried to concentrate on the exchanges between the parties engaged at the tent on the parade ground, but the softness of her breast pressing against my side made that impossible. I did hear Colonel Carrington pose a question to Chief Black Horse. "Why do the Sioux and Cheyennes occupy land that the Crows claim?"

Black Horse's translated answer was simple. "We stole the land from the Crows because it was the best hunting ground." Implied in the response was a warning to the army that the soldiers now encroached on these same grounds.

Late in the afternoon, a commotion from the Bozeman Trail interrupted the proceedings. Captain Haymond's four infantry companies, along with the dozens of repaired freight wagons, were arriving from Crazy Woman's Fork. They halted along Big Piney Creek, a half mile from the parade ground. The assembled Indians appeared noticeably agitated by this sudden doubling of the military force available to Colonel Carrington.

Chief Black Horse indicated it was time to end the discussions. He offered to provide one hundred Cheyenne warriors to fight alongside the Eighteenth Infantry against the Sioux.

Colonel Carrington responded that he had enough troops to accomplish his mission without the addition of Indian fighters. Because the Cheyennes had made the friendly offer, the colonel would provide a written document to the assembled chiefs granting them safe passage when they were hunting in the Powder River region as long as they did not molest travelers on the Montana Road. Adjutant Phisterer, whom the Indians had named "Roman Nose," according to Stead's translation, wrote out multiple copies of this pass and distributed them among the chiefs.

"Captain Brown," Colonel Carrington said, "bring the presents."

"Yes, sir." The quartermaster signaled to a sergeant standing behind him, and a half-dozen soldiers stepped forward with armloads of second-hand uniforms, tobacco, coffee, sugar, flour, and bacon. They placed the offerings in front of the tent and stepped back while the Indians picked through the goods in evident descending order of their authority.

As the Cheyennes ascended the slope of the Sullivant Hills, the sun descended in blazing fury over the Big Horn Mountains.

CHAPTER 22

Whooping, shouting, and pounding of hooves woke me early the next morning, Tuesday, July 17. I sat up on my folding cot, my blanket falling from my shoulders. "What's going on?" I mumbled. "Buffalo stampede?"

"No." One of my tent mates was looking out the door flap. "Indians are making off with Captain Haymond's mule herd."

I pulled on my brogans and grabbed my slouch hat from beneath the cot. "What time is it?" Early morning light shone through the open tent flap.

"Five o'clock," another of my tent mates who owned a pocket watch responded.

We four tent mates scrambled outside in time to watch a dozen Indians drive a couple hundred mules and a dozen horses across Big Piney Creek and up the Bozeman Trail. From where we stood on the plateau, we had a clear view down to where Captain Haymond had set up camp the day before in the flat where the two branches of Piney Creek joined.

Below us, Captain Haymond mounted a horse and took off after the disappearing herd and the Indians. A lone soldier, perhaps his orderly, followed him closely in the pursuit. Other soldiers were trying to saddle the few skittish horses that remained. Singly and in pairs they raced off after their commander.

"What's going on?" The shouted question came from Colonel Carrington.

The commanding officer ran across the new parade ground from his living quarters tent in trousers and a shirt. He stopped not far from us and scanned the scene below.

The Indians, the stolen animals, and the strung-out pursuing soldiers disappeared up the Montana Road heading north.

One of Haymond's teamsters came panting up the slope to where the colonel stood. After he'd caught his breath, the teamster said the Indians had infiltrated the mule herd at sunrise and made off with the bell mare. They evidently knew the other animals would follow her.

Less than an hour later, a trooper on horseback raced back down the Montana Road, splashed across Big Piney Creek, and lashed his steed toward the plateau.

After breakfast, I had gathered up a ledger book and was at work cataloging piles of material that had been accumulated outside the tent warehouses. I pretended to be writing something in the journal as I slipped to the northern end of our row of warehouse tents to get closer to where the incoming rider would report to Colonel Carrington.

The horseman reined in at the headquarters tent where the colonel waited. The courier breathlessly gave Captain Haymond's message calling for reinforcements. He said the captain had managed to assemble his scattered soldiers, but they were under attack from dozens of Indians.

"Lieutenant Bisbee!" Colonel Carrington shouted.

The lieutenant appeared from inside the headquarters tent. The colonel ordered him to get Lieutenant Adair's fifty mounted infantrymen and two additional companies of foot infantry on the way to relieve Haymond's embattled troops.

"Captain Brown!" Carrington called in my direction for his quartermaster.

"Sir." Brown appeared from behind one of the tents where he had been working on sorting through inventory.

"Send an ammunition wagon and an ambulance with Lieutenant Bisbee."

"Yes, sir." Brown exchanged salutes with Carrington. When he turned away, he saw me. "Wakefield, get an ambulance ready."

"Yes, sir," I replied.

I hurried into the tent we used as the quartermaster's office and dropped the ledger book onto a folding table. Then, I headed into our herd of mules, which were confined within a temporary rope corral. Within minutes I had my Gospel mules hitched to an ambulance and drove the rig up near the headquarters tent where Lieutenant Bisbee was inspecting the assembled soldiers. A wagon loaded with ammunition pulled up beside me.

"Ambulance driver!" A white-smocked doctor called out as he approached.

"Name's Wakefield."

"I'm Doctor Baalon, Assistant Surgeon. Colonel Carrington's directed me to go along."

He handed me his satchel, and I helped the contract surgeon climb up and get settled on the bench beside me.

A half hour later, our relief column, having followed the Bozeman Trail along Lodge Trail Ridge, dropped down into Peno Valley. Haymond's messenger guided us off the main trail, across Peno Creek, and up a wooded slope. Scattered firing came from the site where Captain Haymond was holding off the Indians. Upon seeing us approach, the Indians broke off and herded the captured mules farther up the hillside into the trees. Lieutenant Bisbee ordered the foot soldiers, along with my ambulance and the ammunition wagon, to remain in place. Haymond, Bisbee, and Adair led the mounted infantry in pursuing the retreating Indians and the mule herd.

Two of Haymond's men had been killed. We laid their bodies

163

on top of ammunition cases in the wagon. Two privates were slightly wounded but still capable of walking. Another private, John Donovan, was brought to the ambulance. He'd been shot in the chest once with a bullet and once with an arrow. Donovan squirmed and groaned on the stretcher bench where we placed him. I held a canteen to his lips. Most of the water dribbled out of the side of his mouth.

"We think the arrow's poisoned," one of the soldiers who'd carried Donovan to the ambulance told Doctor Baalon.

"If that's the case," the doctor said, "there's not much I can do for him here. Maybe not at camp, either."

Thirty minutes later, Captain Haymond and Lieutenants Bisbee and Adair returned with the mounted infantry. They drove four mules before them. Haymond's mule herd had been eliminated.

To provide easier traveling, we moved back across Peno Creek and picked up the Bozeman Trail farther north than where we had initially left it. We had not gone far when we came upon a grisly scene at the shattered remnants of a portable trading post. It had to belong to French Pete Gazeau. We'd learned from Joe Donaldson earlier that the itinerant trader had relocated here. Six naked bodies lay sprawled in front of the ruined structure. Multiple arrows pierced each body. Thigh and bicep muscles had been lacerated, scalps were missing, and throats cut. In two cases the heads had been almost severed from the torsos.

Gazeau was identified easily because of his swarthy skin. Joe Donaldson we recognized from his earlier visit to our camp. The officers and a few of the soldiers collectively identified the other victims. Henry Arrison had been French Pete's partner. Thomas Burns was one. A man known as Dowaire and another named Moss comprised the remainder.

The bodies of Arrison and Burns, less mangled than the others, were loaded into the ammunition wagon with the dead soldiers for transport to camp. A detail of soldiers dug a single, shallow grave. Scraps of the canvas walls from Gazeau's shanty were used to wrap the remains of the four other men before their burial.

While the burial was going on, I stepped among the destroyed shelves of trade goods. Bolts of drab cloth lay strewn about. The savages had taken the brighter patterns. Pottery utensils lay smashed on the ground. No iron skillets or pots remained. The Indians would convert their metal into arrowheads. I paused at the broken jar of hard candy from which I'd offered pieces to French Pete's children down on Sage Creek. I picked a handful of the remaining sweet treats out of the shattered glass. Where were Pete's wife and children? The only bodies were men.

I walked behind the ruined trading shack. Broken branches and trampled grass revealed where several had recently fled. I followed the trail.

A couple minutes later, I spotted a patch of bright red that didn't belong among the browns and greens. "Come out," I said. "It's all over." I held out my hand, in which lay the hard candy. "Here."

The bushes rustled, and one by one the five Gazeau children came forth. Mary Gazeau followed. The children stood before me and stared at their mother until she indicated it was all right to accept the candy. The pieces in my hand disappeared.

I led Mary Gazeau and her children back to Captain Haymond and Lieutenant Bisbee. She told them in broken English what had happened.

The Cheyenne chiefs who'd met with Colonel Carrington the day before had stopped at French Pete's place last night on their way north to their camp on the Tongue River. The Indians were trading with Gazeau when Red Cloud and a party of Sioux and Arapaho warriors arrived. Black Horse answered Red

165

Cloud's questioning about what the "Little White Chief" had given the Cheyennes. Black Horse said Colonel Carrington had fed them well and had given them presents, including letters of safe passage. When Black Horse said the soldiers did not plan to return to Fort Reno, the Sioux and Arapahos unstrung their bows and beat the Cheyennes about their heads and shoulders. After the warriors rode away, Black Horse advised French Pete to move closer to the protection of Colonel Carrington's soldiers. French Pete had told his wife he would consider going there the next morning.

Mary Gazeau said not long after the Cheyennes left, some of Red Cloud's warriors returned, murdered her husband and his associates, and looted the trading post. She said the most brutal of the attackers was Arapaho Chief Running Bear. I recognized that name, and Katy O'Toole would most definitely remember him when I related today's experiences.

Captain Haymond took Mrs. Gazeau and her children, two of French Pete's wagons that hadn't been destroyed, and twenty cattle remaining from the trader's herd to our camp and turned them over to Colonel Carrington. The colonel appointed John Hugus, the sutler, to serve as administrator of Mary Gazeau's estate. On her behalf, he negotiated the sale of the cattle, the wagons, and their contents to the quartermaster. I inherited the task of working those items into our inventory. Mrs. Gazeau and her children disappeared later, never to be heard from again.

Colonel Carrington designated a site across Little Piney Creek on the slope of Pilot Hill as a cemetery. The bodies of the two traders and the two soldiers became its first occupants.

CHAPTER 23

"Captain Brown," Duggan Maguire said, "I don't care how much paperwork Wakefield has to do. I need all the muleskinners I can lay my hands on, and Wakefield's a muleskinner. Colonel Carrington is sending thirty-four wagons to Fort Reno this morning to pick up additional supplies, and I can't spare teamsters from the wood detail. You're the one who put me in charge of building the stockade, and the colonel's pressing both you and me to work faster."

On that Thursday morning, July 19, I sat at the folding table that served as my desk and listened to Maguire and Brown argue. The captain lifted his slouch hat and ran fingers over his balding head, as if he were brushing his hair.

"Maguire," Brown said, "the colonel doesn't realize how far behind we are in getting our inventory records straightened out."

"Your inventory problems don't interest me, Captain. You'll have to take that matter up with the colonel." Maguire stuck his head farther into the tent and looked at me. "Get a move on, Wakefield. You'd better select mules other than your ambulance mules. They haven't had enough jerk-line training to be trusted on a trip to Fort Reno and back."

I looked from Duggan to Captain Brown. "Sir?" I addressed the quartermaster.

"Aw, hell. Go on. We haven't inventoried what supplies we have, and Carrington's bringing up more." The captain pulled

167

his hat down atop his ears and shoved past Maguire, who still stood in the tent's doorway. "I need a drink," Brown grumbled as he stalked away.

"Get a team and wagon and report to Captain Burrowes at the headquarters tent. I've got to get to the north wall. Daylight's a wasting, and I've got to set another seventy-five logs into the trench by sundown."

Maguire had been placed in charge of erecting the stockade wall. In the short time he'd been at the job, his ability to get things done had impressed everyone—except maybe some of the soldiers assigned to work for Duggan.

The Ponderosa pines that crowded the lower slopes of the Big Horn Mountains provided perfect timber for the fort's perimeter wall. The evergreens grew straight for two hundred feet with thick trunks of the ponderous wood from which the tree took its name. It proved easy for the woodsmen to select and fell one-foot-thick trees with trunks extending over eleven feet and bearing minimal lower side limbs. Those limbs and the slash from the toppings were combed through for pieces suitable for the never-ending requirement for firewood.

The trimmed trunks were lashed with chains onto the underframe of a freight wagon and hauled five miles to the plateau. They were delivered to the horse-driven sawmill adjacent to Little Piney Creek. From sunup to sundown, we suffered through the high-pitched whine of the saw's blade ripping through wood. On Carrington's journey west, a steam-powered sawmill had been wrecked at Scotts Bluff in Nebraska when the ox team pulling it had stampeded down a hillside. That mill had been left behind for repairs and had not yet reached our site. Even without the bigger mill, Engineer J. B. Gregory did wonders in preparing the logs for the stockade wall, slabbing them to a four-inch touching surface on two sides. The sawn sides joined so smoothly calking was not required. Leaving the bark on the outer- and inner-facing surfaces reduced the preparation time.

Duggan's crew of a dozen soldiers first dug a trench three feet deep. When a trimmed log was tipped in, eight feet extended above ground. Where every fourth and fifth log touched, the men cut a firing notch one foot down from the top to accommodate a rifle. Extending along the inner surface of the wall, the workers attached a banquette three feet above the ground to provide a continuous walkway for sentries.

I selected six mules and hitched them to a freight wagon, then I drove the rig out of the quartermaster yard into the main fort's site. The route took me past the hospital tent, where I hoped to get a glimpse of Miss O'Toole. I got a glimpse, but not the one I expected.

When I passed the tent, Katy was engaged in close conversation with Duggan Maguire. Her back was to me. Duggan was fondling that gold shamrock down by his right leg. So much for Maguire's urgency to return to the construction of the stockade wall.

I drove to the end of the line of wagons forming on the road along the south side of the parade ground. A first sergeant directed me to swing my rig to the right of the seventeen wagons already lined up and continue until I was next to the first wagon in the line. I thus wound up as one of the two wagons to lead a double file down the Bozeman Trail. The first sergeant was probably not aware of my inexperience with a jerk line, or he would not have placed me in that position.

Captain Burrowes's forty-six enlisted men of Company G stood in formation ready to escort the wagon train. Jim Bridger arrived to serve as guide. His decrepit old gray mare was the epitome of Steven Foster's song.

"Morning, Zach," Bridger said as he came abreast.

"Good morning, Major Bridger," I replied. "Think we'll

encounter hostiles on the way?"

"I don't *think* so. I *know* so. Seen plenty of sign they ain't backing away from a fight."

Captain Burrowes rode to the front of the column and waved an arm forward to put us into motion. Bullwhips cracked, and we lumbered down the slope off the plateau. I'd done a little practicing with a whip and could now make a sharp sound with it.

We headed southeast on the Montana Road. Driving two abreast, we barely fit on the narrow track. No grading had produced this road, just hundreds of churning wagon wheels. Iron tires on our wagons crunched over rocks littering the roadway. Greased axles squealed, wooden wagon beds creaked, canvas covers slapped in the breeze, mules snorted, teamsters cursed. A dust cloud rose behind us.

Throughout that day, small bands of Indians shadowed us from nearby ridges. The savages did not approach closer. We presented a large force with adequate armed protection.

Even though we stopped every hour to water the mules and stretch our legs, when we got to the end of that first day, my rear end burned with blisters. I was not an experienced horseback rider, and I found myself constantly adjusting my bum in the saddle. Driving an ambulance while sitting on a padded seat was a piece of cake in comparison.

That first night we camped at Clear Creek at the same spot where Mrs. Carrington and the ladies had sat over the rattlesnake. This wasn't a good place to sleep under the stars. I spread my blanket in the empty bed of my wagon.

The next morning, as was his custom, Bridger departed our camp before sunup to ride ahead to scout the route. About noon, we overtook him where he sat on a large rock smoking his pipe. Captain Burrowes halted the column and dismounted. My lead mules stopped just short of the two men. I dropped out of my saddle and worked my way forward, pretending to adjust harness as I went, but with the intention of getting close enough to hear better.

"Captain," asked Bridger, "see this buffalo skull?" He pointed at his feet.

"Yes. What of it?"

"Message on that skull says there's a big battle gonna take place up ahead."

"How do you know that? I thought you couldn't read."

"Don't read English, but I do read Injun. Them markings are inviting passing warriors to hurry over to Crazy Woman's Fork to kill whites."

"I find that hard to believe. It's just an old buffalo skull with pictures scratched on it."

"Oh, it conveys a message. I suggest you pick up the pace and get your soldiers to that creek to help whoever's in trouble. Road goes that way anyhow."

The first sergeant had ridden up from his normal position trailing the wagons. "What does he mean, trouble?" the sergeant asked Captain Burrowes.

"The old coot claims the pictures on that skull predict a battle up ahead and inviting Indians to congregate there."

"I've heard the Indians communicate that way," the sergeant said.

"You have?" the captain responded.

The sergeant nodded. "Maybe we should press on, Captain. Forgo the noon meal break. The skinners can eat in the saddle. We can water the mules less frequently, too."

"You agree with Major Bridger?" the captain asked.

"I don't disagree," the first sergeant answered.

Burrowes looked to the guide, then back at the sergeant. "Well, Sergeant, I guess it won't hurt. We'll press on. Pass the word we'll water the mules every two hours."

I fished a strip of jerky out of my saddlebags when I remounted and chewed on it after we got underway. The combination of hot weather and salty meat dried out my mouth. I reached for my canteen, which hung from a hame on the mule's collar. The canteen's strap slipped through my sweaty fingers, and when I grabbed for it my sore bum raked across the saddle leather. I raised up in the stirrups to relieve the pain to my rear end and inadvertently jerked the line.

The lead mules responded to my command and pulled to the right. "No! Whoa!" I pulled hard on the line, and the mules turned back to the left. Too late, the right wheels dropped off the narrow roadway and dug into the soft berm. When the mules pulled the weight the opposite direction, the wagon tipped.

I kicked my feet clear of the stirrups and bailed off my mule. The wagon teetered momentarily, then rolled over into the ditch, dragging the braying mules with it.

Shouts of *whoa* hurtled down the line of wagons as the other teamsters brought their rigs to a halt. Several muleskinners came forward to help me unhook the mules. Five of the animals were soon back on their feet, shaking dust from their coats.

The off-side wheel mule was down hard. The tongue had knocked his legs out from under him when the wagon rolled. The left rear leg was broken above the fetlock. The mule's eyes stared at me, flaring nostrils emitting labored breathing sounds. How could I have done this? Why did I have to hurt this animal?

"Wakefield." Captain Burrowes sat his horse behind me. "Shoot the poor damned thing."

"I don't have a gun, Captain."

"Here." The captain extended his revolver, butt first.

I knelt beside the mule, placed the end of the barrel between his eyes, cocked the hammer, and pulled the trigger. The pistol bucked in my hand. White smoke at the muzzle momentarily obscured the mule's unseeing eyes.

I stood and handed the revolver back to Captain Burrowes.

"Captain Brown is not going to be happy you killed one of his mules and destroyed one of his wagons."

"No, I suppose not."

"He'll make you pay for it, I imagine. Salvage the wheels, the top canvas, and anything else worthwhile off the wagon. We'll abandon the rest. Get the harness off the dead mule. Leave his carcass for the wolves and the buzzards. Climb onto that mule you were riding and fall in behind me, so I can keep an eye on you."

The sun had set that evening when we reached Crazy Woman's Fork. Twilight revealed five wagons and two ambulances formed into a square corral on the opposite, higher bank. Within the enclosure, soldiers, civilians, women, and children, mingled with some mules and a couple horses.

Captain Burrowes kicked his horse in the ribs and rode on ahead. Since he'd commanded me to ride where he could keep an eye on me, I followed. We splashed across the shallow stream and up the steeper south bank.

When we reached the wagons and ambulances, a young second lieutenant stepped over a wagon tongue used to block an opening into the square. The lieutenant, hatless and wearing a dirty, torn blouse, held a Henry repeating rifle. He saluted. "Lieutenant Alexander Wands, temporarily commanding this detail, sir. We're mighty glad to see you, Captain Burrowes."

Burrowes returned the lieutenant's salute. "What's going on here, Lieutenant? How did you know my name?"

"Major Bridger rode in a half hour ago with word you were coming. We've been under attack all day. The hostiles left when the dust from your train became visible. We had a devil of a time holding them off."

"Sioux?" the captain asked. "Large force?"

"Yes, sir. A hundred fifty, by my estimate."

"How many of you are there, Lieutenant?"

"Thirty-seven originally. We left Fort Reno with six officers, ten enlisted men, nine teamsters, a chaplain, a surgeon, a photographer, and nine dependents."

"What are your casualties?"

"Lieutenant Templeton, the detail commander, is badly wounded. One enlisted man is dead. Lieutenant Daniels is missing, and I suspect he's dead because his horse came in riderless. We have some wounded. I don't have a count."

"The dependents safe?"

"Yes, sir," Lieutenant Wands said. "One other thing, sir. I sent two men off to Fort Reno for help."

"When?"

"An hour ago. Chaplain White and Private Wallace rode out on the two serviceable horses we had left. They were chased by Indians over that far ridge. I don't know their fate."

"Two horses you had left?"

"We only had four horses to begin with. The officers took turns riding. When we approached Crazy Woman, Lieutenant Templeton and Lieutenant Daniels rode off on two of them to chase what they thought were buffalo. Turned out to be Indians. Both of their horses have been seriously wounded with arrows . . . not fit for service."

"Why are you on this road with such a small force?"

"Well, sir," Lieutenant Wands said, "Captain Proctor gave us permission to proceed from Fort Reno when Lieutenant Templeton told him the authorities at Fort Laramie were convinced everything was quiet because of the new treaty."

Captain Burrowes snorted. "Quiet? Wagon trains are under attack all the time. My train's been under continual surveillance for two days. On the seventeenth, the savages stole Captain Haymond's entire mule herd right from under our noses. French

Pete Gazeau and his workers were all murdered. It's not quiet, Lieutenant."

When Lieutenant Wands had said one of his party was a photographer, I was certain Ridgway Glover was somewhere inside that corral.

"The army issuing Henrys now?" Captain Burrowes pointed to Lieutenant Wands's Henry repeating .44-caliber rifle that carried fifteen rounds in its magazine.

"No, sir. This is my personal weapon. The enlisted men are armed with Springfields. The officers and teamsters have pistols. There's one other Henry. Captain Marr, former Missouri Volunteer, now a teamster, has one. I don't mean to brag, sir, but without the two Henrys we might not have survived. The single-shot Springfields are too slow. A hostile can launch three or four arrows while a soldier is reloading for a second shot."

"Not good," Captain Burrowes said. "I agree."

"Chaplain White was armed with an old pepperbox," Lieutenant Wands continued. "Damnedest thing, sir. The Chaplain and Private Fuller charged a bunch of Indians down in that ravine there, and all seven barrels of the pepperbox went off at once." The lieutenant laughed. "You should have seen the savages scatter. Chaplain claimed he killed two and wounded some others with one shot."

While the two officers had been talking, our wagon train had arrived on the far side of Crazy Woman's Fork. Captain Burrowes signaled to his first sergeant to bring the wagons across and circle them around the square.

"You say Lieutenant Templeton is the commander of this unit?" the captain asked.

"Yes, sir."

"Where's Captain Fetterman? We've been expecting him."

"He's still at Fort Sedgewick, sir. He hasn't received orders to come forward yet."

"Take me to Lieutenant Templeton," Captain Burrowes said. "Let me see how he is. I can't let you continue with so few and the condition you're in. You'll have to go to Fort Reno with me. You can go north again as part of my command when I return."

The two officers stepped over the tongue of the wagon and left. I decided to find the photographer. I tied the reins of the captain's horse and my mule to the tongue and entered the corral. I spotted Glover's pale-blond locks near one of the ambulances where he was rinsing bloody rags in a bucket of water.

"Ridgway." I came up behind him.

He looked up. A grin brightened his dirt-streaked features. "Zach," he said. "You missed all the fun."

"Didn't sound like fun from what I heard."

"You're right. I wasn't that scared at Gettysburg."

"What are you doing?" I asked. "Can I help?"

"I just rinsed out these bandages for Mrs. Wands. She, Mrs. Fessenden, and Mrs. Hannibal have been treating the wounded."

"Who are all these dependents?"

"There's Lieutenant Wands's wife and their four-year-old son, Bobby. They have a black servant, Laura. Mrs. Fessenden is the wife of Sergeant Frank Fessenden, a bandsman. They have a three-month-old baby girl named Sedgwick. Named that because she was born at Fort Sedgwick. Then there's Mrs. Hannibal and her three small youngsters. She's the wife of Andrew Hannibal, an enlisted man."

"Why were they sent forward with all the trouble that's brewing?"

"When we left Fort Laramie, we were assured everything was peaceful."

I glanced around the corralled wagons and ambulances. If the Sioux had possessed firearms, there might not have been anybody for us to rescue.

"Where's your perambulator, Ridgway?"

"In one of the wagons. I wanted to photograph the Indians attacking, but Lieutenant Wands said I'd better shoot the savages with a gun instead of a camera."

"Did you?"

"Yes, I shot one. I hated to take a life."

"I know the feeling," I said, "when you shoot the first man."

I went with Ridgway and helped him carry buckets of water from the stream. He said they had trouble getting to the water during the fight because the Indians kept them pinned down in their corral.

The next morning, several of us fanned out to search for Lieutenant Daniels. I accompanied Lieutenant Link, one of the new officers. We found Daniels in a ravine two hundred yards away. His body lay stark white against the brown sand. He had several bullet holes in his torso. Twenty-two arrows pierced his body. His scalp and fingers were missing. A lance had been shoved up his rectum.

CHAPTER 24

We wrapped Lieutenant Daniels's mutilated body in canvas and loaded it into a wagon. Captain Burrowes's column combined with that of Lieutenant Wands headed south on the Bozeman Trail. We'd barely gotten underway when Chaplain White and Private Wallace appeared with First Lieutenant Thaddeus Kirtland and thirteen mounted infantrymen. The preacher and the private had safely accomplished their ride to Fort Reno the night before.

Our train arrived at Fort Reno on Saturday, July 21. Early the next morning, the military buried Lieutenant Daniels with full honors. We spent the rest of Sunday loading the wagons with supplies, and on Monday morning, July 23, we headed north.

No longer having a freight wagon to drive, and being an experienced ambulance driver, I was assigned duty as the latter. I drove the ambulance of Musician Sergeant Fessenden. Each evening, I helped the sergeant gather wood for the family's cook fire and fetched water from the closest source. In appreciation, they let me eat with them. Mrs. Fessenden was a better cook than any of the teamsters.

On July 26, we crossed Big Piney Creek and ascended the new road that climbed the slope to the plateau where the fort's stockade walls were nearing completion. Portions of all four sides of the main palisade presented a clear outline of what the finished enclosure would look like. The side posts for the main gate were in position, and we drove our vehicles through the entrance to line up on the streets encircling the parade ground.

Captain Burrowes had sent a courier ahead earlier that morning to alert the commanding officer of our approach. Colonel Carrington and the other officers stood next to a flagpole that had been erected in the center of the parade ground. Behind the headquarters' staff, the seven infantry company commanders were arrayed. The band was formed up in one quadrant of the square. They loudly tooted and thumped their way through martial music while our wagons rolled into position. The arriving officers dismounted and fell into their own line facing the commanding officer, with whom they exchanged salutes. The colonel signaled for Bandmaster Samuel Curry to stop the music.

Sergeant Fessenden went to report to his new boss, the bandmaster. I remained seated with Mrs. Fessenden and her baby. We were parked close enough to the flagpole we could hear the officers reporting individually to Colonel Carrington. As each officer introduced himself, he handed over a copy of his orders, and the colonel informed him to which company he would be assigned. The appropriate company commander raised his hand to identify to whom the new lieutenant was to report.

While these assignments were being made, Captain Burrowes gave the dispatch pouch to Adjutant Phisterer, who busied himself sorting through the official papers. He handed one document to Colonel Carrington, who quickly scanned it.

"Gentlemen," he announced loudly enough for everyone around the square to hear. "The Department of the Platte informs me this post will be known as Fort Philip Kearny."

Colonel Carrington pointed a finger at Bandmaster Curry, who directed the band in playing a flourish.

Colonel Carrington raised the paper above his head. "Three cheers for Fort Phil Kearny!"

"Hip, hip, hooray! Hip, hip, hooray! Hip, hip, hooray!"

From that moment on, the fort was called Phil Kearny, not Philip Kearny. Kearny had been a popular, one-armed general who was killed at the Battle of Chantilly in Virginia in 1862. His men knew him affectionately as "Phil."

"Morning, Zach." Katy appeared beside the ambulance wearing her hospital matron's apron. Her arm still rested in the sling. Her dimpled smile, as always, mesmerized me.

"Katy O'Toole," I finally said. "Meet Mrs. Fessenden and her daughter, Sedgwick."

"Welcome," Katy said. "The musicians have erected a double tent for your quarters, Mrs. Fessenden. Not much, but it beats sleeping in an ambulance."

"Thank you. I am weary of this mode of living."

Sedgwick Fessenden uttered a small cry, and Mrs. Fessenden turned the edge of the blanket away from the baby's face. "Shh," Mrs. Fessenden said. "I'll feed you soon."

"Oh, what a beautiful baby," Katy said. "And such an unusual name."

Mrs. Fessenden laughed. "Captain Fetterman insisted we give her the name Sedgwick because she was born at that fort."

"Is Captain Fetterman here?" Katy looked toward the assembled officers at the flagpole. "Many of the other officers here speak highly of him. I'm looking forward to meeting him."

"No," Mrs. Fessenden answered. "Captain Fetterman has not yet received orders."

"Well, Zach," Katy said. "What do you think of the work Duggan Maguire has accomplished since you departed?" She waved a hand at the walls of the stockade. "Everybody says he's really done a great job."

"Humph!"

I helped Katy settle Mrs. Fessenden into her new quarters, then I drove the ambulance to the quartermaster yard and took care of the mules. I was surprised when I walked over to the row of temporary storage tents to see the foundation laid out for our permanent warehouse. I paced around the planned wood-framed structure and found it to be twenty-four feet wide and eighty-four feet long. Katy was right. Great progress had ensued while I was traveling to and from Fort Reno. I was sure it wasn't all the doing of Duggan Maguire, though.

"What's this?" Ridgway Glover asked. He dragged his perambulator behind him. He wasn't wearing a hat, and his long blond hair blew about his face in the afternoon breeze. He pushed strands away from his mouth.

"Quartermaster office . . . temporary office. My place of work."

"I did not expect to see such a large fort being constructed here?"

"Come on, let's walk around. I'll point out the structures that're planned. I want to see the progress made while I was away."

Ridgway left his photographic rig parked beside the quartermaster's office tent, and we spent the next hour touring the inside perimeter of the fort's growing stockade. Our quartermaster warehouse tent sat slightly to the south of the fort's main gate. From there, Ridgway and I walked along the road that paralleled the expanding east wall. We passed tents currently serving as the guardhouse, the headquarters, and the sutler's store. Foundations were in place for the permanent structures.

In the evenings, the sutler's tent walls did not contain the singing, shouting, and cursing that arose from within. It was still a little early in the day for such rowdiness, however.

"Would you like a drink?" I asked Ridgway.

"No, thanks. Quakers don't drink spirituous liquids."

He didn't expand on his comment, and I didn't press the matter. We continued with our walk.

At the corner, we reached the building sites for the band and the bakery. Here we turned left following the road paralleling the north wall. This was the wall Duggan Maguire had started first, and it was almost complete. Fronting this wall, we passed the tents and construction sites of future barracks for two of the infantry companies. Looking south, down the long expanse of the parade ground, two other infantry barracks would form a mirror image from the far end. Behind each of these company barracks, latrine sinks had been dug.

There were seven infantry companies at Fort Phil Kearny now. Three of them would be sent farther north to build an additional fort in Montana Territory. The men of these three companies were still camped where the Piney creeks intersected.

In the corner where the north and west walls met, an artillery bastion was being built. A similar one was under construction at the southeast corner behind the quartermaster warehouse tent. Turning to the south, we walked down the west road passing a dozen double tents that served as temporary quarters for officers and families. Eventually, they would be replaced with bungalows. In the southwest quadrant of the parade ground initial excavation revealed where a subterranean ammunition magazine would be located.

A few paces farther on brought us to the hospital tent. I stopped to inquire if Katy were present. She was not. She was probably helping the Fessendens get settled.

Continuing, we passed the tents housing the non-commissioned officers and the cavalry corral. The corral currently consisted of ropes strung between posts. We used the same arrangement to confine the mules in the quartermaster yard. We turned left again and proceeded along the south road, returning to our starting point.

I told Ridgway the quartermaster yard would be outside the main fort, extending to the south down to Little Piney Creek. It would be surrounded by a yet-to-be-built wall of lesser height than the main stockade. The combined length of the quartermaster yard and the main post stretched fifteen hundred feet. The widest portion of the main post measured six hundred feet.

We'd just returned to the quartermaster's office tent when Captain Brown came storming out, nearly knocking me over. "Where have you been?" he demanded. "Take this and come with me." He tossed a Springfield rifle-musket and a cartridge belt to me. "Bloody hostiles are making off with part of our mule herd. Let's go!"

I waved goodbye to Ridgway and stumbled along beside the captain, trying to buckle the belt around my waist without dropping the rifle. "Did they get into our corral?" I asked.

"No. I had sent a detail with some of the mules out to the pasture to graze. Too many savages swooped in for the handful of herders to fend them off. We're going after them. I want those mules back!"

In addition to me, Captain Brown had rounded up a dozen teamsters to mount the pursuit. By the time we saddled our horses, the Indians and the captured animals were more than a mile away on the far side of the Bozeman Trail heading east.

A half hour later we got close enough to fire shots at the warriors, who shook blankets and shouted at the stolen mules to keep them moving.

Fortunately, the musket the captain had given me was loaded. I tried to aim, but the mule bouncing up and down beneath me made a most unstable platform. I pulled the trigger, and the rifle jumped in my hands as the bullet shot out through a white cloud that gathered around the muzzle.

I hadn't hit anything. Now, what was I supposed to do? I had no idea how to load this cumbersome thing while mounted. I could halt and drop the butt onto the ground to get the ramrod into the barrel to ram the charge home, but if the mule moved, he'd yank the musket out of my hands. The only way to reload was to get off the damned mule and stand on the ground.

I halted and dismounted. The mule shied against me, knocked me sideways, and the rifle fell out of my hands. I grabbed the reins and threaded them through my belt to keep the mule under control before picking up the rifle.

A well-trained infantryman could complete the nine reloading steps in twenty seconds. It took me twice that long. When I finished, the Indians were well beyond the one-thousand-yard range of my weapon. I remounted.

It was apparent why the small contingent of men who rode horses in the Eighteenth were called "mounted infantry." They only rode to get to a position from where they could dismount and fight. The Springfield rifle-musket was useless as a cavalry weapon.

I was the only teamster armed with that unwieldy weapon. All the others possessed pistols. The captain had a government issued revolver. The teamsters privately owned theirs. I needed to buy one for myself when next I got paid . . . if there would be any money left after Captain Brown deducted for the dead mule and the destroyed wagon.

After pursuing the Indians for eight miles, they drew farther and farther away. The captain signaled a halt. "It's no use," he shouted. "Let's go back."

We'd recovered six mules. We'd lost fifty.

We returned to the quartermaster's mule coral and inventoried the animals. It was then I realized the bastards had gotten away with John. I only had three Gospel mules left.

CHAPTER 25

A week later, Ridgway and I entered the sutler's tent on Thursday evening, August 2. The pungent odor of cigars, the sweet aroma of pipe tobacco, and the stench of sour beer assailed my nostrils. A trapped cloud of smoke hovered against the roof of the tent, obscuring the weak light emitted by a dozen oil-burning lanterns strung between tent poles.

"I'll buy you a drink, Zach," Ridgway said.

"I thought you didn't drink."

"Don't drink alcohol. I do like a good sarsaparilla. That's what I'm offering to buy. You want whiskey? Spend your own money for that."

I laughed and slapped him on the shoulder. "Fine. Sarsaparilla it is."

While we sipped lukewarm sarsaparilla from pint bottles, I couldn't take my eyes off a gleaming revolver displayed on a shelf behind the counter. Highly polished walnut grips and a shiny brass trigger guard added contrast to the long, blued barrel that extended from a black, case-hardened frame.

"That's the Colt Army model eighteen-sixty." John Hugus, the sutler, offered me the pistol. I set my bottle on the counter and grasped the Colt with both hands. I was afraid my fingers would leave a stain on the shiny metal.

"It's a six-shot, cap and ball, forty-four-caliber, single-action revolver," Hugus said.

"How much?"

"Twenty dollars."

"Twenty dollars! I saw one at Fort Laramie for seventeen."

"Well, there's shipping charges involved. Freighters don't haul goods out here from the States for nothing."

"I know, but twenty dollars seems excessive."

"I tell you what, Mr. Wakefield. I'll let you have it for nineteen-fifty."

It was just what I wanted. I grasped the grip and extended the pistol in front of me. My hand wavered slightly. "It's heavy."

"Two pounds, eleven ounces, unloaded. I can special order you a Navy model if you prefer. Weighs a couple ounces less. It's thirty-six caliber . . . not as much kick as a forty-four. Colonel Carrington carries a Navy."

"No, I like the Army." I returned the revolver to the sutler. "I don't have any money. Maybe on payday I'll come back."

"It's the only pistol I have, right now," Hugus said. "Don't know when I'll be getting more. Somebody else might buy it before payday."

I shrugged.

"Tell you what, Mr. Wakefield. You're an honest man. I'll let you have it on your IOU."

"How do you know I'm honest, Mr. Hugus? We hardly know each other."

"You came back, didn't you?"

"Came back? What do you mean?"

"I heard about you wrecking a wagon and killing a mule. You could have skedaddled once you got to Fort Reno. You didn't have to return to face Captain Brown. You could have shirked your responsibility for the damages, but you didn't. That tells me you're honest."

"Well, that's mighty kind of you, sir."

"But the IOU will have to be for twenty dollars. Interest, you might say." He chuckled.

I smiled. "All right, Mr. Hugus. I'll sign an IOU."

"Ammunition?" Hugus asked. "I recommend using combustible paper cartridges for faster loading."

"Captain Brown will issue me ammunition. He provides it to all teamsters."

The sutler handed me a paper and pencil, and I scribbled out an IOU.

"How about you, Mr. Glover?" Hugus asked. "I don't have any more pistols, but I have rifles and a shotgun."

"No, thanks. I don't need a weapon."

"I wonder about that, Mr. Glover," Hugus said. "With these frequent Indian raids, how are you going to defend yourself?"

"With my camera. I had no trouble at Fort Laramie. The natives liked to have their picture taken. Once they realized my camera couldn't steal their soul, they were friendly."

"I believe you'll find quite a difference between the Sioux of the Powder River country and those Laramie Loafers," the sutler said.

I stuck the Colt into my waistband and took the final swallow of my sarsaparilla. It was dark outside when Ridgway and I left. The last quarter moon would not rise until midnight. Overhead, the blue-black sky was ablaze with shimmering stars. I took a deep breath to clear my lungs. A person had to really crave liquor to linger long in the confines of the sutler's tent.

The next morning, August 3, Captain Brown did a double take when he saw the revolver at my waist. I told him how I'd acquired it and asked if I could draw ammunition.

"Certainly," he said. "I'll give you a voucher to give the ordnance sergeant, but you can't go around with that thing stuck down your pants. Take a holster and pistol belt from stock. I can't sell it to you. Just make an entry in the ledger that you have the loan of it."

"Thank you, sir."

When I approached the hospital later, I wore a brand-new flapped holster strapped around my waist, complete with cartridge and percussion cap boxes affixed to the belt. There wasn't any reason for me to be at the hospital around noontime, but I might catch Katy O'Toole before she went to the Fessendens' to play with the baby during her lunch break.

She nearly bowled me over rushing out through the tent flap door.

"Whoa," I said. "What's the hurry?"

"I have to see Colonel Carrington right away."

"What for?"

"I have to get his permission to accompany Captain Kinney and Captain Burrowes. They're taking their companies north this afternoon for Montana. They're going to build the new fort where the Bozeman Trail crosses the Big Horn River. I want to go with them. It will put me closer to my fiancé."

She hadn't paused for breath while she sped through her explanation. I followed her across the middle of the parade ground. She was in such a hurry, she didn't follow the road like we were supposed to.

Colonel Carrington stood in front of the headquarters tent engaged in conversation with Captain Kinney, Captain Burrowes, Jim Bridger, and Jim Beckwourth. Katy and I slipped in close and waited.

Bridger and Beckwourth had met when they were young trappers with William Ashley's fur trading company in the 1820s. Over the past four decades, Beckwourth claimed to have had ten Crow wives. Bridger was pointing out that since the new fort would be located smack dab in the center of Crow country, it was important to have Beckwourth along.

"Captain Kinney," Colonel Carrington said, "as a brevet lieutenant colonel, it's natural you be commander of the new Fort C. F. Smith. With Captain Haymond being transferred to the States for recruiting duty, that makes you the senior company commander. The Eighteenth is short on officers, but I can't get General Cooke's attention on that matter. With Phisterer's recall for recruiting duty, too, I've had to assign some lieutenants to double duty as adjutants as well as company commanders. With the transfer of Company F to Fort Reno, when General Cooke decided he wanted it to be a two-company post, and with you taking two companies north, I'll be left with four companies here."

Each infantry company was authorized one captain, one first lieutenant, and one second lieutenant. No company in the Eighteenth had more than a single officer. All the officers openly grumbled about the extra responsibilities they had to assume.

"I'm sorry I don't have any cavalry to send with you," Carrington said. "The promised company hasn't arrived. I'm giving you some of our horses and one of the mountain howitzers. That's all I can spare."

"I understand, sir," Kinney said. "With your permission, Captain Burrowes and I will head out. I do appreciate having Major Bridger as our guide, since none of us have been beyond Goose Creek."

The officers exchanged salutes, and the group broke apart.

"Colonel, sir?" Katy asked.

Colonel Carrington turned around. He apparently had not realized Katy and I were standing nearby.

"Good afternoon, Miss O'Toole," he said. "What can I do for you?"

"I want to go with them."

"With Captain Kinney?"

"Yes, sir. That will take me closer to my fiancé in the goldfields."

"Miss O'Toole," the colonel said, "I can't allow that. These troops will be traveling through hostile territory. It's not safe."

189

"We encountered hostiles getting to here." She tapped her collarbone indicating she'd suffered personally from such an encounter. "What's the difference?"

"The difference is that Red Cloud has now declared war on us."

"There are two civilian wagon trains going with the soldiers, Colonel," she said. "I can go with one of them."

"You have not fully recovered from your wound, Miss O'Toole," the colonel said. "You would be a burden to those folks. I simply cannot allow it until you are declared fully recovered by Doctor Horton."

CHAPTER 26

On Saturday, August 18, I was once again drawn away from clerical duties to serve as a driver. This time I took the officers' wives and children on a picnic. In addition to the army freight wagons, the command possessed a few farm wagons. Colonel Carrington sent instructions that I was to hitch up a farm wagon for the task. As usual, Captain Brown grumbled about my absence from quartermaster work.

Since I'd lost John to the thieving Indians, an experienced muleskinner recommended a replacement. Moses was one of the oldest mules in the herd. His mottled brown hair was shot through with gray. I'd been assured he was an experienced off-wheel mule. When I hitched him into place alongside Matt, Mark, and Luke, they accepted him. I now had the Bible team.

This time of morning the fort was alive with activity. The steam sawmill had arrived, and in addition to the pulsating chugging of its engine, the screeching of saw blades from two mills now penetrated the eardrums from the meadow beside Little Piney Creek. Inside the stockade, dozens of handsaws buzzed their way through lumber. An equal number of hammers pounded nails into boards, punctuated by the occasional curse when a thumb got in the way.

Driving the farm wagon was like driving an ambulance. Reins instead of a jerk line controlled the mules. I first went to the sutler's tent to load food and beverages. Mr. Hugus had recently sold the concession to John Fitch Kinney. Kinney had donated the items for the picnic, and he supervised me loading them. He was a short, heavyset man with a flat nose, pronounced pouches beneath piercing eyes, and a gray goatee. A gold stickpin featured prominently in his silk shirt, and he carried a gold-headed cane. He didn't lift any boxes.

"Is that the last of it, sir?" I asked.

"Son, you will address me as Judge," Kinney said.

Kinney had been the Chief Justice of the Utah Supreme Court until President Lincoln had dismissed him during the war. I'd heard from others that he never let anybody forget how important he'd once been.

"Is that the last of it . . . *Judge*?"

"That's it." He tapped my holster with his cane. "See that you take good care of that Colt. Mr. Hugus transferred your IOU to me. If you don't redeem it come payday, I'll expect that revolver to be returned in like-new condition."

"I'll take care of it."

I swung the wagon around the parade ground and brought it to a halt in front of Mrs. Carrington's tent quarters. She and the other wives awaited my arrival there.

Mrs. Carrington's boys, Harry and Jimmy, stood to one side with Calico. At nine and six, they were the oldest children at the fort. Mrs. Bisbee held the hand of two-year-old son Gene. Mrs. Wands's four-year-old son, Bobby, clutched her skirt. Mrs. Fessenden cradled Baby Sedgwick. Katy O'Toole stood beside the bandsman's wife holding a small satchel—probably baby things. Surgeon Horton's wife, Sallie, the only wife without a child present, caressed her pet antelope fawn, Star.

I dropped down from the front seat of the wagon. "Good morning, Mrs. Carrington. Let me help you ladies get on board."

I'd lined the boxes of food and beverages down either side of the wagon to provide temporary seating. I removed one of the wooden boxes and turned it on its side to serve as a stepstool, then helped each lady and child climb into the wagon.

When I handed Mrs. Carrington up, she said, "I wish I'd thought to ask Ridgway Glover to come so he could photograph our picnic. Do you think he's available, Zach?"

"No, ma'am, I doubt it. He needed to earn some money, and the colonel arranged for him to work at the sawmills. I saw him heading down that way earlier this morning."

"Well, next time," she said. "Oh, Mr. Wakefield, my boys will take turns riding Calico."

I returned the makeshift stepstool to the wagon and lifted Jimmy Carrington onto the tailgate. The boy not riding the pony would perch there awaiting his turn. The other children would ride with their mothers in the wagon. Star would be left behind.

"Come, Katy," Mrs. Carrington said. "Join us."

"I should get back to the hospital, ma'am."

"Don't be silly," Mrs. Carrington said. "There are no patients. Mrs. Horton will vouch for you serving us today in a 'nursing' capacity . . . shall we say?"

Sallie Horton nodded and responded, "Of course."

Despite the long hours and hard work building the new fort, the entire month of September had seen only six men report to the hospital for sick call. They'd all been work-related injuries, and the men had quickly returned to their jobs.

"It's rather crowded in the rear, ma'am," Katy said. "Why don't I ride up front with Mr. Wakefield?"

"That's a good idea, dear. It will preclude the children accidently bumping your shoulder."

Katy joined me at the front of the wagon, and I offered her a hand.

"I can manage," she said. She stepped on a rung of the front wheel and grasped the edge of the toe board with her good hand. When she tried to lift herself higher, she lost her balance and swayed to the side. I instinctively threw my hands up to catch her and found myself holding two soft derriere cheeks.

"Watch where you place your hands, sir!"

"Sorry." I gave a final shove to Katy's butt and boosted her onto the seat. I looked up and smiled.

She grinned, dimples accenting the corners of her mouth. She busied herself straightening her hospital matron's apron over her skirt, then tucked a stray blonde curl back inside the confines of her bonnet.

Mesmerized with her beauty, I stood there, my mouth open.

"Well," Katy said. "Aren't you coming?"

Jolted out of my reverie, I hurried around the wagon, climbed up, gathered the reins, and snapped them. The Bible mules pulled us down the parade ground's western road past the other officers' tents and the big hospital tent. After entering the quartermaster yard, I swung the wagon to the right and exited the fort. I halted beside twenty-four empty wagon frames ready to depart for the pineries. Each morning a work party made the five-mile trek on the road leading west along the lower slope of the Sullivant Hills. In the evening, after the wagons were loaded with timber that'd been logged by the teams who camped continuously at the two cutting locations, the teamsters drove back to the fort. A platoon of infantrymen stood at ease nearby, prepared to accompany the wagon train.

Katy waved to Duggan Maguire, who was supervising the planting of additional logs into the stockade wall not far from where I'd stopped. He waved with his slouch hat.

"I do wish Mr. Maguire could come with us," she said. "He is such a strong individual. He's an older version of my fiancé."

"Humph!" If she heard my exclamation, she ignored it.

We hadn't waited long before the wives' husbands rode past us to take up position in front of the caravan. Colonel

Carrington's thoroughbred, Gray Eagle, pranced at the head of the group. The ordinary mounts of the other officers plodded along obediently behind the commanding officer. This was going to be a family outing—for the officers. Sergeant Fessenden was not among the party.

I pulled our wagon in behind the mounted officers. The colonel raised a hand and motioned forward. The logging wagons fell in behind us in a double column, a formation that allowed for rapid corralling in case of an Indian attack. The infantrymen spread out on each side of the wagons to provide a deterrent. We were fortunate to be first in line, protecting my passengers from eating the dust churned up by the large, timber-hauling wagons.

On the way to the picnic site, the ladies examined the boxes of delights provided for their picnic lunch.

"My heavens!" Mrs. Carrington exclaimed. "Look at the treats provided by Judge Kinney. Isn't he wonderful to do this?"

The ladies enumerated in detail the endless variety of delicacies they uncovered. There was canned lobster, oysters, and salmon. Fresh elk meat and other game had been included to be roasted over a campfire. These specialties were accompanied by jellies, pineapples, tomatoes, sweet corn, peas, pickles, and other items. Desserts of puddings, pies, cakes, doughnuts, and gingerbread completed the seemingly unlimited assortment of viands. Pipe tobacco, cigars, and champagne had been included for the officers.

The chatter of the ladies in the wagon bed exclaiming over the bountiful feast awaiting them, plus the fussing of the children, provided enough noise that Katy and I could talk without being overheard.

"You still fretting over not being able to go with Captain Kinney?" I asked.

"No. I'll be going soon enough. Do you suppose Captain

Kinney and Judge Kinney are related?"

"I doubt it."

Katy withdrew the laudanum bottle from her apron pocket, twisted out the cork, and sipped from it. "I saw you shaking your head," she said.

"When're you going to stop using that?"

"Soon." She slipped her arm out of the sling and raised it in front of her. "I'm almost one hundred percent."

"But it still hurts?"

"Sometimes. It'll soon be good enough for me to go to Montana."

"Have you heard from your fiancé?"

She didn't reply right away. Finally, she said, "No."

"Well," I said, "that doesn't mean he hasn't written. Last week the mail courier between here and Fort Laramie was ambushed and killed. The troops who found his body said mail was scattered all over the countryside. They weren't able to recover all of it."

Harness leather creaked, iron-rimmed wheels crunched gravel, mules snorted, teamsters shouted—all adding to the chatter that continued from the bed of our wagon. To keep the children entertained, the ladies sang nursery rhymes.

"Zach," Katy asked, "have you ever had a special someone . . . of the female persuasion?"

Now, that was some question to ask a fellow. Out of the corner of my eye, I watched her turn to look at me. Had my coloring reddened?

"Well, have you?" she asked again.

"No, not really."

"What do you mean by that?" she asked.

I'd slept with a prostitute in New York when I went there to enlist in the army, but I could never tell Katy about that. "I've been to parties where girls were present," I said, "but I never had a special female friend."

After a moment, she continued. "I never had any special male friend either until I met Brandon."

She didn't ask me any more questions, which was good. I didn't know how to continue this discussion. I pretended to concentrate on the mules. I jiggled the reins, stared straight ahead, and kept my mouth shut.

After we'd traveled four miles along the south slope of Sullivant Hills, we came to a fork in the road. Here, the colonel led my ambulance and the right half of the timber wagons onto a road that angled off to northwest. The left half of the wagons continued straight west toward the foothills. Each road led to a pinery. The road we followed descended to a crossing of South Piney Creek. One of the pineries lay less than half a mile beyond this ford.

I flicked the reins and clucked to the mules to encourage them to step into the rapidly flowing stream. We splashed across the pebbly bottom of the shallow water and emerged onto Piney Island. The "island" was just a long, broad stretch of land bordered on this side by South Piney Creek and on the other by North Piney Creek. They joined three miles to the east to form Big Piney Creek.

On the north bank of South Piney Creek, Colonel Carrington signaled a halt. We'd arrived at the picnic site. Towering ponderosa pines predominated here, interspersed with equally tall lodgepole pines. Their canopies kept the island in perpetual shade. Shorter spruce, juniper, and fir trees appeared intermittently below the forest giants. White-barked aspens grew in scattered clumps where clearings might otherwise exist. It was too early for the aspen leaves to turn brilliant gold. When a gust of wind swept through the grove, the aspen leaves fluttered, displaying a pale-green luster as they flipped over.

The half of the mounted infantrymen who'd remained with

us scattered out in a perimeter defense. One soldier picketed the officers' horses after watering them. I unhitched the mules and led them to the stream. After they drank, I returned them to the wagon.

The officers unloaded the boxes and distributed them among several blankets the wives spread along the creek's shaded bank. I gathered an armload of fallen branches and built a campfire for the picnickers.

After ensuring the party no longer needed my assistance, I selected a delicacy from the vast assortment and slipped away. I moved among the trees about a hundred yards to the west until the picnic tableau was hidden from my view. Only the occasional sharp laugh reached my ears.

I spotted a flat-topped boulder embedded in the bank of the stream. A profusion of red, yellow, and purple flowers grew around its base and spread along the low creek bank. I'd gained some knowledge of tree species from associating with the timber cutters. But, not being a student of botany, I had no idea what variety of flowers wafted their fragrances into the breeze. If I leaned close to a ponderosa, I could pick up the mild aroma of vanilla emanating from the bark.

A squirrel sitting atop the boulder scolded me as I drew near. It jumped onto the trunk of a nearby tree and scampered up to an overhanging branch, from where it continued to berate my intrusion. I settled down on the rock and used my pocket knife to cut through the top of a tin of lobster. I hadn't eaten lobster since I'd left New York.

An occasional songbird flitted among the branches chirping annoyance at my presence. A woodpecker tried unsuccessfully to compete with the sharp whack of axes heard striking tree trunks at the nearby pinery.

As I savored my lobster, I pondered the dilemma that haunted me. How could I tell Katy I was in love with her? How could I tell her I wanted to be the man she married? She was already engaged, for God's sake. How do I court a woman who's affianced?

When I slept, I dreamed about us being together. While I worked, I daydreamed about us being together. No girl had ever affected me this way. Why did she flirt with Duggan Maguire? Every time she mentioned her fiancé, my gut tightened. Was she that much in love with this Hollister fellow? After all, she'd obeyed Colonel Carrington and hadn't run away with some wagon train to go to Montana. Maybe she would be amenable to hearing a proposal from me. First, I'd have to stir up the gumption to ask.

"There you are." Katy's voice startled me.

"What are you doing out here?" I stammered.

"I didn't want to intrude on the families any longer," she answered, "so I came searching for you. I saw you head off in this direction."

"It's not safe for you to wander off from the group like that."

"You did."

I slapped the holster at my waist. "I've got a revolver. What if you came across a bear or, worse yet, an Indian?"

"I'd run to the block house. Colonel Carrington said it's only a short distance up the road."

I shook my head.

"What are you eating?" she asked.

"Lobster."

"Good?"

"Yes. Want a bite?" I held out my pocket knife with a chunk of meat on the end of the blade.

"No, thanks. I've already eaten more than I normally do."

"Come sit down. This boulder's big enough for both of us."

"I think I'll go to the water. I want to soak my feet."

"That water's mighty cold."

"I believe that's just what I need. These brogans are blistering my toes. My feet are so hot, I need to cool them off."

She settled below me on a bed of pine needles that had accumulated between the creek's edge and the boulder. She slipped her arm out of the sling and unlaced her army shoes. I hadn't paid much attention to her footwear until this moment. Her shoes were usually concealed beneath the hem of her skirt.

When she pulled off the brogans and stockings, bloody, red blisters were visible on the tops of her toes. She hiked up her skirt, revealing well-turned calves.

She dropped her feet into the fast-flowing current. "Wow!" When the cold water had splashed against her skin, she'd jerked her feet upward. Slowly, she immersed them again and let the water flow around her ankles.

"Not too bad," she said, "once you get used to it. I can hardly wait for payday when I can buy that pair of ladies boots the sutler has on his shelf."

She looked over her shoulder. Dimples graced the corners of her mouth when she smiled. "Mr. Wakefield, you should be ashamed staring at a girl's legs . . . not to mention what you did earlier when I was boarding the wagon."

My cheeks burned. I dropped my gaze to my lobster and fished another morsel out of the can.

She giggled. "But you've already seen me in the altogether, so I guess it doesn't matter."

She was referring to when I had helped remove her dress when the paymaster extracted the arrow from her shoulder. It was a vision permanently burned into my brain.

"Excuse me for staring," I said. "I am sorry you're experiencing pain from those blisters."

"Oh, forget it." She turned away and swished her feet more vigorously in the water.

We neither one said anything for a couple of minutes. Maybe

I should ask her now.

"This quiet place reminds me a little of being home . . . in Pennsylvania," she said.

"Do you miss your family?" I decided that was a safe question.

"Aye," she said. "I miss my mother, my father . . . my brothers."

"Brothers? You never told me you had brothers."

"Aye," she said, "I do . . . but, then again, I don't."

"What does that mean?"

"My brothers, both older, didn't emigrate when my parents came from Ireland. I was born on the ship, so I've never seen them. I don't know them personally. It would be nice to have a brother with whom I could confide. You don't have brothers, do you, Zach?"

"No. Five sisters."

We lapsed into silence again. She continued to swirl her feet in the stream. I ate the last of the lobster and tossed the can into the underbrush.

"Katy, I notice sometimes you say 'aye' but not always."

"At home, my parents always said 'aye.' I grew up hearing and saying 'aye.' But the teachers at college insisted I say 'yes' when instructing young Americans. I try to remember, but sometimes I forget."

"You seem to say 'aye' when you're excited or agitated."

"Aye." She looked over her shoulder at me, her dimples broadening her delightful smile. "You know, Zach, I like talking with you. I can share my feelings and thoughts with you. You are like a brother to me."

A *brother*?

CHAPTER 27

Colonel Carrington had established a look-out post on Pilot Hill, a promontory south of Little Piney Creek, a mile from the fort. Sentries posted there could observe the wood road along the Sullivant Hills. They could also see as far as the upper pinery. Because of the dense tree cover, they could not see movement on Piney Island. The sentries' job was to watch the wood road, as well as the Bozeman Trail, which passed below them, and signal activity to the fort.

Early Wednesday morning, August 22, the flag on Pilot Hill waved furiously for the first time. Indians were attacking the lumber train on the Sullivant Hills road.

Captain Ten Eyck happened to be in the quartermaster's office tent talking with Captain Brown when the alert occurred. Rifle fire could be heard coming from the wood road.

Captain Ten Eyck, as garrison commander, dispatched Corporal George Phillips with a platoon of mounted infantry to the relief of the train. Two hours later, Corporal Phillips led the wood train back to the fort. The Indians had made off with one set of mules, but Phillips and his men recovered the animals, and in the process, the corporal shot and killed an Indian. Corporal Phillips became an instant celebrity.

Colonel Carrington issued an order forbidding any further picnics.

Not long after noon that day, a courier arrived from Fort Reno bearing the first mail in three weeks. Work stopped for the next hour while those lucky enough to receive letters devoured their contents. I didn't receive any mail, not that I'd expected to. I hadn't written any letters.

I did get my hands on a ten-week-old *New York Tribune* and caught up on the news. Republicans were lamenting their inability to impeach President Andrew Johnson. Their attempt had ended May 26 when the Senate failed to achieve the necessary two-thirds majority for conviction. Other than typical intrigues surrounding politics at the New York state capital and the usual obituaries, there was nothing in the paper about Albany. I'm not sure why I'd hoped I might see news of my family.

Captain Ten Eyck returned to the quartermaster's tent, sank down on a camp stool, removed his glasses, and tried to clean them by wiping them on his blouse. "Fred," he said, "the colonel received an interesting letter from General Cooke."

"What about?" Captain Brown asked.

"Two companies of the Second Cavalry are being assigned here."

"It's about time. Now, maybe our commanding officer will feel he's got enough force to go after the Sioux. He's been wasting time building this fort while the Indians keep stealing my mules and cattle. It's time the savages got what's coming to them."

"I agree Carrington's cautious, but I doubt anything will get him moving."

"Time's wasting, Tenodor. Summer will soon be over. We're strong enough to go out and whip the savages. How can a bunch of half-dressed Indians armed with bows and arrows stand up to a veteran fighting force like the Eighteenth?"

Ten Eyck and Brown ignored the fact I was sitting only ten feet away.

"Did you hear from your wife?" Brown asked.

"Yes, six letters. All of them misrouted through Salt Lake City. Every letter bore a Utah postmark."

"I don't know why you stay in the army, Tenodor," Brown said. "You have a wife and how many children in Green Bay?"

"Five."

"As for me," Brown continued, "doesn't matter where I go. I'm not married."

Ten minutes later, Captain Ten Eyck rose and headed for the tent-flap door. He stopped in the opening and looked back. "Oh, Fred, almost forgot. Inspector General Hazen is at Fort Reno now, but he's on his way here."

"Oh, no. My records are in such disarray." Captain Brown turned to me. "Wakefield, you're going to have to work overtime to catch up."

I doubted any amount of overtime would *catch up* with the mess these records were in. Numerous times I've checked the inventory and told a customer we had the items he desired only to find half the quantity existed. Soldiers and teamsters helped themselves to things to get their jobs done building the fort. It wasn't as if they were stealing for their own use. With no lockable warehouse, it was easier to pick up the tools and parts and get on with work, instead of filling out army requisitions.

After Captain Ten Eyck left, my boss headed for the doorway himself. "Damn it. That's all I need. Bloody inspector general reviewing my records. I need a drink."

An hour later, Captain Brown returned. With him he brought three men who'd arrived with the mail courier—James Wheatley, Isaac Fisher, and John Phillips.

"Wakefield," my boss said, "add these men to our roster of quartermaster employees. They were headed for the goldfields, but I've convinced them to stay and help us."

Captain Brown departed and left the newcomers in my care. I wrote their names in a ledger for payroll purposes. After they signed papers as employees, I said, "Come with me. I'll show you to your quarters . . . such as they are."

When I stepped out of the tent, I almost bumped into a beautiful young woman and two toddlers who stood quietly to one side of the doorway.

"Mr. Wakefield," James Wheatley said, "meet my wife, Elisabeth. I call her Liz. And these two rascals"—he ruffled the hair of the two boys—"are our sons, John William and Milton Henry. Say hello to Mr. Wakefield, the quartermaster clerk."

"Hello, Mr. Wakefield," Liz said.

"Please call me Zach." The young woman had to be younger than Katy, but just as fetching in her own way. "I'll find a separate tent for you and your family, Mr. Wheatley. Mr. Fisher and Mr. Phillips will have to share a tent with others, however."

"Zach," John Phillips said, "most folks call me Portugee."

It took me an hour to get the two bachelors and the young family into tents that would be their temporary homes. I'd no sooner returned to my desk than Captain Brown came dashing in.

"Hurry up, Wakefield!" he shouted. "The savages are making off with part of our mule herd again."

He buckled on his dual-holstered gun belt while I fastened my borrowed holster around my waist. As we raced toward the horse corral, Captain Brown shouted at half a dozen workers to join us.

In less than five minutes, ten of us were saddled and dashing down Little Piney Creek in pursuit of a dozen warriors who herded fifty mules ahead of them. Surprisingly, Wheatley, Fisher, and Phillips were part of our group. Phillips was armed with a revolver, but the other two carried Henry repeating rifles.

After splashing across Big Piney Creek, above its confluence with Little Piney Creek, we headed east toward Lake DeSmet. We slowly gained on the thieves, who were hampered with the need to keep the mules moving.

I drew my revolver. I didn't keep a percussion cap on the cylinder that lay under the hammer in the event the weapon was to fire accidently. I drew the hammer to full cock, pulled the trigger to drive the hammer against the chamber that could not fire, then jerked the hammer again to rotate a loaded chamber into firing position. This would be the first time I'd fired the revolver. Colonel Carrington forbade target practice because of the shortage of ammunition.

I leveled my revolver above my horse's head and hoped he didn't stumble. I'd hate to shoot him. I singled out a trailing Indian and urged my mount to greater speed. I almost dropped my pistol when the fellow looked at me. He was white.

His skin was sunburned, and he wore a breach cloth and moccasins like the others with whom he rode. A headband secured a single eagle feather against his skull. Paint streaks marked his cheeks. There was something familiar about him.

My selected target rode next to another familiar figure, who was mounted on a large, black pony. The feathers on his war bonnet pointed straight up. He carried a lance adorned with feathers. Here was Running Bear, the Arapaho chief who'd attacked the paymaster's wagon train—the chief who'd led the band that'd wounded Katy and killed the Hollister family.

The white man pointed a pistol in my direction. I heard the shot's explosion almost at the same time I heard the bullet whistle past me. A puff of white smoke lingered briefly at the muzzle of his weapon.

I brought my revolver to full cock, aimed, and pulled the trigger. My pistol roared, and the barrel jumped. White smoke engulfed my pistol and hand. The white Indian rode on. I'd missed.

My adversary pointed his pistol toward me once more. That's when I saw the tattoo. The skull and crossbones stood out on his forearm. The letters *K.G.C.* were indistinctly visible at this distance. Here was the galvanized Yankee I'd seen with Duggan Maguire. What was he doing riding with Arapahos?

I snapped off another shot. Again, I missed. I could fire more often with the Colt while riding, but I was no more accurate than I'd been with the Springfield rifle.

Running Bear raised his spear high above his head, twirled it rapidly, shouted a command, and the band of Indians broke away, abandoning the mules. Their small ponies were more agile than our heavier mounts in negotiating the broken ground. They soon outdistanced us.

Captain Brown signaled a halt. We hadn't killed any warriors, but we'd recovered the mules.

By the time we herded the mules back to the fort, the sun was dropping behind the Big Horn Mountains. We paused when we forded Big Piney Creek and let the mules and our mounts drink. Then, I helped get the animals into our makeshift rope corrals.

I went to the hospital tent to tell Katy I'd encountered her old nemesis, Chief Running Bear. I found her standing in front of the hospital talking with Duggan Maguire.

"I saw someone you know, Maguire," I said.

"Who's that?"

I described the chase and the white man.

"I have no idea who that is," he said. "It's not anyone I know."

He turned to Katy, nodded, and said, "Good evening, Miss O'Toole. I enjoyed our conversation, as always."

Maguire pocketed the gold shamrock when he walked away.

CHAPTER 28

After work on Saturday, August 25, Ridgway Glover and I joined Portugee Phillips in the sutler's tent for a sarsaparilla. A half-dozen officers engaged in a card game at the far end of the tent. At the counter, opposite where the three of us had settled on a bench, a handful of soldiers and a couple of laundresses haggled with Judge Kinney over the prices for goods.

Jim Bridger entered the tent and paused. "Evening, Zach."

"Evening, Major," I said. "Didn't know you'd returned."

"A few hours ago. Won't be here long. Colonel's sending me out again tomorrow."

"Major Bridger," I said, "meet the quartermaster department's newest employee, John Phillips."

"Mr. Phillips." Bridger touched the rim of his battered slouch hat.

"Folks call me Portugee," Phillips said.

"Care to join us for a sarsaparilla?" I asked Bridger.

"No, thankee. Just came to pick up a plug of tobaccer."

After purchasing his tobacco, Bridger came to our bench. He looked at Portugee. "Phillips ain't a Portuguese name that I heard of," he said.

"Born in Portugal. Came to America fifteen years ago. When I landed in San Francesco aboard a whaling vessel, I changed my name to Phillips and took up gold mining instead of sailing. I was on my way to the Montana diggings, but I ran short of spending money, so I decided to stop here for awhile."

"Well, Portugee," Bridger said, "welcome to the Powder River country."

"I thank you," Portugee replied.

"You're leaving again tomorrow, Major?" I asked.

"Yep. The colonel wants to hire fifty Injuns as scouts. Henry Williams and Jim Beckwourth are going with me to Montana Territory to see if the Crows want the job. The colonel prefers Winnebagos or Pawnees, but they're too far away."

Bridger excused himself and left. We three finished our drinks, then headed off to bed.

The next morning, Sunday, August 26, should have been a day of rest. Colonel Carrington, however, issued instructions that following church services work must continue in sprucing up the place for the upcoming visit from the inspector general. The stockade around the main fort was complete. Foundations and partial walls revealed where permanent barracks, quarters, and offices would replace tents.

After breakfast, I headed toward the quartermaster's office tent to make more entries in the inventory ledgers. Officers and their families were making their way across the parade ground. Since no dedicated tent served as a church, Chaplain David White made use of whatever he could find. Today, folks headed for the headquarters tent. I'd seldom attended church after leaving Albany. I should feel guilty, but the omission hadn't seemed to harm me.

Trailing the officers' families, Katy O'Toole walked arm in arm with Duggan Maguire. She no longer wore the sling. Might not be a bad idea for me to listen to one of Chaplain White's sermons.

I strolled over to the headquarters tent, but the attendance was so large I couldn't get near. Soldiers even surrounded the outside of the tent so they could hear the preaching and sing the hymns. Standing there with a bunch of men didn't interest me. I returned to my desk.

Monday morning, August 27, the flags on Signal Hill announced the arrival of the inspector general. The main fort's inhabitants crowded the interior banquettes on the southern and eastern walls to observe the arriving party. The wall around the quartermaster yard had not yet been started, so we teamsters had an unobstructed view of the Bozeman Trail.

Captain Brown stood beside me observing the approaching procession through his Jumelle Marine field glasses. The French made these expensive binoculars for their navy. The captain frequently commented he considered them better than any German-made field glasses.

"That's not cavalry," Captain Brown said. "That's Lieutenant Kirtland with Fort Reno's mounted infantry. Where's the promised cavalry? How're we ever going to get Colonel Carrington to pursue the Indians if we don't have cavalry?"

The captain rubbed the front lenses of the glasses on his blouse. After the supposed cleaning, he refocused the binoculars.

"Zach, you know the paymaster," he said. "Do you see Major Bonnet with that column?" He handed me the field glasses.

A quick look convinced me there was no ambulance. "No, Captain, he isn't with them."

"Going to be a lot of disappointed soldiers who'll stand Muster Call the end of the month unpaid again," the captain said. "And I won't get reimbursed for invoices and affidavits. I won't be able to pay the teamsters or the contractors, either."

Would Judge Kinney call in my IOU? Hopefully, he'd prefer a delayed payment rather than the return of a used revolver.

From inside the stockade, a bugler sounded Officers' Call. Captain Brown headed back inside the fort's walls.

I returned his binoculars to the quartermaster's tent and

went out again to await the inspector general's arrival.

Ridgway Glover stood near the open front gate.

"Morning, Ridgway," I said as I came up beside him.

"Good morning, Zach."

"Where's your camera? This is a big moment in the history of Fort Phil Kearny. Don't you want to document it?"

"Can't," Ridgway said. "My last batch of chemicals wasn't good. The shots I took in the mountains didn't develop. I expect new chemicals to arrive with the next medical supplies."

"The mountains?" I asked. "You didn't go up into the Big Horns by yourself, did you?"

"Last week. All the way to the top of Cloud Peak."

"Why'd you do that? What's up there except snow and rocks?"

"Unobstructed view in all directions. Marvelous mountain meadows covered in wildflowers. Herds of deer and elk. Even saw mountain goats . . . at a distance."

"Indians?"

"No Indians."

"You shouldn't go that far on your own, Ridgway. The colonel has forbidden picnics."

"Wasn't on a picnic. I was doing my job. The Smithsonian expects me to capture images of nature, in addition to people and forts."

"Not a good idea, Ridgway."

"We've had this discussion before, Zach. No Indian is going to bother me."

Further conversation was drowned out when the band blared out a martial tune as General William Hazen and his party entered the fort.

The infantry companies were arrayed on the parade ground in full dress uniforms. Plumes fluttered in the breeze above helmets. Officers sported red sashes beneath their sword belts. Sunlight reflected off polished brass buttons and buckles.

We civilians stood on the perimeter roads and observed the ceremonies welcoming the inspector general. Ridgway and I moved close enough to hear the words exchanged between Carrington and Hazen.

The adjutant called the troops to attention, and Colonel Carrington saluted. "General Hazen, the Second Battalion, Eighteenth Infantry, is ready for inspection."

The inspector general dismounted and returned the salute. "Thank you, Colonel."

Hazen and Carrington walked to the front of the formation.

Hazen wore eagle epaulettes like Carrington, but the officers and men addressed Hazen as "general." He'd been breveted a major general for service on the battlefield. Perhaps the courtesy title had something to do with Hazen being a West Point graduate. Or perhaps it was because Hazen had been an Indian fighter before the war—something the officers of the Eighteenth aspired to become. In any case, not addressing Carrington with the same courtesy title was an obvious snub by his men.

The review of the troops consumed the rest of the morning. After the formation broke up and the soldiers dispersed, word spread that Colonel Carrington had authorized a dance for the evening entertainment of his guest.

After the noon meal, Duggan Maguire supervised a detail in building a temporary wooden dance floor on the parade ground. At each corner of the floor, posts were installed on which flares could be mounted. Wires stretched between the posts provided a place to string oil-fired lanterns.

After supper, I scrubbed the mud off my boots and donned my other, clean shirt. One of the laundresses washed my shirts in exchange for a few choice items I slipped her from the commissary warehouse.

Captain Brown appeared just as I stepped out of my tent to head for the dance.

"Wakefield," he said, "the colonel wants a detail to keep the stoves in the officers' tents burning during the dance so folks have a place to warm up. The evening promises to be cool. Round up a couple of teamsters to help you keep firewood supplied to the stoves. Also, replace any sputtering torches with fresh ones and refill the oil in the lanterns, if they need it."

I stood there with an open mouth.

When he walked away, he glanced over his shoulder. "Don't let those stoves go out, Wakefield."

Cords of firewood were stacked in the quartermaster yard. I spent the evening goading my two helpers into keeping the fires stoked and the dance stage lit.

I couldn't blame my fellow workers for wanting to stop to watch the ladies twirling with their partners. Shoes and boots pounded rhythmically on the wooden dance floor. A dozen enlisted men wore bandanas around an arm to indicate they were substitute females. Bandmaster Samuel Curry led the musicians in transitioning from waltz to schottische, from galop to polka.

Kathleen O'Toole proved quite popular with the lieutenants and captains. She didn't miss a dance. At one point, Duggan Maguire swung her about. He resembled a riverboat gambler, dressed in a black frock coat and tan vest.

Katy exhibited no discomfort at having her injured arm pulled back and forth and up and down with the dance steps. Her army brogans didn't slow her down. Either her blisters were healed, or she didn't care.

Later in the evening, as I stepped out of the Carringtons' tent after ensuring George had adequate wood to keep the commanding officers' stoves burning, Duggan Maguire sauntered up. I brushed soot off my shirtsleeves.

"Not dancing, Wakefield?" Duggan caressed the shamrock

suspended on a gold chain between the pockets of his vest.
"Pity. Miss O'Toole is particularly charming this evening."

Chapter 29

I had just turned the wick down on my lantern in the quarter-master's office tent on Wednesday, August 29, prior to going to lunch, when approaching voices got my attention.

General Hazen, Colonel Carrington, Captain Ten Eyck, and Captain Brown entered the tent and stood together near the entrance. My end of the large tent was dimly lit, and if they saw me, they ignored me.

"Colonel Carrington," General Hazen said, "I am impressed with your stockade. It's probably the best I've seen except for one in Canada. I understand you designed it yourself."

"Yes, General," Carrington said, "I'm the architect of the fort." His voice expressed a definite pride.

"Well done," Hazen said. "I congratulate you. Had it been me, however, I'd have constructed the buildings first and then erected the walls. I consider the comfort of troops and the security of supplies to be of utmost importance. I can't believe Indians pose much threat to a force as large as yours. Fort Laramie has no walls, and they've never been attacked."

"General," Carrington said, "the Laramie Loafers will never be a threat. Red Cloud is a different matter. A day seldom passes that the savages don't raid our grazing herds, attack our timber wagons, or assault our hay mowers. Last week, Major Bridger reported the Crows discovered over five hundred Sioux lodges along the Tongue River. That's a lot—"

"Colonel," Hazen abruptly cut off the conversation. "I'm not convinced there are that many Indians in one place. My experience on the frontier is that the savages live in small, isolated villages so as not to deplete the grass for their grazing ponies."

Even in the dim light, I perceived the frustrated look on Colonel Carrington's face.

Hazen spoke to Captain Brown. "As for your quartermaster records, Captain, they're a disgrace."

I tried to sink farther into my chair. I was glad the feeble light from my lantern didn't vividly illuminate my corner of the tent.

Captain Brown removed his hat and ran a hand over his balding head. He didn't respond to the criticism.

"You're also the commissary officer, I believe?" General Hazen asked Brown.

"Yes, sir. The Eighteenth is short officers, and we've all been assigned additional duties."

"Since the war ended, the army is short officers everywhere." Hazen waved a hand to brush aside the issue. "We make do with what we have. General Cooke informed me he will soon assign additional officers to the Eighteenth."

"General Cooke also promised to send two companies of cavalry," Colonel Carrington said. "We hoped they would arrive with you."

"Well," Hazen said, "I don't know what's causing that delay."

"Neither do I," Carrington said. "Mounted infantry using Springfield rifles are ill suited to combat with Indians mounted on fleet ponies. We need cavalry armed with carbines."

"What condition are your Springfields?" Hazen asked.

"Bad," Carrington replied. "Fortunately, I have a good armorer. Private Maddeon, through cannibalization, can make one good rifle out of two bad ones. Omaha hasn't sent any spare parts."

"Who serves as your ordnance officer?" Hazen asked.

"I double in that capacity," Carrington answered. "I only have an ordnance sergeant."

"That submerged magazine you're constructing looks like a good place to store your ammunition," General Hazen said.

"We don't have much to store right now," Carrington said. "We only have enough rifle ammunition to equip each man with eight rounds. Many of our new recruits have never fired a weapon, but I can't afford to waste ammunition on target practice. I've installed small flags on stakes around the perimeter of the fort at specified distances so the men can set their sights at known ranges when they shoot at Indians. The flags help aim the howitzers, too."

"Are any of your officers artillerymen?" Hazen asked.

"No, sir," Colonel Carrington said. "I fill that capacity, too."

"Are you trained in artillery practice, Colonel?" Hazen asked.

"Not formally. I have studied the matter and am capable of cutting Borman fuses to the proper length."

"I must say," Hazen said, "I am impressed with the bastions you've constructed at two corners of your stockade. They will serve as admirable platforms for artillery to place enfilading fire along your walls."

"That was the intent, General," Carrington said.

Hazen did not comment for a moment.

"What else would you like to inspect, General?" Carrington asked.

"Actually, I'm finished here. I want to depart in the morning for Fort C. F. Smith and go as far into Montana as Fort Benton on the Missouri River. I'm responsible for inspecting there as well. I'll need you to provide me an escort since Lieutenant Kirtland took his detachment back to Fort Reno."

"Captain Ten Eyck," Carrington said, "assign Lieutenant Bradley and twenty-six of our best mounted infantrymen to serve as General Hazen's escort, even though that's going to leave us short horses and men."

Second Lieutenant James Bradley was one of the new officers who had been with the Templeton party at Crazy Woman's Fork. He had acquitted himself well there when he led a dozen men in driving the Sioux away from the corralled wagons and ambulances.

"You won't need to be concerned about the shortage long, Colonel," Hazen said. "I'm sure your two companies of cavalry will arrive any day. What about a guide?"

"We only have two left. All the others are out on assignment. I'll have James Brannan be your guide. He knows the Tongue River region. He scouted for one of General Connor's columns up that way last year."

"Fine," Hazen said. "I'll submit my written report to General Cooke once I return to Omaha. Headquarters will send you a copy."

After the officers departed, I went for lunch. I knew from having talked with Katy the night before, she'd gotten Colonel Carrington's permission to travel north with General Hazen's party. Katy could now get to the Montana goldfields to rejoin her fiancé.

I sat alone in the teamsters' mess tent pushing lukewarm beans around a tin plate while I pondered going with her. She'd given no indication she was interested in me—other than as a "brother." My original plan had been to go to the goldfields. I had that excuse to justify going to Montana. But I hadn't been paid yet for my work as a quartermaster clerk. I had an outstanding IOU with Judge Kinney. If I couldn't reclaim the IOU, I'd have to return the Colt. I still owed money to the army for the wrecked wagon and the dead mule. If I tried to leave, Captain Brown might have me arrested.

"Wakefield, you gonna eat that?" One of the muleskinners

stood in front of my table.

I shoved my plate toward him. "No, don't have much appetite."

I took a final swig of cold coffee and left. I went to the quartermaster's office tent and collapsed into my chair. My head dropped forward onto the desk, and I fell asleep.

"Wakefield, wake up!" Captain Brown's voice jerked me upright.

I noticed half a dozen scruffy looking civilians standing outside the tent's entrance.

"What do you mean sleeping on the job?" he demanded.

"Sorry, sir. It's been a difficult few days with the inspector general criticizing everything we've tried to do."

"It's all right, Zach," he said in a lower voice. "I understand. But you have to look alive now. These miners passing through from the Montana goldfields are possible employees."

Captain Brown returned to the waiting men. "Take it or leave it, gentlemen. That's the best I can offer. We need workers, but I'll not be held up for exorbitant wages."

The men grumbled among themselves, then one of them spoke up. "I reckon we'll keep moving on to the States, Captain. The men have agreed we don't want to be stuck out here in Indian country during the winter."

"Suit yourselves," Captain Brown said.

All of them walked away except one. "Sir?" the remaining man asked. "Forgive me, but I was wondering if you could tell me whether a certain young woman might be here."

"Young woman?"

"Yes, sir. I'm looking for Miss Kathleen O'Toole."

I stood up so fast I knocked my chair over.

"Kathleen O'Toole?" Captain Brown asked.

"Yes, sir. A letter I had from her was postmarked from here."

"Yes," Captain Brown said. "There is a young lady here by

that name. And who are you, sir?"

"Dennis Sawyer."

"Dennis Sawyer?" I blurted out his name. Katy's future brother-in-law.

Sawyer nodded. "I'd like to talk to her. I have news."

He must have word from her fiancé.

"Mr. Wakefield," Captain Brown said, "take Mr. Sawyer to Miss O'Toole."

"Follow me, Mr. Sawyer."

I preceded him as I strode purposefully toward the hospital tent. On the way we did not talk. I had no idea what to say to this man who was going to give Katy news about her fiancé.

Inside the hospital tent's entrance, Doctor Horton sat at a desk sorting through paperwork. He looked up when we entered.

"Afternoon, Mr. Wakefield," the doctor said. "What can I do for you?"

"This gentleman wants to speak with Katy."

Doctor Horton scrutinized the disheveled fellow standing beside me. He turned toward the interior of the hospital tent and called out, "Miss O'Toole!"

"Yes, Doctor?" Katy's answer came faintly from the far end of the large enclosure.

"Someone here to see you," Doctor Horton shouted.

"Be right out."

Katy brushed aside a curtain separating the front from the rear of the hospital and came to an abrupt halt.

"Dennis!" She smiled broadly, her dimples deepening at the corners of her mouth.

She hurried across the space that separated us, holding out her arms to him.

He just stood there.

"Dennis?" Katy dropped her arms when he did not respond. Her dimples faded.

"I received your letters," he whispered, "about Megan's death . . . about the baby . . . and her parents."

"I'm so sorry I had to write to you about that," Katy said. "Why are you here, Dennis? Are you alone?" She looked to either side of him, as if someone else should be there.

"I'm with other fellows." His voice grew stronger. "We're going back to the States. We didn't do well in the goldfields."

"Where's Brandon?" Katy asked. "Is Brandon with you?"

Sawyer shook his head.

"Did you bring word from him? Do you have a letter for me?"

He shook his head again.

"What's happened?" Katy demanded. "Is Brandon alive?"

"He's alive . . . yes, he's alive."

"Well?" Katy prompted.

Sawyer took a deep breath and blew it out through pursed lips. "He's living with a Blackfoot squaw!"

Katy swayed. I stepped forward and grasped her around the waist to steady her.

The next morning, Katy stood beside me in front of the quartermaster's office tent as we watched General Hazen's party depart for Fort C. F. Smith. Before the gates closed, the party of Montana miners also shambled out of the fort to head south. Dennis Sawyer did not look at Katy when he trudged past.

"I don't know what to do, Zach," Katy said.

"Do you want to go with those miners to the States?" I asked.

She shook her head. "I'm not ready to make that decision. Maybe I'll return to Pennsylvania. Maybe I'll go to Montana. I had such dreams of becoming Brandon's wife. I looked forward to a future of teaching school for the miners' children. Now . . . I'm not sure. I just don't know. So . . . I'll stay here and help Doctor Horton while I weigh my options."

"Of course." What else could I say? I knew I didn't want her to go in either direction.

Katy abruptly leaned closer and laid her cheek against my shoulder. I wrapped an arm around her while she wept. Wetness soaked the wool material beneath her face. I decided never to wash the shirt again.

Across the way, standing beside the front gate, Duggan Maguire glared at us and caressed the shamrock pendant.

Katy straightened up, reached into the pocket of her hospital apron, and withdrew the bottle of laudanum. She popped out the cork and took a long swig.

"I thought your collarbone was healed," I said.

"It is. My heart is broken now."

CHAPTER 30

On September 1, a Saturday, snow blanketed the higher slopes of the Big Horn Mountains. With this harbinger of winter, everybody was aware of the need to get roofs on the buildings. Each evening after supper, Captain Brown and Duggan Maguire supervised men in riving shingles from bolts of wood using mallets and froes. The band entertained the workers, who augmented the music with their own percussive effort.

The walls of the barracks were up, and the commissary warehouse neared completion. Colonel Carrington wanted to get the flour, hardtack, and bacon under shelter to protect them from the elements. Hardware items could remain in crates and under canvas until the quartermaster warehouse could be built.

A week later, a blinding snowstorm swept down from the mountains, and we experienced our first dose of harsh weather. Even though we couldn't see more than a hundred yards beyond the stockade walls, a band of Indians swept through the flat land between the fort and the foothills where our herds were grazing and made off with dozens of cattle, mules, and horses.

On Monday, September 10, freighter A. C. Leighton arrived with a wagon train of goods for the sutler. Late that afternoon the Indians raided his camp outside the fort and made off with forty-two of his mules. Lieutenant Adair led a mounted contingent in pursuit for twenty miles. They returned without any of the freighter's animals. Without corn to feed them, our mounted infantrymen's horses were undernourished and could not effectively pursue the nimbler Indian ponies.

Colonel Carrington informed Leighton to see Captain Brown about his loss. I helped the wagon master complete an Indian Depredations Claim form. He valued the mules at two hundred fifty dollars each. The loss of ten thousand five hundred dollars would probably wipe out Leighton's profits.

That afternoon, another band of Indians stole thirty-three horses and seventy-eight mules from our quartermaster herd. Pursuit by Captain Brown and a detachment of soldiers and teamsters failed to recover any of these animals. I posted monetary losses in the inventory ledgers valued at more than double what Leighton experienced. The real impact on the Eighteenth Infantry was the loss of working mules for timber hauling and the reduction in horses available to pursue the thieves.

Early Tuesday morning, September 11, the slow thumping of muffled drums caused me to leave my breakfast plate on the table in the teamsters' mess tent and step outside.

I brought my cup along and took a sip of coffee while I watched the band pass through the water gate at slow march pace heading toward the cemetery at the foot of Pilot Hill. An ambulance followed, and bringing up the rear, a squad of infantrymen marched with muskets on their shoulders.

"Wonder what that's all about?" I casually asked a teamster who stood beside me.

"Bandmaster Curry died last night," he answered. "He's the first person to be buried in the cemetery who wasn't killed by Indians. I heard he had typhoid pneumonia."

The colonel promoted Peter Damme to replace Samuel Curry.

★ ★ ★ ★ ★

Shortly after midnight on Wednesday, September 12, the nightly chorus of howling wolves was drowned out by shouting from the front gate, which was located not far from my sleeping tent. I roused myself and went out to determine the cause of the disturbance. Captain Brown hurried past me on his way to the headquarters tent, so I followed him.

John Jost, known as the "stuttering blacksmith," stood in front of headquarters holding the reins of a lathered horse while he talked with Colonel Carrington. Jost worked for Leviticus Carter and Beebe Crary, whom Captain Brown had under contract as hay cutters working on Goose Creek, twenty miles north. Colonel Carrington frequently asked Jost to stop stuttering so he could understand him.

Jost described how the eighty-man hay-cutting crew had been attacked at noon the day before by two hundred warriors. The force of the attack caused the workers to retreat to the shelter of a circle of wagons where they spent the rest of the day fending off repeated charges. Jost knew one man had been killed. The warriors covered the six mowing machines with hay and set them on fire.

Carter had offered Jost five hundred dollars to race to the fort for help. Jost said he had to try twice before he slipped past the Indians after dark.

Colonel Carrington assigned Lieutenant Adair to lead forty mounted infantrymen to the relief of the embattled hay cutters.

Not long after Adair's force disappeared heading north up the Bozeman Trail, Indians coaxed a small herd of buffalo into the midst of the fort's grazing cattle and stampeded the entire mixed herd. The sentries patrolling the stockade wall shouted the alarm, and many of us climbed onto the banquettes to see for ourselves.

"Zach, help me," Katy called from below me.

I pulled her up beside me. A sergeant and ten men who had been standing guard over the cattle watched helplessly, as did we.

"Look." I pointed to the band of Indians chasing the stampeding animals. "That's Running Bear. They're Arapahos."

"Zach," Katy said, "that one's a white man."

"He's the galvanized Yankee who shared whiskey with Duggan Maguire at our campsite at Fort Reno. But why is he riding with the Arapahos?"

Captain Brown led a pursuit of the stampeded animals with a detachment of soldiers and teamsters. When they returned later without any of the cattle, I estimated the Indians had made off that day with over two hundred head of prime beef. The garrison's supply of meat intended for the coming winter season had been seriously diminished.

On Saturday, September 15, I spotted Ridgway Glover dragging his perambulator out the quartermaster's gate that led to the wagon park. His long blond hair trailed over his shoulders beneath the brim of a straw boater hat.

"Hey, Ridgway," I called. "Where'd you get the new hat?"

"It arrived in the shipment for the sutler the other day. I couldn't resist."

"What're you doing leaving the fort alone?" I asked.

"Going to take some pictures up at the pineries."

"I thought you didn't have chemicals."

"The sutler got in a small assortment, and I managed to piece together enough to develop a dozen plates."

"Who's going with you, Ridgway? You know the colonel forbade anyone leaving the fort alone."

"The timber train left only a half hour ago. I'll catch up to them."

"Not a good idea."

"Stop worrying, Zach. I've told you before, the Indians aren't going to bother me."

"Do you have a weapon in that rig?"

"Don't need one. I'll just point my camera at them, and they'll pose."

Ridgway was a grown man. Although I questioned his judgment, who was I to stop him? He rolled his rig past the sawmills, where he picked up the wagon road that led toward the lower slope of Sullivant Hills.

On Sunday morning, September 16, a train of twelve farm wagons made a trip down the Bozeman Trail to a hay cutting location near Lake De Smet. This caravan went protected with a rifleman sitting next to each wagon driver and six mounted infantrymen riding on the flanks. After the wagons were loaded and headed back to the fort, Private Peter Johnson moved out on horseback to ride point. He allowed the distance between himself and the wagons to widen to over three hundred yards.

An Indian rushed out of a ravine and after a short chase captured the private. Then, dozens of Indians appeared on the hills on either side of the wagon train. The riflemen riding wagon-guard and the mounted infantrymen had been issued only three rounds each. The teamsters were mostly unarmed. The leader of the wagon train wisely chose to return to the fort rather than confront a large Indian party with his limited armaments.

Shortly after the train returned, Captain Brown led a detachment out to rescue Private Johnson. I rode with them.

A mounted infantryman who'd been with the wagon train guided us to the spot where the incident occurred. Even though we searched the ravines and hills for several hundred yards on both sides of the road, we found no trace of Private Johnson.

★ ★ ★ ★ ★

Later that Sunday afternoon, Captain Brown entered the quartermaster's office tent and stopped just inside the entrance. I had been concentrating on making entries in the inventory ledgers, and it took me a moment to realize he hadn't moved farther into the tent. I looked up.

"Zach . . . you may want to go to the hospital tent."

When he didn't elaborate, I asked, "Why?"

"An ambulance just brought in what's left of Ridgway Glover."

I laid my pen in the crack of the open ledger and inserted the cork stopper in the ink bottle. I pushed my chair away from the camp desk, got slowly to my feet, and retrieved my hat from where it hung on a nail in a tent pole.

When I reached the hospital, Katy stood to one side of the entrance, her hands pressed against her cheeks. I walked to the rear of the ambulance. A corporal held the edge of a blanket up, allowing Surgeon Horton and Lieutenant Bisbee to see beneath it while they talked.

I stepped up behind the two officers and peered over the doctor's shoulder. On the floorboard of the ambulance lay a face-down, naked body. Bare feet extended toward the tailgate. Dried blood discolored the stark white back. Clumps of black feces clung to the buttocks and thighs. A severed head leaned against the body's shoulder. Folds of skin slumped down the forehead pressing the eyebrows low over Ridgway Glover's wide-open, unseeing, blue eyes. The top of Ridgway's skull showed exposed bone, devoid of hair except for a blond fringe above the ears. Rivulets of blackened blood streaked the severed head's cheeks and chin.

The stench assailed my nostrils. My stomach revolted. Bile rose in my throat, and I gagged down the threatening vomit.

Tears blurred my vision. My fingernails cut into the palms of my hands.

I listened as Lieutenant Bisbee described to Surgeon Horton how his detachment had discovered Ridgway two miles from the stockade. The stripped body lay face down in the middle of the road, the backbone cleft with a metal-bladed tomahawk, like those distributed at the Fort Laramie peace conference. Lieutenant Bisbee stated that, from the position in which the Indians had left Ridgway's body, it appeared they didn't think he'd been brave when he faced death. Bisbee's soldiers found Ridgway's head several feet away from the body. In addition to the tomahawk wound, his men removed a dozen arrows from Glover's back. Bisbee said a wide search by his troopers of the surrounding area failed to locate the perambulator, camera, or photographic plates.

Some warrior now boasted a prize of long blond curls attached to his war lance. Another brave was probably trying to incorporate the straw boater into some outlandish costume.

"The goddamned sons of bitches!" I gritted my teeth. "I hope we kill them all."

I said those words louder than I'd intended, because Surgeon Horton turned around and laid a hand on my shoulder. "Easy, Zach," he said. "Come with me."

He led me over to where Katy stood. "Miss O'Toole," he said, "take Mr. Wakefield inside and pour him a cup of strong black coffee."

Later that afternoon, when the wood train came into the fort, we learned Glover had reached his intended destination on Saturday. Several pinery workers observed him taking photographs and making sketches that afternoon. On Sunday morning, he decided to head to the fort. No wagon train was scheduled to make the journey until evening. The woodcutters claimed they advised Glover against going alone, but he countered that he'd made it out their way safely without accompaniment.

That evening, I hitched the Bible mules to an ambulance and drove toward the cemetery with Ridgway's body. The sawmill workers, with whom Ridgway had worked, had nailed together a pine-board coffin for his remains. Chaplain White rode beside me. We had no muffled drums nor marching band. Portugee Phillips and some sawmill workers trudged behind us carrying shovels on their shoulders.

As we passed through the water gate and splashed across Little Piney Creek, Chaplain White spoke to me. "Mr. Wakefield, Mr. Glover would appreciate your taking him to his final resting place. You were probably his best friend here."

"Chaplain, if I'd been Ridgway's true friend, I'd have reported his unauthorized departure to the sergeant of the guard."

CHAPTER 31

On Monday morning, September 17, Colonel Carrington grinned more broadly than I'd ever seen. He was usually aloof, allowing nothing to faze his stoic demeanor.

"Open this one." The colonel almost danced when he tapped the top of the wooden crate.

I jammed the crowbar beneath the lid and pried up. The nails securing the cover squealed as they released their grip. The top flew up, revealing row upon row of paper packets, each containing ten .58-caliber rifle-musket cartridges.

"Now do this one," the colonel said.

The second crate was also packed with cartridges. Captain Brown reached into this crate and handed one of the packets to the colonel.

"Magnificent!" The colonel fondled the lacquered paper container. "Finally, we have ammunition. Now, we must expedite construction of the magazine. Captain Brown, assign that fellow Duggan Maguire to supervise the work. He did a good job on the stockade walls."

"Yes, sir."

Earlier that morning, a wagon train had arrived with sixty thousand rounds of Springfield rifle ammunition. The train also contained dozens of sacks of corn destined for the goldfields in Montana. Captain Brown persuaded the wagon master to sell several bushels at an inflated price.

Now the troops had extra bullets but Colonel Carrington

wanted a hundred thousand more. The horses would get their first taste of corn in weeks, but it wouldn't last long. For the moment, however, the garrison commander was ecstatic.

"Colonel Carrington!" A sentry yelled from the bastion at the stockade's southeast corner.

We all looked in that direction. Colonel Carrington raised a hand in acknowledgement.

The sentry pointed south. "Pilot Hill is signaling the arrival of a party, Colonel."

The colonel and Captain Brown headed for the bastion.

"Zach," Captain Brown said, "fetch my binoculars."

"Yes, sir."

I dropped the crowbar and hurried to the quartermaster's office tent a dozen paces away. Two minutes later, I climbed onto the bastion and handed the field glasses to the captain.

"It's the mail escort returning from Fort Laramie," Captain Brown explained as he studied the approaching column through the binoculars. "There's also an ambulance and a wagon. A woman is sitting beside the ambulance driver. An infantry lieutenant is riding alongside. Looks like we have an addition to the garrison, sir."

"That would be George Washington Grummond," Colonel Carrington said. "I received notice in the last mail he was being sent forward. He was a lieutenant colonel of the Fourteenth Michigan Infantry during the war, but he's joining us as a second lieutenant."

"That would be his wife, I presume," Captain Brown stated.

"Probably. General Sherman is determined we operate a normal garrison here. Even though the general doesn't want us to start a war, we may not be the deciding factor in that matter."

A half hour later, the ambulance party approached the open

front gate. I had returned to inventorying the ammunition crates nearby.

"Halt!" The gate sentry had stopped the ambulance short of the entrance. He signaled the driver of a wagon approaching from the pinery road to enter the fort ahead of the ambulance.

Had I been closer, I probably would have heard some exclamation escape the lips of the female occupant of the ambulance. The woman clasped a hand over her mouth as she observed an arrow-riddled, naked corpse pass by in the wagon. Red Cloud's warriors had butchered another soldier or teamster.

After the wagon from the pinery proceeded with its grisly contents to the hospital tent, the sentry motioned the mounted lieutenant to swing his group over to the headquarters tent.

Colonel Carrington had been so enthused with the arrival of the ammunition shipment that he'd not left our worksite. With the arrival of Lieutenant Grummond's party, the colonel said he had to return to headquarters. He paused to give Captain Brown instructions.

"Captain," the colonel said, "we don't have quarters under construction for another family. We'll have to house them in a tent for the time being. See to it, please. And ask all the officers' wives, mine included, to join me at headquarters to greet our new arrivals."

"Yes, sir."

The colonel strode away, and Captain Brown turned to me.

"Is the inventory finished?" he asked.

"Yes, this is the last of it."

"Good. Get a crew and erect a double wall tent for the Grummonds. There's room between the colonel's quarters and the bungalow north of it." He followed Colonel Carrington toward the headquarters.

I chose Portugee Phillips and two other men to help me erect the tent. I hitched Mathew and Mark to a farm wagon, and we hauled two standard army wall tents and some furniture items to officers' row. We erected the tents end to end, replacing the rear wall of the front tent and the front wall of the rear tent with a canvas-fly divider. In the front section we placed two camp stools and a mess chest to serve as a table. In the rear section we installed two hospital bunks. Extending behind the rear tent, we affixed a tarpaulin on poles to serve as a roof over a woodburning cook stove and a half cord of firewood. This eighteen-foot long by nine-foot wide tent shelter would be the Grummonds' home until a cabin could be built.

We'd no sooner finished our chore when Mrs. Carrington came into the tent with Mrs. Grummond. I'd sent two of the men to return the wagon to the yard. Only Portugee and I remained to help the Grummonds unload their ambulance.

Portugee's mouth fell open. I followed his gaze. His eyes were fixed on Mrs. Grummond. The dark-haired young beauty, engaged in conversation with Mrs. Carrington, was oblivious to the effect she was having on my friend.

I poked an elbow into Portugee's ribs, and he jumped.

At that moment, Katy O'Toole entered the tent. She nodded to Portugee and me.

"Mrs. Carrington," Katy said, "you sent for me."

"Yes, Katy, thank you for coming. Let me introduce Mrs. Frances Grummond, wife of Lieutenant Grummond, newly assigned to the Eighteenth. Mrs. Grummond, this is Miss Kathleen O'Toole."

"Mrs. Grummond," Katy said. "Welcome."

"Thank you, Miss O'Toole. Friends call me Fannie." The words rolled slowly off Mrs. Grummond's tongue. I'd heard similar melodious accents on my tour of the South after the war.

"Miss O'Toole," Mrs. Carrington continued, "is a hospital matron. She has also been helping Sergeant Fessenden's wife with her new baby. Katy will be of great assistance to you in your condition."

What condition? She'd had a shock when she'd seen the naked body at the gate, but she looked fine now.

"It will be a pleasure to assist you, Fannie. Please call me Katy."

"Now, ladies," Mrs. Carrington said, "if you will excuse me, I'll let you get better acquainted."

I held the tent flap open to allow the commanding officer's wife to pass through.

Katy guided Mrs. Grummond through the sleeping portion of the tent and out through the rear flap. Portugee and I followed, staying back a discrete distance.

"My goodness," Mrs. Grummond said, "whatever will I do with this?" She pointed to the cook stove we'd placed beneath the fly.

"Cook your breakfast?" Katy suggested.

"Oh, I don't cook. We had slaves who did that in Tennessee."

"Well," Katy said, "since your husband's an officer, he can employ an enlisted man as a striker. The striker can prepare meals and do other chores."

"What a good suggestion," Mrs. Grummond said. "The wives of the other officers invited us to share meals with them. So, I suppose I'll make do."

Lieutenant Grummond arrived next, escorting the ambulance and the baggage wagon. Portugee and I helped the drivers bring the trunks and cases into the tent. The lieutenant obviously considered carrying items beneath his rank. He did not speak to us except in a grunt when he pointed to where we were to place things.

While we'd been unloading the ambulance, the ladies remained engaged in quiet conversation. When we finished, Mrs. Grummond thanked us.

"I'm sorry your welcome involved seeing a dead man first thing," I said.

"Oh," she said, "it wasn't that the poor man was dead. I saw many dead men during the war. I helped nurse the wounded following the Battle of Franklin. It's just that this man was being transported like a side of beef."

I nodded as a way of indicating I understood. Portugee, Katy, and I departed.

Walking away from the newly erected tent, Katy said, "I'm afraid she's going to find life here a little difficult, especially in her condition."

"What condition?" I asked. "She doesn't look sick to me."

"She's expecting, Zachary! I'm surprised at you. You surely saw your mother's condition when she was expecting the birth of your sisters."

"My mother got fat when she was in the family way."

"Well, Fannie Grummond will get fatter. She's only two months along now."

Later that afternoon, a man named William Bailey and forty miners arrived from the Montana goldfields. They all accepted Captain Brown's offer of quartermaster employment. They established a camp on the far bank of Big Piney Creek. The men were well armed and each was mounted on a sturdy horse. Colonel Carrington was quite pleased, saying they could serve as his cavalry until the real thing arrived.

Jim Bridger, who was still at Fort C. F. Smith, had sent a message with Bailey confirming earlier information that five hundred Sioux lodges were located along the Tongue River. The message also indicated white men had been seen riding with the Indians.

That night it snowed. The next morning, Captain Brown sent Portugee and me back to the Grummonds' tent. We hadn't secured the gap in the roof line between the two tents, and snow had drifted into the bedroom section.

"When I awoke," Mrs. Grummond explained in her soft drawl, "wetness trickled down my cheeks. My word, I thought I was shedding tears. Then I realized my face was covered with snow. My pillow, my blanket, everything was white with snow."

"Mrs. Grummond," I exclaimed, "I'm so sorry. We'll clean up the mess and fix the problem."

Portugee spent most of his time trying to get a glimpse of Frances Grummond. Next time I came to the Grummonds' abode to do work, I'd bring a different helper.

CHAPTER 32

One of the newly arrived officers, Second Lieutenant Winfield Scott Matson, came into the quartermaster's office tent late on Saturday afternoon, September 22. Captain Brown and I were wrapping things up for the week. Tomorrow being Sunday, we'd have a day off. I'm not sure what I was going to do with a day off except listen to a long-winded sermon by Chaplain White. The colonel had forbidden pleasure journeys outside the stockade walls.

"Well, Lieutenant," Captain Brown asked, "did you get my hayfield workers back safely?"

"Not without some difficulty, Captain," the lieutenant answered. "We'd just gotten the machinery and wagons lined up in the road for the trip back from Goose Creek when we were attacked by at least three hundred warriors. Mainly Sioux, but some Arapahos were mixed in with them."

"I can't afford to lose more mowing machines. Did you save the equipment . . . and the men?"

"Yes, sir. The column will arrive shortly. I rode ahead to report to Colonel Carrington."

"You've seen the colonel already?"

"I reported to him before coming here, sir."

"You say three hundred savages attacked you. Where was that? What'd you do?"

"About five miles north. We were spread out along the road when they jumped us from the mountain side. If they'd hit us from both sides simultaneously, I'm not sure we'd have been so fortunate. As it was, we saw them coming and circled the wagons. They kept us pinned down for awhile, but they gave up after an hour and drifted away to the north. We unwound the corral and had just started down the trail when I was confronted by a strange apparition."

"How's that?"

"I'd ridden ahead to make sure the point man knew what I wanted him to do when we came face to face with a white man dressed like an Indian. He held up a hand to signify we should halt. He had no fingers on that hand—just a thumb. Without my asking, he identified himself as Captain Bob North."

"Captain?"

"Former Confederate officer, probably. He had a pronounced southern drawl."

"What'd he want?"

"I didn't find out. At that moment, two scouts from a contractor's wagon train, traveling south from Fort C. F. Smith, raced up on lathered horses demanding I come to their aid. They claimed a contractor named Grull and two of his drivers had been killed during an Indian attack not far behind my column. I imagine the Indians who'd attacked me shifted their assault when they identified an easier target in the contractor's train. While the scouts were relating their predicament, Captain North disappeared."

"Well," Captain Brown said, "that confirms what Jim Bridger relayed earlier about white men riding with the Indians."

"Captain, one other thing," the lieutenant said. "Colonel Carrington said I'm to replace you as quartermaster."

"He did?"

"Yes, sir. He said you have orders to report to Fort Laramie."

"I can't get shed of being a quartermaster, it seems. Omaha has appointed me Chief Quartermaster, Mountain District,

Department of the Platte. Promotion with a fancy title, but I'd rather be here fighting Indians."

"What do you want me to do, sir?" Lieutenant Matson asked.

"Nothing, right now. Mr. Wakefield and I need to clean up the inventory records before I dump this mess in your lap. My orders didn't specify a reporting date. I figure I've got some time. Did the colonel happen to mention you'll also be the commissary officer?"

"No, sir."

"Well, you will. Colonel Carrington complains we're short officers—which we are. But being quartermaster should not be that important. Our priority should be to kill Indians. Maybe once the colonel's satisfied construction of the fort is far enough along, he'll lead us out to challenge the savages. For me, I don't plan to leave here until I've got Red Cloud's scalp."

I did not sleep well that night. Rain commenced pounding on my tent around midnight and never let up. I rolled out of my bedroll early, slipped a rain slicker over my head, and slogged through the muddy field over to the teamsters' mess. A dozen early risers had beaten me there. I'd barely managed to take two sips of coffee before Captain Brown stormed in.

"Come on, boys!" he shouted. "I need every one of you. The goddamned savages are making off with a cattle herd. Let's get 'em."

The colonel had issued orders that all horses were to be saddled and bridled at first light to cut down on delays in instigating pursuits. I stopped by my tent on the way to the corral and grabbed my revolver. I belted it around my waist as I ran through the rain to get a horse.

A small contingent of infantry were already mounted by the time we teamsters climbed into the saddle. Captain Brown led us out the east gate of the quartermaster yard at a trot. It was then I realized Duggan Maguire rode beside me. To my knowledge, this was the first pursuit in which he'd participated.

We raced east toward Lake DeSmet. The sun would be rising ahead of us, but the rain blurred its presence. A cold wind pushed the storm from behind our backs, trying to lift my slicker. I grabbed the bottom of the flapping gutta-percha material and jammed it between my buttocks and the saddle leather.

As we rode, word circulated that the raided cattle herd belonged to a civilian wagon train camped near the fort. The Indians had used the cover of the rain to get the herd moving before the train's night guard realized what was happening. Why was it our responsibility to recover this herd? Maybe Captain Brown thought Red Cloud was present, and he'd have a chance to collect the scalp he sought.

We rode hard for two hours. In places the mud made it slow going, but by my estimation we rode ten miles. We struggled through water rushing down what would normally be a dry gulch. We urged our horses up a slippery slope toward a ridgeline ahead. That's when we got our first view of the cattle. The animals were being herded over the top of the ridge by a dozen Indians waving blankets.

Suddenly, the scene changed. Where I'd seen mostly cattle, now I saw a long line of warriors on ponies extending well beyond our flanks on both sides. They outnumbered us three to one.

Captain Brown shouted as he raised a hand to bring us to a halt. "Back to the gulch!"

We swung around and dashed down to where water raged down the center of the usually dry bed.

"Dismount!" the captain commanded. "Form two skirmish lines! Half on each bank." He extended his arms to indicate the eastern and western banks of the creek.

We dropped out of our saddles and spread out along the two

banks. The captain moved along each line directing each of us into position. Most of the teamsters had served in the war, and we quickly assumed skirmish positions alongside the soldiers, with ten feet between us.

Captain Brown designated three of the troopers who were armed with single-shot Springfields to serve as horse holders. We couldn't allow the Indians to stampede our mounts. These men gathered up the horses' reins and held them in the creek bed between our lines.

"Shelter behind the embankments," the captain shouted, "and prepare to receive a charge."

I drew my pistol and lay forward against the wet earth. Only my head and shoulders rose above the rain-soaked bank.

A white man rode in the center of the line of warriors. He signaled the charge with the forward snap of an upraised arm. There were no fingers on the hand. I'd heard the dreaded Rebel yell during the war but it didn't compare to the shriek of the savages who now charged.

The Indian mass split, half riding in either direction around our position. Each warrior slid to his animal's offside, hooked a heel over the pony's flank, and launched arrows from beneath his mount's neck. Only a few bullets flew in our direction. The Indians possessed few firearms. On the first pass, I recognized Arapaho chief Running Bear. I tried to single him out for a shot, but he raced past too quickly.

Arrows bounced off nearby rocks or buried themselves into the muddy soil. Two of our horses were hit, neither severely injured. The rain had soaked the Indians' bowstrings, and their firing was not effective.

After they completed the first pass, the Indians regrouped on the ridgeline, then came at us again. On this second pass I saw the galvanized Yankee. At least two white men rode with this band of Arapahos.

Each time the Indians passed, our volleys dropped one or two of them. When an Indian went down with a wound, or his pony was shot from beneath him, a fellow rider scooped him up, and the two rode together to safety. When a warrior did not rise, two others reached down and hefted the dead man up between them and bore him off.

I had shot three times on each of the two passes, and now my revolver had to be reloaded. In the falling rain it would be difficult handling paper cartridges. I unbuckled my gun belt and let it fall to the ground. I squatted over the belt and held my pistol under the umbrella-like protection I created by spreading out the skirt of my rain slicker with my knees. I couldn't see what I was doing, but by feel I loaded each of the six chambers. I rammed each round down hard with the loading lever. Then I fumbled the tiny percussion caps onto their nipples. I dropped two because of wet fingers. It took me two minutes to load all six chambers—twice normal time. Fortunately, the Indians had given me that time while they reassembled on the ridge.

After they regrouped, the Indians charged a third time. On this pass, one of our men shot Captain Bob North off his pony. Two warriors swept in and retrieved him. I watched this action transpire out of the corner of one eye while I concentrated on locating the galvanized Yankee.

Most of the savages had passed before I spotted my target riding down the slope. He would pass from left to right across my front. I laid my left forearm on the embankment and steadied the barrel of the revolver on it. I doubled-cocked the piece and waited.

I led my target and slowly squeezed the trigger. Something jostled me, and my hand jerked to the side. My shot plowed into the ground in front of me. I kept myself from tumbling over by digging my left elbow into the muddy embankment.

"Sorry, Wakefield. Lost my balance."

Duggan Maguire stood above me with a hand on my shoulder. What was he doing here? Why had he moved from his position on the opposite bank?

Shortly after noon we returned to Big Piney Creek driving a hundred head of cattle before us. Captain Brown basked in the wagon master's thankful praise at having recovered his entire herd. The captain then led us into the fort.

We were greeted at the gate by Captain Ten Eyck. He reached up and shook Captain Brown's hand. "Great job, Baldy. That'll show them savages we're not to be trifled with."

We'd all passed through the gate when our group came face to face with Colonel Carrington. He stood in the middle of the road. We rain-soaked riders reined to a halt. Captain Brown exchanged salutes with the colonel.

"What did you think you were doing chasing after a civilian's cattle herd without my orders?" the colonel demanded.

"I thought our duty was to protect the immigrant trains, sir."

"Protecting the immigrants and risking the lives of my men without proper authority are two different things, Captain. See that it doesn't happen again."

"We killed five Arapahos and Captain Bob North," Captain Brown said. "We also wounded at least a dozen more of the hostiles."

"Humph," Colonel Carrington grunted. He swung around and walked away without another salute.

Captain Brown clenched his teeth so tightly his dark beard protruded up and away from his chin. "That lily-livered coward," the captain muttered. "He's afraid of a few bedraggled Indians. He'll never lead us in an attack against the savages."

CHAPTER 33

About midmorning, Thursday, September 27, while Captain Brown and I observed workers put a roof on the commissary warehouse, a sentry on the banquette signaled for the main gate to be opened. After the wooden doors swung back, an ambulance rolled into the fort. Acting Assistant Surgeon Edwin Reid sat on the front seat beside the driver.

Two soldiers on woodcutting detail had returned to the fort from the pinery at midmorning to ask for an ambulance and a physician to go to one of the blockhouses to bring in wounded Private Patrick Smith of Company H. Shortly after sunrise, a dozen Sioux swept down on the loggers and cut off three soldiers from the main workforce. Two of the soldiers sneaked through the attacking Indians and made it safely to the blockhouse. Private Smith had not been so lucky.

"Doc Reid," Captain Brown called out as the ambulance passed. "How's he doing?"

"Poorly. He's scalped, his nose and fingers are broken, and partial shafts of five arrows are still in his back. He broke off the shafts to keep them from snagging in the bushes while he crawled to the blockhouse. It's a miracle he's still alive."

The ambulance proceeded to the hospital tent, and Captain Brown and I returned to the quartermaster's office tent.

Following lunch, I sought out Katy to learn about Private Smith's condition. I went to the front entrance to the hospital tent and asked for her from the orderly on duty. She came out drying her hands on a towel. Dark-red stains stood out starkly on her white apron.

"Zach." Katy's shoulders slumped. Her usually neatly pulled-back hair had escaped its bun, and strands of golden locks scattered across her shoulders in disarray. "We're kind of busy. What do you need?"

"I'm sorry. I didn't mean to draw you away from your duties. I was anxious to find out how Private Smith's doing."

"He's not going to make it. We're trying to ensure his final moments are comfortable."

"Has he said anything?" I asked.

"Not to us. He's been unconscious since he was brought in. He apparently was coherent enough when he dragged himself into the blockhouse to describe what happened. The soldiers who requested the ambulance said an old Indian woman beat his face with an unstrung bow and snapped each finger backward to break it."

Tears glistened at the corners of Katy's eyes. She brushed the moisture aside with a finger. "He apparently knew he'd been scalped," she continued. "He told the woodcutters he couldn't see the squaw clearly through the blood running into his eyes. He claimed he pretended to be dead. I remember what I went through when I was shot, and that was with one arrow, not five. I don't see how he stood the pain without screaming."

"He must possess a strong desire to live," I said.

"That's not going to do him any good." Katy's chin dropped, and she clasped her fingers together. I gathered her cold hands into mine. She slowly raised her head, then glanced down at our joined hands. I'd never touched her for so long. Her gentle smile brought familiar dimples to her cheeks. She slowly withdrew her hands from mine.

"I heard they were Sioux," I said.

"Surgeon Horton and Doctor Reid agreed the arrowheads were bound to the shafts in a wrapping style known to be Sioux."

The whistle at the steam sawmill shrieked. A sentry on the banquette near the hospital tent shouted, "Indians attacking Pilot Hill!"

The lower slope of Pilot Hill was obscured from view by the fort's stockade. The upper stretches, including Pilot Knob, halfway to the summit, were visible over the top of the wall. Fifteen warriors urged their ponies up the trail along the ridgeline. This one route provided the only easy access to the signal station. The slopes of Pilot Hill dropped away steeply on all sides except for this approach ridge.

At the signal station, three hundred feet above the elevation of the fort, four pickets were assigned on a rotating basis. One now frantically waved a flag indicating they were under attack.

The two soldiers who'd arrived earlier that morning from the pinery came out of the hospital tent and joined Katy and me. "They're probably the Sioux who attacked us," one of the soldiers announced.

"You're right," the other soldier responded. "That's the same band that attacked us at the pinery this morning. There's a squaw trailing behind them, too. She must be the one who tortured Smith."

The cavalry corral stretched along the south wall of the main fort between the hospital tent and the quartermaster's office tent. Captain Brown came racing to the corral gate from his office. "Come on, Zach!" he shouted when he spotted me. "We're going after them."

I waved goodbye to Katy and ran to join Captain Brown in selecting a horse. With the increased readiness, I'd taken to wearing my revolver all the time. I and two dozen soldiers and teamsters climbed into saddles. Lieutenant Adair was one. It required only a few minutes for twenty of us to race through the open main gate and turn south.

I was close enough to hear Lieutenant Adair shout to Captain Brown. "The picket leader is Private Rover! Smart soldier."

The Sioux warriors had passed Pilot Knob and neared their goal at the top. On the summit, Private Rover and his men chased their horses down the ridgeline's path toward the approaching Indians. Then, Rover and his men disappeared, evidently going down the steeper southern slope of Pilot Hill, away from the attackers.

Rover's loosed horses raced through the midst of the attacking Indians, forcing them to pull their ponies aside to avoid being driven off the ridge.

Behind us a boom indicated Colonel Carrington had fired one of the howitzers. The whistling shot passed over our heads, and a second later, the spherical case shot exploded in a ball of fire and smoke over the Indians, showering them with shrapnel. None of the Sioux fell, but the Indians had developed such a fear of *the gun that shoots twice*, they turned their ponies off the trail. They struggled to stay astride their animals as the ponies slid on their haunches down the steep bank.

When the Indians reached the low ground at the base of Pilot Hill, they took off toward Lake De Smet. Captain Brown waved a hand to lead us in pursuit.

We continued our chase until almost dark. Captain Brown signaled us to pull up. It appeared he was on the verge of turning us back to the fort, when one of the men pointed and yelled that another band of Indians was joining those we were pursuing.

Captain Brown studied the situation through his binocular. He returned his field glass to its case and signaled us to resume the chase. "Forward!"

We pounded on toward the combined group of Indians. The first band suddenly separated from the newly arrived band and scattered individually in different directions, mostly heading east. The newly arrived band did not move. We slowed our pace as we came up to them. These Indians waved white papers overhead.

"Oh, my God!" Captain Brown exclaimed. "It's the Cheyenne riffraff bearing Colonel Carrington's good conduct passes."

Three elderly chiefs headed the band. Captain Brown identified them from names written on their good conduct papers. Through broken English and crude sign language, Two Moons indicated he was now the leader. Black Horse, the band's senior leader who'd visited the fort earlier, had taken ill and retired to the mountains. The other two chiefs were The Rabbit That Jumps and The Wolf That Lies Down. None of the middle-aged warriors in the band wore face paint. None of their ponies bore paint. No bows were strung. One old squaw sat astride a ragged pony that dragged a heavily loaded travois.

We escorted the band to Fort Phil Kearny. The ribs of the Cheyenne's ponies were clearly visible. The small animals trod slowly with lowered heads. Our own horses, which still hadn't had much corn to eat, were exhausted following our long chase after the Sioux raiders. We took our time on the return journey to give all the animals a breather.

The sun disappeared slowly behind the Big Horns as we approached the main gate. Captain Brown signaled for the Indians to remain outside the fort. We passed on through the gate, and Captain Brown and Lieutenant Adair swung over to the headquarters tent. The soldiers and the other teamsters headed for the corral with their horses. I stayed with Captain Brown and Lieutenant Adair. When they dismounted to talk with Colonel Carrington, I took the reins of the captain's horse.

After Captain Brown described the chase of the Sioux and the encounter with the Cheyennes, the colonel sent an orderly to find Jack Stead. The Indians respected Stead because of his

Cheyenne wife.

The "black white man" led the Indians into the fort. At the headquarters tent cordial greetings were exchanged between the parties. Stead ascertained the reason they had sought this interview with the "Little White Chief." They desired permission to hunt along the Tongue River.

"Jack," Colonel Carrington said, "tell Chief Two Moons he does not need my permission to hunt along the Tongue River. The army is not here to control who hunts where. Our job is simply to ensure safe passage for travelers heading to Montana."

After Stead translated the colonel's remarks, smiles replaced frowns on the faces of the Indians.

"Tell Chief Two Moons," the colonel continued, "they can camp tonight on the island in the center of Little Piney Creek, opposite the sawmills."

Gestures and nods from the three chiefs indicated their pleasure with this information. Two Moons informed Jack Stead they could use rations. Hunting had not been good in the Powder River country from whence they had come.

"Captain Brown," Colonel Carrington said, "issue them bacon and coffee, please."

"Yes, sir."

"Oh," the colonel continued, "and sugar. I know they like a little coffee with their sugar." He chuckled at his own joke.

Captain Brown turned and pointed at me. I knew I'd been given the assignment to issue the rations. I pulled on the reins of my horse and the captain's horse, then stopped.

"Lieutenant Adair," I asked, "would you like me to take your horse to the corral?"

"That's most kind of you, Mr. Wakefield, thanks." The lieutenant handed me his reins.

I led the three horses and signaled the old squaw to follow me. I assumed she'd be the one to accept the rations for the band. She followed with her pony and travois to the commissary warehouse. When I handed her the slab of bacon, the layer of fat sloughed off and fell into the dirt. She sneered and shook her head.

I shrugged. "It's the same meat we have to eat, squaw lady."

She picked up the fat, brushed the sand off on her dirty buckskin dress, and tucked the two parts of the bacon in between other bundles on the travois. She led her pony out the front gate.

After the Indians left the fort, I took the three horses to the corral and unsaddled them. I changed their bridles to halters and gave each a quick brush with a curry comb.

I'd just finished the effort when a soft, sweet voice spoke to me.

"What're you doing, Zach?" Katy O'Toole leaned her chin on the top rail of the corral and dazzled me with the dimples of her smile.

"Why, I have this important duty of taking these three horses down to the creek to get them a drink. Care to join me?"

"I don't mind if I do."

Katy took the halter rope of one of the horses, and we walked through the gate leading from the main fort into the quartermaster yard. I made sure the gate was closed behind me, and we headed down the gentle slope, through the quartermaster yard, to the water gate.

"How's Private Smith?" I asked.

"He died."

I couldn't think of anything appropriate to say.

Opening the water gate that gave access to the creek, I motioned for Katy to proceed first. The horses were soon quenching their thirsts, and from where Katy and I stood, we had a good view of the island opposite the sawmills.

The squaw had wasted no time getting her pony and its travois onto the island, where she was now engaged in erecting a teepee. Even though I'd seen the Laramie Loafers erect teepees and knew the job could be done in less than thirty minutes, it was fascinating to see the ease and rapidity with which she executed the job. She already had the main tripod poles standing and was in the process of positioning the interspersing, smaller poles. A few minutes before, those same poles had been part of her travois.

The Cheyenne chiefs and the braves sat around a small campfire smoking pipes and watching the squaw work.

"Humph," Katy grunted. "I suppose she'll have to cook the meal for them, next."

She'd stated the obvious. Although cooking was considered women's work in most societies, it wasn't a topic I cared to debate with Katy.

"You know," I said, "some of the soldiers with whom I was riding this afternoon believed this band was involved in the murder of Private Smith. It's about the same number of warriors that attacked Pilot Hill. They think this squaw could have been the one who tortured Private Smith."

"What?" Katy demanded. "Look at them! Three old chiefs and five middle-aged, fat men? I watched them straggle into the fort. These so-called warriors couldn't wait to squat down and smoke their pipes. And the woman? She's got her hands full serving that ragtag bunch. This band doesn't have the gumption to attack anyone."

"Well, it's just something I heard being circulated among the men."

"Somebody needs to get the men to exhibit some common sense," Katy said. "Come on, Zach. It's supper time. These horses have drunk their fill."

Katy had the timing right. From inside the main stockade, a bugler sounded Supper Call.

For some reason, I felt restless after the evening meal and not in the mood to return directly to my lonely tent. The sun had disappeared behind the mountains, and it would be a few hours before the moon rose. The fading light of dusk illuminated my stroll to the sutler's store. Lanterns visible in windows around the parade ground created flickers of bright light. At the guardhouse, dim light shone through a single window. The pending guard shift would be trying to sleep until called to take up positions around the stockade. Shadows flitting across a window in the headquarters indicated the adjutant was working late. Perhaps the commanding officer still toiled there over reports.

Chaplain David White approached the entrance to the sutler's store from the opposite direction when I reached there. "Good evening, Mr. Wakefield," he said. "Care to join me in a sarsaparilla? My treat."

"Why that's kind of you, Reverend. Thank you."

Inside the store, soldiers crowded the counter. It required several minutes for the chaplain and me to get served. We eventually settled on a bench. Judge Kinney's employees, in addition to stocking goods and waiting on customers, were engaged in erecting his building. They were making good progress. The exterior walls now stood, with only the roof still requiring the use of canvas.

The bottle of sarsaparilla was cold and damp in my fingers. Someone in the sutler's staff had disobeyed the orders about not straying from the fort. Only snow brought down from the mountains could render the beverage this cool. I took a refreshing sip and smacked my lips.

"Katy told me Private Smith died," I said.

253

"Yes," the chaplain said. "Sad case. Poor fellow suffered grievously before passing. We'll bury him in the morning."

Among the crowd, I recognized a couple of soldiers who'd ridden beside me in the afternoon's pursuit of the Sioux warriors. One, a burly corporal, kept asserting his belief the Cheyennes camped on the island were the Indians who'd murdered Private Smith.

"I say we make them pay!" the corporal shouted.

"I agree," another soldier added. "The colonel shouldn't give them safe passage any longer. They're murderers!"

"That's not true, Reverend," I said to Chaplain White. "They're not the warriors we were chasing this afternoon. They're not the killers of Private Smith."

"I know," he replied. "Best you stay out of this, though."

"We'll kill them all," another soldier added. "Especially the squaw. She's the one what tortured poor Private Smith."

"Yeah! Yeah!" The noise level increased as soldiers shouted to be heard.

I swallowed the last sip of the bittersweet liquid. "Chaplain," I said, "thanks for the sarsaparilla, but I'm going to turn in. This place is too rowdy for me."

"Don't blame you," he said. "I'll stick around to see if I can talk some sense into these men before they do something foolish. If not, I'll alert the colonel to possible trouble."

I weaved my way through the throng of soldiers, returned my empty bottle to the counter, slipped out the door, and headed for my tent.

The bugler blew taps at eight-thirty. It'd been a busy day, and I was tired. I hadn't been asleep long, however, when something bumped into the wall of my tent. I instantly awoke and grabbed my revolver from beneath my pillow.

"Careful, Paddy," a voice whispered outside my tent. "You'll wake the whole fort. You're too drunk to be out here with a loaded rifle."

"Ah, shut yer mouth, John," the slurred response said. "I'm as sober as ye are."

I heard the shuffling of multiple pairs of feet and the occasional rattle of weaponry. Several men were obviously groping their way around in the dark.

I pulled on my trousers and slipped my feet into my brogans. I retrieved my gun belt from beneath the bed, belted it around my waist, and returned the revolver to the holster.

Waiting a moment for the noise to subside, I stepped out of my tent in time to see the last of several dozen soldiers armed with rifle-muskets slip through the nearby postern gate connecting the main fort with the quartermaster yard. After they'd moved away from the tent housing area, I followed, keeping a safe distance. I didn't want one of them confronting me with a loaded weapon.

The men went out of the quartermaster yard through the west gate that led to the wagon park and the sawmills. I slipped across the yard to the water gate from where I'd have a good view.

At least a hundred soldiers assembled in a ragged formation along the north bank of Little Piney Creek. Opposite them, on the island, the old chiefs and warriors sat around their campfire smoking pipes. The Indians surely knew the soldiers were there, but they made no attempt to look in the direction from which danger threatened.

"Double time, march!" The shouted command came from near the main stockade. Two squads of guards hustled across the quartermaster yard at the double quick. "Close it up!" the sergeant of the guard ordered. "Move sharply!"

The guard unit trotted through the west gate of the quartermaster yard—the same one used earlier by the mob. The moon

Robert Lee Murphy

had risen, and from its light I made out Colonel Carrington, Captain Van Eyck, and Chaplain White following the column of guards. The chaplain had made good on his promise to alert the commanding officer.

The sergeant of the guard directed his men into a double-file formation about twenty yards from the creek. Captain Ten Eyck stepped between their ranks with a drawn pistol. "You men along the creek bank!" he shouted. "Lay down your arms and face about."

The men did not obey the captain's command. As if someone had issued a different order, they suddenly broke to the side and raced down the edge of the creek toward the water gate. I decided I'd better step aside and let them pass.

"You men, halt where you are!" Colonel Carrington shouted.

The mob continued to surge toward me in a rush to reach the gate.

Two pistol shots dominated the noise of shuffling feet. The men halted. The colonel stood with his revolver raised above his head. He'd fired into the air.

"What in the world are you men doing?" the colonel demanded, dropping his weapon to his side. "This is insubordination! It verges on mutiny. You almost committed murder because you are attacking the wrong Indians."

Colonel Carrington stalked up and down the file of men who were lining up to pass through the water gate. He shook his finger at various non-commissioned officers. "I recognize you and you. I should take your stripes—maybe even court-martial you."

He stopped pacing and shoved his revolver into its holster. "Get to your barracks, now! All of you. I'll have no more of this nonsense."

I suppose the colonel realized he couldn't arrest a hundred armed men with twenty members of the guard detail. The line of soldiers ceased being a mob at that time and trudged single file through the water gate, crossed the quartermaster yard, and disappeared into the main fort.

The raids on our herds continued unrelenting each day. When I prepared the month-end inventory report for Captain Brown, it revealed we had only one hundred left of the seven hundred cattle that had been driven from Nebraska to Fort Phil Kearny. The size of the loss was not attributable to consumption.

One good thing happened the last day of September. A wagon train from Omaha delivered corn and oats for the few starving horses and mules that remained.

CHAPTER 34

By the first day of October, the infantry barracks were almost finished. Four-inch-thick plank roofs were topped with empty corn sacks on which was piled six inches of turf. Both the commissary and the quartermaster warehouses neared completion. The commanding officer's quarters would soon be ready for occupancy. It was considerably larger than the half-dozen two-room cabins being erected for other officers. The only officer who would have to continue occupying a tent a while longer was Lieutenant Grummond. Construction of his cabin had only begun.

Duggan Maguire's team was making quick work on the ammunition magazine. The central pit, four feet deep, was lined with timbers. A sloping wooden roof would be erected above this cellar. Any explosion should be well contained. Colonel Carrington stopped by the site several times a day to check on progress.

The temporary corral for the horses had been supplanted with stables made in the jacal style, using a wattle and daub method. The structure consisted of closely set poles lashed together and chinked with a mixture of mud and grass. This adobe-like structure was roofed with dirt-covered poles. Similar stables were under construction in the quartermaster yard for the mules.

During the first week of October, three contract wagon trains arrived with corn and oats for our animals. Our inventory of

258

their cargo revealed shortages. Colonel Carrington appointed Lieutenants Bisbee and Wands to a board of survey. After three days of investigation, they ruled the losses were due to spillage from poor quality sacks. All three freighters were exonerated of responsibility, and I proceeded to make the appropriate entries in the inventory records.

On Saturday, October 6, two privates of Company A, John Wasser and Christian Oberly, were killed at the pinery by Indians. They had been part of a small force assigned to protect the wood cutters. The remaining soldiers confronted what they claimed to be a hundred Sioux and Arapaho warriors. The observers on Pilot Hill signaled an alert to the fort, and Colonel Carrington took a thirty-man detachment and a howitzer to confront the attackers. The colonel's artillery shelling of the woods and hillsides drove the Indians away. In addition to a squad of infantry regularly stationed at each of the two pinery blockhouses, the colonel now left the howitzer and a trained three-man gun crew at one of them.

Later that same day, the sentinels on Pilot Hill alerted the stockade to the approach of a procession coming up the Bozeman Trail from the south. The dust cloud rose higher and broader in the sky than one produced by a wagon train.

Colonel Carrington ordered Captains Ten Eyck and Brown to ride out to intercept the party. I rode with them.

The cattle herd Carrington's Overland Circus had driven north from Fort Reno three months ago had impressed me, but it didn't compare to what moved toward us now. I'd heard Texas longhorns described, but I'd never seen one. Here came hundreds of them. Their massive horns forced them to spread apart farther than the short horns of our cattle.

We approached the huge herd three miles from the fort. The leading rider held up a hand, and mounted men surrounding the cattle brought the moving mass to a halt.

Captain Ten Eyck used both hands to press his reins against the pommel of the McClellan saddle as he steadied himself. His wandering left eye drifted closed with each nod of his head. The drooping right eye had not opened since we rode out of the fort. Was his hangover left over from last night, or had he been drinking this morning?

"I'll handle this, Tenodor," Captain Brown said.

"Right," Captain Ten Eyck responded.

The two captains rode up to the leader, and I stayed abreast of them. "Good afternoon, sir," Captain Brown said. "I'll have to ask you to halt here until the commanding officer provides you clearance to proceed farther."

The man before us appeared to be a few years older than I. From how he sat in his saddle, he was probably close to my height and weight. Revolvers filled open holsters on both hips.

"Good afternoon, Captain," the man replied. "The name's Story, Nelson Story."

"I'm Captain Brown, quartermaster at Fort Phil Kearny, and this is Captain Ten Eyck, garrison commander."

"I was told Colonel Carrington was commanding officer," Story said.

"Colonel Henry Carrington is the commanding officer of the Mountain District and the Eighteenth Infantry," Captain Brown replied.

Story glanced at me.

"This is my clerk," Captain Brown said, "Zach Wakefield."

Story and I exchanged nods.

"Regulations require each party moving north into Montana to contain forty armed men," Captain Brown said. "I don't count forty men."

"Now, Captain . . . at Fort Laramie's sutler's store I bought each of my twenty-seven men a Remington breech-loading, rolling-block, single-shot rifle. When we encountered a band of

Sioux a few miles south of Fort Reno, we drove them off hand-
ily, even though I did lose two men. Still, with my remaining
twenty-five men armed with Remingtons, I reckon I've got more
firepower than any forty of your soldiers armed with Springfields."

"Regulations don't say anything about what kind of weapon
you're carrying. Has to be forty armed men."

"And if I don't care to comply with your *regulations*?"

"Then Colonel Carrington will be obliged to send out a
company of infantry to hold you in place."

"Well, I don't want to cause the colonel any bother. Why
don't I discuss the matter personally with him?"

"Fine."

"I'll move the herd down a little closer to the fort. If the
army is supposed to provide protection to travelers on the
Montana Road, it would be easier for you to do that if we
weren't so far away."

"Sorry, Mr. Story. This is as far as you can come. There's
inadequate grass for more animals close in. The area for three
miles on all sides of Fort Phil Kearny is reserved for the army's
herds."

"I see. Then, I'll have my men move the longhorns off the
road and set up camp here . . . for the time being."

"Why don't you sell me some of those cows?" Captain Brown
said. "I'll be glad to take them off your hands. The army will
pay top dollar."

"I know what the best army price is. The quartermaster at
Fort Laramie tried to buy from me, too. In Montana, I can get
five times what the government pays. And the miners will pay in
gold, not with a requisition I have to submit someplace far off
for eventual payment in greenbacks."

"Suit yourself," Captain Brown said.

"Captain," Story said. "I would like to ask one favor."

"What's that?"

"I have a sick man in my group. I would like him to see a doctor."

"Certainly. Mr. Wakefield will guide him to our hospital to see Surgeon Horton."

"If it's all right," Story said, "I'll ride along and talk with Colonel Carrington now."

"Fine," Captain Brown said.

A short time later, the captains, the sick man, Nelson Story, and I entered the fort. Captain Brown pointed out the headquarters building to Story and excused himself, saying he had to report to the commanding officer.

"Tell the colonel," Story said, "after I get my sick man tended to, I'll stop by to visit."

Captains Brown and Ten Eyck turned their horses away.

At the hospital, Surgeon Horton took the sick drover into an examination area. Story and I remained at the tent's entrance. Work had just begun on a permanent structure for the hospital, so the large tent still served that purpose.

Katy O'Toole joined us, and I introduced her.

"Mr. Story," she asked, "would you like a cup of coffee?"

"That would be nice, ma'am. Just black, no sugar."

Katy poured three cups of coffee. In response to my quizzical look, she stuck her nose in the air. "I drink coffee in the hospital because the men prefer it. I drink tea with the ladies."

The three of us sat on camp stools in the kitchen area.

"You're driving those cattle to Montana?" Katy asked Story.

"Yes, ma'am."

"How far have you come?"

"Well, I bought a thousand head in Fort Worth, Texas, several weeks ago. I've lost quite a few on the trail. Some got sick and died. Kansas Jayhawkers stole some. Indians took some. I've got maybe seven hundred head left. I expect to get a good return on my investment when I get them to Virginia City."

"Virginia City," Katy said. "Have you been there?"

"That's where I started."

"You wouldn't happen to know Mr. Brandon Hollister, would you?"

"No, ma'am. Can't say that I do."

"He's my fiancé. He went to Montana over a year ago to prospect for gold."

"Lots of folks did that, ma'am. Most haven't found any. I was lucky and hit a good vein. I used the proceeds to invest in this herd. Beef's in short supply in Montana. Folks up there will pay plenty to get beef, even if it is stringy longhorn."

Surgeon Horton released the sick cowboy back into Story's care, and they left to go to headquarters to seek out Colonel Carrington.

"What are you thinking, Katy?" I asked, after Story had departed.

"I might go to Montana with Mr. Story."

CHAPTER 35

Late the next afternoon, October 7, I departed the new headquarters building after delivering Captain Brown's daily report to the adjutant. I was returning to my office desk in the now completed quartermaster warehouse when I crossed paths with Katy O'Toole and Duggan Maguire. They were headed for the main gate.

"Good evening, Zach," Katy said. "Come, go with us to Wheatleys' for supper. Word is Mrs. Wheatley has prepared an Irish stew. I haven't had a good Irish stew since I left home. Liz Wheatley's reported to be an excellent cook."

Maguire glanced at Katy, then glared at me, daring me to accept the invitation.

I had not partaken of any of Liz Wheatley's meals, but several teamsters did so regularly and praised the excellent cuisine. I only had a couple dollars left, and Mrs. Wheatley charged twenty-five cents for her meals. Payday should take place the end of the month. We'd received notice to expect Major Bonnet then. I couldn't think of anything I'd have to pay cash for, other than sarsaparilla. My meals at the teamsters' mess were on credit. I'd settle that bill come payday.

I returned Maguire's glare. "Sure," I said. "I'm finished with work for the day, and Irish stew sounds better than another round of bacon and hardtack." I wasn't about to let Duggan Maguire think he had a monopoly on Katy's attention. After all, she considered me to be her *brother*. So, I'd do my *brotherly* duty and make sure Maguire kept his hands to himself.

Maybe I'd see Portugee Phillips tonight. I hadn't seen him lately. He'd switched jobs and taken employment with a hay contractor who maintained an independent camp for his workers down by Big Piney Creek. Since he no longer ate in the teamsters' mess, he might be taking his meals at Wheatleys'.

Colonel Carrington had granted James Wheatley permission to erect a building outside the fort. There, the Wheatleys operated a civilian mess hall halfway between the main gate and Big Piney Creek. Several muleskinners and contractor employees ate there. Young Mrs. Wheatley must work herself ragged preparing three meals a day for all those customers.

Katy, Duggan, and I entered the spacious room, where James Wheatley greeted us. Duggan and I hung our hats on pegs beside the front door. Katy pushed her bonnet off and let it hang down her back. Wheatley escorted us to one of a dozen tables that each accommodated a half-dozen diners. Two men sat on one side of the table engrossed in consuming their meal.

"Sit here," Wheatley said. "These two gents are part of Nelson Story's crew. You folks introduce yourselves, and I'll tell Liz to hustle up your meals."

I pulled the bench away from our side of the table so Katy could slide into place between Duggan and me. We scooted the bench forward and exchanged greetings with Story's two heavily bearded cowboys. Both men offered their names and stared at Katy, who had her blonde hair drawn into a neat bun. She offered them a dimpled smile.

Katy, Duggan, and I each placed a twenty-five-cent shinplaster in front of us. The smell of stale sweat and cow manure emanating from our table companions' clothing didn't eliminate the enticing aroma wafting from their stew.

Across the room, I spotted Portugee at another table. I raised a hand in greeting. He acknowledged me with a nod, gathered up his bowl, and came to join us. The cowboys obligingly slid to one side to make room for him on their bench.

"Miss O'Toole," Portugee said. "How is Mrs. Grummond faring?"

"She's well enough," Katy answered. "Why do you ask?"

"Just concerned about how she is getting along in a tent in her condition."

"The construction of the Grummonds' quarters is being expedited," Katy said. "They will soon be able to move in. I imagine the chill in that tent can be unbearable."

Through a curtained doorway, Liz Wheatley came out carrying a tray loaded with three bowls of stew and a platter of warm bread. She set a bowl and spoon in front of each of us and replaced the drovers' empty bread platter with the fresh one. She scooped up our paper money and slipped it into an apron pocket. A crock of butter already occupied a place of honor in the center of the table. We seldom saw butter in the teamsters' mess. The aroma from our tablemates' stew had set my saliva to working. Now that a bowl of savory goodness appeared before me, it seemed to take forever to get my spoon to my mouth.

"Oh, my," I said, my mouth full of hot beef, desiccated vegetables, and wild onions. "This is good." It was amazing what Liz Wheatley had concocted without fresh potatoes or carrots.

The occupants of the fort made do with the government's desiccated vegetables. The canned mixture contained dried potatoes, cabbage, turnips, carrots, parsnips, beets, tomatoes, onions, peas, beans, lentils, and celery. The can was about the size of a house brick, weighed about as much, and probably could have been used as such. Once water was added to the can's contents, they swelled multiple times. Mrs. Grummond, well known as an inexperienced cook, had to hurry to fill multiple pots during her first encounter with the expanding concoction.

Throughout the room, the clicking of spoons against bowls accentuated the humming of contentment. Those eating at our table remained absorbed in savoring their food. Conversation waited.

After we'd finished eating, Liz Wheatley rapidly cleared the table. A couple of minutes later she returned with a pot of coffee, a sugar bowl, a small pitcher of milk, and six cups.

"Help yourself, folks," she said. "Now, for a nickel extra, I'll serve you a slice of peach pie. Sorry it's not included in the regular menu, but I have to buy the canned peaches from the sutler, and the old skinflint doesn't give them away."

Liz's gentle giggle at her own joke about Judge Kinney brought smiles to us four residents of Fort Phil Kearny. The two cowboys looked at each other in bewilderment. Duggan Maguire explained Liz's reference to the curmudgeonly sutler.

Duggan laid nickel shinplasters beside his and Katy's coffee cups.

Story's two drovers laid out five-cent Shield Nickels. I imagine they'd paid for their meals with metal quarters, too. Mrs. Wheatley would have been greatly pleased to get them.

I was sorely tempted to try the pie, but decided I'd rather save my remaining money for sarsaparillas. Portugee evidently made a similar decision because no money appeared before him.

While we concluded the meal with our coffee, and with dessert for those who'd paid extra, the cowboys relaxed and told us about the cook who accompanied their herd. They said they enjoyed steak every evening on the trail, but it didn't compare to Mrs. Wheatley's cooking.

"When do you think you'll go on to Montana?" Duggan asked.

"Don't rightly know," the cowboy who'd introduced himself

as Landers answered. "We've been hoping a wagon train would come along and bring us up to the forty men your colonel demands."

"Mr. Story ain't happy about laying around here," Rupert, the other cowboy, offered. "He's a pusher and a doer. That man's got more energy than anybody I ever seen afore."

The cowboys' Remington rifles leaned against the bench beside them.

"Is that rifle as good as Mr. Story claims?" I asked. "I was with Captain Brown yesterday when Mr. Story said twenty-five herders armed with Remingtons had more firepower than any forty infantrymen armed with Springfields."

"I'd say we have more firepower than a whole company of infantry armed with Springfields," Landers said. "I fought in the war. I know how long it takes to load and fire a rifle-musket. With the Remington, I can get off thirteen shots per minute. The fastest I ever fired a Springfield was three shots a minute."

"Mr. Story hasn't stopped complaining about this forty-man regulation," Rupert said. "He thinks your colonel's rule is plain arbitrary. Mr. Story's not much for foolish thinking. I expect we'll be moving on shortly."

Katy had been quiet during the meal, and I'd observed the two disheveled cowboys giving her the once over. With the last cowboy's comment, she spoke up. "I've been thinking about asking Mr. Story to accompany you to Montana."

"You and your husband?" Rupert asked. He inclined his head toward Duggan.

"He's not my husband," Katy replied.

Rupert shifted his gaze to me. "*He* is?"

"No," she said. "I'm not married,"

The two roughly dressed characters looked at one another, and broad smiles brightened their leathery faces. I was tempted to punch both of them in the nose.

"Well, ma'am," Landers said. "I can't speak for Mr. Story. But if it were me making the decision, I'd be mighty proud to have a pretty, young filly like you riding with us."

We finished our coffee and dessert, bade one another a good evening, and departed Wheatleys' mess hall.

The following morning, October 8, a small wagon train arrived along with the mail courier and his escort from Fort Laramie.

"Wakefield," Captain Brown said, "that wagon train's medical resupply. How about going over and helping Surgeon Horton inventory and store the items?"

"Yes, sir." I grabbed my hat and left.

A half-dozen wagons were drawn up in front of the hospital tent. Teamsters were unhitching their mules prior to taking them to the quartermaster yard for water and feed.

Doctor Horton stood at the lead wagon talking with a mounted civilian, who most likely was the wagon master. The civilian handed the doctor a memorandum book, waved, and swung his horse away.

"I'm sure glad to see you, Mr. Wakefield," the doctor said. "We desperately need these supplies, but I'm at a loss as to how to sort them out."

"That memorandum book probably contains the manifest, sir," I said. "May I see it?"

"Here." Doctor Horton shoved the book into my hands as if it were on fire. "I can face dying soldiers with bloody wounds easier than I can the paperwork associated with keeping track of inventory."

"I'll take care of identifying the items and supervising the unloading. A couple of your hospital stewards to tote and carry would be helpful."

"I'll send them right out. I'll ask Miss O'Toole to lend a hand, too. She'll know where to tell the stewards to place the items in the hospital better than anyone else."

"Fine, sir. We should be able to finish this by lunch time."

Katy came out a moment later, along with two hospital stewards. Together we commenced to unload and store the medical supplies that had been needed at Fort Phil Kearny for a long time.

The inventory consisted of liniments, tonics, wound dressings, cough syrups, castor oil, Epsom salts, expectorants, emetics, and antiseptics. In one of the wagons, I picked up a box labeled *carminatives.*

"What's a carminative?" I asked one of the hospital stewards.

"Combats flatulence," he answered. "Cuts down on farts."

"Maybe I ought to take a bottle of this stuff and give it to my tent mates."

Katy had evidently heard our exchange, because her checks were red, and she was biting her lower lip.

"Never mind," I said. I moved over to another wagon.

The manifest for this wagon listed two hundred fifty-eight bottles of porter for use as a tonic for invalids. I could only find fifty-two bottles. Colonel Carrington would have to appoint another board of survey. If I'd found two hundred six broken bottles, I could provide an answer for the shortage. I didn't find any glass shards.

In addition to the medicines, we identified hundreds of bandages and adhesive plasters. We unloaded seventy-two hair mattresses and one hundred hair pillows. We unpacked seventy-three dressing gowns and twenty-seven chamber pots. One box contained sixty-six meteorological report forms. Surgeon Horton now had the required forms for recording the daily weather statistics.

"Katy?" I called from the interior of the last wagon.

She appeared at the rear. "Yes, Zach."

"What shall we do with this box?" I asked.

"What is it?"

"Ridgway Glover's photographic chemicals."

We completed the job of offloading the medical supplies shortly before noon. I turned the memorandum book containing the inventory over to Doctor Horton and stopped by the teamsters' mess for a quick meal before returning to the quartermaster warehouse.

When I entered the new building and headed for my desk, I heard a heated conversation coming from the corner office that had been installed for Captain Brown. My stand-up desk had been placed just outside the entrance to the captain's office so he could easily call for me. I slipped onto my tall stool and made as little noise as possible.

I recognized Colonel Carrington's voice. "Captain, this order from General Cooke directs that, because we now have cavalry horses, I'm to return ninety-four of our original horses to Fort Laramie. We haven't received any cavalry, and your report yesterday stated only forty of our horses are considered serviceable. Doesn't General Cooke pay any attention to my requests for cavalry or replacement horses? I've been asking where our cavalry is for weeks. But there's been no response from Omaha. How can we send horses we don't have to Fort Laramie?"

"I don't know, sir," Captain Brown answered.

"Somehow, I have to write an explanation to General Cooke. If you have any suggestions, I'd appreciate hearing them."

"Yes, sir. I'll think on it."

"The mail also contains an order from General Cooke abolishing the Mountain District effective the thirteenth of the month."

"Well, that does eliminate some of the paperwork, Colonel," the captain said.

"True . . . true." I heard a distinct sigh from Colonel

Carrington. "One other thing that arrived in the mail is a letter from the adjutant general in Washington City complaining that our post returns for June have not been received."

"What's the matter with those people, Colonel?" Captain Brown asked. "We didn't arrive here until July."

"Frustrating, Captain, frustrating. I have to get back to my office now and compose a response to General Cooke's order to return horses that don't exist."

I dipped a pen into an open ink bottle and pretended to make entries in an open ledger book. The colonel walked out of the warehouse without looking at me.

My job had just gotten easier. In less than a week, I'd no longer have to maintain separate records for the Mountain District.

No sooner had Colonel Carrington left, than Captain Ten Eyck came in. He staggered slightly, bumping against the door jamb, as he entered Captain Brown's office. The aroma of alcohol lingered in the air after he passed. He pushed the door closed, but in his inebriated condition, he didn't get it completely shut. I could easily hear their conversation.

"What's the matter, Tenodor?" my boss asked.

"Carrington took command of the fort away from me, Baldy." Ten Eyck slurred his words.

"Well, what'd you expect. You've been hitting the bottle harder than ever."

"Can't help it, Fred. Can't stand this place."

"Tenodor," Captain Brown said, "you have it better than most of us. You've got Black Susan to cook and clean for you. She takes better care of you than your wife probably would back home. And, a lot of folks think she takes care of your other needs, too."

"Oh, stop it, Fred," Ten Eyck said. "You know very well there's no intimacy between Susan Fitsgerald and me. She takes care of my quarters and my meals, but she's fully occupied being the laundress for Company H. She annoys me with her constant complaining that Colonel Carrington has forbidden her to bake pies for the men."

The captain referred to a long-standing arrangement where Black Susan had drawn ingredients from the commissary supplies, then used Captain Ten Eyck's kitchen facility to bake pies she sold to the soldiers for fifty cents each. Liz Wheatley would be jealous if she realized she was undercharging for her pie.

"She may complain," Captain Brown said, "but she at least made money out of the affair. When the colonel shut her down, he issued me a severe reprimand for allowing her access to the ingredients in the first place. I still don't understand what difference it makes if she or the soldiers draw the ingredients for pies. The soldiers eventually eat them. In effect, they just hired her to cook them."

"Wish I had the gumption to do what Adair's doing," Captain Ten Eyck said.

"What's this wonderful thing Lieutenant Adair's doing?" Brown asked.

"Resigning."

"What? Resigning? Why?"

"Claims he has to go home to care for an invalid mother."

"Well," Captain Brown said, "you've got a wife and five children to take care of back home in Wisconsin. Use that as your excuse to get out of here."

"That'd be dishonest."

"What is dishonest is you getting soused every night and most mornings."

"I can't leave," Captain Ten Eyck said. "I'm still in command of the Second Battalion, plus I'm to reassume command of Company H from Lieutenant Wands."

"What's Wands going to do?"

"He's to be post adjutant for Carrington."

"Who's going to replace Adair?" Captain Brown asked.

"Lieutenant Bisbee becomes regimental adjutant."

"Bisbee's going to love that assignment." Brown said. "He's more vocal than I am about wanting to get out there and lick the tar out of the damned savages."

"Well," Ten Eyck said, "I feel insulted that I've been relieved of garrison command."

"Look at it this way, Tenodor. You've been relieved of some onerous tasks you really didn't like anyway. Now, if you'll excuse me, I have work to do. The colonel hasn't shifted any tasks off my back."

At the end of the day, I wandered over to the hospital. I wanted to see how Katy had done storing the new medicines and supplies. I found her sitting alone at a table in the kitchen alcove. She stared at a letter that lay before her on the table.

"Why so glum?" I asked, sitting opposite her.

"I received this letter today from my folks." She picked up an envelope and handed it to me. "It's a month and a half old. It's got postmarks from Salt Lake City."

"Is this the first you've heard from your parents?" I asked.

"Yes. I wondered why they hadn't written. I sent them a letter telling them about Megan's and her family's deaths at the same time I wrote to Brandon in Montana to tell him."

"Do they want you to come home?"

"Aye."

"Have you written to tell them about what your fiancé's doing in Montana?"

"No."

"What are you going to do?" I asked.

"I'm thinking seriously about going to Montana with Mr. Story. I came out here to teach school to the miners' children.

Maybe I should just do that."

"Or are you more interested in confronting this Brandon Hollister about how he's apparently treated you?"

"That's none of your business." She clenched her fists and glared at me.

"Probably not. But someone has to get you to think through your decision and realize why you are making it."

"Go away, Zach. I have to think." She got up and went back through the hospital ward.

On Thursday, October 18, although the interior was not yet completed, the Carringtons moved into their new quarters. The substantial frame house of board and batten siding boasted a wood-shingle roof and two brick fireplaces. Mrs. Carrington celebrated by hosting a dance that evening for the other officers, their wives, and a few invited guests.

I didn't receive an invitation, but Katy did. She invited Duggan Maguire to be her escort. Duggan had finished the construction of the ammunition magazine on the tenth, and Colonel Carrington was duly impressed. A construction supervisor would be welcome at the soirée, but not a lowly quartermaster clerk.

As it turned out, Captain Brown arranged for me to witness the party by assigning me the task of keeping George provided with food from the commissary warehouse. I slipped into the rear door of the new quarters to coordinate requirements with the Carringtons' servant.

Select members of the regimental band provided a private orchestra. Their music could be heard everywhere inside the fort that evening. Soldiers and teamsters lingered in the street to get a glimpse through the double-sashed windows. Lanterns and candles illuminated the house's interior.

From the doorway between the kitchen and the living room,

I saw Katy had a different partner for almost every dance. At least, Duggan Maguire couldn't monopolize her attention.

During one of my eavesdropping opportunities, I overheard Katy tell Mrs. Carrington she had talked with Nelson Story about going with him when he went on to Montana.

On the morning of October 22, a Monday, Colonel Carrington stormed into the quartermaster warehouse.

"Where's Captain Brown?" the colonel shouted at me after finding the office vacant.

"Back in the warehouse, sir." I pointed behind me.

"Get him out here."

"Yes, sir." I hurried off.

A minute later, Captain Brown reported to the commanding officer. He closed the office door, but that did not preclude me hearing the loud conversation.

"Well, he's done it!" Colonel Carrington shouted.

"Who's done what, sir?" Captain Brown asked.

"Nelson Story stole away last night with his herd in direct contravention of my orders."

"What are you going to do about it, sir?"

"I've dispatched fifteen men and a sergeant to catch up to him and escort him to Fort C. F. Smith. I insist on obedience to my forty-man requirement before undertaking travel on the Montana Road. I've issued a regulation to preclude anyone else emulating what Story has done."

"What regulation, sir?"

"First, no one will be permitted to enter or leave the gates of this fort after retreat, except authorized members of your quartermaster department and the sutler's staff. Second, all gates and wickets will be locked at retreat, except for your quartermaster gates, which will be closed at tattoo. Third, all soldiers absent from quarters after tattoo will be arrested. And, fourth, all civilian travelers will be required to reside within the walls of this fort until they receive proper authorization to proceed north."

Footsteps stomped across the wooden office floor, the door flew open with a bang, and Colonel Carrington stalked out.

I walked over and looked through the open doorway into the office.

"Did you hear that?" Captain Brown asked.

"Yes, sir."

"I can't imagine what some people are going to think when they hear these new restrictions limiting their travel."

I couldn't imagine what Miss Kathleen O'Toole was going to think when she learned Nelson Story had left without her. I didn't want to be the one who told her.

CHAPTER 36

On a chilly October 27 morning, Katy O'Toole came into the warehouse.

"What a surprise," I said. "Are you on a business visit or a pleasure trip?" I gave her my best smile.

She returned my smile with that beguiling dimpled one that always set my heart thumping.

"Good morning, Zach. Officially, I came to get office supplies, but I also wanted to get out of the hospital for a while."

She handed me a requisition for stationery items that bore Surgeon Horton's signature.

I looked down the list. "Yes, we have these. I'll get them for you."

"May I go with you?"

"Certainly. Let's walk through the shelves while I gather up the items."

A short time later, we returned to the front of the warehouse. She reached out to take the stack of paper and envelopes, but I shook my head.

"This paper stuff is heavy, Katy. I'll carry it to the hospital for you."

"Thank you."

I slipped into my jacket and plopped on my slouch hat. We walked in silence until we were halfway to the hospital.

"I can't sleep lately, Zach," she finally said. "At times I curse Nelson Story for leaving me behind, and at other times I thank my lucky stars I didn't have to go to Montana."

"*Have* to go?" I asked.

"I feel an obligation to my family and myself to confront Brandon and ask him what he was thinking when he asked me to marry him. Did he know he didn't plan to go through with our wedding? Did he think I'd willingly share him with a squaw after we married? I have so many questions."

"I don't know how to advise you, Katy. I will say I'm glad you're still here. You make my days brighter."

"Shortly after midnight last night," Katy went on, "being unable to sleep, I took a walk around the outside of the hospital. When I passed between the tent and the stockade wall, I came face to face with Colonel Carrington."

"The colonel was out that late?"

"Yes. He said he makes the rounds of all the sentry posts and gates every night."

"That hardly seems necessary," I said. "The Indians raid the herds every day, but they've never attacked the fort. They seldom raid the herds at night, either."

"What about that sentry the warrior shot through the heart with an arrow?"

"That was one Indian dressed in a wolf skin who sneaked up to the stockade undetected. The sentry probably thought it was another wolf prowling around."

"Well," Katy said, "the colonel seems to be concerned."

"I know he's frustrated because his cavalry hasn't arrived. Sometimes I overhear his problems when he comes to the warehouse to discuss them with Captain Brown."

"I hear similar complaints about the lack of cavalry when I visit Fannie Grummond. Her husband is particularly vocal about the colonel not going after the Indians. Yesterday, the lieutenant said things will change after Captain Fetterman arrives. Colonel Carrington has apparently notified the captain to come forward from Fort Sedgwick."

"There'll be a lot of soldiers happy about that," I said.

We paused at the entrance to the hospital, and Katy summoned one of the stewards to come take the stationery supplies.

"I need to get back now." I turned to leave, but her hand tugged on my forearm.

"Wait, Zach," she said. "There's something else I want to talk to you about."

"Yes?"

"Duggan Maguire told me that after payday he plans to leave and go north. He's offered to take me with him."

"No! Absolutely not!"

"I thought that would be your response."

"What did you expect a *brother* to say? I don't trust that damned Reb as far as I can throw him. Going with Maguire alone would be worse than if you'd gone with Nelson Story's gang."

"Well, I *am* going to think about it." She spun on her heels and flounced into the hospital.

I stalked down the road toward the quartermaster warehouse with gritted teeth and clenched fists.

"Open the gate!" The shouted alert came from the main gate a few yards straight ahead of me. Hoofbeats and jangling bridle chains revealed riders approaching.

General Hazen was returning from his inspection tour. Following him rode Lieutenant Bradley and his detachment. There had been twenty-six mounted infantrymen when they departed two months ago. I counted twenty-three in the arriving column.

Colonel Carrington stood at the road intersection a couple of yards ahead of me. He had evidently been forewarned of the arrival, probably by a sentry stationed on the newly completed observation platform atop the headquarters building.

"Welcome back, General Hazen," Colonel Carrington said.

"I see you're short a few men."

"Three deserted in Montana . . . probably for the goldfields. The only man we lost to the Indians was Jim Brannan. He was scouting out ahead of our column one day and got ambushed. We buried him where we found him."

"That's too bad," Carrington said. "Brannan was a good guide."

"Word reached you earlier from Jim Bridger as I recall," Hazen said, "but I promised him I'd tell you again."

"If you mean about several hundred Sioux lodges pitched along the Tongue, yes."

"I question that bit of intelligence," Hazen said. "During my time on the frontier, I never encountered that many Indians in one place. It's not in their nature to assemble like that."

"Well," Carrington said, "there must be a lot of them someplace, because they raid us every day."

General Hazen pointed to the southwest quadrant of the parade ground. "I see you've finished your magazine."

"Yes, sir. We received sixty thousand rounds of ammunition after you departed. Now, all I need is a hundred thousand more. Then, I'll rest more comfortably."

"Looks like you've made good progress on completing the fort's buildings." General Hazen surveyed the interior of the stockade. "Good work."

"Thank you, General. But forgive me. You've been in the saddle a long time. Please step down and come in for some coffee. I'll send over to see if Margaret has some sweets available."

General Hazen dismounted. Even though I wasn't a member of the army, he handed the reins of his horse to me. He followed Colonel Carrington into the headquarters building.

Lieutenant Bradley laughed. "Ever think you'd be mistaken for a hitching post?"

I shrugged and grinned.

"Is there room in the stable for our horses, Mr. Wakefield?" The lieutenant remembered my name.

"Room for yours and a lot more, Lieutenant. I'm sure Colonel Carrington's glad to have you fellows back."

"We're glad to be back." He held up a hand and shouted, "Dismount!"

The groaning of tired soldiers and the snorting of horses mingled with the squeaking of leather as the men executed the command.

Lieutenant Bradley handed the reins of his horse to a private and took the reins of General Hazen's horse away from me and handed them to the private, also.

"Any word on payday?" the lieutenant asked.

"Yes, the paymaster is coming. To celebrate payday and the completion of most of the construction, the thirty-first has been declared a holiday. Dress parade in the morning and dances in the evening. Captain Brown is issuing new uniforms to the men."

"That's good. The rags my men are wearing are about to fall off their backs."

"Oh," I said. "I heard something else that might interest you, Lieutenant. Do you know Captain Fetterman?"

"Not personally, but the men talk about him all the time. He has a great reputation as a battle-tested fighting man."

"He's been called forward by Colonel Carrington."

"Aha. The relationship between the colonel and the brevet lieutenant colonel will be an interesting one to follow."

Chapter 37

On the morning of the last day of October 1866, Katy and I stood on the southeast artillery bastion and watched the regimental band lead the four infantry companies out the front gate. They formed up for inspection and review on the grassy plain between the stockade wall and Big Piney Creek. This early autumn morning proved unusually balmy with a clear, azure-blue sky overhead—perfect conditions for parading. To the west, the turning leaves of the aspen speckled the slopes of the Big Horns with gold.

Katy and I had arrived early to this viewing platform, and for a while it appeared we would enjoy it in private. The approaching chatter of ladies' voices quickly dispelled that idea.

Mrs. Carrington, Mrs. Horton, Mrs. Grummond, Mrs. Wands, and Mrs. Bisbee joined us. Mrs. Wands had four-year-old Bobby in tow. Mrs. Bisbee carried two-year-old Gene. The addition of these new arrivals filled the ten-by-ten-foot space to capacity. Had there been a howitzer positioned on the bastion, there would not have been room for so many. All three of the howitzers had been placed on the parade ground in preparation for the upcoming ceremonies. Katy and I moved to the rear to let the officers' wives press against the log retaining wall for a better view.

"You boys be careful!" Mrs. Carrington shouted down to her sons as they passed out the front gate and down the road to the battalion's formation. Harry perched on Calico with James trotting alongside. Mrs. Horton's pet antelope, Star, accompanied the boys.

Mrs. Carrington looked at us. "I'm sorry we took your spots," she said.

"We're fine," I responded.

Since the day was pleasantly warm, Katy threw back the ends of the shawl she wore. When she did, she revealed the gold shamrock suspended around her neck on a thin gold chain.

"Oh, Katy," Mrs. Grummond said. "What a lovely necklace."

"Thank you, Fannie," Katy replied. "Mr. Maguire gave it to me last night."

Why had Duggan Maguire given Katy the shamrock I'd seen him fondle so many times?

"What occasioned that?" Mrs. Wands asked.

"He gave it to me as a birthday present."

Oh, no. I'd forgotten Katy's birthday.

"Happy birthday!" All the ladies chirped the greeting together.

Fannie Grummond lifted the pendant, turning it over. "There are initials on the reverse, Katy. *AB* on one leaf and *LK* on the opposite one. I wonder who they were. Lovers maybe . . . husband and wife?"

"I don't know. Mr. Maguire said he didn't know either. He said he acquired the shamrock during the war, but he didn't elaborate."

Stolen plunder from some Confederate raid was my surmise.

"Well," Fannie said, "a jeweler can buff those initials out and re-engrave it however you want."

Conversation came to an abrupt halt as the band burst forth with martial music. One shouted command after another reached our ears from the plain below, and the units stepped off to pass in review. The brilliant sunlight reflected off the shoulder scales and bayonets of the three hundred sixty men of the

Eighteenth Infantry. That count was accurate, because I'd issued new uniforms to each of them yesterday.

Their old uniforms had already shown considerable wear
when we'd first arrived on this plateau fifteen weeks ago. In the
interim, the constant logging, hauling, and building, not to
mention chasing Indians, had virtually destroyed those
uniforms. The fresh uniforms seemed to raise the soldiers' spirits
a notch or two. The men stepped smartly through their maneu-
vers.

"No, Bobby," Mrs. Wands said. "Where did you get all that
candy?" She fished a handful of hard candy out of his pants'
pockets.

"You can blame Judge Kinney," Mrs. Carrington said. "I
relieved my boys of pockets full of sweets awhile ago."

Bobby whined, and Mrs. Wands glanced in my direction.
"Well, here," she said. "One more now, but we'll save the rest
for later." Perhaps she gave in to his protest because she thought
the youngster was disturbing Katy and me.

The troops completed the gyrations of the review and
marched back into the fort. The units halted in front of their
respective barracks and were dismissed for the noon meal. On
previous weekdays, the men would have returned to construction work after eating. Today, they were granted a little free
time.

Early in the afternoon, the troops formed around three sides of
the new flagpole and bandstand that had been erected in the
center of the parade ground. Wives, children, and selected guests
gathered on a temporary platform in front of the headquarters
building. The band entertained with popular and light classical
music as everybody took their places for the dedication
ceremonies. Duggan Maguire escorted Katy onto the guests'
platform. I stood at the south end of the parade ground with

285

the other teamsters.

Colonel Carrington, Chaplain White, and Judge Kinney occupied a temporary speakers' platform beneath the flagpole, which towered one hundred twenty-four feet above them. The seven officers of the line stood at parade rest in front of their respective infantry companies. The two regular army surgeons sat with the guests. In total, only eleven officers were assigned to Fort Phil Kearny. That was half the number Carrington should have. His repeated complaints to higher headquarters about being short officers, cavalry, ammunition, and other essentials went unanswered.

Judge Kinney rose and recited a chaste, but spirited, poem written by Miss Sarah Carmichael, a Mormon lady he'd probably known from his earlier days in Utah. Chaplain White offered a prayer, then Principal Musician John Barnes stepped away from his customary place on the new bandstand to read an original poem he'd written for the occasion. Barnes had been a ship's carpenter before joining the army, and he and Private William Daley, an expert woodworker, had constructed the mammoth flagpole after the fashion of a ship's yardarm.

Finally, Colonel Carrington rose and delivered a long-winded, patriotic speech, in which he lamented those who had recently given their lives battling the Indians. Chaplain White offered a short benediction.

Then, Adjutant Adair shouted out commands in preparation for raising the flag. "Battalion—*Attention!* Present—*Arms!*" Infantrymen snapped to attention and brought their muskets to the position of respect in front of their bodies.

"*Play!*" the adjutant commanded. A drum roll brought the regimental band to its feet. Band Master Damme handed his baton to Principal Musician Barnes as a token of appreciation for his efforts in the construction of the flagpole. Barnes waved the baton, and the band played "The Star-Spangled Banner."

"Hoist!" A detail of sergeants along with Private Daley pulled on the halyard and slowly raised the thirty-six-star garrison flag. The flag's thirty-six-foot fly floated free into the breeze as the twenty-foot hoist rose to the masthead. The colonel had ordered cheering would not be tolerated during the ceremonies, but a smattering of applause came from members of the audience.

"Ready, *Fire!*" The adjutant voiced his next command. All three of the garrison's howitzers blasted a simultaneous salute. White smoke drifted across the parade ground.

"Pass In Review!" The adjutant commanded.

Each company marched past the speakers' platform. Officers saluted with their sabers, and the men executed "Eyes—*Right"* as they came abreast of the commanding officer.

When all companies had returned to their starting point, the adjutant gave his final command. "Parade—*Dismissed!*"

The band struck up "Hail Columbia," and the troops marched to their barracks. The spectators dispersed from the parade ground.

I'd no sooner returned to the quartermaster office than Captain Brown burst through the door shedding his dress uniform.

"Come on, Wakefield! The damned savages are making off with the invalid horses. Get a couple mounts."

At three o'clock, a band of Indians had raced around the foot of Sullivant Hills and stampeded a small herd of unserviceable horses grazing outside the stockade. Captain Brown had assigned two muleskinners to guard the herd so all soldiers could participate in the ceremonies. Two teamsters were no match for a band of determined Indians.

I dashed to the cavalry stables to get two serviceable horses that were kept saddled. I rode one and led another toward the warehouse. The captain had completed his uniform change, and we met halfway. He hauled himself into the saddle.

Lieutenant Grummond and half a dozen mounted infantry privates joined us. We charged out the front gate in pursuit of the Indians. The thieves were hindered in moving the stolen herd because of the condition of the horses.

We easily closed the gap between us and the Indians. Shortly after we splashed across Big Piney Creek, I identified the raiders as Running Bear's Arapahos.

We pursuers were armed with revolvers or rifles except for Lieutenant Grummond. When we came within pistol-shot range, the lieutenant drew his saber and spurred his horse ahead.

"Hold up, Lieutenant!" Captain Brown shouted the order. "Stay with the detachment. They'll surround you if you get close enough to them to use that saber."

Lieutenant Grummond reined in, and the rest of us caught up to him. I was riding behind Captain Brown and had a good look at the lieutenant's face. His cheeks flamed red. He'd been a lieutenant colonel during the war, while Brown had never risen above the rank of captain. It was hard for Grummond to take orders from someone he probably thought he should outrank.

As we drew nearer, I spotted the galvanized Yankee, dressed as an Indian, riding with Running Bear.

I swung away from our pursuing detachment and jammed my heels hard into my horse's flanks. My mount leaped ahead. I was doing what the captain had ordered the lieutenant not to do. I didn't care. I wanted that ex-Rebel.

An Indian riding close to my intended target launched an arrow at me. It embedded in the pommel of my saddle. The force of the impact jolted my crotch. An inch to the side and the missile would have been in my groin.

I ignored the Indian and fired my revolver at the white man. From my bouncing position, it would have to be a lucky shot—and it was. He slumped to one side and slid off his mount. Dust flew into the air when his body bounced on the ground. His pony raced on without him.

The Indian who'd shot at me swung his pony around and headed for the downed white man. I snapped off a shot at the savage. This bullet missed its mark, but it must have been close, because the Indian turned away from trying to rescue the galvanized Yankee.

I stepped out of the saddle before my horse halted. I kept my revolver pointed at my victim and approached. He wasn't dead. He wore a breechclout only. His long hair was pulled into a braid, and his cheeks bore streaks of red and yellow paint.

"Don't move," I said.

"I can't." Bright frothy blood stained his breast, and a sucking sound came from the wound. "You back-shot me."

"What'd you expect me to do? Wait until we came face-to-face?"

He groaned, spit out more blood, and tried to reach beneath himself with a hand. Was his revolver under him?

I stepped forward and placed a boot on his elbow, pinning his arm down. "Don't try it," I said.

The Arapahos abandoned their attempt at stealing the horses and raced to the east. The soldiers rounded up the herd.

Captain Brown and Lieutenant Grummond rode up to where I had my prisoner on the ground. "What's this?" the captain asked.

"The galvanized Yankee I told you I'd seen during other chases. I first saw this fellow at Fort Reno talking with Duggan Maguire. This former Reb was recently mustered out of the Fifth U.S. Volunteers."

"Let's get him on a horse," Captain Brown said.

The captain shouted instructions to one of the soldiers who cut a horse out of the herd and brought it over.

Lieutenant Grummond got down and helped me lift the

injured man onto the horse. "He's bleeding badly," the lieutenant said.

The bullet had passed completely through him. Blood oozed from his naked chest and back and began dribbling from his lips.

"Without a saddle or a bridle," Captain Brown said, "he'll have to be supported."

The captain instructed two privates to ride on either side of the former Rebel, and we returned to the fort at a walk.

A half hour later we passed through the front gate. I proceeded with the two soldiers who supported the wounded man to the hospital tent. Lieutenant Grummond and the others herded the rescued horses into the stable area.

"I'll have the sergeant of the guard find Maguire and send him to the hospital," Captain Brown said. "Maybe he can identify this man."

Work was underway to erect a wooden structure for the hospital, but the tent facility was still in use today. The two soldiers carried the galvanized Yankee into the hospital, and I followed.

Doctor Horton was examining the now-unconsciousness man, when Captain Brown and the sergeant of the guard escorted Duggan Maguire into the treatment area.

"Do you recognize this man?" Captain Brown asked Duggan.

"Never saw him before."

"You're lying!" I exclaimed. "I saw you with him at Fort Reno, and you know it. When you showed him that shamrock pendant you gave to Katy O'Toole, you both laughed."

"You're mistaken, Wakefield." Maguire glared at me. "I've no idea who this is. If you'll excuse me, Captain, I have work to do."

Maguire left the hospital.

Captain Brown looked at me and cocked his head to the side.

"You sure about this?"

"Yes, sir. Look at the tattoo on the man's forearm. I described that tattoo to Major Bonnet at Fort Reno, right after I first saw the man. The paymaster said the tattoo's the symbol of the Knights of the Golden Circle."

Captain Brown lifted the comatose man's arm. "That is the symbol of the KGC." The captain turned to the sergeant of the guard. "Ask Colonel Carrington to come to the hospital. He may want to interrogate this fellow."

Ten minutes later, Colonel Carrington entered the treatment area. I briefed the commanding officer about my prior experience with the galvanized Yankee.

"This man's tattoo is the symbol of the KGC," the colonel said. "During the war, I investigated the secret group's activities in harboring deserters, discouraging enlistments, and obstructing the draft. My efforts helped court martial that infamous anti-war Copperhead Democrat, Clement Vallandigham. That's what earned me the brevet brigadier general's rank."

The colonel looked at me. "You say you saw him with Mr. Maguire at Fort Reno?"

"Yes, sir."

"I've been informed," the colonel said, "the KGC is raising money to finance a resurrection of the Confederacy in Mexico. An element of the organization under a lawbreaker named Jesse James has been robbing banks and trains in the States. Mr. Maguire said his original destination was the Montana goldfields. I wonder if he was going there to prospect for himself or for the KGC?"

The colonel turned to the sergeant of the guard. "Please escort Mr. Maguire here, Sergeant. I want a word with him."

Five minutes later, the sergeant of the guard came into the hospital tent. "He's gone, sir. His quarters have been cleaned out."

"Well," Colonel Carrington said, "I'll just have to talk with this man about why two members of the KGC are hanging around the Bozeman Trail."

"Sorry, Colonel," Surgeon Horton said. "He's dead."

CHAPTER 38

Captain Brown had gone to headquarters and left me to handle the incoming wagon train from the hay cutting contractor. Portugee Philips was the leader of this train. I walked in front of the five wagons, guiding them into the quartermaster yard. Once there, the teamsters forked the dry grasses from their wagons into the hay yard. We had erected a fence around the area where we stored the hay to keep the mules from eating the fodder indiscriminately.

Portugee walked with me to the quartermaster warehouse, so I could give him a receipt for the delivery. We had almost reached the doorway when Katy O'Toole strolled up.

"Good morning, Portugee." She gave him a bright, dimpled smile. She ignored me.

"Morning, Miss O'Toole," Portugee said. "I trust you are well?"

"Yes, thank you. I am."

Katy shoved a requisition in my direction. She just held it out and didn't say a word. I took the paper that bore Lieutenant Grummond's signature.

"Mrs. Grummond wants a new cast-iron skillet?" I asked.

"Aye," Katy said.

"The authorization is one skillet per family, Katy. What happened to the one we issued when she arrived?"

"Threw it away."

"If I'm to issue her a replacement, I'll have to have the old one as proof that it's damaged. Why did you throw it away?"

"Mrs. Grummond burned her supper so badly last night we couldn't clean it. I took it out and threw it in the sinks."

"Tossing it into the latrine is not the proper way to dispose of a damaged skillet, especially if you're seeking a replacement."

"If you must have the old one before you issue a new one," she huffed, "you'll have to fish it out of the sinks yourself."

I shook my head at her sarcasm. "When he returns, I'll get Captain Brown's approval to issue a replacement. I can't do it myself without having the damaged item."

"Fine. You take the skillet to Fannie when you get approval." She turned to leave.

"Miss O'Toole, how is Mrs. Grummond?" Portugee asked. "Now that I'm working outside the fort, I don't get to see her . . . or you, very often."

Portugee's face flushed. Katy and I had talked before about how it was obvious Portugee was infatuated with Fannie Grummond. He was much too polite, however, to approach her directly. Perhaps he was afraid of a confrontation with her short-tempered husband.

"Mrs. Grummond is doing well," Katy answered. "They will move into their new quarters tomorrow. Perhaps she won't have as much trouble with household chores once she is settled into a regular cabin instead of that tent."

Katy left, and Portugee looked at me with a shrug of his shoulders. "What's that all about, Zach?" he asked.

"What's what all about? The skillet?"

"No. She snubbed you. I thought she considered you to be like a brother."

"*Brother.* Ha! She gave me a tongue lashing the night Maguire left four days ago, and she hasn't spoken a decent word to me since. She blames me for Maguire not taking her to Montana."

"Speaking of Maguire," Portugee said, "everybody's heard

about the incident with the Knights of the Golden Circle. I thought you killed that galvanized Yankee?"

"I did. Why?"

"You know that raid last night on the wagon train circled down by the creek?"

"Yes. Colonel Carrington fired a howitzer and drove the Indians away. What does that have to do with the KGC?"

"Well, there was a white man riding with those Indians."

Late that same afternoon, November 3, every occupant of the fort turned out to welcome the arrival of one of the two promised cavalry companies. Sixty-three men wearing yellow piping down the seams of their trousers rode through the main gate and formed up in the street in front of the headquarters building. Following them through the gate rode two infantry captains and the paymaster. An ambulance and a supply wagon brought up the rear.

Even from where I stood at the quartermaster warehouse, I saw the broad smile that brightened the usually dour face of Colonel Carrington.

The officer leading the mounted unit saluted. "Second Lieutenant Horatio Bingham reporting with Company C, Second Cavalry, sir."

"Welcome, Lieutenant Bingham. We've been expecting you . . . for a long time."

Captain Ten Eyck and Lieutenant Adair stood beside the colonel.

"Adjutant Adair will guide you to the stables and show you where to set up your tents."

"Thank you, sir."

"I don't see any new model carbines," the colonel continued. "Your men seem to be carrying an assortment of older weapons."

"Yes, sir. Some have Starr carbines, but most have Enfield rifles."

"I don't understand," Carrington said, "how the army can field a cavalry unit with old British-made single-shot rifles and obsolete single-shot carbines. But that's my problem, not yours. Welcome, again, Lieutenant. Report to me after you get your men settled."

The two officers exchanged salutes, and the adjutant led the cavalry unit away.

"Ah, Major Bonnet," Colonel Carrington said. "Welcome to Fort Phil Kearny. We will assemble for pay tomorrow."

"Thank you, Colonel." Major Bonnet dismounted and saluted. "Meet my two traveling companions. They're both assigned to the Eighteenth."

The two captains dismounted and saluted the colonel. I judged them to be about equal in height. They both stood an inch or two shorter than my six feet.

"Captain William Fetterman, reporting for duty, Colonel." The captain removed his tight-fitting kepi and shook Colonel Carrington's extended hand. Fetterman's erect posture exuded that of the professional soldier. His jet-black hair exhibited a temporary crease around his scalp from wearing a hat for hours on end, but the hair was neatly combed back and pomaded. His black mustache and muttonchop whiskers revealed no streaks of gray.

"Welcome, Captain," the colonel said. "You know Captain Ten Eyck from your previous service. Since you are the senior captain now, you will assume command of the Second Battalion and take over Company A from Captain Ten Eyck."

Captains Fetterman and Ten Eyck exchanged nods.

"Sir," the other officer said, "Captain James Powell reporting." He, too, removed his hat when he shook hands with the colonel. His shoulders stooped slightly, his face clean-shaven.

Captain Brown, who knew this officer from prior service together, had told me Powell still suffered from two bullets that remained lodged in his body from war wounds.

"Captain Powell you will take over command of Company C from Lieutenant Adair. That will free him to concentrate full-time on his duties as adjutant, until he departs. Gentlemen, it's time for you to settle in and get cleaned up. I invite all of you"— the colonel paused to indicate Bonnet, Fetterman, and Powell— "to join my wife and me at our quarters this evening for supper. I'll see that Lieutenant Bingham receives an invitation as well. Now, Captain Ten Eyck will show you to the bachelor officers' quarters."

The officers exchanged salutes, and Captain Ten Eyck led the way toward the BOQ tents pitched near the hospital. The construction of the bachelor officers' permanent building would be the last to take place at the fort. Priority extended to housing the enlisted men.

When the group made the turn at the south end of the parade ground, they came abreast of where I stood at the corner of the quartermaster warehouse. The officers led their horses, followed by the paymaster's ambulance, which was driven by someone I assumed to be the current paymaster clerk.

Major Bonnet spotted me and motioned me to join him.

"Welcome, Major," I said. We exchanged handshakes, and I fell in beside him.

"How have you been, Zach?" he asked.

"Fine, sir. It's nice to see you getting around so well."

His limp hadn't improved since I'd last seen him, but he kept pace with the others even with his wooden leg.

"Can't complain," he said. "Glad to get out of the saddle, though. That's one heck of a ride from Fort Laramie. One doesn't realize how far north this place is until you undertake the journey."

When we passed the hospital, Katy O'Toole was standing by the entrance.

"Major Bonnet," she called and waved.

The major led his horse away from the others, who proceeded on to the BOQ tents.

"Miss O'Toole," the major said. "So nice to see you without a sling. You're fully recovered?"

"Aye, thank you."

"I am surprised to see you here," he said. "I thought you would have gone on to Montana."

"That's a long story." Katy glared at me.

I shrugged. Why was she blaming me because Maguire abandoned her?

"What are you wearing around your neck, young lady?" The major pointed at the shamrock pendant. "That looks so much like one I gave my wife on our honeymoon years ago."

Katy's mouth dropped open, as did mine. I remembered the initials engraved on the reverse of the pendant—*AB* and *LK*. Armond Bonnet?

Katy cleared what was obviously a dry throat. "Sir?"

"Yes?" He prompted her when she didn't immediately continue.

"What was your wife's maiden name?"

"Leila Kennedy."

CHAPTER 39

Katy lifted the pendant, attached to the chain around her neck, and turned it over so Major Bonnet could see the reverse.

The major rubbed a thumb over the initials and blinked several times. "How did you come by this, Miss O'Toole?" he asked, his voice barely a whisper.

"Mr. Maguire gave it to me as a birthday present a few days ago." Tears glistened at the corners of her eyes.

Major Bonnet clenched his teeth and dropped the pendant. It fell against Katy's breast.

"Then how did that wagon master come by it?" he asked "Everyone in Rocheport, Missouri, knew Leila wore that pendant every day. When her body and my daughter's body were found following the raid by Bloody Bill Anderson's men, the pendant was missing."

I reminded the major of our discussion at Fort Reno about the possible connection between Maguire and the Knights of the Golden Circle. I apologized for failing to tell him about the incident with the pendant. I described the recent events involving the galvanized Yankee and Maguire's disappearance.

"Zach," Major Bonnet said, "remember in Major Van Voast's office at Fort Laramie, Maguire said he'd been in the army, but not ours?"

"Yes, I remember."

"We all knew he meant he'd been a Confederate soldier, but I never asked him any details about his service. He told us he's half Cherokee. I'm guessing that when the war started, he joined up with Stand Watie."

"Who's Stand Watie?" Katy asked.

"A Cherokee chief," the major said, "who raised a cavalry unit of Cherokees, Muskogees, and Seminoles in Indian Territory. The Confederates made Watie a brigadier general. He led those Indians in battles in Texas and the western states. He was the last Confederate general to surrender."

"I thought you believed it was Bloody Bill Anderson's men who murdered your family," I said. "How could Maguire be riding with that outfit if he was with Watie?"

"Maguire could have quit Watie and joined Quantrill's Raiders in Texas. When Anderson's bunch split off from Quantrill late in the war, Maguire went with Anderson to Missouri. That's conjecture on my part, but something else makes me believe it could be true."

"What?" I asked.

"The citizens who survived the raid in Rocheport claimed the leader of the gang that terrorized the town exhibited the features of an Indian."

We three stood silently for a moment, then Katy lifted the pendant and chain from around her neck and offered it to the major.

"No," the major said. "You keep it, dear. Knowing you are wearing it will bring me happiness each time I am reminded how much you resemble my wife and daughter."

Katy curled the chain around the pendant and dropped it into the pocket of her hospital matron's apron.

"I will wear it on special occasions, Major," she said, "and say a prayer for you and your family when I do."

The next morning, Sunday, November 4, was payday. The battalion marched into position on the parade ground to the music of the regimental band. One after another, the companies lined up in single-file formation before the bandstand where Major Bonnet had set up his table. First, the company commander approached and presented his muster roll, then each man came forward to accept his pay.

After the troops had been paid, Captain Brown and I received reimbursement for the quartermaster and commissary vouchers. The captain and I retired to the quartermaster warehouse, where the teamsters and contractors were waiting impatiently. The contractor supervisors were paid in lump sum, and they in turn paid their own employees. Portugee Philips was one of several entitled to be paid by both the quartermaster and their current contractor employer.

Captain Brown grew bored with the details and retired to his office, leaving me to pay the handful of guides remaining at the fort.

The last guide to present himself was a welcome sight. "Major Bridger," I said. "When did you return?"

"Today, Zach. Just today. You got some pay for this old man?"

"I sure do. Sign here."

He took the pen and marked his X where I indicated. I counted out his money, which was more than even the colonel received. Bridger's wage was a bone of contention with Omaha headquarters, but Colonel Carrington had continued to refuse an order from General Cooke to fire the frontiersman.

"What did you find up north?" I asked.

"There's one heap of Indians gathering along the Tongue," he replied. "The Crow chiefs say it takes half a day to ride through the villages. I've never known so many to camp together before. There are Sissetons, Bad Faces, Oglalas, Hunkpapas, Arapahos, and Northern Cheyennes. Crow Chief Yellow Face said he even saw a few Gros Ventres."

Unexpectedly, Captain Fetterman and Lieutenants Bisbee

and Grummond barged past us and went into Captain Brown's office. They slammed the door behind themselves.

I placed a finger against my lips, and we listened to the conversation among the four officers.

"Fred," Captain Fetterman asked, "who's the old codger out there with your clerk?"

"Major Bridger," Brown answered.

"That old farmer is the famous Jim Bridger?"

"That's 'Old Gabe' himself. He just returned from Fort C. F. Smith. He claims hundreds of Indians are assembling along the Tongue River."

"That's good news," Fetterman said.

"Good news?" Lieutenant Bisbee asked.

"Of course," Fetterman continued. "With the savages congregating like that, it will make our job easier. A single company of the Eighteenth can whip a thousand Indians. The full regiment can wipe out *all* the hostiles."

"That's what I like to hear," Lieutenant Grummond said. "Let's get rid of the bastards for good. When do we start?"

"Colonel Carrington is not going to start anytime," Bisbee said. "We need your leadership, Bill."

Bisbee, although a lieutenant, addressed Fetterman by his first name. The officers did that when they were together privately. In public, they would probably address Fetterman as colonel because of his brevet rank.

"You've seen the reorganization plan?" Fetterman asked.

"We've only heard rumors," Captain Brown said.

"Come the first of the year," Fetterman continued, "the Second Battalion of the Eighteenth will be re-designated the Twenty-seventh Regiment, and I expect to be its commander. The Third Battalion, out in Utah, will become the Thirty-sixth Regiment. Carrington will continue as commander of the Eighteenth, but it will consist only of the First Battalion. He will move the regiment's headquarters down to Fort Caspar on the North Platte. I'll be in charge of all activity along the Bozeman Trail."

"I can't wait," Captain Brown said. "Then we will see some *real* action."

"We're not going to wait," Fetterman said. "I've got a plan for tonight."

"Tonight?" Captain Brown asked. "You just got here yesterday, Bill. Don't you want some time to get settled in?"

"No. We're going to get started right away. The sooner we show the Indians who's stronger, the better."

"What do you have in mind?" Bisbee asked.

"We'll hobble a dozen mules down by Big Piney Creek and conceal a detachment of mounted infantry in the cottonwood thicket there. When the savages come to steal the mules, we'll spring the ambush."

"Now you're talking," Grummond said. "I'll assemble the best of the mounted men. Most of the privates are raw recruits and can barely stay in the saddle. But I do have a handful of experienced noncoms we can count on."

"Good," Brown said. "I'm going along. I've chased after the thieving bastards almost every day since we got here. I have more experience fighting Indians than most of the company commanders. No offense to any of the officers. The colonel just hasn't given them many chances to engage the enemy."

"I'd like to go, too," Bisbee said, "but the colonel has me working with him tonight to respond to complaints received in yesterday's mail."

"What complaints?" Fetterman asked.

"General Cooke's continuing to complain about the length of time it takes our dispatches to reach Omaha," Bisbee answered. "Along with a host of other questions, the adjutant general in Washington City is asking 'where is Fort Phil Kearny?'"

Laughter from the others responded to Bisbee's last comment.

Major Bridger pushed his old hat back and slapped his fingers to his forehead. "I've heard all I care to," he said. "These officers who fought down south don't know nothin' 'bout fightin' Injuns. Colonel Carrington's the only one with common sense."

Bridger resettled his hat atop his gray head and slipped out the door of the warehouse. I stayed at my desk to continue eavesdropping.

"Wakefield!"

Captain Brown's shouted command took me to the door of his office. I knocked and went inside when invited.

"Captain Fetterman needs a dozen mules, Wakefield," Captain Brown said. "Go with him to the yard and halter the ones he selects. Bring them here to the warehouse and tether them outside. We'll be using them tonight."

Lieutenants Bisbee and Grummond left the warehouse, Captain Brown remained in his office, and I escorted Captain Fetterman through the postern gate between the main fort and the quartermaster yard.

"You been here long, Mr. Wakefield?" Captain Fetterman asked.

"From the beginning, sir. I was originally Major Bonnet's pay clerk, but after we paid the troops at Fort Reno in July, I joined up with Quartermaster Brown."

"What do you think of these Sioux and Cheyennes?"

"They've proven formidable . . . and elusive, sir. The Arapahos are just as bad, if not worse. There aren't as many of them."

"You've fought them personally?"

"Yes, sir. I've chased hostiles with Captain Brown on a few occasions."

"What's this I hear about members of the Knights of the Golden Circle being in the neighborhood? Colonel Carrington said at supper last night that you killed one of them."

"Yes, sir. I did shoot one of the galvanized Yankees who was riding with the Arapahos. I'm also of an opinion that Duggan Maguire may be involved."

I briefly explained who Maguire was and the recent activities that led to his departure.

"What do you think the KGC's after?" Captain Fetterman asked.

"Money to start a new Confederacy, sir."

We had reached the stables that had been erected against the east and south walls of the quartermaster yard to shelter the mules.

"I'll point out the ones I want for the stakeout," the captain said. "Halter them and round up hobbling ropes."

"Yes, sir."

The captain went through the herd and picked out some of the best. He knew his equines. I cringed when he selected Matt and Mark to be two of the dozen. Why risk losing our best mules? Maybe he thought Indians would be smart enough not to be tempted by weak ones.

Not long after Taps, I realized I wasn't going to sleep. I was worried about losing two of my Bible mules if Captain Fetterman's plan failed to keep the Indians from stealing them.

I crawled out of my bunk, tugged on my boots, shrugged into my jacket, and headed for the southeast artillery bastion. My breath hung in front of me in a fragile white cloud. The temperature already hovered well below freezing.

On the bastion, I leaned back against the barrel of a howitzer that occupied most of the small space. I jumped away. The bronze barrel was frigid. The air I sucked into my lungs added to my chill. I shoved my hands beneath my armpits. Why hadn't I worn gloves?

Smatterings of light glowed from random lanterns and candles in windows inside the fort's walls. Beyond the stockade, all remained black. Dozens of meteors streaked overhead. They didn't provide enough light for me to see the mules. Somewhere in the distance a wolf howled. Or was it a wolf?

Shortly after midnight, the waning crescent moon rose and bathed the area along the creek with moonlight. The hobbled mules grazed in the open meadow between the fort and the stream. None of Fetterman's ambushers was visible. They'd done a good job concealing themselves in the cottonwoods lining Big Piney Creek.

"Zach?" That was Katy's voice. She stood at the base of the bastion.

"What are you doing here?" I asked.

"I could ask the same of you," she replied.

"I'm watching to see if the Indians take Captain Fetterman's bait."

"I'll watch with you," she said. "Help me up."

I steadied the top of the ladder leaning against the parapet that provided access to the top. After she'd climbed the first two rungs of the ladder, I was able to grasp her outstretched hand and assist her the rest of the way.

"Any activity?" she asked after joining me beside the howitzer. The fine mist from her breath partially obscured her nose and lips.

"No. All quiet. You can see the mules grazing yonder." I pointed toward the scene of the hoped-for action.

"Isn't Captain Fetterman wonderful?" she asked. "Everybody is so excited he's here. He's so handsome . . . and articulate."

Had everybody but Major Bridger, Colonel Carrington, and me fallen victim to the spell cast by this newly arrived officer?

"I was helping Fannie get settled into her new quarters this afternoon," Katy continued. "Lieutenant Grummond couldn't stop talking about how impressed he was with Captain Fetterman's plans for leading the battalion in the fight against the Indians. I heard him tell Fannie what he was going to be doing tonight. When I couldn't sleep, I thought I'd come watch the fun."

"Fun?" I exclaimed. "I don't think it's fun that we could lose a dozen of our best mules. Not to mention the Indians might kill some of the men."

The longer we stood there the colder we became. Both Katy and I shivered. My muscles shook. I noticed her head jitter as she scrunched her shoulders up toward her ears. If I only had the courage to wrap my arms around her, I could keep her warm. I moved closer. I'd never hugged anyone other than my mother. I gradually raised an elbow with the intention of slipping my arm around her shoulder.

Katy reached a hand up and touched my cheek with her fingertips. "Even in the moonlight," she said, "I can see you haven't shaved. Trying to grow a beard?"

"Well, no." I froze with my elbow cocked to the side. "I don't shave every morning. I've never thought about growing a beard."

"You might look handsome with a beard, Zach. Observe Captain Fetterman's neatly trimmed beard. It's quite attractive."

Fetterman again! I dropped my elbow and forgot about putting an arm around her.

Two hours later, with nothing happening in the meadow, we called it a night.

At sunrise, Captain Fetterman led his mounted infantrymen and the mules back into the fort. The Indians had been smart enough to know the army wouldn't leave hobbled mules unattended.

The returning infantrymen led the mules by halter ropes

even though the soldiers could hardly remain upright in their saddles. What a bedraggled lot. The ambushers undoubtedly hadn't gotten any shuteye.

I met them at the front gate and took charge of the mules. I'd no sooner taken possession of the twelve animals, with a special pat of relief on the necks of Matt and Mark, when the shrill yells of Indians shook me out of my pastoral reverie.

A sentry at the front gate pointed to the east and shouted. "Indians are making off with Wheatley's cattle herd!"

CHAPTER 40

Payday had occurred three days previously, and even after deductions for the dead mule and the destroyed wagon, I had money in my pocket. At the sutler's store, I'd retrieved my IOU from Judge Kinney, so the Colt revolver was mine, free and clear. I invited Katy to join me at Wheatleys' for supper that Wednesday evening, November 7. I'd thought she and I would have a chance to talk about the future and how I might figure in that. But all she could talk about was Fetterman!

That morning, the *handsome* captain had almost gotten himself killed. I couldn't understand why *not* getting killed made him such a big hero.

The incident occurred when Captain Fetterman made his first trip to the pineries in the company of Captain Ten Eyck, Lieutenant Bisbee, Lieutenant Link, and an escort of twelve cavalrymen. The four officers had ridden ahead of the dozen soldiers. When the officers approached the crossing of South Piney Creek, Indians sprang an ambush.

From the volume of fire heard, the sergeant leading the escort assumed the worst and dispatched a messenger to the fort with word he suspected the officers had been killed. Colonel Carrington mounted an immediate relief party, which encountered Fetterman and the other officers returning unharmed to the fort.

"Can you imagine how frightening that must have been for Captain Fetterman?" Katy asked.

"He's a soldier, for heaven's sakes," I said. "He's been shot at before."

"But," she continued, "if something would have happened to him, I don't know how the men of the garrison would handle it. They are counting on him to lead them."

Our supper conversation didn't get any better. I couldn't get Katy interested in discussing her plans other than she intended to accompany the paymaster to Fort C. F. Smith. I voiced my concerns about her going that far and not being able to proceed to her final destination. The suspicion voiced around the fort was the last wagon train of the season had already passed.

We finished what was probably a good meal Liz Wheatley had worked hard to prepare. I couldn't remember what it was. I walked Katy to the hospital, said goodnight, and headed for my quarters. Impulsively, I swung over to the sutler's store, where I ordered a beer—something I rarely did.

I sat alone and enjoyed a beer that'd been hauled all the way from St. Louis. The sutler's staff had obviously disobeyed orders again and brought snow from the mountains, because the brew was chilled just right. My hand was cold and slick with the moisture that ran down the side of the glass bottle.

Smoke hung thick against the rafters. The usual sour smell of beer didn't assail my nostrils tonight because I was enjoying a bottle of the stuff myself. Suddenly, the door burst open and Captain Fetterman strode in.

Captains Ten Eyck and Brown were playing cards with Lieutenants Bisbee and Link at the far end of the room.

"Captain Fetterman!" Brown shouted. "Join us."

Fetterman removed his hat and went to the table. Bisbee confiscated an extra chair from a neighboring table and dragged it over for Fetterman. Ten Eyck scooped up the cards, ending the game, while Link went to the counter and returned with a beer for Fetterman. The five officers commenced a lively conversation, making no attempt to keep it private. One boast after another rose from the group.

"So, Colonel Carrington went to your rescue," Brown said, "when it wasn't even necessary." He punctuated his statement with a guffaw.

"What we should have done," Fetterman said, "was join forces right then and pursue those savages. We could have punished them severely for their insolence."

"I agree," Bisbee said. He raised his bottle. "Here's to more aggressive action!"

It occurred to me that Captain Ten Eyck should have known better than to let the four officers get separated from their support force. Was this an example of what some perceived to be Ten Eyck's faltering judgment?

"It is my firm belief," Captain Fetterman announced, "that any well led group of soldiers can whip these ragamuffin Indians easily. Colonel Carrington's lack of command experience has made him overly cautious. What's needed is a forceful approach!"

The officers cheered. I'd had enough. I downed the last of my beer and left.

Two days later, Major Bonnet came to Captain Brown and arranged to have me serve as paymaster clerk for the trip to Fort C. F. Smith. Major Bonnet's present clerk had come down with ague and was confined to hospital.

On Friday morning, November 9, I hitched the Bible mules to the paymaster's ambulance and waited at the main gate with a forty-man cavalry escort. Jim Bridger would guide us up the Bozeman Trail to the Big Horn River. He sat on his old gray mare near the ambulance.

Ten other cavalrymen were also departing to guard a mail courier on his trip south to Fort Caspar. Suddenly, Colonel

Carrington's newly arrived cavalry command would be reduced to thirteen men at Fort Phil Kearny.

The colonel had taken steps to improve the efficiency of the cavalrymen. First, he'd put them through saber drills, which none of the recruits had previously undergone. Second, he'd traded some of their obsolete single-shot Starr carbines for the regimental band's Spencer repeaters, resulting in twenty-five improved weapons. Half of our escort had the better weapon swinging from their shoulder slings.

Colonel Carrington came out of headquarters and approached the column.

"Good morning, Colonel," Major Bonnet said. The major was in the process of mounting his horse. It always amazed me how he could swing that wooden leg over the back of his mount and shove its boot into the stirrup without assistance.

"Major Bonnet," Carrington said, "keep a sharp eye out once you cross Goose Creek. Beyond there you'll be deep into Sioux territory. Major Bridger believes there are hundreds of lodges assembled along the Tongue River. You still hold with that opinion, Jim?"

"Not an opinion, Colonel," Major Bridger answered. "It's a fact."

I looked beyond the line of cavalrymen behind the ambulance. In the distance, Katy O'Toole stood in front of the hospital. Although she was some distance away, it was obvious from the way her arms were folded across her chest she was giving me the evil eye.

Yesterday, she'd approached Major Bonnet with the idea of going with him as far as Fort C. F. Smith. The major had deferred to the judgment of Colonel Carrington, who adamantly refused to give permission for her to leave the fort. Katy had gotten it in her head that I was to blame for it. Women!

Major Bonnet signaled the column forward. I snapped the

reins harder than necessary. The mules jumped when they pulled the ambulance into motion.

I drove the ambulance behind Major Bonnet as he led the column across the shallow crossing at Big Piney Creek. On the far side of the stream, the Montana Road climbed up Lodge Trail Ridge. After following the ridge for four miles the road dropped sharply down into the valley of Peno Creek.

We continued north all day following Peno Creek, which some folks called Prairie Dog Creek. Major Bridger said the name *Peno* was that of an old French-Canadian trapper he'd known who'd been badly mauled alongside the creek by an enraged buffalo bull. There were colonies of prairie dogs in the vicinity, but I agreed with Major Bridger that Peno was a better name.

The day's journey proved quiet and pleasant. A cool breeze blew steadily from the west off the Big Horn range. Clouds scudded off the mountain tops and shredded themselves into streamers as they flew overhead. We stopped every couple of hours to water the animals.

Nearing the end of the day, after traveling twenty-five miles, we reached the point were the road turned sharply to the west away from Peno Creek. Here, we climbed a narrow divide and a mile and a half later dropped down the opposite slope toward Goose Creek. Major Bonnet and Major Bridger agreed we should cross the creek and set up camp for the night on the west bank. We forded Goose Creek just beyond where Little and Big Goose Creeks joined.

That evening, we picketed our animals between our campsite and the creek, allowing them to graze on abundant grass along the bank. It was such grass that contractors had mowed here over the past months to provide fodder for the animals at Fort Phil Kearny. It was here, Indians had frequently raided the harvesters.

I built a small cook fire, and using the utensils from the kitchen box, I prepared a meal of salt pork and hardtack. The cavalrymen built their fires and prepared their own rations. Major Bonnet invited Major Bridger to join us for supper, such as it was.

The three of us sat around the fire and dipped hardtack in the skillet's hot grease to soften it. I pounded coffee beans with a hatchet and dropped them into a pot of boiling water. I wasn't about to pound the beans with the butt of my new revolver. The two majors, one actual and the other honorary, lit their pipes and enjoyed their smokes along with a cup of steaming coffee.

"It's been a peaceful trip," Major Bonnet said.

"That's what bothers me," Major Bridger responded.

"How's that?" Major Bonnet asked.

"When you don't see the rascals, that's when they're the closest. They're out there watching. You can bet on it."

"The sergeant has set up pickets around our perimeter," Major Bonnet said. "They'll sound off if anyone comes near."

After supper, I cleaned the utensils with sand and creek water. Then, Major Bonnet and I spread our blanket rolls out on opposite benches in the ambulance and climbed over the pay chests to stretch out.

Bridger refused Major Bonnet's offer to join us. "Can't abide sleeping inside when there's a good tree available," the old guide said. He spread his blanket under a nearby cottonwood.

The soldiers had paired up and joined shelter halves to make their temporary quarters. Idle talk diminished, and campfires died down to smoldering coals. Snores soon accompanied the burbling of Goose Creek's water racing past on its way to the Tongue River.

Shouts and yells, punctuated by gun shots, jerked me awake. I bolted straight up on the bench where I'd been sleeping. An arrow whizzed through the canvas cover above my head and swished through the opposite side. Fingers of light crisscrossed the dark interior of the ambulance through the resulting holes. Shrill screams confirmed we were under attack by savages. Early morning light illuminated the campsite as cavalrymen crawled out of their low-slung tents, dragging carbines with them.

I tossed my blanket aside and rolled over. Instead of my feet landing solidly on the floor, they thumped on the lids of pay chests. I grabbed my pistol belt and holster from where I'd left it on a chest the night before and belted it on. I crawled over the chests to reach the rear of the ambulance. Major Bonnet was doing likewise. He and I dropped off the ambulance's rear gate and ducked beneath its body.

With our campsite backed up against the creek, the sergeant directed his troopers to spread out around the ambulance and the tents in a semi-circular skirmish line to confront the Indians coming toward us from the west.

The cavalrymen soon found the range with their carbines, and the savages broke off their attempt after three of them were shot. Other Indians gathered up the wounded and dead and returned to an embankment that rose several feet above the far side of the meadow.

By my estimate, fifty Indians spread out along the embankment, about a hundred yards away. Behind them foothills rose to the snowcapped peaks in the distance. The rising sun revealed the painted faces and bodies of the assemblage. They were close enough I could tell most were armed with bows and arrows.

I soon identified an old antagonist. Running Bear, the Arapaho chief, raised his feathered spear and stabbed it forward. The yelling warriors surged down the slope toward us.

"Hold your fire!" the sergeant shouted. He walked seemingly unafraid behind his skirmish line calming the recruits, many of whom were confronting Indians for the first time.

Robert Lee Murphy

"Fire!" the sergeant yelled. "Give 'em hell!"

The skirmish line of reclining and kneeling soldiers discharged a volley. A few warriors fell, but most shots missed their mark.

The Indians' charge abruptly came to a halt as the cavalrymen unleased a second and a third volley at them. The Indians obviously assumed they faced Springfield single-shot rifles, and the soldiers would have to pause to reload. The hostiles hadn't expected the rapid fire from the Spencer carbines.

The Arapahos regrouped at the embankment. If the untrained recruits had better aim, more of the savages would have fallen. The Indians' ponies pranced in circles while warriors yelled and shook bows above their heads.

A white man dressed in buckskin rode up beside Running Bear. Duggan Maguire rose in his stirrups and shouted. "Bonnet! I'm going to get that payroll and put it to a better use! Long live the Confederacy!"

Running Bear, Maguire, and the attacking Indians whirled and raced away.

316

Chapter 41

After paying the troops at Fort C. F. Smith, we returned to Fort Phil Kearny late on Sunday, November 18. We encountered no Indians after the fight at Goose Creek.

On the return journey, Major Bonnet had deliberated about Duggan Maguire riding with the Arapahos. Maguire's shouted challenge confirmed he was a member of the Knights of the Golden Circle. Rather than prospect for gold and perhaps fail, Maguire had decided to steal the army payroll.

The major was now convinced Maguire had been one of Bloody Bill Anderson's gang who had raped and murdered his wife and daughter. It explained why Maguire possessed the shamrock pendant.

After we entered Fort Phil Kearny that evening, Major Bonnet and Major Bridger reported to Colonel Carrington. The mounted infantrymen took their horses to the stable for feeding and grooming. I, with four mules to care for, volunteered to handle the horses for the two majors. Nobody offered to help me, so I drove the ambulance into the quartermaster yard and took care of the six animals.

It was dark when I finished and went past the hospital with the intent of seeing Katy. The white hospital building had been completed while I'd been gone and the big tent dismantled. A hospital steward told me Katy had gone to console Mrs. Horton. Earlier in the day, the pet antelope, Star, had mistaken a bucket of white paint for milk, drank it, and died. The steward, with a wry grin, said the hospital's patients had enjoyed fresh meat for supper. That would not put Katy in a good mood. I decided to wait until tomorrow to see her.

During breakfast the next morning at the teamsters' mess, I ate with the paymaster clerk who'd stood in for me as quartermaster clerk during my absence. He had recovered from his bout of ague and would drive Major Bonnet's ambulance to Fort Laramie. He said the major planned to depart midmorning with a train of empty wagons making a trip back to Fort Leavenworth. The muleskinners would provide adequate protection for the paymaster on his trip south since the pay chests were empty.

When I reached my desk in the quartermaster warehouse, I stared at the piles of paperwork and realized my substitute had simply arranged invoices and requisitions in stacks. He'd made no entries in the ledgers. I found my ink bottle and pen and sat down to face the unfinished work.

As had become his practice lately, Captain Brown strolled into the warehouse late. Lieutenant Bisbee accompanied him. My boss raised a hand to acknowledge my presence before the two officers disappeared into the office behind a closed door. My pen remained poised over the open ledger while my attention stayed glued to their loud conversation.

"Stop complaining about 'Bully 38,' William," Captain Brown said.

"Baldy," Lieutenant Bisbee said, "it's just another example of how weak Carrington is."

"Well, the colonel never served in the line. He doesn't know sergeants maintain discipline in the ranks by beating the shit out of enlisted men from time to time."

What was "Bully 38"? That was a new term to me.

"I know you're right, Fred. But it galls me that the order is in my handwriting."

"What'd you expect, William?" Captain Brown asked. "When Adair resigned and Carrington made you adjutant, writing orders is part of the job."

"Still," Lieutenant Bisbee continued, "the message conveyed in General Order Number 38 is directed squarely at me. I wrote my own reprimand!"

"Well," Captain Brown said, "what about Colonel Carrington's reprimand? The mail that arrived the next day must have provided some vindication for you."

"Some," Bisbee said. "General Cooke's telegram threatening him with a court-martial if our reports didn't reach Omaha faster really upset the colonel. I stood across the desk after handing him the message. I couldn't keep the grin off my face."

"I understand Carrington wasn't chagrined for long though," Brown said.

"Just a few minutes. There was a second telegram telling him to disregard the prior instructions since they'd found the reports. Too bad that second courier from Fort Laramie caught up to the first one at Bridger's Ferry. If that second telegram had been delayed until the next mail courier, Carrington would have sweated for days about the threat of a court-martial. That would've been fun to watch."

Captain Brown chuckled. "Get out of here, Bisbee. I've got work to do. I can't sit around listening to you complain all morning."

I had to learn more about what happened while I was gone. Katy would have all the gossip.

Knowing the paymaster planned to depart at midmorning, I asked Captain Brown if I could have a few minutes to say goodbye to Major Bonnet. He consented.

First, I headed for the hospital. Katy came outside to join me at the front entrance.

"What's this 'Bully 38' thing?" I asked.

"I was walking to church Sunday morning with Fannie Grummond," Katy said, "when it happened. Right in front of all the ladies, the children, and of course, Colonel Carrington."

"*What* happened, Katy?" I prodded. "Don't just tell me *it* happened."

"Lieutenant Bisbee's Company E was performing close-order drill on the parade ground. Sergeant Garrett was shouting orders to his men, but Private Burke turned the wrong way. Before you knew it, the sergeant knocked the private down, cursed him repeatedly, and continued to beat him."

"What happened next?"

"Nothing. Nobody did anything. Lieutenant Bisbee stood to the side of the formation with Captain Fetterman. They just watched."

"What'd the colonel do?"

"He hurried us all along to the chapel. After the services, Colonel Carrington issued the general order admonishing the officers and sergeants about the evils of swearing and fighting. I think he was particularly upset that the wives and the children had witnessed everything."

"Nobody was confined to the guardhouse?" I asked.

"Not that I heard," she answered.

"I saw similar things during the war, and I never knew any sergeant being punished for enforcing *discipline.*"

"After the order was posted," Katy said, "the men called it 'Bully 38.' "

At that moment, Major Bonnet joined us. "Sorry to intrude," he said. "I wanted to ask Miss O'Toole if she would like to return to Fort Laramie with us."

"Oh, Major," Katy said, "thank you for asking, but I've decided to stay."

"You still thinking of going on to Montana?" he asked.

"Perhaps." She glanced at me before turning to the paymaster.

"For the time being, I can help here. Mrs. Grummond, and the other ladies, need assistance. I can continue to lend a hand at the hospital. With winter approaching, the men will encounter more ailments."

"It's the approach of winter that concerns me," Major Bonnet said. "Winters here in Dakota Territory are brutal. You may get snowed in for days, and you won't have a chance to depart."

"I've thought about that, Major," Katy continued. "I'll stay, just the same."

"Very well. I'll say goodbye, for now. I'll see you both in a couple of months when I return with the next payroll . . . weather permitting." He laughed.

The major extended a hand, and I clasped his firm grip.

"Thanks, Zach," he said. "You were a big help. I appreciate it."

"My pleasure, Major."

He tipped his slouch hat to Katy, bowed slightly, and limped back across the parade ground to the headquarters building, where his ambulance and horse awaited.

"You're sure about staying?" I asked Katy.

"No. I'm not *sure.*"

Judge Kinney departed with Major Bonnet. No one understood why the judge decided to leave his position as sutler. The judge seemed to hold a grudge against me. He treated me indifferently whenever I was in the store. Perhaps he thought he could have sold the Colt for more money than his predecessor had charged me. His absence, however, made it more pleasant for me to visit the store to enjoy my occasional sarsaparilla.

It was during such a visit on the evening of November 26 that I overheard the latest in the ongoing argument between the officers and Colonel Carrington.

"Damn it, Fred," Captain Fetterman said, "why didn't you

321

tell me we were that short on horses?"

"I thought everyone knew we only had ninety-two horses," Captain Brown replied. "And that half of them aren't fit to ride."

"Well, I didn't know," Fetterman continued. "Otherwise, I would not have gone to Carrington with a plan to lead a raid along the Tongue River."

"I thought it was a good plan," Lieutenant Grummond said. "Why don't we just reduce the number of men to match the horses that are available and go anyway."

"What plan?" Lieutenant Link asked.

"I proposed," Captain Fetterman said, "that, in order to comply with General Cooke's latest telegram directing the Eighteenth to strike the hostiles by surprise in their winter camps, I would lead fifty soldiers and fifty civilians on a raid."

"A hundred men could easily wreak havoc with the Sioux camps," Lieutenant Bisbee said. "But it's obvious Carrington isn't going to move against the savages."

"Hell," Captain Fetterman said. "With eighty men I could whip all the Sioux."

The next morning, November 27, the last planned courier for the winter departed to carry mail and dispatches to Fort C. F. Smith.

Katy and I waited in front of the headquarters building with Major Bridger. He would serve as guide for Lieutenant Horatio Bingham and twenty-four cavalrymen. The mounted men were drawn up in formation in the road waiting for the lieutenant to receive his final instructions from the colonel.

"This is your last chance to get partway to Virginia City," I said to Katy in a teasing way. We'd discussed her plans the evening before, and she'd decided not to leave Fort Phil Kearny until spring.

She jabbed me in the ribs with an elbow. "Hush!" She chuckled. "Don't tempt me."

Lieutenant Bingham came out of the headquarters building with Colonel Carrington. Major Bridger mounted his flea-bitten old mare, and the lieutenant climbed aboard his spirited horse. Lieutenant Bingham signaled the advance. "Column of twos. Forward, *Ho!*"

As they swung past us, Major Bridger waved goodbye. "See you in the spring." He'd been ordered to remain at Fort C. F. Smith through the winter to serve as liaison with the Crow Indians.

Colonel Carrington turned our way after the cavalry exited the main gate. "I'm glad you've decided to remain, Miss O'Toole," he said. "Fort Smith is not suitable for a single female. It's less than half the size of Fort Phil Kearny. There's no doctor, no sutler, no families. It's not the place to get stuck for the winter. Besides, we're glad to have your help here."

CHAPTER 42

I'd just finished my noon meal at the teamsters' mess on Thursday, December 6, when a bugler blew "Boots and Saddles." Sergeants shouted orders while soldiers assembled on the parade ground with their horses.

I hurried to the quartermaster warehouse, where I encountered one of Colonel Carrington's orderlies exiting Captain Brown's office.

"Wakefield!" the captain shouted upon seeing me return to my desk.

"Yes, sir?"

"Find me a horse." The captain buckled on his sword belt and checked the loads in his pistols. "Pilot Hill pickets report the wood train is under attack four miles out. They repeated the signal five times, indicating a large war party. They also signaled Indians on Lodge Trail Ridge, two miles to the north. Colonel Carrington is assembling men for pursuit of the savages. That orderly brought instructions for me to go to Pilot Hill to verify the signals. I need a horse, quickly."

After Captain Brown and two infantrymen rode off toward Pilot Hill, I took his binoculars to the southeast bastion. There I found three soldiers loading a howitzer. I nodded and stepped out of their way. From an isolated corner of the retaining wall, I had a good view of the parade ground. I turned my jacket collar up, thankful I'd brought my gloves.

Captain Fetterman sat mounted in front of seventeen foot

soldiers from Company A, Eighteenth Infantry, mounted on horses. Drawn up next to Fetterman was Second Lieutenant Horatio Bingham with thirty troopers of Company C, Second Cavalry. Lieutenant Bingham had returned from Fort C. F. Smith with his detachment four days ago after setting a record seven-day round trip. Next to the cavalry, Second Lieutenant George Grummond headed twenty-one mounted infantrymen from Company C, Eighteenth Infantry. Three orderlies sat their horses in front of the headquarters building. One of them held the reins of Colonel Carrington's thoroughbred.

Saddle leather squeaked, bridle chains jangled, sword scabbards clanked, carbines on shoulder slings rattled, and horses stamped and snorted. The white mist of men's and beasts' breaths was blown away rapidly by the frigid wind coming off the Big Horn Mountains. Beards reflected specks of ice when sunlight broke momentarily though the thick cloud cover.

Colonel Carrington mounted and faced the assembled troops. "Men!" he exclaimed. "You've been issued thirty rounds of ammunition in addition to your normal load of twenty. We're dividing our force today into two wings to execute a pincer movement to entrap the enemy. Captain Fetterman commands the left wing. His and Lieutenant Bingham's men will relieve the wood train and drive the savages away. Lieutenant Grummond's men will go with me over Lodge Trail Ridge and down into Peno Valley, where we'll take up a blocking position. Lieutenant Wands will ride with me. Move out!"

The columns passed through the main gate at a trot. Beyond the fort's walls they broke into a canter. The two wings divided, Fetterman's turned west, and Carrington's headed north.

Lieutenant Wands struggled on the parade ground to control an unruly horse. He finally gave up and headed back to the stables. Wands's Henry rifle would provide Colonel Carrington with the most powerful weapon in either wing. A few minutes later, Wands trotted to the front gate on a different horse. When he asked the gate sentry for directions, the sentry waved a hand toward the northeast corner of the stockade. The sentry was stationed inside the gate and may not have observed that the two columns had divided later.

From my vantage point, I watched Lieutenant Wands swing around the end of the fort and head west. Colonel Carrington had gone north.

Below me the two infantrymen who'd accompanied Captain Brown to Pilot Hill rode back into the fort. The captain wasn't with them.

I pointed the binoculars to the west and focused on Captain Brown urging his horse through the deep grass of the meadow. He was riding to intersect Fetterman's column advancing west on the Sullivant Hills road. The quartermaster continued to ignore demands from Fort Laramie to report for his new assignment. In the sutler's store, after he'd consumed more whiskey than prudent, he bragged about his plan to collect Red Cloud's scalp.

I turned the binoculars north and refocused on Colonel Carrington leading his wing toward the ford at Big Piney Creek. A flash of light burst into the binocular lenses. I squeezed my eyes shut to block out the momentary blindness, then shifted my view up to Lodge Trail Ridge above Big Piney Creek. A dozen Indians came into view on the ridge. A red blanket waved above the head of one, then a flash of light shot out from another. They were signaling the wood train attackers with blankets and mirrors.

Captain Brown's Jumelle Marine field glasses were too heavy to hold steady for long by hand, so I rested them on the top rail of the retaining wall. I adjusted the focus and studied the Indians atop Lodge Trail Ridge. One of the riders wore a feathered headdress that flowed over the tail of his pony. Red

Cloud? Major Bridger said Red Cloud coordinated many of the attacks directed against the fort. I'd seen this famous Sioux once before when he'd stormed out of the peace conference at Fort Laramie in June. I remembered he stood taller than his companions. The Indian on whom I now concentrated sat taller in the saddle than those around him.

The Indian sitting next in line was Arapaho Chief Running Bear, easily identified because the feathers of his headdress stood straight up. Dressed in buckskins and wearing a slouch hat, Duggan Maguire sat behind Running Bear.

I swung the field glasses down to Big Piney Creek as Colonel Carrington's party approached the ford. The colonel led his detachment to the creek, where he encouraged his thoroughbred to plunge into the ice-covered stream. The horse shied momentarily, then jumped forward. His forehooves struck the glazed surface, and shards of ice flew into the air. The animal's forelegs penetrated the frozen covering and plunged into the water. Carrington pitched forward over his mount's neck, slammed through the cracked ice, and sank. He immediately rose, standing knee deep in the stream. Water dripped from the brim of his hat and streamed from the sleeves of his buffalo overcoat.

Lieutenant Grummond rode to the edge of the creek and motioned repeatedly toward the fort. The lieutenant was apparently trying to convince the colonel to return to the dryness of headquarters. Colonel Carrington shook his head, pointed up the Bozeman Trail, and swung into his saddle.

Carrington's horse splashed on across the creek, breaking additional ice as he went, and surged up the far bank. The colonel motioned for the soldiers to follow him—which they did, except for Lieutenant Grummond.

The lieutenant whirled his horse in a couple of circles and waved a hand to indicate he wasn't going to cross there. He put spurs to his mount and galloped up the near side of the creek, leaving his mounted infantrymen with the colonel on the far bank. Did Grummond think his horse incapable of fording the stream there?

Colonel Carrington waved his troops forward. They climbed up the south end of Lodge Trail Ridge on the Montana Road heading north. The Indians who'd been signaling from there earlier were gone.

I turned the binoculars toward the mountains and watched Fetterman's men chase the Indians away from the wood train and pursue them up and over the Sullivant Hills. Captain Fetterman and Lieutenant Bingham led the mounted soldiers up the slope, while Captain Brown and Lieutenant Wands brought up the rear. The wood train unwound its circle and proceeded toward the pineries.

With nothing further to see, I waved goodbye to the soldiers manning the howitzer and returned to the quartermaster warehouse and some welcome warmth.

Midafternoon, a little more than two hours after the troops had departed, a shout from the main gate's sentry brought me hustling out of the warehouse. A messenger galloped through the gate on a lathered horse. His mount skidded to a stop at the headquarters building. The rider dismounted and disappeared inside. Shortly thereafter, Captain Ten Eyck hurried out shouting instructions to an orderly to summon Captain Powell.

Ten Eyck spotted me standing near the main gate. "Wakefield!" he shouted. "Get an ambulance. Stop by the hospital and pick up a doctor. I'll have one waiting for you. Report here to join the relief column."

What had gone wrong? I raced into the quartermaster yard and harnessed the Bible mules to an ambulance. When I drove up to the new hospital building, Assistant Surgeon C. M. Hines waited there with his medical bag. He climbed up and sat next to me.

"What's happening?" the doctor asked.

"Captain Ten Eyck ordered me to get an ambulance, pick you up, and get ready to follow a relief party somewhere."

At the headquarters building, Captain Ten Eyck paced back and forth in front of an assorted group of forty mounted men assembled there in a haphazard fashion.

An orderly ran directly across the parade ground from the direction of the officers' quarters. "He refuses to go, sir," the orderly shouted.

"What?" Captain Ten Eyck stopped walking and shook a sheet of paper he held in his hand. "Colonel Carrington specifically requested Captain Powell to lead the relief party."

The orderly halted in front of the captain, came to attention, and saluted. "Begging the captain's pardon, sir, but Captain Powell says he's not able to go. He didn't give any reason."

Captain Ten Eyck slapped the paper against his thigh. "Go fetch Lieutenant Arnold."

The orderly saluted and dashed back across the parade ground.

Ten minutes later, First Lieutenant Wilbur Arnold trotted up on a horse and saluted Captain Ten Eyck. Arnold, who'd been breveted a captain during the Civil War, had only reported for duty at Fort Phil Kearny four days ago. This would be his first encounter with Indians.

Ten Eyck issued brief orders, and Arnold motioned the column forward. The messenger who'd brought the instructions from Colonel Carrington led the way on a fresh horse. I pulled the ambulance in behind the mounted men.

Thirty minutes later, we descended the steep slope of the Bozeman Trail that took us down into Peno Valley. Soldiers were spread out in a circular skirmish pattern along the far, west bank of Peno Creek. In the center of this semicircle, a dozen soldiers held the reins of four horses each—standard practice for dismounted units.

We'd heard firing before we came in sight of Peno Creek. It'd diminished in volume as we drew closer. The Indians undoubtedly saw we were bringing additional fighting men, and they'd broken off their attack.

Colonel Carrington motioned us to come ahead to where he, Captain Fetterman, Captain Brown, and Lieutenant Wands stood near the horse-holders. Off to one side, Lieutenant Grummond held the reins of his own horse.

We splashed across narrow Peno Creek and halted inside the perimeter of defenders.

Lieutenant Arnold saluted the colonel. "Sir, the relief party as requested."

"Where's Captain Powell?" Colonel Carrington asked.

"I don't know, sir," the lieutenant answered. "Captain Ten Eyck ordered me to bring you this relief force and an ambulance."

"Very good," Colonel Carrington said. He looked at Surgeon Hines where we sat on the ambulance seat. "We've got wounded, Doctor. Please look after them. Sergeant Bowers is in bad shape. The savages split his skull with a tomahawk. We also have a dead man, Lieutenant Bingham, a half mile away. I'll take the ambulance and retrieve the lieutenant's body."

The doctor climbed down with his bag and hurried to where three men sat next to four others who lay stretched out on the ground. Dried, black blood streaked their disheveled uniforms.

"Mr. Wakefield," Colonel Carrington said, "follow me with the ambulance around that rock outcropping at the bend on the right side of the creek there." He pointed north along Peno Creek's east bank.

I followed the colonel and ten mounted men. After recrossing the creek and maneuvering the ambulance around the rock outcropping, the colonel ordered us to halt. What I saw forced me to swallow bile that surged into my throat.

Lieutenant Bingham's body lay slumped face down over an old stump. His naked back resembled a porcupine. Dozens of arrows protruded from his white body. Puddles of dark blood lay at the ends of his outstretched hands and feet.

The colonel detailed two men to dismount and prepare the body for removal. He directed the others to form a mounted defense around the site.

The two designated men set about pulling arrows from the lieutenant's back. No further bleeding occurred as they did so. He'd already bled out. Where the arrows were stubborn of removal, the soldiers broke off the shafts.

I took a stretcher and a blanket from the ambulance and placed the items near the stump.

When the men finished with the arrows, they lifted the body, wrapped it in the blanket, and laid it on the stretcher.

"Colonel," said the older private who'd worked on the body, "we removed fifty arrows in total. I served on the frontier before the war, sir, and I never seen that many in one man afore."

Colonel Carrington nodded.

"His ring finger is missing, Colonel," the younger of the two men said. "The savages must have wanted his ring badly."

I helped the two men lift the lieutenant's body into the ambulance and place it in the upper stretcher position above the bench I'd left in place beneath it. One side of the upper stretcher attached to brackets on the frame of the ambulance while the inside was supported on metal rods fitted into slots in the floor. The bench on the opposite side would provide a space for wounded to sit. It was cramped but useable.

Colonel Carrington led the detachment and my ambulance

back to the circle of skirmishers beside Peno Creek. Here, we laid wounded Sergeant Gideon Bowers on the bench beneath Lieutenant Bingham's body. I tucked a blanket around the sergeant's torso.

"How is Sergeant Bowers, Doctor?" Colonel Carrington asked.

Surgeon Hines shook his head. "I can't do anything for him, sir. The tomahawk blow cleaved his skull clear through to the brain. I forced laudanum between his lips. Hopefully, that will ease his pain."

"Make him as comfortable as you can," the colonel said. He glanced at the overcast sky. "We need to start back. It'll be dark before we get there—and much colder."

Doctor Hines helped the two most gravely wounded men, Sergeant Aldridge and Corporal Kelley, both of the Second Cavalry, climb into the ambulance. They sat on the bench opposite Sergeant Bowers.

The four privates who were less severely wounded were lifted onto horses behind other riders. The command was short three horses that'd been killed. Another five horses had to be led because they were wounded too badly to carry a man. In addition to the wounded soldiers, the men who no longer had their own mounts also doubled up for the return ride.

The colonel detailed a half-dozen men to serve as flankers, then he ordered the formation forward by columns of twos. Captain Brown motioned me to pull the ambulance in behind the last of Captain Fetterman's men. Lieutenant Grummond and his troops fell in behind the ambulance. We were thus positioned in the middle of the column.

Surgeon Hines sat between the two wounded cavalrymen. The lowered stretcher and the iron rods supporting it limited the doctor's ability to clean and dress the wounds of the injured.

I drove the ambulance as carefully as I could, but I didn't

have much choice about where the wheels went. Once they dropped into the ruts that'd been created by hundreds of covered wagons, that's where they stayed. The weight of the ambulance forced us to continue to roll in the ruts.

"What happened out there?" the doctor asked the two wounded men. "How'd the lieutenant get killed?"

"Captain Fetterman led us down the north side of the Sullivant Hills pursuing the Indians we'd chased away from the wood train," Sergeant Aldridge said. "When we reached the upper forks of Peno Creek we were surrounded by at least a hundred Indians."

"More than a hundred," Corporal Kelley added. "They came out of the ravines on all sides. I never seen so many savages."

"We were struggling down a steep slope," Aldridge continued, "and Lieutenant Wands's horse fell and slid down the slope with him toward the creek. We had to shoot fast to hold off the rascals long enough for the lieutenant to remount and climb back up the hill."

The ambulance bounced upward. Sergeant Aldridge groaned loudly.

"Sorry, Sergeant," Doctor Hines said. "I'm almost finished with this bandage. Didn't mean to hurt you."

"Oh, it don't hurt that much, Doc."

"Wakefield," the doctor called to me, "can't you keep this ambulance steady?"

"Sorry, Doctor. There was a big rock in the middle of the rut, and I couldn't avoid it."

"What happened next, Sarge?" the doctor asked.

"Captain Fetterman organized us into a horseshoe formation with the creek on the open side. He ordered us to dismount, but suddenly, Lieutenant Bingham took off on horseback racing for the Bozeman Trail, which was on the ridge above us to the east. Half the lieutenant's men, those who hadn't dismounted yet, went with him. I was in the process of remounting to follow the lieutenant . . . he was my commander, after all . . . when Captain Fetterman, Captain Brown, and Lieutenant Wands pointed their weapons at me and the others and ordered us to stand down or they would shoot us. I stood down."

"I did follow Lieutenant Bingham," Corporal Kelley said. "I thought he was leading us back to the fort. Then, ahead of us, on the ridge, coming down the road, I saw Colonel Carrington and his men. I thought then we were heading over to join the colonel, but Lieutenant Bingham turned his horse back the way we'd come and motioned for everybody to follow."

"Did they?" asked the doctor.

"Lieutenant Grummond broke away from Colonel Carrington and shouted for his men to follow. Only a couple did. I raced after the two lieutenants, thinking that's what I was supposed to do. In the end, only five of us went with the lieutenants. We chased a half-dozen warriors who led us around a bend in the creek and deep into a rocky formation. That's when we were flanked by dozens of the savages who came at us from both sides. Lieutenant Bingham fired at them with both his revolvers, and I saw him throw one away."

"We didn't find any weapons with Lieutenant Bingham's body, Doc." I turned briefly to speak into the rear of the ambulance. "The savages would have them by now."

"Undoubtedly," he responded. "Go on, men. What happened when you got surrounded?"

"I had one of the Spencers," Corporal Kelley continued, "so I kept up a steady fire. The two men with us from Lieutenant Grummond's command had those damned single-shot Springfields. Once they fired, they were finished. The warriors knowed them two were in trouble, 'cause they tried to lasso them by dropping their strung bows over the boys' necks. Them two boys were lucky to get away, I tell you."

334

"How're they doing, Doc?" a loud voice called from behind us.

I looked over my shoulder and saw that Lieutenant Grummond had ridden up to the rear of the ambulance and was addressing Doctor Hines.

"These two will be all right." The doctor indicated the men sitting on either side of him. "Sergeant Bowers won't make it."

"The sergeant was a brave man today," Lieutenant Grummond said. "He rode beside me part way."

"Why did so few of you go after the Indians?" the surgeon asked.

"I thought all my men were right behind me," the lieutenant answered. "But that damned Carrington had Bugler Metzger sound recall, and most of them halted."

Adolf Metzger served as the Second Cavalry's bugler. He was a little, fun-loving German fellow who could blow his horn louder than any of the players in the regimental band.

"Did you see Lieutenant Bingham get killed?" the doctor asked. "Do you know he had fifty arrows in his body?"

"I saw him fall from his horse, but I didn't see anything after that. I yelled at the other men to follow me, and we turned and headed back. We had to cut our way out. At least I did. I'd left the fort without my revolver."

"Corporal Kelley tells me Lieutenant Bingham had two revolvers," the doctor said. "But he threw one away."

"I saw that," Lieutenant Grummond said. "My guess is he didn't have ammunition for the empty one."

"How is it they got Lieutenant Bingham," the surgeon asked, "and not the rest of you?"

"Bingham and Bowers had ridden ahead," Lieutenant Grummond said. "After we were surrounded, Bingham got cut off. Bowers managed to get turned around and rode with me for a short distance, but his horse tuckered out. He fell behind, and I

335

couldn't stop to help. The bastards were closing in on me from both sides. I just closed my eyes and slashed left and right with my saber to fend off the sons of bitches. I heard a *click* every time my saber cleaved a skull."

"You're fortunate, Lieutenant," Doctor Hines said. "We could have lost you, too."

"It didn't have to end this way. That damned Carrington is responsible. He's either a fool or a coward to allow his men to be cut to pieces without offering to help. I yelled at him to come down to our aid, but he just sat on his horse up on the road. By God, Doc, I tell you that's one hell of a way to treat your soldiers."

Lieutenant Grummond reined in his horse, and the ambulance pulled away from him. I'd allowed the mules to follow the horses in front of them and stay to the road while I'd kept my concentration focused on the conversation between the surgeon and Lieutenant Grummond.

A choking, ragged cough came from Sergeant Bowers. I looked at Surgeon Hines, who shook his head. The doctor pulled the blanket up over the sergeant's face.

CHAPTER 43

Early Sunday morning, December 9, three days after I'd driven the ambulance that'd borne the bodies of Lieutenant Bingham and Sergeant Bowers back from Peno Valley, I helped load their coffins into an ambulance. Two tin-lined, pine-board caskets were shoved into the bed of the ambulance side by side. Chaplain White climbed up next to me. This sharing an ambulance seat with the preacher was occurring too frequently.

The chaplain signaled to Bandmaster Peter Damme we were ready. Sergeant Damme shoved his ceremonial baton forward, retracted it to his chin, then extended it quickly again. The regimental band stepped off at the slow march pace without verbal command. Muffled drums thumped out a rhythmic cadence, and the band led the way to the expanding cemetery at the foot of Pilot Hill. Colonel Carrington and the officers marched between the band and the ambulance. Following us, the enlisted men of Company C, Second Cavalry, and Company E, Eighteenth Infantry, joined the procession.

At the cemetery, the band played "Nearer My God to Thee" while the troops aligned themselves in company formation. Chaplain White recited the traditional military funeral service over the open coffins. Lieutenant Grummond conducted Masonic Order honors for Lieutenant Bingham. Before the lids were nailed closed, Captain Brown placed his personal Army of the Cumberland service medal on the chest of Sergeant Bowers. Brown, Bisbee, Powell, Fetterman, and other veterans of the Eighteenth had soldiered through the war with Bowers.

After the caskets were lowered into the graves, details of enlisted men shoveled frozen earth over the coffins, then piled rocks atop the mounds to fend off wolves.

Later that morning, I walked beside a canvas-covered, blue army wagon that a teamster drove out of the quartermaster yard. We took the road around the south end of the parade ground and proceeded to the headquarters building. A mail escort of a corporal and eight privates from the cavalry company sat there on horseback awaiting our arrival.

The day before, carpenters had double-boarded the floor and sides of this wagon, installed a hinged, wooden door at the rear, and stretched a double canvas cover over the bows. The mechanics had fabricated a small sheet-iron stove and extended a smoke vent through the canvas cover. While that work was progressing, I'd gone to a sawmill and brought back a bushel basket full of pine knots to serve as fuel. Near sundown, members of Company E had packed the personal belongings of the Bisbee family into the wagon, leaving open a central living space next to the stove.

The teamster halted the wagon next to the mail escort. Colonel Carrington and newly promoted Captain William Bisbee came out of headquarters. The captain shook hands with the other officers who'd gathered nearby. Few words were spoken.

Bisbee clasped the hand of Lieutenant Wilbur Arnold longer than any other. "Lieutenant," Captain Bisbee said, "I gladly turn over the duties of adjutant to you, and I wish you good luck under the circumstances."

"I'll do my best, Captain," Lieutenant Arnold said.

"Is your wife ready?" Colonel Carrington asked Bisbee.

No sooner had he asked the question than Lucy Bisbee came

out of her quarters and walked directly across the parade ground in contravention of orders not to do so. She held her two-year-old son, Gene, by the hand. Both were bundled warmly in buffalo coats against the cold days ahead of them. An enlisted man walked behind her carrying a carpetbag.

Frances Grummond and Katy O'Toole also accompanied Lucy Bisbee. Perhaps it was the chill wind blowing down from the mountains that kept Mrs. Carrington and Mrs. Horton indoors.

Mrs. Bisbee approached the rear of the wagon along with Katy and Fannie.

"What am I to do with that little black cow, Lucy?" Fannie asked.

"You're going to feed its milk to that baby of yours," Lucy Bisbee said.

"I know that," Fannie continued, "what I mean is, how do I get the milk out of it?"

"You don't know how to milk a cow?" Mrs. Bisbee laughed.

"Heavens, no," Fannie said. "I assume the slaves did the milking. Milk came to me in a pitcher."

"We'll find a soldier who can milk the cow," Katy interjected. "Fannie can share the milk with him in return for his effort."

"Good idea, Katy," Lucy Bisbee said.

"It's time, Lucy," Captain Bisbee said.

I'd already kindled a fire in the stove to warm the interior of the wagon. I opened the door, and the soldier placed the carpetbag in the rear. Captain Bisbee lifted his son and set him in the specially winterized wagon. He nodded at me for my assistance.

The three women embraced. "I'll miss you both," Lucy Bisbee said. "Are you absolutely certain you won't come with us, Katy?"

"I'm certain. I'll stay and help Fannie with her baby when it comes. There are lots of things besides milking a cow that Mrs. Grummond doesn't know how to do."

The three ladies laughed.

Captain Bisbee helped his wife into the rear of the wagon, and I latched the door. The captain mounted his horse. Once settled in the saddle, Bisbee saluted Colonel Carrington without saying anything and motioned for the mail escort to follow him and the wagon out the front gate.

Captain Bisbee, well known for not being an admirer of Colonel Carrington, had been reassigned to Omaha to serve as aide-de-camp to General Philip St. George Cooke.

Late that afternoon, Captain Fetterman joined Captain Brown in the warehouse office. He didn't bother closing the door. The officers knew their voices carried well through the flimsy walls.

"I told Colonel Carrington," Captain Fetterman said, "this Indian war has almost become hand-to-hand fighting. It will require the utmost caution."

"What!" Captain Brown exclaimed. "Are you siding with the colonel now?"

"No. Just stating the facts. I've begun drilling the men of Company A in infantry tactics and weapons firing. They are ill prepared to respond rapidly to orders."

"The whole battalion's ill prepared, William," Brown said. "I hate to sound sympathetic, but Carrington now has only six officers for six companies. He has no cavalry-trained officer. He's assigned Captain Powell to command the cavalry. That bunch of recruits don't know anything about fighting mounted. They're lucky to stay in the saddle. Powell's the best choice, I suppose, since he fought with dragoons before the war."

"You're probably right, Baldy," Fetterman said. "Grummond will do all right with the mounted infantry. He had command

340

experience during the war, even though it was with foot soldiers."

"The horses may be suffering more than the men," Brown said. "This cold weather on short rations does not bode well. We know what happened to poor Sergeant Bowers when his horse tuckered out."

"With winter on us," Captain Fetterman said, "the Indians' ponies will suffer, too. Even Major Bridger says the Indians stand down during the winter when snow covers the ground and there won't be any grass. That's when we'll have the opportunity to wipe them out."

"Now you're talking. Every time the mail comes, it contains another demand for me to report to Fort Laramie. I don't want to leave here until I have Red Cloud's scalp."

"You'll get a chance soon," Fetterman said. "Be ready, Frederick."

CHAPTER 44

Wednesday morning, December 19, the wood train departed the fort promptly at 9:00 a.m. Less than an hour later, pickets on Pilot Hill signaled the train was under attack. A bugler blew "Boots and Saddles," and the clamor of men retrieving horses that had been saddled since dawn indicated a relief party was rapidly assembling.

"Wakefield," Captain Brown called as he hurried into the warehouse. "Get an ambulance and pick up Assistant Surgeon Hines. The colonel's sending a detachment out under Captain Powell's command, and he wants an ambulance to go along."

"Yes, sir." I gathered up my jacket and slouch hat.

I'd taken to keeping my holster and revolver with me all the time. While I was buckling my belt around my waist, the captain asked, "How are the records progressing?"

"They'll be in good enough shape by the end of the year for you to turn over the account to someone else."

"Humph." He snorted. "That's too bad. I'm in no hurry to report to Fort Laramie. It'll be dull sitting there surrounded by the Laramie Loafers."

By the time I'd rounded up the Bible mules, hitched them to the ambulance, and picked up Surgeon Hines at the hospital, the mounted men had formed up on the parade ground. I drove to the headquarters building.

Colonel Carrington came out and exchanged salutes with Captain Powell, who sat mounted in front of two dozen troop-

342

ers of Company C, Second Cavalry. Drawn up nearby, Lieutenant Grummond had the mounted infantry of Company C, Eighteenth Infantry, ready. These two units would comprise the relief detachment.

"Captain Powell," the colonel said, "heed the lessons of our actions on the sixth. Do not pursue the Indians over Lodge Trail Ridge."

"Yes, sir."

"Lieutenant Grummond," Colonel Carrington said, "adhere to the directions of Captain Powell. Don't let me hear otherwise."

The lieutenant saluted without saying a word.

Captain Powell issued the command to advance by twos. I pulled the ambulance in behind the mounted men, and we moved out the front gate. The column advanced at a trot around the north end of the fort, where we picked up the wood road.

The captain increased the pace to a canter for the next two miles, then increased the speed again to a hand gallop. When we came within sight of the embattled wagons ahead of us, Captain Powell signaled the bugler to sound the charge.

Bugler Metzger, riding beside the guidon bearer, responded with the resounding bugle call. The troopers unhooked rifles and carbines from carrying straps and spurred their horses forward. The soldiers shouted as they charged, probably more to instill self-courage than to frighten their opponents. Lieutenant Grummond outdistanced his unit, brandishing his saber.

I whipped the mules to a faster pace, the closest thing they could come to a gallop while dragging an ambulance. We soon fell behind.

"Slow down, Zach!" Surgeon Hines shouted. He clutched the seat with both hands. "We want to be in one piece if we're needed, not scattered all across the hillside."

I hauled on the reins and stepped against the brake lever. The ambulance swayed as we bounced over the rutted road. We slowed to a trot.

The Indians wheeled their ponies away from the wagon train and dashed toward the ridge of the Sullivant Hills. The savages disappeared over the crest. Lieutenant Grummond and his mounted infantry raced up the hill in frantic pursuit.

Ahead of us, Captain Powell slowed his cavalrymen to a walk as they reached the wagon train. He shouted a command to bugler Metzger, who raised his instrument and blew "Recall."

I brought the ambulance up close to Captain Powell, where I halted. Up the slope to our right, Lieutenant Grummond raised a hand to signal his charging men to stop. He swung his horse around and waved a hand for Captain Powell and his men to come up.

Captain Powell motioned Lieutenant Grummond to come down. Grummond's head shake was noticeable even at a distance, but he signaled his unit to descend the slope.

The mounted infantry came back to where the wagon train remained circled. A half-dozen warriors reappeared on the crest of the hill. They shook lances and bows above their heads. One warrior dismounted, bent over, and flipped up his breechcloth, exposing his buttocks.

Grummond reined in next to Powell. "What's the matter, Captain? Afraid of a few Indians?" Grummond pointed to where the savages continued to shout taunts.

"Those six are decoys, Lieutenant," Captain Powell responded. "Didn't you count the hundred other warriors who disappeared over the hilltop. We have our orders not to pursue."

"Our orders were not to pursue beyond Lodge Trail Ridge," Lieutenant Grummond said. "That's the next hill over. We can trap that bunch in the valley when they cross Big Piney Creek. It's time we make an example of them."

Captain Powell shook his head. "The main party is lying in

wait for you, hoping you'll race into their midst. There's too many for us to attack. I have no intention of disobeying orders."

Captain Powell rode to the sergeant who commanded the wagon train escort and spoke briefly to him. They were too far away for me to hear the conversation, but the sergeant saluted and the captain rode back.

The wood train unwound from its corral, and the sergeant and his detachment led the wagons on toward their original destination of the pineries. We returned to the fort.

That evening it snowed. At dawn on Thursday, December 20, a bright sun shined out of a clear sky illuminating patches of white powder scattered on the ground and clinging to shrubs.

The fort had barely come to full wakefulness when once again I was ordered to get an ambulance and pick up Assistant Surgeon Hines. This morning we were to accompany Colonel Carrington, who was personally leading a special wagon train to South Piney Creek. In addition to the normal train guard of forty men, Carrington had assembled sixty infantrymen and twenty cavalrymen. This group was not in pursuit of Indians. They were a workforce for building a bridge so wood trains would not have to break through icy water to get onto Piney Island.

At the creek crossing, where I had earlier taken the officers and their ladies for a picnic, the men felled pines to serve as stringers for the bridge. The wagons Colonel Carrington led today carried loads of three-inch planks that the sawmills had cut to form the bridge's bed.

By sundown, a bridge forty-five feet long and sixteen feet wide was complete. No Indians harassed us this day.

During the last half hour of our return trip to the fort, Colonel Carrington rode beside the ambulance to inquire of Doctor Hines about the hospital's current operations.

"Since the winter season commenced," the surgeon said, "we've seen an increase in rheumatic complaints, and we've treated several cases of frostbite."

"Some of the men have tailoring experience," Colonel Carrington said. "I've put them to fabricating cold-weather clothing from buffalo hides. They've also been able to make serviceable boots. Maybe that will eliminate some of the frostbite problems. It will have to do, since Omaha has yet to fill my requisitions for winter clothing."

When we reached headquarters that evening, Captains Fetterman and Brown were waiting to talk with the colonel. Lieutenant Arnold, the adjutant, was with them.

The colonel dismounted, and the four officers stood together. Torches on either side of the door illuminated their features.

I raised the reins to snap the signal to the mules to proceed, but Doctor Hines laid a hand on my forearm motioning me to stay in place. He wanted to overhear this conversation.

Somehow, Captain Brown had hung his spurs in the buttonholes of his greatcoat. Belted around his waist he wore his two holstered revolvers.

"Colonel," Captain Brown said, "Captain Fetterman and I have a plan."

Colonel Carrington glanced to Captain Fetterman, who nodded agreement.

"Fifty of my civilian employees who have horses," Captain Brown continued, "have volunteered to join fifty veteran mounted soldiers to attack the Indians in their camps along the Tongue. Now is the time to strike, Colonel, while the savages are standing down for the winter."

"Fifty mounted soldiers?" the colonel asked.

"Yes, sir," Captain Brown replied.

"Lieutenant Arnold," the colonel said, "bring me a copy of the *Morning Report.*"

The lieutenant stepped into the building and returned with the document.

"Here." Carrington handed the report to Brown. "Notice the number of serviceable horses. Did not your office provide that number to the adjutant?"

"Yes, sir. I sent Mr. Wakefield over with the information this morning."

"And what number is on the report?"

"Forty-two, sir," Captain Brown said.

"Then," Colonel Carrington said, "pray tell me, how can I provide you and Captain Fetterman with fifty horses? Even if I had fifty serviceable horses to give, that would leave me with none for mail escort, courier service, or wood train guard."

Captain Brown glanced at Captain Fetterman, then at Colonel Carrington.

"You propose to take fifty seasoned veterans," the colonel continued. "That's almost every veteran in this outfit? That would leave me mainly with recruits."

The colonel took the *Morning Report* from Captain Brown and returned it to the adjutant.

"Gentlemen," the colonel said, "I appreciate your desire to bring the Indians to heel, but now is not the time. We've had this discussion before. Not only are we short horses, we are short men. Every company is under strength, not to mention being short officers to command them. We are still short ammunition and weapons. The armorer informs me we need at least one hundred Springfields to replace broken ones. I send requests to Omaha for solutions to these problems but get no response."

Colonel Carrington turned his attention from Captain Brown to Captain Fetterman. "Do you have anything to add to this conversation, Captain?"

Captain Fetterman shook his head. "No, sir."

Robert Lee Murphy

"Are you satisfied now, Captain Brown?" the colonel asked. Captain Brown's shoulder slump was visible even beneath his greatcoat. "It's just, sir, I must depart after Christmas. I can't postpone reporting to Fort Laramie any longer. I was hoping to have one more good fight before I go."

"Well," Colonel Carrington said, "the Indians have harassed us every day, lately. You might still get your chance, Captain."

348

Chapter 45

Friday, December 21, the winter solstice, dawned clear, dry, and cold at 7:00 a.m. The north wind kept the temperature well below freezing. The snow that had fallen two nights ago was gone except in places of perpetual shadow. Captain Brown was busy with paperwork in his office, so he sent me over to headquarters with our feeder information for the *Morning Report*.

When I entered the building, I encountered Colonel Carrington giving orders to Lieutenant Wands, the officer of the day, to delay the normal 9:00 a.m. departure of the wood train for an hour in hopes the temperature would rise.

On my way back to the quartermaster warehouse, a shout from a sentry atop the headquarters' observation platform brought Colonel Carrington and Lieutenant Wands outside. The officers hurried past me to the southeast bastion.

The carpenters had been installing a more permanent wooden-slab roof on the warehouse, and they'd left a ladder leaning against the end of the building. I climbed up the rungs to gain a view over the stockade wall.

On the bastion, the colonel and the lieutenant pointed to the northeast. A half-dozen Indians stood on Lodge Trail Ridge from where they had a clear view into the fort.

"Come out and fight, you sons of bitches!" The Indians' shouted obscenities carried clearly in the crisp northerly breeze. They yelled and gestured toward the fort for a few minutes.

Then, they wrapped themselves in blankets and sat down under a tree. When they did, they revealed a buckskin-clad figure behind them. Duggan Maguire leaned against the tree.

A three-man howitzer gun crew stood on the bastion, also. Colonel Carrington studied the intruders through field glasses, then using a pocketknife, cut the fuse on a case shot. One of the crew shoved a powder bag down the barrel, then rammed the case shot in behind it. The colonel sighted down the barrel and twisted the elevating screw three turns. He stepped back, and another soldier jammed a metal probe down the touch hole to puncture the powder bag. Next, he inserted a primer cap into the touch hole and signaled everything was ready. The colonel yanked on the lanyard that tripped the primer. The howitzer roared and lurched backward on the platform. A cloud of white smoke drifted away from the muzzle.

I followed the trajectory of the shot as it arced across the valley. It exploded in the air a dozen yards beyond the tree. The Indians looked up when the shell exploded, but they remained seated.

The gun crew went through the steps of loading another shot. The colonel adjusted the elevating screw, and the crew shifted the trail a few inches to the left. This shot flew across the valley and burst closer to the tree.

The crew went through the loading and adjusting process again. This time the shell exploded directly over the tree under which the Indians sat. Branches crashed down and fountains of dirt bounced up as two dozen lead balls blasted into the ground. The savages scampered away and disappeared over the crest of the ridge. Duggan Maguire casually walked after them.

Colonel Carrington and Lieutenant Wands descended from the bastion, and I climbed off the ladder. When I stepped from the bottom rung, the two officers passed a few feet from me. The colonel pulled a pocket watch out and checked the time.

"Lieutenant," the colonel said, "It's almost ten o'clock. I think we can get the wood train on its way."

"Yes, sir."

"Add another squad from Company E to bring the total force up to ninety."

"Yes, sir." Lieutenant Wands saluted and hurried toward the infantry barracks.

I had reached the front door of the quartermaster warehouse when a familiar voice shouted my name from the front gate. Portugee Phillips was driving a farm wagon into the fort.

"Where do you want this hay?" Portugee shouted.

"Where's your water wagon?" I asked. Portugee had recently been transporting water in barrels from Little Piney Creek for the fort's use.

"Temporary assignment today. Back on water detail tomorrow."

"All right," I replied, "follow me." I motioned past the cavalry stables.

Once within the quartermaster yard, Portugee and I worked together to pitch the dried hay from the wagon onto the existing pile.

"Boss says this is the last load before spring," Portugee said.

"That's too bad," I said. "The colonel has already reduced the hay allowance per animal from fourteen to eight pounds per day."

The command had almost two hundred mules and less than half that many horses. We only had a few head of cattle left. Grain shipments from Fort Leavenworth were few and far between. Although the colonel kept requesting additional horses, none had been delivered.

It took us thirty minutes to unload Portugee's wagon. I joined him on the seat for the drive into the main stockade. As we came abreast of the hospital, Katy was exiting the door carrying a basket of linens.

"Good morning, Portugee," she said, "it's nice to see you."

"Good morning, Miss O'Toole," Portugee said. "Whoa." He pulled on the reins to stop the wagon.

"Can we help you, Katy?" I jumped down and took the load from her hands. "Where're you going?"

"I'm taking some old sheets over to Fannie Grummond to cut up to make diapers."

"Is she due already?" Portugee asked.

"No," Katy answered. "But we have these old sheets available now."

I set the basket on the tailgate and pointed down the road along the west side of the parade ground. "Straight ahead, Portugee," I said. "The Grummonds' cottage is just beyond Colonel Carrington's house."

The commanding officer's large board and batten quarters, opposite the flagpole, dominated officers' row where all the other quarters were small log cabins. Portugee snapped the reins, and his horses moved forward. Katy and I followed the wagon to the Grummonds' residence.

We'd just pulled up to the cottage when a bugler blew "Boots and Saddles." At the headquarters building, the officer of the day gestured with the sentry atop the lookout platform.

"Wood train must be under attack," I said.

Lieutenant Wands, grasping his saber scabbard to keep it from bouncing, ran across the parade ground toward Carrington's residence.

Troops emerged from the barracks and assembled in company formation on the parade ground near the flagpole.

Lieutenant Grummond came out of his cabin followed by his wife.

"You promised, George." Frances Grummond held onto her husband's forearm.

"I promised to be careful," Lieutenant Grummond said, "I didn't promise not to go. If I'm needed, I *must* go. I'm a soldier." He pulled away from his wife and headed for the commanding officer's quarters. He nodded briefly in our direction.

Fannie realized Katy and I were standing there. "Oh," she said, "good morning." She glanced up at the driver's seat of the wagon but said nothing to Portugee. She probably didn't remember him. "Why are you here?" Fannie asked.

"I brought the old sheets I promised," Katy said.

I lifted the basket to show Fannie its contents.

Fannie grinned but watched to see where her husband went.

"He'll be fine," Katy said. "The Indians are attacking the wood train again. It happens almost every day."

Fannie's gaze was fixed on Colonel Carrington, who stood in front of his quarters with Captain Powell and Lieutenants Wands and Grummond. The colonel was emphasizing points to the officers with repeated chops of one hand against the palm of the other.

"Company, halt!" The command from behind me came from Captain Fetterman. He had marched the men of Company A into formation by the flagpole. Smaller detachments from three other companies also assembled there under the command of sergeants. Private Thomas Maddeon stood alone to one side. As armorer, he wasn't assigned to any company.

Fetterman left his company and hurried past us to join Colonel Carrington and the other officers. They were next door and close enough we could hear their heated conversation.

"I insist on taking command, Colonel!" Captain Fetterman exclaimed. "I'm senior to Captain Powell. Besides, half the infantrymen are from my company."

"I've already given instructions to Captain Powell," Colonel Carrington said.

"Then repeat them to me," Fetterman countered.

The colonel looked at each of his officers in turn, and when none of them offered any comment, he shrugged. "Very well," he said. "Captain Fetterman, your orders are to support the wood train, relieve it, and report back to me. Do not engage the Indians at the train's expense. Under no circumstance pursue them over Lodge Trail Ridge."

"Understood, sir," Fetterman said.

"Captain Powell," Colonel Carrington continued, "you will now be under Captain Fetterman's orders and command your Company C, Second Cavalry."

"I protest, sir!" Lieutenant Grummond exclaimed, snapping to attention. "I request command of the cavalry today."

"What is this?" the colonel asked. "Are you gentlemen conspiring against me? What do you say, Captain Powell?"

"I have no objection to Lieutenant Grummond commanding the cavalry."

"Lieutenant Wands," Colonel Carrington said, "what is the composition of the infantry today?"

"Sir, twenty-one from Company A, nine from Company C, six from Company E, and twelve from Company H. The armorer wants to go. There are two volunteer civilians, James Wheatley and Isaac Fisher. They each have Henry repeating rifles and want to test them."

"Very well," the colonel said. "Counting Captain Fetterman, that makes fifty infantrymen. How many cavalrymen?"

"Don't know yet, sir," Lieutenant Wands answered.

"Lieutenant Grummond," Carrington said, "get the cavalry lined up here so I can inspect them."

"Yes, sir." Grummond saluted and took off for the stables, where cavalrymen were saddling horses.

"Captain Fetterman," Carrington said. "Each of your men has thirty rounds of ammunition. That should be sufficient for relief of the wood train. Get started, now. The cavalry will catch up to your foot soldiers before you reach the train."

"Yes, sir."

Fetterman ordered the infantrymen into double time, and they headed toward the mill gate leading from the quartermaster yard to the wood road. A mangy dog ran beside the column barking incessantly.

"Lieutenant Wands." Colonel Carrington turned to the officer of the day. "Go after Captain Fetterman and repeat my instructions to not cross Lodge Trail Ridge."

The lieutenant saluted, gathered his saber to his side, and ran in pursuit of the disappearing infantry column.

The colonel turned to Captain Powell. "What time is it, Captain?"

The captain flipped open a pocket watch. "Eleven fifteen, sir."

"Katy," Fannie Grummond said, "I'm getting cold. Let's go inside."

I carried the basket of sheets for Katy. We'd only been inside a couple of minutes when Lieutenants Grummond and Wands burst in.

Fannie caught Wands's arm as he followed Grummond across the living room toward the bedroom.

"Alex," Fannie said, "tell him to avoid rash movements and not to pursue the savages." She placed a hand atop her growing pregnancy.

Grummond returned from the bedroom buckling his saber belt.

Wands repeated Fannie's pleas, to which Grummond responded, "I will not make a damned fool of myself this time."

"George," Lieutenant Wands said, "you *have* to be careful."

Grummond pecked a kiss onto his wife's cheek and raced out. Through the open door, which he'd not pulled closed, Colonel Carrington could be seen inspecting the cavalry.

"Frances," Lieutenant Wands said, "do not worry. He will be fine." The lieutenant left and hurried across the parade ground to help with the cavalry inspection.

Katy, Fannie, and I went back outside to watch. Colonel Carrington dismissed a few troopers because of faulty weapons. When a trooper fell out another stepped forward to take his place. Lieutenant Grummond had assembled twenty-seven serviceable horses in addition to his own, and the colonel intended to put a rider on each of them.

The selected troopers mounted and peeled off by twos to follow Lieutenant Grummond, who alone rode a white horse, out the main gate. Bugler Metzger and the guidon bearer rode behind the lieutenant. Most of the cavalrymen were armed with seven-round Spencer carbines. These troopers also carried a Blakeslee quick-loader cartridge box containing six extra tubes of seven rounds each. This firepower should more than make up for the limited capability of the infantry's single-shot Springfield rifle-muskets.

As the last of the horses passed through the gate at 11:30 a.m., Colonel Carrington ran across the parade ground and jumped onto the banquette beside the front gate.

"Lieutenant Grummond!" the colonel shouted. "Under no circumstance cross Lodge Trail Ridge!"

Katy stayed with Fannie to cut old sheets into diapers. I climbed onto the wagon seat next to Portugee, and he headed back the way we'd come. The noon meal at the teamsters' mess would be served in less than half an hour.

"Portugee," I said, "you may as well stay for a bite before you head out for your camp."

"Thanks. I will."

He drove the wagon through the gate into the quartermaster yard.

"Out of the way!" The shout came from behind.

Captain Brown waved as he trotted past on Calico, Jimmy Carrington's pony. "I'm going to get a scalp today, Wakefield." The short stirrups forced the captain's knees waist high. The apparition brought Ichabod Crane to mind.

I motioned for Portugee to pull the wagon to the right, and we followed the captain to the open wood gate, where we stopped. We watched Captain Brown kick the pony into a canter. Was this the first time the little pony had felt the sharp stab of spurs? The captain did not follow the road. He cut across the pastureland at an angle to intercept Captain Fetterman's infantrymen, who were running toward the wagon train at trail arms. Lieutenant Grummond's cavalry had ridden around the north end of the fort, and they were also advancing rapidly along the Sullivant Hills road in their effort to catch up to Fetterman.

"Wakefield!" That shout came from Assistant Surgeon Hines, who ran toward us from the main fort. As soon as he reached us, he bent over with his hands on his knees. He took several deep breaths before straightening up. "The colonel," he gasped, "forgot to send a surgeon with Captain Fetterman. Lieutenant Matson and one of his men are escorting me out to the wood train."

"You need an ambulance?" I asked.

"We don't have time for you to hitch one," Surgeon Hines said. "Is this wagon available?"

"Yes," Portugee put in.

"Fine," the surgeon said. "It's now an ambulance."

"Ready, Doc?" Lieutenant Matson rode up accompanied by a mounted infantryman.

"Ready," the surgeon answered.

Surgeon Hines tossed me his medical bag, and I helped him climb up. I wound up squeezed between Portugee and the surgeon. The farm wagon's seat hadn't been designed to serve as a carriage.

We followed Lieutenant Matson out the mill gate. The lieutenant signaled us to stop, pointing toward Pilot Hill. "The wood train's no longer under attack."

On the Sullivant Hills road, Captain Fetterman had reversed course with his infantrymen and had merged with Lieutenant Grummond's mounted infantry. Captain Brown had joined the group, too. All eighty-one men now headed back to the crossing of Big Piney Creek where the Bozeman Trail advanced up Lodge Trail Ridge.

"Ah," Lieutenant Matson said, "Captain Fetterman's following the same route Colonel Carrington took on the sixth to cut off the Indian retreat. The captain will succeed, where the colonel did not." The lieutenant sniggered.

"We'll follow them," Surgeon Hines said.

Lieutenant Matson and his man led the way around the north end of the fort, and we approached the ford at Big Piney Creek. Fetterman's column had broken the frozen surface when they'd crossed. Rapidly flowing water forced jagged chunks of ice to jam against the still frozen downstream side of the ford.

"Hold up!" Surgeon Hines shouted to the two riders in front of us, as they prepared to enter the ford. Lieutenant Matson and his companion halted and waited for our wagon to pull up between them at the creek's edge.

"Up there." Surgeon Hines pointed to Lodge Trail Ridge above Big Piney Creek. Dozens of mounted Indians streamed north along the Bozeman Trail.

Fetterman and his men were not to be seen. They'd already continued over the ridge to the north, and these Indians were closing in behind them.

A howitzer fired with a boom from the fort. The case shot whistled over our heads and exploded above the warriors. The savages fought to contain their ponies. A second shot immediately followed. When this shell exploded, the Indians scattered off the trail.

"Listen," Lieutenant Matson said, cupping a hand behind an ear. He sat on his horse next to the wagon beside Doctor Hines.

The crisp north wind carried the spattering sound of rifle and carbine fire from the far side of Lodge Trail Ridge. Then we heard the roar of a volley being fired.

"Yes," the lieutenant said. "Captain Fetterman's men are putting their training to fire by rank and file to good use now."

A second round of volley fire ensued.

"Look!" I pointed at the crest of Lodge Trail Ridge. The Indians who'd ridden off the trail when under howitzer fire now returned to the road and continued north, in the direction of the volley fire.

"We can't get through that many Indians to join Captain Fetterman," Surgeon Hines said. "Let's go back to the fort, before those warriors turn and come after us."

It was almost noon when we passed through the main gate. Colonel Carrington met us there. Surgeon Hines explained why he'd considered it unwise to proceed farther.

"Well . . . ," the colonel said, "probably a smart decision. I'm not concerned. Fetterman's got the largest force we've ever sent out at one time. You can hear his volley fire. I'm sure he's got everything well in hand."

An unusually heavy blast of volley fire caused us all to turn our attention to the north, even though we couldn't see anything. This volley was followed in a few seconds by another. The time delay between volleys matched that needed for soldiers to ram cartridges down the muzzles of their single-shot Springfields. Scattered, individual popping from the lighter Spencer carbines could be heard between the volleys. Repeated volleys persisted for the next couple of minutes. The ferocity of each volley diminished. Then, silence.

Colonel Carrington hurried over to the headquarters observation tower, where Lieutenant Wands and a sergeant scanned the north through field glasses.

"See anything?" the colonel shouted up to his adjutant.

"No, sir."

"Come down. Find Captain Ten Eyck and have him report to me immediately. I don't care what condition he's in."

"Yes, sir."

The colonel turned to us. "Surgeon Hines, get a real ambulance ready. I'm sending a relief party out. Lieutenant Matson, load that wagon with ammunition."

Lieutenant Matson saluted and motioned for us to follow him. The magazine lay a hundred yards ahead in the southwest quadrant of the parade ground.

When Portugee halted at the magazine, I jumped down and took off on foot for the quartermaster yard.

When I reached the road intersection at the hospital, I encountered Katy returning with an empty basket following her visit with Fannie Grummond. She clasped the basket against her side with one hand while she tucked a stray blonde curl beneath the edge of her bonnet with the other.

"What's going on, Zach?" she asked. "Why did all the firing stop?"

"Don't know. The colonel's sending out a relief party, and I'm taking an ambulance along."

"You be careful out there." Her soft blue eyes bored intently into mine for a moment. "I mean it, Zachary."

"I will." I reached out and touched the hand she had wrapped around the basket. Even though both our hands were cold, the contact felt warm.

I ran into the quartermaster yard, racing across the hard-packed ground toward the mule stables. Why hadn't I told Katy how I felt about her? She'd given me the perfect opportunity. I shook my head at my own timidity.

Chapter 46

I drove the ambulance toward the main gate and halted between the guardhouse and the quartermaster warehouse on the main road exiting the fort.

Portugee Phillips drove his wagon load of ammunition up next to me.

"How much are you carrying?" I asked.

"Three thousand rounds of Springfield," he answered, "and two cases of Spencer. That's all the carbine ammunition there was."

Acting Master of Transportation, Bill Williams, nodded to Portugee and me as he pulled a second, empty wagon up beside us. Bill hadn't gone on his normal job with the wood train this morning.

Assistant Surgeons Hines and Ould approached carrying medical bags. "Jeremiah," Hines said to Ould, "go with Williams. We'll use his wagon as an ambulance if we have to. I'll ride with Wakefield."

The two doctors climbed into position, and we watched Colonel Carrington complete his inspection of the relief party. Captain Ten Eyck had assembled thirty-six infantrymen and thirty cavalrymen. The only horses left were mostly broken down, and there weren't enough for all the men. Half of the troopers would march on foot. Forty-two teamsters also gathered in a throng near the main gate, some of them mounted on personally owned animals.

"Attention to orders!" Colonel Carrington spoke loudly enough for everybody to hear. "Captain Ten Eyck, take the most direct route to Lodge Trail Ridge and join with Captain Fetterman's column at no hazard."

"Yes, sir." Captain Ten Eyck saluted. He sat on a horse in front of his mixed group of soldiers. Beside him, Lieutenant Matson also was mounted. They were the only officers to go with the relief party.

"I'm sending Private Semple to serve as a courier," the colonel said. Archibald Semple was the colonel's personal orderly. He was mounted on Gray Eagle, one of the colonel's favorite horses. "Move out," the colonel said.

Surgeon Hines, who sat beside me, flipped open the cover of his pocket watch. "Twelve-fifteen," he said. "We haven't heard any firing for half an hour."

Captain Ten Eyck and Lieutenant Matson led the party out the main gate. The soldiers marched or rode behind the two officers. I pulled the ambulance in behind them, and the two wagons followed me. The teamsters, most of whom had served during the war, moved along in a column of sorts at the rear. The relief party totaled one hundred fifteen men. When we joined with Captain Fetterman's eighty-man unit, we truly would comprise the largest armed contingent ever sent out of Fort Phil Kearny to contend with Red Cloud's warriors.

Beyond the main gate, Captain Ten Eyck ordered the column to move at double-quick time. It only took a few minutes to reach the ford at Big Piney Creek. Here, the captain halted for the walking men to remove shoes and stockings before wading into the icy water. On the opposite bank, the reshod men once again advanced at double time.

After crossing the creek, the Bozeman Trail climbed gradually for a couple hundred yards before running through a ravine bordered on the left by the northeast slope of Lodge Trail Ridge.

A slightly lower, unnamed ridge ran along the opposite side of the ravine. We'd proceeded into this gully only a short distance when Captain Ten Eyck raised a hand and brought us to a halt. Because of the distance separating me from the head of the column, I could not hear what he said. The captain and Lieutenant Matson motioned back and forth at the slopes on either side of us. It appeared they were concerned about running into an ambush if we rode deeper into the defile.

Captain Ten Eyck motioned the column forward again and led us off the trail to the right. We climbed steeply to the top of the unnamed ridge and continued in a northerly direction along its summit. Lodge Trail Ridge rose several feet higher on the opposite side of the Montana Road, which ran through the ravine below us to our left.

Doctor Hines consulted his pocket watch again. "Twelve forty-five. It's been almost an hour since we've heard firing."

Captain Ten Eyck signaled a halt at the end of the ridgeline. The slope from here dropped abruptly down to the Bozeman Trail. On this exposed point of land, the north wind cut sharply against my cheeks. I pulled my jacket collar up to shield my neck. My nose ran, and I wiped the moisture on my sleeve.

"Pull up close to the captain, Mr. Wakefield," Doctor Hines said. "I want to hear what he's saying."

I drove around the infantrymen and cavalrymen.

"Holy Mother of God!" Doctor Hines jumped up on the footboard as I pulled up close to the captain.

Now in view below us, hundreds, maybe thousands, of warriors swarmed. I didn't know there were that many Indians in Dakota Territory. The savages raced their ponies up and down the hillsides, shouting, screaming, and brandishing bows, lances, and rifles. An occasional warrior rode a larger horse outfitted with cavalry gear. The Indians had spotted our relief column and taunted us with challenges to come down and fight.

The Bozeman Trail emerged from the ravine at the base of our ridge and continued north along a narrow spur of land for about a mile before descending sharply to Peno Creek.

"I can't see anything other than bloody savages," Captain Ten Eyck said. He removed his glasses and wiped the lenses on the front of his blouse. "Do you see any of our men, Lieutenant?"

"No, sir," Lieutenant Matson answered.

"Private Semple." The captain turned to the orderly, who sat behind him on Gray Eagle.

The orderly saluted. "Sir?"

"Ride to the colonel and inform him I can't see or hear anything of Captain Fetterman. I do see two or three thousand Indians. Tell the colonel I'm afraid Fetterman's command is all gone up."

"Sir!" The orderly saluted again. He swung the thoroughbred back the way we'd come and lashed him into a gallop.

A flash of red drew my attention to the top of Lodge Trail Ridge to my left. The frigid wind flooded my eyes with tears. I blinked and squinted to get a better view of the far ridge that overlooked the valley and road below. If only I'd brought Captain Brown's field glasses. A half dozen Indians wearing headdresses and a white man dressed in buckskin occupied the highest point on the ridge. I recognized Chief Running Bear and Duggan Maguire.

Another flash of the red blanket, and the warriors milling around below stormed off to the north and disappeared down the slope toward Peno Creek. Could that be Red Cloud flashing signals with the red blanket? In a matter of minutes, the Indians disappeared. A glance back to Lodge Trail Ridge revealed the signaling party was gone, also.

Before I had a chance to call Captain Ten Eyck's attention to what I'd seen, one of the soldiers shouted, "There are the men down there, Captain, all dead!"

"Where?" the captain asked.

"Those large rocks down there . . . next to the road, on that little rise." Many of the men broke ranks and crowded forward to get a better view.

Scattered in and around those rocks, I saw what resembled old cottonwood trunks stripped of their bark. Blinking again to clear my eyes of tears, dozens of naked bodies became apparent.

"Boys!" Captain Ten Eyck exclaimed. "That's what we're looking for." He stood in his stirrups, raised his arm, and motioned with his hand. "Forward!"

The walking and mounted men, both soldiers and teamsters, formed an impromptu skirmish line and rapidly descended the steep slope to reach the rocky area. The ambulance and wagons required more caution as we drivers coaxed our teams down the rugged hillside.

Near the large stone outcropping, dozens of naked, mutilated men lay around and within the miniature fortress created by the rocks. Spent carbine cartridge cases and broken arrows and lances littered the ground. Strands of frozen blood clung to clumps of dry grass and bushes.

Puddles of frozen blood lay black on the ground farther away from the rock enclosure indicating where Indians must have died. Not one red-hued body remained, however.

Stretching away to the north, dead horses lay along the ridgeline road, their heads pointing toward us. White bodies near each horse marked where the cavalryman had fallen or been pulled from his mount in what must have been a desperate attempt to retreat to the promised shelter of the rocks.

I stopped the ambulance several yards from the rocky outcropping to keep from driving over bodies. A malodorous smell assailed my nostrils. I dropped down from the driver's seat beside a dead man. I immediately appreciated the horror this soldier had faced in the last moments of his life. A dozen arrows protruded from his torso. The man's nose and ears were missing. His eyes had been pried from their sockets and lay on his cheeks. The top of his head and his chin whiskers had been scalped. His skull had been split open and his brains spilled onto the ground. Deep cut marks separated and exposed his ribs. His heart lay atop his mutilated chest. His bicep and thigh muscles were splayed open to the bone. His hands and feet had been chopped off. His abdomen had been ripped open and his intestines dragged out in a long string extending away from his body. A pile of feces lay between his legs. Dark, frozen rivulets of blood streaked his remains and stained the earth beside him.

Even though the bodies were freezing solid in the brutal cold, the stench from the involuntary bowel evacuations and the exposed intestines remained overpowering. I turned to the side and vomited. Adjacent sounds assured me I was not alone in my retching.

The offending smell affected our animals as well. The Bible mules shuffled and reared in their harness. I grabbed Matt's bridle and led the mules farther away with the ambulance in hopes of separating them from the foul odor. I located a sapling struggling to survive on this windswept expanse and tied my team to the tiny tree.

"Lieutenant Matson!" Captain Ten Eyck shouted. "Form a perimeter skirmish defense around these rocks."

"Yes, sir." The lieutenant quickly spread the thirty-six infantrymen in a wide circle around the location.

"Over here, Captain," a soldier summoned Captain Ten Eyck. "That horse moved."

A gray cavalry horse showed signs of life, raising its head. The body, like those of the men, was full of arrows. How had the animal survived this long?

"That's Dapple Dave, sir," one of the cavalrymen said. "He's

367

in bad shape."

"Put the poor animal out of his misery," Captain Ten Eyck ordered.

A single shot followed.

I walked over to where Surgeon Hines pointed up the Montana Road beyond the rock formation. "Nothing survived," he said. The little dog, filled with arrows, must have been making a run for the fort.

At our feet, the doctor and I stared at one poor fellow who'd had a fire kindled on his stomach. Within the rough circle of the rock shelter, bodies were piled atop one another. Some men had evidently used the corpses of companions for protection. Neither clothing nor weapons were present. The Indians had taken everything except the naked bodies.

Beside me, Private Guthrie pointed to the far side of the rock outcropping. "Captain Ten Eyck!" the private called out. "Over there."

The captain, the doctor, and I followed to where Private Guthrie led. Though mutilated, I knew it was Captain Fetterman and Captain Brown who lay side by side. Both were naked, both filled with arrows.

Captain Fetterman's crushed skull hung suspended down his back, held in place by a strip of neck skin. His throat had been cut all the way through to the cervical spine. His brains hung frozen in stringy icicles off his shoulders. His intestines lay strung out down the hillside from between his legs.

Captain Brown's thighs were slashed open, exposing the bones. His ears were missing. He bore a bullet hole in his right temple. Powder burns around the wound indicated the shot had been at close range. Had he shot himself? A lance had been shoved up his anus, the point of which protruded through the abdominal cavity where his intestines had been dragged out. The sons of bitches had cut off the captain's genitals and stuffed his penis into his mouth! His testicles hung down over his chin.

Doctor Hines was unable to pry the captain's jaws apart. Rigor mortis and the icy weather had frozen everything in place.

The special hatred the savages apparently felt toward Captain Brown for continually chasing their raiding parties extended to the animal he'd ridden. Calico lay in the brown grass several yards away. The Carrington boys' pony had been scalped. Arrows penetrated its flanks.

"Bring the ambulance down here, Mr. Wakefield," Surgeon Hines said. "We'll place the captains' bodies in it. We'll also fill it with as many others as we can. The wagons will have to be loaded, too. Do you agree, Captain Ten Eyck?"

The captain exhaled sharply. "Yes. Yes, of course. Let's get everybody working on gathering up the bodies. It is so damnably cold out here, the rest of us will freeze to death if we don't get back to the fort soon."

Those men who had handkerchiefs covered their noses. Most, like me, did not have one. Nothing remained in our stomachs to regurgitate anyway, so we set to work stuffing intestines into body cavities. A soldier beside me grumbled, "I can't tell if I'm pushing a cavalryman's guts into an infantryman, or vice versa."

We stacked one dead body atop another in the wagons and the ambulance. We were loading the last of the bodies into Bill Williams's wagon when his mules panicked and lunged forward, dragging the wagon against one of the boulders and tipping it over. Frozen bodies tumbled everywhere. Williams calmed his animals, and we once again gathered up the dead and reloaded his wagon.

"Let's get rolling," Captain Ten Eyck said. "We have all the bodies we can carry today. The sun will drop behind the mountains in a few minutes. I want to get back to the fort while we at least have twilight."

Lieutenant Matson directed the infantrymen to spread out

on either side of our vehicles, and we headed toward Fort Phil Kearny. Counting the two captains, we'd gathered up forty-nine bodies in and around the rocky outcropping. Lieutenant Grummond and thirty-one other men still lay along the Bozeman Trail somewhere.

Surgeon Hines wearily climbed onto the seat beside me. He glanced into the rear of the ambulance. "Reminds me of taking hogs to market."

Captain Ten Eyck had sent one of the men ahead on horseback to alert Colonel Carrington about the nature of our return. When we forded Big Piney Creek, with the fort just ahead of us, Indian signal fires could be seen burning on the surrounding hillsides. Complete darkness had set in by the time our macabre procession passed through the main gate.

Armed soldiers were visible at every loophole along the entire length of the fort's walls, not just at the widely spaced sentinel stations. Within the fort, windows in every building revealed light from lanterns and candles. On the parade ground and on the corner bastions, gun crews stood beside each howitzer.

The magazine in the southwest quadrant had been surrounded with three circles of wagon beds turned on their sides to make a secondary barrier within the fort. Every enlisted man and civilian not positioned on the banquettes of the stockade stood guard along the road.

I halted the ambulance in front of the hospital. The two wagons pulled in behind me. Colonel Carrington, Captain Powell, and Lieutenant Wands waited there.

"Sir!" Captain Ten Eyck exchanged salutes with Colonel Carrington. "Reporting after a sad mission."

"I'm at a loss for words, Tenodor," Colonel Carrington said. "The courier said you were returning with forty-nine. Is that right?"

"Yes, sir," the captain answered. "We only had room for those we found clustered around a rocky outcropping, which they apparently attempted to use as a fortress. The others appear to be strung out along the road for a mile or so north of where we found these men. We could see dead horses and bodies in that direction."

"You found Captains Fetterman and Brown, but not Lieutenant Grummond?" the colonel asked.

"Correct, sir," Ten Eyck answered. "The captains are in the ambulance."

Doctor Horton came up beside Colonel Carrington. "Colonel, these bodies are all frozen. We should not allow them to thaw, or we will be overcome by the stench. I do want to examine each man to determine, if possible, the cause of death. I'll need help from other soldiers to identify the remains of their friends. It will be best to place the bodies in unheated structures until we can assemble coffins and bury them."

"I agree, Sam." The colonel used the doctor's first name, as he'd done with Captain Ten Eyck. "Lieutenant Wands!"

The adjutant stepped up and saluted. "Sir?"

"We'll move the bodies a few at a time into the hospital where Doctor Horton can examine them. Empty the guardhouse of prisoners. Have the sergeant of the guard supervise them in taking the bodies into the hospital for the doctor's inspection. After the prisoners complete that job, release them from confinement. If you can find rifles, arm them, and return them to their units. Have the sawmills commence building coffins first thing in the morning."

"Sir?" Lieutenant Wands asked. "Who's going to inform Mrs. Grummond that we haven't recovered his body? The ladies are all gathered in my cabin."

The colonel sighed. "I'll tell Mrs. Grummond," he said. "I give you the responsibility to inform Mrs. Wheatley. Earlier, she went into the Fessendens' quarters with her two little boys."

Lieutenant Wands blew out his breath. "Yes, sir." He exchanged salutes with the colonel and headed for the guardhouse.

"Chaplain White," Colonel Carrington called the preacher forward. "Bring the men coming off guard duty over to identify their friends if they can. Some of the men will need consoling to handle the trauma. Also, ask the men to locate uniforms for the deceased. These men cannot be buried naked."

"Yes, sir." The chaplain saluted and walked away.

Doctor Hines and I climbed down from the ambulance to await the arrival of the prisoner detail. While we waited, Colonel Carrington went to the Wands's quarters, which stood close to the hospital. In a few minutes, the colonel came out of the cabin followed by the women and children. Katy and Mrs. Carrington accompanied Fannie Grummond down officers' row to the Carrington residence, where the three of them went inside.

The Carrington boys slipped away from the group of ladies, and without the colonel knowing, followed their father back to the hospital. They sneaked up to the side of the building. From that surreptitiously achieved vantage point they could see the bodies stacked in the wagons.

I stepped in front of the boys to block their view.

"Harry." I spoke first to the older one. "Jimmy. This is not a good place for you."

The faces of both boys, one nine and the other six years old, were pale despite their sunburned complexions.

"I have another bit of sad news," I said. "Calico won't be coming back. He died on the battlefield with the men."

Where there were none before, tears now welled in their eyes. They wiped sniffles from their noses.

"Come. Let's go home." I took each by a hand, and we

walked to the commanding officer's quarters.

Before the door closed behind the boys, Katy came out of the residence.

"Oh, Zach," she said. "This is absolutely awful."

I extended a hand and helped her down the two steps from the small porch. I did not let go of her hand, and she did not withdraw it.

"How is Fannie taking it?" I asked.

"I don't know how she manages to stay upright . . . but she does. Mrs. Carrington says Fannie will reside with them now, because of her condition. That's good. It wouldn't be right to leave her alone in that little cabin confronting the memories of a dead husband."

"I'll walk you to the hospital," I said. I still held her hand, and I wanted every excuse to continue to do so.

We'd only taken a few steps when Portugee Phillips appeared.

Katy withdrew her hand. "Good evening, Portugee," she said.

"Good evening, Miss O'Toole. Is Mrs. Grummond inside with Mrs. Carrington?"

"Why, yes, she is."

"I would like to speak with her for a moment, if I may?"

"What about?" Katy asked."

"The colonel has hired me to ride to Fort Laramie with news of the massacre and to take dispatches for telegraphing to Omaha."

"In this weather?" I asked. "That's two hundred thirty-five miles."

"I know," he replied. "I'm not going alone. Daniel Dixon volunteered to go with me."

"The half-breed?" I asked.

"Daniel has mixed blood, yes. But that doesn't mean he sides with the Indians."

"Sorry," I said. "I didn't mean to imply that. It's just surprising the colonel didn't order a soldier to go."

"The colonel needs every soldier for defensive duties," Portugee said. He turned to Katy. "Can I see Mrs. Grummond a moment?"

"I don't know, Portugee," she answered. "Let me check first." Katy went into the house.

"You volunteered to go?" I asked Portugee.

"The colonel is paying each of us three hundred dollars."

"That's six months' pay."

Before we could discuss the matter further, Katy opened the door. "Fannie will see you," she said.

Katy and I slipped in behind Portugee and stood with our backs to the door. Fannie Grummond sat on a straight-backed chair next to the pot-bellied stove. Mrs. Carrington stood beside her.

Portugee removed his hat. "Ma'am," he said. "My name is John Phillips. Most folks call me 'Portugee' because I come from the Azores."

"Mr. Phillips," Fannie said. "What can I do for you?"

"I am going to Fort Laramie for help, carrying dispatches. I'm going for your sake, even if it costs me my life."

Portugee had been holding a rolled-up bundle, and he now extended it to Fannie.

"This is my wolf robe. Keep it to remember me if you never see me again."

Fannie took the robe, unrolled it, and draped the dark-gray fur over her lap. "Thank you, Mr. Phillips."

Portugee said nothing else. He bowed, turned, and left the quarters. Katy and I followed.

"You could do me a favor, Zach," Portugee said as the three of us headed toward the bustling activity in front of the hospital.

"What?" I asked.

"Help me select a horse. You've been around the colonel's

animals. I haven't. He's letting me ride whatever horse of his I want."

"Come with me," I said. "The colonel's horses are in the stables."

When we reached the hospital, Katy said goodbye to Portugee and went inside to help Doctor Horton. She was a brave lady. I don't know that I would have the stomach to help the surgeon examine mutilated bodies.

At the stables, Daniel Dixon was saddling one of the few remaining serviceable horses. Portugee took my recommendation and chose Colonel Carrington's prized thoroughbred, Dandy, a black, bluegrass horse with three stocking feet. We had just finished cinching the saddle, when the colonel and Private Samples arrived.

"Here are the dispatches and the last of the Spencer carbines, Mr. Phillips. Be wary out there. The savages are now better armed than we are. Here's a hundred rounds of ammunition in bags. We don't have any more Blakeslee quick-loaders."

"I'll strap the bags to my ankles," Portugee said. "The weight will help keep my feet in the stirrups."

The colonel and the orderly set to work helping Portugee accomplish his unusual dress modifications. I filled two pairs of saddlebags with hardtack for the riders and a couple of sacks with grain for their horses. I also provided each of them with a canteen of partially frozen water. Not much in the way of provisions for the journey ahead, but with all the mess halls closed, it was all I could find.

The colonel led the two horsemen through the quartermaster yard and down to the water gate. I followed with a lantern and the quartermaster's key to open the gate's padlock. The sentry challenged us, but a nearby sergeant hushed him with the admonition it was the commanding officer approaching.

Flakes of snow danced in the reflected light of the lantern.

After I opened the gate, the two riders raised a hand in farewell and rode out. The colonel stood in the open gate listening as Portugee and Dixon rode across shallow Little Piney Creek and disappeared into the falling snow. It was apparent when they reached the Bozeman Trail because the clopping of the horses' hooves reverberated on the hard-packed surface. That sound lasted for a moment only.

"Good," Colonel Carrington said. "They've dropped off to the side of the trail. Best not to make unnecessary sounds that would alert lurking savages."

CHAPTER 47

Dawn on Saturday, December 22, broke over the somber garrison with a bitterly cold wind blowing out of the north and low-lying gray clouds blocking the view of the mountains and threatening a blizzard. When the reveille bugle sounded, I'd already finished eating an early breakfast. The cook in the teamsters' mess had fired up his stove early to cater to civilian workers who'd slept little, if at all. I was among the latter, having never removed my clothes. I had been busy at the warehouse issuing hammers and nails to the coffin makers and sheets to the hospital to serve as shrouds.

I decided to make my way over to headquarters to see if I'd be needed to drive an ambulance. When I exited the teamsters' mess, I checked the thermometer attached to the outside wall. The mercury stood at zero.

On the parade ground, troops not on guard duty had turned out for roll call. Colonel Carrington's four remaining officers, Captains Ten Eyck and Powell and Lieutenants Wands and Matson, gathered in front of the headquarters building to make their reports. Lieutenant Wands assumed his additional duty as adjutant and accepted the information for compilation of the *Morning Report.*

The sentinels still assigned to the banquettes had been accounted for, and the dead from yesterday added to the count. The resulting tally indicated Lieutenant Grummond and thirty-one enlisted men were still missing. None had come in during the night. All were presumed dead.

"Colonel, sir." Lieutenant Wands snapped to attention and saluted. "We have nine officers, counting the three doctors and the chaplain. We have accounted for three hundred twenty enlisted men and one hundred nineteen civilian employees of the quartermaster department. In addition, there are fifty sutler employees, officers' servants, and contract employees. There are five dependent wives and four children. All total, we have five hundred seven people inside the fort."

I stood at the side of the headquarters building next to the scaffolding supporting the observation platform. The colonel had seen me and knew I was there. He made no motion or spoke no words to indicate I should leave.

"Gentlemen," Colonel Carrington said, "I propose to lead a detachment to recover the bodies. I intend to inform Mrs. Grummond I will not leave her husband's remains on the field any longer. What say you?" He looked from one to the other of the four officers.

A shaking of heads indicated no enthusiasm for such a mission. Each officer, in turn, grumbled a comment that the risk of another attack from the Indians was too great.

"I disagree, gentlemen," Carrington said. "The Indians do not leave their dead on the field. I will not allow the Indians to entertain the notion that our dead cannot and will not be retrieved. If we do not do this, then how can we send out details for any purpose? Such lack of action on our part would signal weakness to the Indians and invite them to risk another assault."

Head shaking gradually changed to faintly observable nods.

"Captain Ten Eyck," Colonel Carrington said, "you and Lieutenant Matson gather eighty volunteers, soldiers or civilians . . . makes no difference. Captain Powell, you are designated officer of the day. Lieutenant Wands, you remain here to assist

Captain Powell in maintaining discipline and vigilance at the fort."

The officers saluted and executed an about-face to return to their companies to seek volunteers.

"Captain Powell," Colonel Carrington said, "hold up a minute."

"Sir?" Powell turned about.

"After dismissing your company," the colonel continued, "join me at the magazine."

"Yes, sir." Powell saluted and departed.

"Mr. Wakefield." The colonel turned and addressed me. "I assume your presence here means you are prepared to drive your ambulance today?"

"Yes, sir."

"Good. Pick up Assistant Surgeon Ould from the hospital. Doctor Horton and Doctor Hines worked all night identifying the causes of death. Doctor Ould is the only one in a condition to go with us. Also, arrange for seven wagons. I will not stack the bodies like cordwood as you had to do yesterday."

"Yes, sir."

I hurried over to the teamsters' mess, where I had no trouble getting seven men to volunteer to drive the wagons. I harnessed the Bible mules to the ambulance and drove to the hospital, where Doctor Ould was waiting for me.

The magazine, located in the southwest quadrant of the parade ground, sat diagonally across the road from where I'd parked the ambulance. Colonel Carrington and Captain Powell were approaching from the headquarters building when Surgeon Ould prepared to climb up to join me. He paused and raised a hand to hold us in position.

The colonel saw us and waved for the surgeon to join him. I slipped off the seat, took the medical bag out of the doctor's hands, and used that as an excuse to follow him across the road. I stopped at the outer ring of wagons that formed the temporary barrier around the magazine. Doctor Ould slipped between gaps in the three rings of wagons and joined Colonel Carrington and Captain Powell at the open cellar door that led down into the magazine. They were close enough I could overhear their conversation.

"Captain Powell," Colonel Carrington said, "I have cut the fuses on a dozen spherical case shot and placed them among the cases of ammunition. I have laid a train of powder across the floor connecting all shots. A single match will set off the explosion."

Captain Powell snuck a sideways glance at Doctor Ould.

"If Indians attack in overwhelming numbers," the colonel continued, "put the women and children in the magazine. In the event of a last desperate struggle inside the fort, destroy everyone in the magazine rather than allow them to be captured."

What had possessed the colonel to make the decision to kill his family members and other dependents? What torment had he struggled through to reach the conclusion the Indians would torture innocent women and children?

"At sunset," Colonel Carrington continued, "if everything is well, fire a single cannon shot and run a white lantern to the masthead of the flagpole. If, however, you are surrounded by Indians, fire three cannon shots at one-minute intervals, and hoist a red lantern to the masthead. Understand?"

"Yes, sir."

"Good. Doctor Ould," the colonel asked, "are you up to making this trip?"

"Yes, sir. I'm ready."

"Good. Let's get on with our tasks."

Captain Powell closed the cellar door, and he and Colonel Carrington walked back to headquarters. Surgeon Ould returned to the ambulance with me. By the time we were seated and I clucked the mules forward, the string of seven wagons rolled through the gate from the quartermaster yard and headed toward the main gate with us.

Under a dark winter sky threatening more snow, with the temperature still at zero, the detachment marched out of the fort. The few remaining cavalrymen rode what horses were left on the flanks. Some of the infantry climbed into the wagons, while others were detailed to march alongside. On every high point on our journey to the battlefield, Colonel Carrington left two infantrymen as sentinels to maintain visual contact in relay fashion between him and the fort.

When we reached the little fortress of rocks, we paused long enough for Captain Ten Eyck to point out to Colonel Carrington where we had recovered the bodies the day before. Then, we continued on the Bozeman Trail for a quarter mile and came to a smaller cluster of boulders on high ground to the left of the road. Here we found several dead cavalrymen.

Lieutenant Matson spread a ring of infantrymen around the site in skirmish formation. Surgeon Ould, Colonel Carrington, and Captain Ten Eyck walked quickly from one body to the next, verifying each was dead. Dark pools of frozen blood lay around each body, which had been mutilated like those we'd recovered the day before. Dozens of arrows protruded from each corpse. Limbs had been sliced and extremities cut off. The cavalrymen riding with us were able to identify some of their comrades.

Doctor Ould supervised the loading of the dead into the wagons. Because the mules were spooking at the foul smell, the wagons were brought forward one at a time to accept the bodies. However, once again, a lunging team overturned one of the wagons, dumping its load onto the ground. After that, when a teamster brought a wagon close to the carnage, soldiers were assigned to hold the bridle of each mule.

We proceeded north another half mile. Scattered between the high ground we'd just left and where the road dropped off toward Peno Creek, we discovered six more bodies. The way these men and nearby horses were strung out along the road, they'd obviously been trying to get back to join the infantrymen at the first rocky outcropping.

One of these dead was Lieutenant Grummond. His head had almost been severed. His naked body was filled with arrows, and his fingers had been chopped off.

After we'd loaded Grummond's body into my ambulance, Colonel Carrington used a pocketknife to cut off a lock of the lieutenant's hair. He dropped the strands into an envelope and slid the packet into a coat pocket.

Among a large cluster of boulders, at the point where the road dropped steeply down to Peno Creek, we found Wheatley, Fisher, and four soldiers. Dozens of brass cartridges lay beside the bodies at this site. The two civilians had made good use of their repeating rifles. Surrounding this defensive position, we found half a dozen dead Indian ponies and counted sixty-five pools of dark, frozen blood. Many Indians either died or were wounded trying to overrun this site.

The savages' anger at such stubborn fighting was evident from the one hundred three arrows protruding from Wheatley's scalped body. The markings on these arrows indicated they'd been fired by Oglala and Miniconjou Sioux, Northern Cheyennes, and Arapahos. Every tribe protesting our occupation of the Powder River country had been present at the massacre.

Off to one side of this rocky outcropping, we discovered the only untouched body. Doctor Ould and I lifted a buffalo robe covering bugler Adolph Metzger.

Colonel Carrington and Captain Ten Eyck joined us to stare at this strange anomaly.

"Why do you suppose this is?" Colonel Carrington asked no one in particular.

An older teamster, who'd worked for years on the frontier, stood close by. "It's a sign of respect, Colonel," the teamster said. "When a man fights bravely, the warriors honor him by not mutilating his body. That way he'll be able to find his way unobstructed in the afterlife."

Darkness dropped over our little expedition as we loaded the last body. We had found all thirty-two. The colonel ordered the wagon train back to the fort. We'd not traveled far when we heard a single cannon shot from the south. I, and probably everyone else, counted the next sixty seconds and listened to hear a second and third shot. None was fired.

Doctor Ould sat beside me in silence on the return trip. The snow blew in sheets across the Bozeman Trail in front of us. What were Portugee Philips and Daniel Dixon facing out there alone farther south on this road? How far had they gotten? Was it snowing as hard where they were as it was here? Had they been harassed by Indians? At least we had eighty armed men in our entourage to fend off any attacks.

It was totally dark when we approached the fort and thankfully saw a white lantern hanging from the flagstaff. Even inside the fort, the wind blew the snow in blinding waves across the parade ground where it drifted against the buildings and the stockade wall.

When we reached the hospital with our somber cargo, Doctor Horton joined Colonel Carrington at the rear of my ambulance.

"We recovered all the men, Doctor," Carrington said. "Are you prepared to repeat your work of yesterday?"

"No choice, Colonel. It must be done."

"Damn," the colonel said. "Pardon my language, but it is bloody cold out here."

"When I made the sunset entries in the weather log a short time ago," the doctor said, "the thermometer had dropped to twenty below. It will get colder as the night progresses."

Captain Powell came up and reported to the commanding officer. "Sir, no sign of Indians on any of the hills all day long," he said. "I made the decision to put the guards on half-hour shifts because of the cold."

"Good," Colonel Carrington said. "I don't like the way the snow is drifting against the interior of the stockade wall. If it's doing it on the outside of the wall, the Indians will soon be able to walk right over the top."

"I noticed that, too, sir," Captain Powell said, "and I've put men to shoveling the snow away from the exterior west wall where the drifting is worse."

"Excellent," the colonel said. "Captain, if you will supervise the unloading of these poor men, I must go tell Mrs. Grummond we have returned with her husband's remains."

Under the direction of Doctor Horton, the bodies from the ambulance and the wagons were lined up in the road outside the hospital. Snow soon covered the bodies.

Since I had organized the wagon train earlier, I waited until each wagon had been cleared of its load and thanked the teamster for his help. The last wagon moved through the gate into the quartermaster yard, and I was climbing aboard the ambulance, when Katy appeared.

"Katy," I asked, "what are you doing out here in this cold?"

"I'm returning to the hospital from the Carrington residence. I was with Fannie Grummond when the colonel gave her the lieutenant's lock of hair."

"How did she take it?"

"She broke down and sobbed when she realized the locket bearing her portrait that her husband always wore must now be hanging around some squaw's neck."

384

"It's been hard on all of us," I said, "but she surely must feel the pain the most."

"Zach," she said, "it must have been miserable work out there in this weather."

"Yes." I slapped my hands against the outside of my arms to stimulate the circulation.

"It is so very cold," she said. "I've been worried about Portugee. He's out there somewhere in this brutal weather, and who knows how many Indians are chasing him."

"I've been thinking about that myself," I said. "I have an idea. I can use your help."

CHAPTER 48

The snow fell with increasing intensity as the evening progressed. For those involved in examining and re-clothing the dead, the icy temperature made for miserable conditions. For those engaged in shoveling the accumulating snow away from the stockade wall, it could not have been worse. For my purpose, it could not have been better. I'd decided to go help Portugee fend off troublesome Indians. Katy agreed to meet me at the quartermaster warehouse at midnight.

Around ten o'clock, I quietly transferred Luke to the last stall in the mule stable—the stall abutting the water gate. I saddled and bridled him, fed him a ration of oats, and gave him a drink of water. I slung two sacks of oats over his rump along with my blanket roll and my saddlebags containing my rations. I hung two canteens tied together with a length of rope over his withers. Luke sensed something different was about to happen. I patted his neck and whispered in a long ear to keep him quiet.

Overhead, a sentry paced across the roof of the mule stable, which along this southern-most wall of the fort served double duty as the defensive banquette. No permanent sentry posts had been erected along the walls of the quartermaster yard. Normally, no guards manned these walls at night. But, with the heightened security, an infantryman now patrolled the length of this wall overlooking Little Piney Creek.

I counted the sentry's steps as he picked his way across the roof from the water gate to the southeast corner of the wall.

Here he paused momentarily before returning. At two hundred feet, this was the shortest wall in the fort. The sentry took eighty steps to cover the distance one way. Because of the uneven surface of the stable's slanted roof and the slipperiness created by the accumulation of snow on the shingles, he paced slower than he would have on the banquettes of the main fort's walls. Not having a pocket watch, I counted the seconds mentally and estimated it took him almost one minute to reach the farthest point from the water gate. Not much time for what I needed to do.

Right on the dot of the main gate's sentry shouting *All's well* at midnight, Katy arrived at the quartermaster warehouse.

"Wow!" she exclaimed, brushing snow off her shoulders. "It's brutal out there. Are you sure you want to do this?"

"I'm sure."

I motioned for her to follow me into the quartermaster's office. From a hook on the wall behind the desk, I took down a ring of keys and held them up. "When you bring these back, hang them on that hook."

She nodded.

No fire burned in the stove in the office. I was shivering, and I could see Katy was as well. Outside the temperature was thirty degrees below zero, and it was almost that cold inside.

"Hopefully, you won't have to be out long in this weather," I said.

"Don't worry about me," she said. "You're the one who has to be concerned about the cold. What are you wearing under that buffalo coat?"

"Both of my shirts and my jacket—every item of clothing I own."

Katy pulled the lapels of my buffalo-hide overcoat more closely together. She retied the bulky garment around my midsection with the rawhide drawstrings. The coat made movement somewhat difficult, but it provided welcome warmth. The shaggy outer fur would shed moisture like it did for the animal who originally wore the hide. At the colonel's direction, company tailors had fabricated these coats from hides traded from friendly Cheyennes. Each sentry wore one on duty, and I had confiscated this one from our limited inventory.

From the desk, I lifted the belt that carried my holstered revolver and ammunition and percussion cap pouches. Katy took it from me. While she strapped it about my waist, my nose nestled into the top of her bonnet. I inhaled the aroma of heaven.

She leaned back, looked up, and ran fingertips down my cheek. Then she placed her hands on my chest and pushed. "You haven't shaved. You trying to grow a beard?"

"No. I haven't had time to shave lately."

"You might look good with a beard," she said. "I thought for a long time you couldn't grow one, but maybe you can."

"Humph." Maybe I'd let my beard grow to show her I could.

"You promise me to be careful, Zach."

"I promise."

"You're only carrying a revolver?"

"Even if there were a rifle or carbine available, I wouldn't take it. I don't want my hands encumbered with a long weapon."

"Do you have enough ammunition?"

"My belt pouch is full, and I have another packet in my saddlebags."

"Food and water?" she asked.

"Hardtack, some of Liz Wheatley's bear meat jerky, and two canteens."

"I see you're wearing buffalo-hide leggings over your brogans. Do you have on warm stockings?"

"Two pairs."

Katy slipped a hand into her wool coat and withdrew an

object she dangled in front of me on a chain—Major Bonnet's shamrock. She hung it around my neck. "Wear it for good luck."

"You sure?"

"Aye."

I tucked the charm down inside my shirts. "I'll give it back when I return."

"Hat?" she asked.

"On a peg above my desk."

She stepped through the open doorway, and I followed. She settled my slouch hat on my head.

"Your ears are going to freeze." She lifted the shawl from around her shoulders and draped it over the crown of my hat. She pulled on the shawl, folding the hat brim down over my ears, and tied the ends beneath my chin. "There. That'll help. You can also return the shawl when you come back."

I hung a pair of clumsy buffalo-hide gauntlets around my neck by a cord that joined them. The company tailors had fashioned these oversized mittens to wear over regulation army gloves, which I now pulled on.

"It's time to go, Katy. We don't have a lot of time to accomplish this. We have to work quietly, or the sentry might hear us."

In front of the quartermaster warehouse, we paused to check for passersby. When I was sure it was clear, I grasped her hand and led her through the nearby postern gate into the quartermaster yard. Once through, we paused again, and I checked to be certain the men manning the howitzer on the southeastern bastion were not looking in our direction, and the sentry walking the south wall of the main stockade was at the far end of his round.

We had to pass in front of the teamsters' quarters, which were built against the east wall of the quartermaster yard for about a third of that wall's length. It was after midnight, and only snores came through the flimsy walls. We moved cautiously though because a teamster could stagger out on his way to the sinks.

Beyond the teamsters' cabins, we came to the mule stables that extended in an *L* shape down the balance of the eastern wall, where they turned and followed the south wall to the water gate. We kept under the ledge of the overhanging stable roof and passed to the rear of the mules, who faced into their open-ended stalls. We moved slowly so as not to disturb the animals and start them braying.

As we neared the end of the stables close to the water gate, a loud thump accompanied a shower of snow cascading off the sloping roof, dusting us with white powder. I pulled Katy in tightly against a post separating two mule stalls. A booted foot emerged over the edge of the roof and dangled in front of our faces.

"Damn!" the sentry cursed. He'd lost his footing and slid down the roof, shoving the snow load ahead of him. Luckily, he hadn't dropped his rifle into the quartermaster yard. The sentry struggled to his feet, dislodging more snow. His steps passed overhead as he climbed back to where the roof joined against the yard's wall.

We waited until he'd taken several steps away before we went the last few feet to Luke's stall. We slipped into the stall beside him, and when we reached his head, I stroked his forehead and rubbed his ears.

"Easy, Luke," I whispered. "This is Katy. She's a friend." I took one of Katy's gloved hands and placed it on Luke's mane. He snorted and shook his head up and down.

"Now," I whispered to Katy, "next time the sentry is halfway to the far end of the wall from here, we unlock the gate. Remember, it takes thirty seconds for him to get halfway. After I'm gone, you must snap the lock closed before he returns to the halfway point. Count to sixty after I unlock the gate. That's the total amount of time you have."

The sentry paced overhead and stopped above us next to the water gate. Here he turned and resumed marching back toward the north wall. I started counting.

I counted the thirty seconds it took the sentry to reach halfway in his route. We had thirty seconds before he reached the far end. We had one minute to get me outside the gate and reclose it before he got back to the halfway mark where he could more easily hear us or maybe see the open gate.

I backed Luke out of the stall and led him to the gate. Thick snow cover on the ground muffled the sound of his hoofbeats.

I stuck the reins between my teeth while I inserted the key into the padlock.

CLICK!

That was loud. I didn't wait to determine if the sentry had heard. I handed the key ring to Katy and tugged hard to drag the heavy door through the accumulated snow.

Katy grabbed my arm, reached up, and kissed my cheek.

"You'd better come back to me, Zack," she whispered. "I love you." Then, she pushed me out the gate.

What had she said? I forced myself to concentrate on what I was supposed to be doing. I led Luke through the gate and turned left. I leaned against his side to shove him close to the wall.

The door's bottom scraped loudly through the snow as Katy shoved it closed.

CLICK!

She had snapped the padlock shut.

"Who goes there?" the sentry called out. His quickened steps brought him near the water gate. "Anybody there?"

I hoped Katy was hugging the inside of the gate. I leaned hard against Luke to keep him pressed against the wall. I squeezed his nostrils and rubbed his forehead hoping to keep him from braying or snorting.

A shower of snow dropped onto the brim of my hat. If the sentry looked down, he might see me. I kept my head down even though I desperately wanted to look up. I hoped the white shawl draped over my hat resembled snow.

The first quarter moon had set at midnight, so visibility beyond the lights of the fort was diminished. Would the storm's snowfall obscure the view the sentry had if he peered over the side of the wall? It took a moment for me to realize the deep breathing I heard came from me.

The sentry finally walked away. When the sound of his footsteps diminished, I led Luke down to the north branch of Little Piney Creek and mounted. I urged him across the shallow stream, his hooves crunching through a layer of ice. I prayed the sentry could not hear that noise.

My God! Had Katy said she loved me? Had I heard correctly?

After riding across the narrow island, we crunched and splashed through the icy south branch of Little Piney Creek. Then, my path took me past the cemetery. The crews assigned to dig the massive trench had stopped work for the night. Enough light existed to reveal pickaxes and shovels scattered along the edges of the fifty-foot-long grave. The men had dropped their tools at sunset to return to the safety of the stockade. The frozen ground was yielding slowly to their attempt to reach a depth of seven feet. They were going to have difficulty meeting Colonel Carrington's desire to hold burial services on Christmas day.

I rode beneath Pilot Hill. The sentries there, like the grave-diggers, had been recalled to the security of the stockade. Had they been there, they could not have seen me through the low-lying clouds and blowing snow that obscured the lookout post.

A few yards farther on, I picked up the Bozeman Trail. The passage of wagons and herds over the past three years had eradicated the vegetation that originally grew where the road now existed. By keeping snow-covered bushes on either side, I stayed in the center of the roadway. When Portugee and Dixon had departed the fort, snow did not cover the ground as it did now, so they'd dropped off the road to reduce the noise of their transit. I was a day behind them. I needed to remain on the road to make better time. I kicked Luke into a trot.

Thankfully, I didn't have to face into the north wind. I tucked the loose ends of Katy's shawl around my neck to fend off the chill. From time to time, I slapped my checks and scrubbed my dripping nose with my furry buffalo gauntlets. My breath hung suspended in front of my nose, matching that of Luke's, which scattered in icy beads before his muzzle.

I stopped every hour, climbed out of the saddle, and walked Luke for a few minutes. That took the weight off him and increased the circulation in my feet. I had attached a canvas feed bucket to a D-ring on the pommel of the McClellan saddle and used it to give Luke a drink. The two canteens suspended on a rope over Luke's withers bounced against his warm sides, keeping the water from freezing solid.

Six hours later, the dim glow of the rising sun appeared on the eastern horizon as we approached Clear Creek. We'd come sixteen miles. The low-lying fog hanging among the cottonwood trees concealed the stream from view. I dismounted and led Luke down to the stream. The usual tumbling babble of fast flowing water was muffled by its frozen surface.

I heard something out of place before I saw it. Luke heard or smelled it as well, because his head jerked up, and his ears flexed forward. I squeezed and twisted the ends of Luke's nostrils, hoping the twitch would keep him quiet.

The mysterious noise proved to be ponies' hooves clopping on the frozen ground. A dozen Indians rode single file along the far bank. Each had a blanket wrapped around his hunched shoulders. The fog concealed the lower extremities of the animals, giving the illusion the riders were floating by.

I seldom prayed, but I prayed now to keep Luke and me concealed in that stand of cottonwoods. At this location, Clear Creek meandered away from its general flow to the northeast and flowed directly north. The prevailing wind pushed Luke's and my scents southward, parallel to the creek's western bank. If the wind shifted and blew across the stream to the east, the ponies and warriors would pick up our smell.

The Indians passed on, and the clopping sound ceased. I released Luke's nostrils. I waited for a count of ten minutes before leading him to the stream's edge. I picked up a downed limb and whacked the surface to test its strength. It didn't shatter, so I led Luke across the frozen surface and remounted on the far bank. We were still fifty miles from Fort Reno.

Portugee planned to travel only at night to diminish the chance of running into Indians. But if I was going to catch up, I had to press on during daylight.

The falling snow made the going difficult, but it also served to conceal my presence. In dips in the road, drifts had accumulated three feet deep. Luke occasionally sank to his barrel, but he plowed on through. In places, the wind swept the road clear of snow, and we were able to maintain a steady trot.

Twenty miles past Clear Creek the terrain changed drastically. We now approached Crazy Woman's Fork. Bushes lining the sides of the trail were short. The different vegetation indicated we'd reached the dry plains. The path we followed grew more difficult to identify.

We crossed Crazy Woman's Fork about noon using the same ice testing technique I'd used at Clear Creek. On the south bank of the stream, I rode through the site of the ambush where Lieutenant Daniels had been butchered on a blistering hot day in July. I wished we had a little of that heat now. The snow continued to fall, and the north wind blew unceasingly against my back. We were more than halfway to Fort Reno, having come thirty-six miles in twelve hours.

A couple of miles south of Crazy Woman's Fork the road climbed up a cliff and continued in virtually a straight line to the southeast along a high plateau. The wind, as uncomfortable as it was, blew the snow off the road in many places.

The blizzard raged on. Visibility dropped to near zero. When Luke wandered off the road and bogged down in softer ground, I'd steer him back until I could feel his hooves pound down on harder surface. Our progress had slowed to a walk. I still hoped to reach Fort Reno before dark. I also hoped the Indians were smarter than me and stayed under shelter.

Toward nightfall, the road descended from the plateau, and we approached Dry Creek. We were now a half-dozen miles from the fort. My teeth chattered unceasingly. Luke snorted more frequently.

An hour later I spotted a dim light through intense fog that indicated we were approaching our destination on the Powder River. Ten minutes later, the speck of light grew into a glow from a lantern hanging above the front gate of Fort Reno. A stockade now surrounded the buildings. General Hazen's inspection had stimulated the necessary activity to enclose the compound.

"Halt! Who goes there?"

"Zachary Wakefield from Fort Phil Kearny."

A few moments later the main gate was opened, and a sentry beckoned me forward. I dismounted and led Luke into the fort.

"What are you doing out here alone?" The light from a lifted lantern revealed shoulder boards bearing silver oak leaves. I was confronted by Lieutenant Colonel Henry Wessells, who had been sent out from Omaha in November to replace the ailing Captain Proctor as Fort Reno's commanding officer.

"I'm trying to catch up to John Phillips, sir," I answered.

"Well, you missed him by a couple of hours. Phillips went on to Fort Laramie at sundown. He said he wanted to travel at night. Are you carrying additional dispatches from Colonel Carrington?"

"No, sir. I came on my own authority because I thought Portugee might need help fending off Indians."

"Phillips didn't say anything about encountering any savages on his trip. What do you know of the effort to locate survivors after the battle on the twenty-first?"

"There were no survivors, sir. I helped bring in the last of the bodies."

I turned Luke around and headed for the gate.

"Where are you going?" the officer asked.

"After Portugee."

"No, you're not."

CHAPTER 49

"Colonel, you can't stop me!" I exclaimed. "I'm not a soldier. I'm not even a civilian employee of the army anymore. I abandoned my job when I rode away from Fort Phil Kearny."

"Calm down, son. I won't detain you long. But it'd be inhumane if I let you ride on without food and coffee in your belly. You also need to dry out those clothes before they freeze fast to your skin."

I took a deep breath. "I'm sorry I lost my temper, sir."

"Forget it. Come along with me. I've got hot coffee on the stove, and I'll have my orderly rustle up some grub. The sergeant of the guard will select the best horse we have left and switch your saddle and gear."

"Sir, I don't want another mount. I want to continue on with Luke."

"Luke?"

"My mule." I reached over and scratched his forehead. He shook his head and snorted.

The officer gave a half-hearted laugh. "All right. I'll have the farrier check Luke over to be sure he's fit to go on."

The officer sent one of the sentries away with Luke and escorted me into his office. He helped me out of my buffalo overcoat and draped it over a straight-backed chair next to a sheet-iron stove. Steam rose from the melting ice that coated the garment.

Lieutenant Colonel Wessells asked if I'd run into Indians on my trek from Fort Phil Kearny. I told him about my encounter at Clear Creek but said I'd not seen any others.

"You must keep vigilant," he said. "Yesterday, a band of Arapahos made a stab at stealing some of our horses from a water detail that had gone down to the spring. The troops said a white man was riding with the band."

"Duggan Maguire," I said.

"How's that?" he asked.

I described Maguire's history.

"Knights of the Golden Circle, you say?"

"The evidence seems to point in that direction, sir." I explained what had led Colonel Carrington to decide the KGC was operating in the Dakota Territory.

"Well," he went on, "Colonel Carrington was instrumental in frustrating the efforts of the Copperheads. He would know about the KGC."

In response to a knock on his door, Lieutenant Colonel Wessells said, "Come in."

A rush of cold air preceded a captain who pushed the door closed behind him.

"General," the captain said, "I heard another man arrived from Fort Phil Kearny."

"Yes, General," Wessells said. "Meet Zachary Wakefield."

"Mr. Wakefield," the captain said. "Good evening. My name is Dandy. I've been assigned to replace Captain Brown as quartermaster at Fort Phil Kearny."

"Sir," I said, "I'm not sure how to tell you this, but I was Captain Brown's clerk."

I repeated my involvement in recovering the bodies of Fetterman's command, including that of Captain Brown. I admitted to deserting my post but hoped that trying to help Portugee Phillips was an acceptable excuse.

"Mr. Wakefield," Captain Dandy said, "since you plan to

return to Fort Phil Kearny, we will evaluate your position at that time."

"Yes, sir."

"General," Dandy spoke to Wessells, "I will leave at first light. I have two lieutenants and twenty-two enlisted men. Based upon the conditions Mr. Wakefield has described, we can probably reach Fort Phil Kearny in under three days. If you'll excuse me, I want to get a little sleep."

"All right, General," Wessells said. "I'll see you off in the morning."

After Captain Dandy left, I posed a question to Lieutenant Colonel Wessells. "Am I correct in assuming that both of you were brevetted generals in the war?"

"Brigadier generals," he answered. "Both of us."

The orderly brought in a plate of food, and I devoured salt pork and hardtack, washed down with a cup of thick, black coffee. I thanked my host for the nourishment and retrieved my buffalo coat. A puddle of water lay under the chair. The outside fur still felt damp, but the heat from the stove had warmed the inside.

The farrier returned with my mule. "Ye've got yerself a fine mule, so ye have." The farrier spoke with a thick Irish brogue. "Sure, and I fed and watered him for ye, and curried him a bit before replacin' the tack. I had to reseat two nails in his left front shoe. Them nails may've worked loose from poundin' on frozen ground, ye know. Ye'll be needin' to keep an eye on that hoof. Iffen he throws that shoe, he'll go lame on ye."

"You're sure you want to go on?" Lieutenant Colonel Wessells asked. "Portugee has two others with him already."

"Two others?" I asked. "I knew Dixon was with him."

"When Phillips and Dixon arrived, they hooked up with William Bailey. He was waiting here for the weather to clear, but when Phillips insisted on pressing ahead, Bailey joined them."

William Bailey was the mail carrier who regularly traveled between Fort Phil Kearny and Fort Caspar.

"I'm glad Portugee has another to accompany him, but I'm going just the same."

I was about three hours behind Portugee when I said goodbye to the commanding officer and rode out the fort's gate.

The Powder River's current flowed fast enough past Fort Reno to keep the surface from freezing completely. Chunks of ice that had broken away from the banks of the creek farther upstream bumped against Luke's legs as he waded across the ford below the fort.

I'd gotten away from Fort Reno a little after eight o'clock on the evening of December 23. The snow had stopped falling, and the wind had abated somewhat, so the chill on my back was less brutal. Luke seemed rejuvenated. The Irish farrier had treated him well.

Without a watch, I couldn't be sure, but it was probably the witching hour when I reached Sand Creek. Christmas Eve day had begun.

Luke lumbered up the embankment on the south side of the creek, where I came upon a well-remembered site.

"Whoa." I halted Luke at the base of a large cottonwood tree. Two wooden crosses stood partially buried in snow beneath its branches. I didn't need to dismount to decipher the faded lettering on the cross pieces. They marked the graves of Reverend Hollister and his wife.

"Well, Preacher," I said aloud. "Back then I cursed you for bringing Katy O'Toole into this wilderness. Now, I guess I have to thank you."

If the reverend had succeeded in his stubborn plan to travel alone to Montana, Katy would have disappeared from my life. As it was, she'd become very much a part of it. In fact, I was fairly sure I'd heard her say she loved me.

I clucked, and Luke had taken only a dozen paces when I halted him again beside the burned-out wreckage of the Hollisters' wagon. Bits of charred wood and blackened iron thrust their skeletons above the drifting snow.

I rode around the wagon's remains and paused at the top of the bank above Sand Creek. Below me, I made out the clump of bushes where I'd found Katy hiding. I returned to the Bozeman Trail and continued my pursuit of Portugee Phillips.

The effect of the coffee had worn off, and my eyes wanted to close. When they did, my chin dropped, jolting me awake again. I dismounted every hour or so and led Luke at a walk. His head sagged. We both needed to sleep, but we still had miles to go. My fingers lacked feeling. My toes were numb. Each breath hung in a suspended cloud before me. My nose ran. My eyes watered. My teeth chattered. I didn't need a thermometer to tell me the temperature remained well below zero.

When the first glow of sunrise appeared in the east, we were descending the long, gradual slope to the Dry Fork of the Cheyenne River. We'd come seventy miles from Fort Reno. I decided it wasn't safe to go farther without rest.

I guided Luke into a clump of stunted cottonwood, juniper, and scrub oak. This would shelter us from the north wind and hopefully provide concealment from any passing Indians. I tied Luke's reins to a low-lying branch. I removed the saddle but left the blanket on to provide him warmth. I gave him some oats and a little water. I had to be stingy with the water. The Dry Fork of the Cheyenne River was living up to its name. The only traces of water were frozen patches of thin ice.

With my pocketknife, I hacked branches off a juniper tree and piled them up to keep me out of the snow that covered the ground. I placed my saddle at one end of the pile to serve as a pillow. I wrapped my blanket around me and stretched out on my makeshift bed. The faint aroma of Katy remained on the shawl. I drew an end of it over my nose and imagined her beside me. I pulled my slouch hat over my face and fell asleep.

Several hours later, a rumbling sound and a shaking of my flimsy bed woke me. It took a few seconds to realize a herd of buffalo was making its way down the slope toward the river. The animals were moving south, same as I. John Bozeman had probably selected this ancient buffalo path as the logical place to cross the dry riverbed when he'd first explored the route.

I shook newly fallen snow from my blanket and slouch hat. The inside of the blanket had absorbed moisture from the wet surface of my buffalo overcoat, but I had been so tired, I'd slept soundly. I stomped my feet to get the blood flowing in my frigid toes and slapped my arms around my body to force circulation into my cold fingers. I laid a gloved hand on Luke's mane to keep him steady while hundreds of great shaggy beasts flowed by us on either side. The thicket had kept them from trampling over us.

The herd required the better part of an hour to pass. They headed due south, keeping their rumps turned to the north wind. They climbed straight up the opposite bank of the dry riverbed and continued cross-country. Fortunately, I wouldn't have to contend with them when I proceeded, because the Bozeman Trail ran southwest paralleling the river course.

After the buffalo passed, I fed Luke more oats and gave him another drink. I softened hardtack with my precious water and gummed the cracker more than chewed it. I washed the mushy substance down with a swig from a canteen. I saddled Luke, and we resumed our journey.

I must have slept seven or eight hours, because the low position of the sun's glow through the snow flurries indicated it was evening again. The force of the wind had dropped, as it usually did at sundown. I was forty-five miles from Bridger's Ferry.

Hopefully, I could catch up to Portugee there.

Sometime after midnight, in the early hours of Christmas day, I arrived at the mouth of Sage Creek where the Bozeman Trail joined the Mormon Trail. I had thirty miles to go to Bridger's Ferry. I turned east and rode past French Pete's old site. At times, off to my right down a steep embankment, I caught a glimpse of the North Platte River. Chunks of ice and downed cottonwood limbs drifted in the rapidly flowing water.

The sun had risen when I rode into the army encampment that provided guard services for Bridger's Ferry. Sunrise occurred around seven thirty this time of year. Soldiers were forming up for guard mount. That provided another clue as to the time of day. I estimated it to be about eight o'clock.

A sentry stepped in front of me pointing a rifle-musket at my chest. "Halt! Who are you, and where are you going?"

"Zachary Wakefield from Fort Phil Kearny. I'm looking for Portugee Phillips. He should have come through here on his way to Fort Laramie carrying news about the Fetterman fight."

The sentry lowered his rifle and pointed toward the river. "You might catch him if you hurry. He went down to the ferry a half hour ago."

403

CHAPTER 50

When I headed down the slope to the ferry landing, the raft was pulling away. In addition to the ferryman, three men and their horses stood onboard.

"Portugee!" I stood in the stirrups, jerked off my hat, and waved it overhead. "Portugee, wait!"

My voice carried well in the crisp morning air, because Portugee reached out, touched the ferryman, and pointed toward me. The ferryman shook his head and continued to haul on the rope to pull the craft farther into the current.

Portugee grabbed the ferryman's sleeve, shook a gloved finger in his face, and pointed again in my direction.

By the time I reached the boarding ramp, the ferryman had reversed course and, with the help of the other three men, pulled the raft into the landing. The ferry had barely stopped when I dismounted and led Luke on board.

"Zach Wakefield," Portugee said, "what are you doing here?"

"I was worried you might be attacked by Indians, and with only two of you . . . three after you left Fort Reno . . . I thought you could use another hand."

Portugee laughed. "Well," he said, "as you can see, we are safe. But you're welcome to join us, nonetheless."

Benjamin Mills, the ferryman, whom I recognized from when I'd crossed the river in June, held an open palm out to me. "One dollar," he said. "Folks on official government business ride for free. You have to pay one dollar . . . fifty cents for you, fifty cents for the mule."

"Mr. Mills," Portugee said, "he's joining me."

"Mr. Phillips," the ferryman said, "you and Mr. Dixon are carrying dispatches for the government, and Mr. Bailey is an official mail carrier. This feller just rode up and wants a free ride across, as I see it."

The ferryman turned to me. "You carrying dispatches?"

I shook my head.

"One dollar or get off my ferry."

I dug into my saddlebags, retrieved my tri-fold wallet, and unrolled it. I extracted a greenback dollar and slapped it into Mills's extended hand.

We crossed the North Platte River, and the four of us headed east on the Oregon Trail for the nine-mile ride to Horseshoe Station and its telegraph office.

The snow, which had stopped falling earlier that Christmas morning, now returned with a vengeance. The wind, howling from the north across the expanse of river water, intensified its bitterness.

We rode two abreast to stay on the hardened road. We didn't have to look for foliage to mark the sides of the path here, we followed the wires strung overhead between the telegraph poles. The snow-covered ruts created by years of passing wagons provided treacherous footing for our mounts. Their hooves would drop unexpectedly and cause them to stumble, forcing us riders to grab the saddle.

About ten o'clock, the telegraph lines led us into the enclosure of Horseshoe Station. We surprised the small contingent assigned there.

I'd met John Friend, the telegrapher, the past summer on my trip north. I introduced John to Portugee. The soldiers and the telegrapher listened wide-eyed to our story about the Fetterman battle. It did not take long for them to understand the urgency of Portugee's mission.

Friend read through the dispatches. "This rambling message from Colonel Carrington is too long for me to guarantee correct transmittal over the wires," he said. "Plus, you've got this other message Lieutenant Colonel Wessells wants transmitted to the commanding officer at Fort Laramie. I'll do the best I can, Mr. Phillips."

While Friend got busy with his key, some soldiers fed us a makeshift lunch of sow belly and hardtack. Other soldiers fed and watered our mounts. The strong black coffee restored me more than the food did.

About two o'clock, Friend announced he'd completed the transmission. "I condensed portions of Colonel Carrington's message. It was just too long."

"I'll take the dispatches now," Portugee said, holding out a hand to Friend.

The telegrapher passed them over with a quizzical look.

"I'm riding on to Fort Laramie," Portugee said. "Thank you, Mr. Friend, for sending what you could, but I promised the colonel I'd deliver his message to Fort Laramie. I intend to see every word gets to Lieutenant Colonel Palmer just as the colonel paid me to do."

Portugee donned his buffalo protective clothing.

"I won't go with you, Portugee," Dixon said. "This is as far as I'm going."

"I can't go with you either," Bailey said. "I have mail to deliver to Fort Caspar, so I'm going to head west."

"I'll go with you, Portugee," I said. I gathered up my buffalo coat and gauntlets from where they'd been drying in front of a sheet-iron stove. I tugged Katy's shawl over the top of my slouch hat and knotted it beneath my chin.

Shortly after two o'clock on Christmas afternoon, Portugee and I rode east. Fort Laramie lay forty miles down the Oregon

Trail. The blizzard had grown worse during the time we'd spent in the warmth of Horseshoe Station. The wind pummeled my face, so I drew an end of Katy's shawl across my nose and mouth.

The sun grew dim over our backs as we kept our mounts at a trot. Portugee and I did not speak. We would have needed to shout to be heard over the wind even though we rode side by side.

We dismounted every hour to walk our mounts and pound feeling into our own limbs. We fed the animals oats the soldiers at Horseshoe Station had provided. Portugee and I nibbled hardtack and shared canteen water with the animals.

About four thirty in the afternoon we reached Bitter Cottonwood Creek. The light from the sun had disappeared, meaning we'd have to ride the rest of the way in darkness. We'd come eighteen miles from Horseshoe Station and had twenty-two ahead of us. Little water flowed in this creek, and what there was of it was frozen solid. We dismounted and led the animals across. We didn't want to take a chance of them slipping on the ice with us in the saddle.

When we reached Nine-Mile Ranche, I hoped we would stop to warm up and get a bite to eat. But the place was dark. On a holiday, lights should be blazing, and noise from shouting, singing, and brawling should be making the walls shake. But the weather was so bad, no soldiers had made the trek from the fort to partake in wine, women, and song, even though it was Christmas day.

"Why don't we knock?" I asked Portugee. "Someone will wake up and let us in."

"No, we need to move on."

So, we continued. As the name of the location implied, we had nine miles to go.

The storm assailed us with blasts of frigid wind. The blizzard alternated between wet, heavy snow and icy sleet. I continually brushed snow out of the gap between my crotch and the pommel of my saddle. The frosty stuff wanted to create a drift against my privates, and I didn't particularly like it accumulating there.

Finally, we turned off the Oregon Trail onto the approach road leading to Fort Laramie. One more mile to our destination. We'd come two hundred and thirty-four miles from Fort Phil Kearny.

Suddenly, Luke jolted to a halt. I flicked the reins, kicked his flanks with my heels, and clucked for him to proceed. He took one step and stopped again.

"Hold up, Portugee!" I yelled.

Portugee had gotten several paces ahead of me. He heard my call and turned back.

I dismounted as he approached. I knew without looking what caused Luke to not want to move. I lifted his left front hoof. No shoe.

"Ah, damn!" I looked up at Portugee. "He's thrown a shoe. The farrier at Fort Reno warned me it might happen."

"Climb up behind me," Portugee said.

Colonel Carrington's thoroughbred, Dandy, stood with his head hanging down, foam blowing from his muzzle.

"No, that horse is too tired to carry two. You go on. It's only a mile. I'll lead Luke in."

Portugee nodded and turned his horse around. He gradually pulled away.

Eventually, I saw the lights of Fort Laramie. I was tired and cold, but I staggered ahead, and Luke plodded behind me. He probably would have followed without me holding his reins.

"Halt! Who goes there?" A sentry confronted me.

I did as he commanded. "Wakefield," I replied. "Zachary

Wakefield from Fort Phil Kearny." I could hardly keep my eyes open, and I swayed on my feet.

"Lieutenant Haas!" The sentry shouted over his shoulder.

An officer appeared out of the dimness.

"It's Wakefield," the sentry said. "He's the one Mr. Phillips told us would be coming along."

"Mr. Wakefield," the lieutenant said, "I'm Lieutenant Haas, officer of the guard. Follow me. Major Bonnet is waiting for you at Old Bedlam."

I opened one eye. Then, I opened the other. There wasn't any snow anyplace. No whiteness surrounded me. A dark, wool army blanket was tucked under my chin. My teeth no longer chattered.

"Ah, sleeping beauty awakens."

I took a deep breath and inhaled the sweet aroma of tobacco. Major Bonnet sat on a chair a few feet away puffing on his pipe.

"How do you feel?" he asked, holding the pipe away from his mouth.

"Fine. Where am I? How long have I been here?"

The major laughed. "Well, you're coherent again. You're in my bed, and you've been sleeping for fifteen hours."

"Fifteen hours! How? Why?"

"You staggered into Old Bedlam around midnight last night and collapsed. It's approaching sundown on the day after Christmas."

I realized I wore only my drawers. Someone had undressed me and put me to bed . . . just like my mother used to. I rolled over and swung my feet onto the floor. When I did, the shamrock suspended on its chain swung free and dangled before my bare chest. I looked at the major.

His eyes sparkled, and a grin raised the corners of his lips while his teeth still gripped the stem of his pipe. He laid the pipe on the table beside him. "I take it Miss Kathleen O'Toole still resides at Fort Phil Kearny?"

"Yes, sir." I told him how I came to be wearing the pendant and offered to return it to him.

"No," he said. "I gave it to Katy, and it's hers to do with as she pleases. Now, you just relax and get your strength back."

"I can't stay here," I said.

"Why not?"

"It's your bed, Major. I need to go to the teamsters' quarters."

"There'll be time for that, soon enough. How about a cup of coffee?"

"Coffee sounds good, sir."

Major Bonnet filled a cup from a pot perched on a pot-bellied stove. "Sugar?" he asked.

"No, sir. I drink it black."

He handed me the cup and I winced when I wrapped my fingers around it. My fingers stung, but not from the heat of the cup. The pain was internal. I studied the backs of my swollen, red knuckles. The tips of my fingers were pale, almost pure white.

The major returned to his chair and retrieved his pipe. He drew deeply on the stem and coaxed smoke to curl up from the bowl. "Fingers hurt?"

I nodded as I took a sip of coffee.

"Frost nip. You're lucky you don't have frostbite, like Mr. Phillips. He's in the hospital. He'll be lucky if he doesn't lose some fingers or toes. The doctor says you'll recover. Going to ache a bit while you do, though."

I took another sip of coffee, remembering the time months ago when I'd observed the paymaster sitting on this bed to strap on his wooden leg.

"Still snowing?" I asked. I turned to glance out the single

window, but the pane was obscured behind a spidery pattern of frost.

"Yes. Still snowing," he said. "Longest blizzard I've ever endured. The thermometer on the balcony reads twenty-five below. Been that way for days."

We sat in silence a moment, me sipping coffee and the major smoking his pipe.

"You got a razor?" the major asked.

I ran the fingers of my free hand over my cheek. "No, but I won't need one."

I hadn't shaved for five days. That was the longest I'd ever gone. I told the major Katy had said I might look good with a beard, and I had decided to let it grow.

"Where's Luke?" I asked.

"Your mule?"

"Yes, sir."

"He's in the stables. The farrier replaced his shoe. Your mule did better than Mr. Phillips's horse."

"Dandy?"

"That the name of the horse?"

"Yes, sir. He's one of Colonel Carrington's thoroughbreds."

"Was one. The horse dropped dead in the street shortly after Mr. Phillips arrived."

"Portugee delivered the dispatches all right?" I asked.

"Yes, around eleven o'clock last night. An hour before you came in."

The major described how Portugee had disrupted a full-dress garrison ball underway in Old Bedlam where the officers and their ladies were celebrating Christmas. Lieutenant Colonel Palmer had received the telegram from Horseshoe Station earlier that afternoon. He had found the telegram hard to believe even though it corroborated a rumor being circulated by the Laramie Loafers about the Fetterman fight. When Portugee

Phillips stumbled into the ballroom wearing his frost-covered buffalo overcoat and heavy gauntlets, the rumor became reality.

CHAPTER 51

One week later, January 2, 1867, I sat at what doubled as Major Bonnet's dining table and office desk at Fort Laramie. We were creating payroll records for the reorganization of the regiments that had gone into effect the day before. The pay period ending December 31, 1866, was the last payroll for the Eighteenth Infantry in its old configuration.

My fingers had recovered enough from frost nip that I could write legibly. I flexed my fingers and blew on them frequently . . . for what purpose, I didn't know. The doctor assured me the phantom pain would soon disappear. I hoped so.

The major knew I intended to return to Fort Phil Kearny, and since I was no longer officially employed as a quartermaster clerk, he offered me a temporary position as a payroll clerk. His current payroll clerk was again down with ague and not fit to travel.

In the reorganization of the army, directed by Congress, the First Battalion of the Eighteenth Infantry retained that regimental designation. Colonel Carrington would continue as commanding officer of the Eighteenth but would move his headquarters to Fort Caspar. The Second Battalion, currently occupying the three forts along the Bozeman Trail, was now the Twenty-Seventh Infantry. Lieutenant Colonel Wessells would assume command of this new regiment with his headquarters at Fort Phil Kearny. This was the regiment Captain Fetterman had boasted he would command. The Third Battalion, largely stationed in Utah, became the Thirty-Sixth Infantry. It had played no role in the fight with the Indians along the Bozeman Trail.

Lieutenant Colonel Innis Palmer came to see Major Bonnet in his quarters late on the afternoon of January 2. Palmer had replaced Major Van Voast as Fort Laramie's commanding officer a few weeks earlier.

"Major Bonnet, can you be ready to travel tomorrow?" Lieutenant Colonel Palmer asked.

"I'm afraid not, General." The major addressed Palmer with the brevet rank awarded to him during the war. "The pay chests have not arrived. They're stranded at Fort Sedgwick because of the blizzard."

"Today is the first break we've had in the weather," General Palmer continued, "and I can't delay the relief column any longer. Major Van Voast will lead Companies B, C, E, and G of the Eighteenth north tomorrow. Lieutenant Gordon will follow on the fifth with Companies D and E of the Second Cavalry. The cavalry's struggling to get their horses properly shod. Hopefully, your pay chests will arrive in time for you to travel with the cavalry as your escort."

"That would be desirable," Major Bonnet said.

"I'm concerned," General Palmer continued. "Omaha has ordered me to send extensive reinforcements to Fort Phil Kearny, but it will leave only Company K of the Eighteenth and Company F of the Second here at Fort Laramie. True, there hasn't been the threat here that was experienced farther north. Still, I don't trust these Laramie Loafers camped so near the fort."

"General," Major Bonnet said, "I'm going to need two ambulances to transport the payroll. With so many troops departing tomorrow . . . troops that I normally would pay here . . . I'll have to transport more pay chests up the line."

"You can have two ambulances. That's not a problem. If your pay chests don't get here before the cavalry leaves, what's your contingency plan?"

"You're also sending fifty wagons with supplies, ordnance, and ammunition along with the troops, right?"

"Yes."

"That will slow the column's march through the snow. With my two lighter ambulances, I can move rapidly. All I require is Sergeant Marley and a squad of infantry for security. The sergeant is familiar with the route. He's accompanied me before. With this weather, I don't perceive any real danger between here and Fort Reno."

"Sir." It was highly unusual for me, a civilian clerk, to interrupt the discussion of two senior officers.

Major Bonnet raised his eyebrows. "Yes, Zach?"

"Sir," I continued, "you recall Lieutenant Colonel Wessells at Fort Reno told me his men thought they'd seen Duggan Maguire with a band of Arapahos in the area."

"Yes," Major Bonnet said, "I recall what General Wessells told you. So what?"

The major used Wessells's brevet Civil War rank. Carrington, Wessells, Dandy, Palmer—there were a lot of former generals in the area now.

"Just thought I'd mention it, sir."

"We'll catch up to the main column long before we get to Fort Reno. With this bad weather, the Indians will stay north of the Powder River."

The pay chests arrived January 6, a few hours after the Second Cavalry companies had departed Fort Laramie. We spent the rest of the day paying the troops remaining at Fort Laramie.

On Monday, January 7, we prepared to head north. I sat on the driver's seat of one of two ambulances parked in front of

415

Old Bedlam waiting for Major Bonnet to appear. Sergeant Marley, along with a corporal and a squad of ten privates, stood at ease alongside the ambulances. Snow drifts on the parade ground lay six feet deep, and the temperature stood at forty below zero.

"Sergeant Marley?" Major Bonnet called from where he appeared on the second-floor balcony. "Are these the same men who went with us before?"

"No, sir. They're new recruits. Half of them are German and don't speak much English. The other half are straight off the boat from Ireland. They speak English, so they tell me. I can't understand their brogue. Except for the corporal, none of them have ever shot at an enemy."

The major sighed and shook his head. "God, help us," he said. "Let's get moving." His wooden leg thumped along the balcony floor as he headed toward the stairs.

The enlisted men wore standard wool overcoats. The major at least had the addition of a cape over the shoulders of his officer's overcoat. I'm sure I was warmer than any of them as I snugged my hand-made buffalo coat closer around me.

On my ambulance, I had hitched Luke in the near-wheel position, his usual spot. The other three mules were new. Hopefully, Luke's presence would help me shape them into a responsive team.

The major had left the selection of the driver of the second ambulance to me. I'd chosen a young German recruit. Franz Stroebel had never handled a four-team hitch, but he'd been raised on a farm near Dusseldorf where he'd driven two-horse teams.

We proceeded to the adjutant's office, where we hauled the pay chests out and loaded them into the beds of the ambulances. As on our first journey, the major entrusted me with a lanyard containing the second set of keys for the two dozen chests. I hung the lanyard around my neck and dropped the keys down the inside of my shirt, where they clinked against the shamrock pendant.

Then we drove over to the stables and laid sacks of oats and shelled corn for the mules on top of the chests. We should have enough feed to see us through to Fort Reno if another blizzard didn't delay our progress.

That first day we covered twenty-five miles and camped on the banks of Bitter Cottonwood Creek. The puddles remained frozen, just as Portugee and I had previously experienced. The soldiers slipped and slid along the stream's bed to its confluence with the North Platte River, where they chopped ice away from the edge in order to fill buckets and canteens with water.

Franz Stroebel handled his teams well, even though all he had to do was follow me down the center of the Oregon Trail. "Good job, Franz," I said while we watered and fed the mules.

"Ja. Thankee."

As before, I served as the paymaster's cook. Franz joined us, and he helped me by gathering firewood and tending the blaze. The other soldiers divided into small groups and prepared their own meals. Everybody shared the same menu of bacon, hardtack, and coffee.

The second day, January 8, we covered twenty-seven miles. At midday, we paused at Horseshoe Station, but the major kept pressing us forward. It was an hour after sundown when we reached Bridger's Ferry. Benjamin Mills refused to bring his ferry across, shouting it was too dark for a safe crossing of the icy river. We went into camp.

We were three days behind the cavalry when we crossed the North Platte at Bridger's Ferry on January 9. I gave Mills a sneer when I drove my ambulance on board his ferry. The old skinflint wasn't going to get a greenback off me again.

We paused for a couple of hours to pay the troops stationed

at the crossing site. It was midmorning by the time we headed west along the Mormon Trail skirting the north bank of the North Platte. By nightfall, we'd come a little more than thirty miles and camped at Sage Creek, where the Bozeman Trail started. Overhead the Milky Way sprayed glitter across the sky.

On the morning of January 10, the temperature remained below zero. We made good progress because the infantry troops of Van Voast's command had shoveled the deep drifts off the trail to allow their fifty wagons to pass. Dirty piles of snow remained along the sides of the road, but the main course was clear.

Major Bonnet rode Hector, while Franz and I drove the two ambulances. Sergeant Marley and the squad of infantry marched ahead of us. Because of the deep snow alongside the road, placing flankers out was impractical. That security precaution probably wasn't necessary because it was unlikely Indians could travel through the drifts of snow either.

Late in the afternoon, we reached the South Fork of the Dry Fork of the Cheyenne River. This was where the Arapahos had attacked us last summer. The temperature that long-ago day had been one hundred fifty degrees warmer.

We parked our ambulances ten yards apart on a slight rise, with the bed of the dry creek to our north. On the opposite side of the stream crossing was the thicket where Luke and I had waited out the passing of the buffalo herd.

Only stunted vegetation grew this far above the stream's bank. We had an unobstructed view in all directions. We strung rope between the front and rear of the ambulances to form a corral for the animals.

By hammering the ice off frozen ponds in the creek bed, we uncovered enough water for the mules to drink. I filled a bucket, which I used to make a pot of coffee and then to wash the dirty skillet and the tin plates and cups.

After supper, Franz and I spread a tarp on the ground under one of the ambulances. Major Bonnet, sitting beside the dying cook fire, finished his evening pipe of tobacco before joining us. We three wrapped ourselves in our blankets and stretched out side by side in anticipation of another night of shivering.

Sergeant Marley posted four of his men as sentries several yards out in a semi-circular perimeter defense to the south. The stream would suffice as defense to our north. The sergeant and the remaining infantrymen crowded under the other ambulance to get some sleep before it was time to change the guard.

It seemed I would just drift off to sleep when a wolf howled in the distance. Perhaps that buffalo herd I'd encountered earlier was passing through the area again, and the wolves were stalking the weaker bison. It became a long, cold, restless night.

The sudden howling of many wolves caused me to sit up quickly, banging my head on the undercarriage of the ambulance. They weren't wolves.

The approach of sunrise that January 11 morning lightened the sky to the east, revealing dozens of Indians on ponies racing toward us. The screech of war cries accompanied the snap of carbine fire. Bullets whizzed through our campsite and smacked into the sides of the ambulances. Arrows swished through the canvas side curtains.

We all scrambled out from under the ambulances as the sentries came running back from their exposed posts. Mules jostled with men for space inside the makeshift corral.

"Get the pay chests," Major Bonnet commanded. "Spread them along the outsides of the ambulances."

"You heard the officer!" Sergeant Marley shouted.

Soldiers dragged the heavy pay chests out, two men to a chest. They lined them up on the exposed east side of one ambulance and west side of the other. In the process, two infantrymen were killed. Finally, everybody else crawled beneath the ambulances, using the chests as barricades, weapons pointing outward in opposite directions from our corralled animals. Sergeant Marley and two privates crawled under to my left. Major Bonnet crouched to my right with the rear of the ambulance above his head.

We were most vulnerable where the makeshift corral ropes extended between the two ambulances. The northern roped end abutted the creek. The other open end jutted to the south. The Indians found this weak point and shot down its length. Mules brayed and screamed when hit with bullets or arrows. Two mules went down with their wounds. The remaining mules and the major's horse panicked. They surged against the barricade on the creek side and broke through. The rope line could not contain them.

The infantrymen, armed with single-shot Springfield riflemuskets, experienced the same frustration I had the summer before. It was impossible to reload that weapon while prone. Two of the men were wounded when they backed out from under their ambulance to reload in the standing position.

I quickly fired the six bullets in my revolver. I had extra ammunition in my belt pouch and rolled onto my back to reload. I'd become adept at the procedure, but it still took a full minute to complete.

The Indians raced back and forth along the three sides of our makeshift fortress that faced away from the creek bed. The winds that howled persistently through this part of the country had kept our chosen higher ground clear of snow. Although it had made for a good campsite, it benefited our attackers more than us. No drifts impeded our enemy's maneuvering their ponies.

I extended the reloaded revolver across the top of the pay chest and waited for a target to get close. Over my sights, sitting on ponies on a hillock three hundred yards beyond the circling warriors, I spied a familiar pair. The upright feathered head-dress identified one as Running Bear, the Arapaho chief. Beside him sat a man wearing buckskins.

"Major," I asked, "do you recognize that white man out there?" I used my pistol to point toward the rise.

"Don't tell me it's Duggan Maguire," he responded.

"It is."

"That bastard swore he'd get the payroll someday," the major said. "If he succeeds, the Knights of the Golden Circle may crown him king."

The Indians made another charge at us. I dropped one of the warriors with a shot. I did not see any other savages fall from their mounts even though rifle fire blazed from beneath our ambulances. Sergeant Marley had warned us that his recruits had not had target practice.

Twenty-five or thirty Indians rode in the attacking force. They outnumbered us two to one. We were concealed behind barriers, but our marksmanship was inferior to that of our opponents. It might be only a matter of time.

"Those are Spencer carbines those bastards are firing!" Sergeant Marley exclaimed.

"Weapons they took off the cavalry at Lodge Trail Ridge," I said.

"They may have the carbines," the sergeant said, "but they surely don't have much ammunition."

"They're doing pretty well with what they have," Major Bonnet said.

The major, like me, was armed with a revolver. We were the only two of our force with repeating-type weapons. Our pistols, although each contained six shots, had relatively short range. The Indians' Spencer carbines held seven rounds with a range twice that of our Colts. And the Arapahos had at least a half dozen carbines. While a savage might not be the best shot with

421

a firearm, he was incomparable with bow and arrows. An Indian was so good at shooting from beneath the neck of a pony, he could get off a half dozen arrows while a soldier fired once with his Springfield.

To my right, I heard a *whap* and felt a bump against my side.

"Ah, damn!" the major exclaimed.

No pay chest had been positioned across the rear of the ambulance, and Major Bonnet's right side lay exposed. An Indian had identified that weakness in our defense and shot an arrow into the opening. It had slammed into the major's right leg, driving him against me.

"Why couldn't they have hit the wooden leg like they did the last time."

"Are you hurt badly?" I asked him.

"It's not good," he replied. "Here, you can make better use of this than me." He wheezed as he handed me his revolver.

I now had two revolvers.

"Sergeant," I said, "take the major's pistol. Give me your rifle. I want to try something that might discourage the bastards."

We exchanged weapons.

I returned my revolver to its holster and checked the Springfield to ensure it was loaded. I untied Katy's shawl from around my ears and laid it and my slouch hat atop the pay chest. I nestled the barrel of the rifle-musket into the crushed crown of the hat. The Springfield was notorious for being slow to load but was famous for being accurate up to five hundred yards.

Duggan Maguire would know the effective range of a Springfield from his war experience. He also knew that current army recruits were not receiving target practice. Perhaps that's why he and the Arapaho chief had allowed themselves to take up their present position.

My intended target was well within the effective range of my weapon. Still, I would have only one shot. I raised the rear leaf sight and brought my target into focus. I took a deep breath, exhaled half, and squeezed the trigger.

The discharging weapon slammed into my shoulder. White powder obscured my view. When it cleared, Duggan Maguire lay motionless on the ground.

Chief Running Bear twirled his feathered lance above his head, and the braves broke off their attack. They'd already gathered up the warrior I'd shot earlier. Now, two of them scooped up Maguire between them, and the Arapahos rode away.

"Good shot, Zach," the major said through labored breathing.

"We'll get that arrow out now, Major." I laid a hand on his arm. "Hang on."

"Sergeant." I motioned for him to crawl out from under the ambulance with me. "We need to get the mules back, or we'll be stuck here."

"Corporal," the sergeant called. The soldier summoned climbed out from under the other ambulance.

"Sarge?" the corporal asked.

"Take half the men and find the mules and the major's horse."

"Take Franz with you," I said. "He knows animals."

The corporal nodded.

"Franz," I addressed the German private, "detach those ropes from the ambulances and cut them in two to make some lassos. Take the bridle for the major's horse. He hung it on the far side of that ambulance." I pointed behind Franz. "Hector's a gentle horse. If you can get a bridle on him, the mules will follow you. Let's hope they're not scattered all the way to Sage Creek."

The corporal, four privates, and Franz headed off on their assignment.

"You other men," the sergeant said, "form a perimeter defense twenty yards out." He swept his arm in an arc around the outside of the ambulances.

"Sergeant Marley," I said. "We need to get the arrow out of the major's leg."

Major Bonnet was braver than I might have been under the circumstances. He gave me a wry grin when I crawled up beside him again.

"Hurt?" It was a dumb question but the only thing that came to mind.

"Not as much as when the cannon ball tore my leg off. I keep reminding myself of that difference."

Sergeant Marley crawled up on the other side of the major.

"Sergeant, have you done this before?" I asked.

"Yes. When you're battling savages on the frontier a man gets shot with an arrow every now and then."

"I saw one extracted once," I said.

The sergeant was busy examining the major's leg, and I decided I didn't need to describe the details of the major extracting the arrow from Katy O'Toole's shoulder.

"Major," the sergeant said, "it passed clear through the fleshy part of your calf, just above your boot top. You're bleeding, but not from an artery."

"Well, it's a good thing the bastard didn't shoot lower and ruin these new boots. I'd be really mad, then."

All three of us chuckled at the major's humor.

"I have to cut that arrowhead off so I can pull the shaft out," the sergeant said. "I'll need a sharp knife. My bayonet won't do."

"There's a butcher knife in the mess kit," I said. "It's plenty sharp."

"Fetch that," the sergeant said. "I'll get his boot off."

While I'd gone to get the knife, the sergeant had stripped a short branch clean of its bark, and the major clamped it between his teeth. I grasped the major's ankle and steadied his leg while the sergeant sawed at the shaft. The major kept blowing his breath out around the stick in sharp bursts. Even though I held his ankle to keep his leg stretched taut, it moved slightly with each stroke the sergeant took with the knife. A couple of minutes later the arrowhead fell to the ground.

The sergeant moved to the other side, grasped the feathered end of the shaft with one hand, and placed his other against the major's knee. "Keep his leg straight, Mr. Wakefield," he said. "Deep breath, Major. Going to hurt. Ready? Now!"

The major let out a whopping yowl when the sergeant pulled the arrow out. Blood flowed from the wound on both sides of his calf. The sergeant used the butcher knife to slice the major's pants leg up to the knee and rolled the material up above the wound. I wrapped Katy's shawl twice around the major's leg, tied it tightly, and pressed on both sides. Blood seeped through the material.

"Is that Katy O'Toole's shawl?" the major asked.

"Yes, sir. She gave it to me to keep my ears warm. I told her I'd bring it back to her."

"Huh!" he snorted. "She's probably not expecting to get it soaked in my blood."

After the bleeding had subsided, we helped the major get out from under the ambulance. We'd just gotten him settled on a pay chest when Franz and the others returned with the animals.

"That didn't take long," I said to Franz, who rode the major's horse. The corporal and the other soldiers were mounted on mules.

"They were in a bend in the creek about a mile away drinking unfrozen water," Franz said.

"We're short two mules," I said, indicating the two dead ones lying between the ambulances. "We need to redistribute the loads. Let's put all the pay chests in this one, and we'll hitch four mules to it. We'll place the wounded men and the grain sacks in the other. Two mules will be able to pull it."

"Let's get these two soldiers buried," Sergeant Marley said, pointing to the dead men. "Corporal, take two men and dig a grave down there." He pointed to a spot near the creek's edge. "The rest of you load the pay chests into this ambulance. You'll have to double stack them."

Fifteen minutes later the corporal returned. "Sarge," he said, "it's no use. That ground's frozen solid. We can't get a shovel into it."

"Bring them back," the sergeant said. "We'll take them to Fort Reno for burial."

We configured one of the ambulances with stretchers one above the other on one side and left the bench in place on the opposite side. We laid a body wrapped in a blanket on each stretcher, and the two wounded men sat on the bench. On the floor, around the feet of the wounded men, we piled the remaining sacks of grain. The loaded weight of this ambulance would be about half of the one carrying the pay chests. Franz shouldn't have any trouble driving a two-mule hitch to pull the load. I would drive the four-hitch ambulance.

By the time we'd gotten reorganized, the sun had set. Major Bonnet and Sergeant Marley decided we would remain where we were overnight.

CHAPTER 52

January 12 dawned cold and clear. The blinding glare off the snow made me wish we had goggles, but none were available when we departed Fort Laramie.

We got underway early and reached Dry Creek about midday. The snow had piled deeper since I'd ridden through there on Christmas Eve.

"Major," I asked, "recognize this place?"

"No."

"That snow bank to the right is Reverend Hollister's burned-out wagon. Those sticks visible under that cottonwood tree are the tops of the crosses over the preacher and his wife."

We did not pause but pressed on.

That night, we camped on Antelope Creek. Shortly after noon on the following day, January 13, we caught up to the tail end of Major Van Voast's column. One company of infantry, comprising the rear guard, stood in loose formation in the road behind the supply wagons that were at a standstill.

We pulled the ambulances up behind these troops and halted. Sergeant Marley, riding the major's horse, went on ahead to report to Major Van Voast that the paymaster had joined his force.

The soldiers in our squad struck up a conversation with the men in the trailing company and learned why Van Voast's caravan wasn't farther along. They'd confronted snow that had covered the Bozeman Trail to a depth of six feet on the flat.

When the road dipped between ridges, they often encountered ravines filled with ten-foot drifts. A company of soldiers would spend an hour shoveling a path through the snow, then those exhausted men would rotate to the rear while another company replaced them.

The head of the column lay a mile ahead of us. Fifty wagons pulled by six-mule teams stretched half a mile by themselves. Four companies of infantry marching four abreast, and two companies of cavalry riding two abreast, stretched another half mile.

Van Voast's units had run out of forage for their animals. The mules were eating the manes and tails of their companions. When out of harness, they gnawed chunks out of the wooden sides of the wagons and chewed holes in wagon tongues.

That night, the command camped in the road where the Dry Fork of the Powder River joined the main stream, sixteen miles from Fort Reno.

Midafternoon on Monday, January 14, we reached Fort Reno. Fording the Powder River proved miserably cold and wet for man and beast. We were glad to reach the high plateau where the fort sat. There wasn't room to accommodate our large force within the stockade, so the wagons went into circles of ten each. The animals were corralled within the circles. Attempts at driving tent pegs into frozen soil met with failure. The men would sleep under the wagons.

The frozen bodies of our two dead were placed in wooden coffins and stacked between the fort's wall and the hospital alongside the caskets of two local deceased soldiers. Burials would have to await warmer weather.

The hospital steward replaced Major Bonnet's makeshift shawl bandage with regular medical dressings. The major refused laudanum. He said the pain was slight compared to his memory of the time he'd lost his leg. He did accept a pair of crutches.

Before the day was over, Major Bonnet and I set up the folding pay table under a tent fly in front of the fort's headquarters. We paid the troops who would be left to garrison Fort Reno, but the major deferred paying all others until we reached Fort Phil Kearny.

Sergeant Marley and the remaining men of his squad were assigned to escort mail back to Fort Laramie. A private from Company B replaced Franz Stroebel as the driver of our second ambulance. The major would ride in my ambulance with Hector tied to the tail gate.

Early the next morning, January 15, Lieutenant Colonel Wessells led the way north. Major Van Voast had brought the orders for Wessells from Omaha appointing him commanding officer of Fort Phil Kearny and the Twenty-Seventh Infantry Regiment. He was also designated commander of the Mountain District, which was being reestablished. Although he served in a lower rank, Lieutenant Colonel Wessells would now be Colonel Carrington's superior.

The closer our column drew to the mountains and Fort Phil Kearny, the deeper the snow had drifted. Soldiers now shoveled snowdrifts seven to ten feet deep on the level. Swales were packed solid. Fortunately, the blizzard had ceased, and no additional snow was accumulating.

Despite the terrible conditions, we made it to Crazy Woman's Fork the first night and were able to get water for the men and the animals. One sentry froze to death that night. The men managed to dig a shallow grave in the hard ground, and we buried the deceased soldier beside the creek that continued to be the scene of repeated grief.

Two days later, January 17, we crossed Clear Creek and

passed Lake DeSmet. Late that afternoon, the sentries on Pilot Hill wigwagged to alert the fort of our arrival. Now that the storm had let up, Cloud Peak and the Big Horn Mountains loomed above us in majestic white splendor.

The garrison band greeted our passage through the main gate with "The Star-Spangled Banner." Cheers from the fort's residents almost drowned out the musicians. Jumping, hand waving, and hat tossing by the fort's occupants expressed their relief.

On the journey from Fort Reno, I'd kept the paymaster's two ambulances in line behind a cavalry squad that accompanied Lieutenant Colonel Wessells at the head of the column. When we entered Fort Phil Kearny, he and his escort turned right and halted at the entrance to the headquarters building. I stopped my ambulance in front of the guardhouse.

The three arriving infantry companies marched past us and formed up on the snow-covered parade ground. The two cavalry companies lined up behind the infantry on the west perimeter road in front of the officers' quarters. The fifty supply wagons rumbled through the gate and headed for the quartermaster yard.

Major Bonnet and I had a front-row ambulance seat from which to observe Colonel Carrington and Lieutenant Colonel Wessells exchange salutes and shake hands. Wessells was fifteen years older than Carrington. Neither officer was the young firebrand the soldiers considered best suited to fighting Indians. Colonel Carrington's shoulders slumped more than I'd remembered. Both he and Wessells were slender of build. The captains and lieutenants who congregated nearby stood a head taller than their two senior officers.

"That has to be hard," Major Bonnet said. "Colonel Carrington probably wasn't aware until now that General Wessells, as a lieutenant colonel, would be his superior."

"Didn't Colonel Carrington know this reorganization was going to happen?" I asked.

"He knew he'd retain command of the Eighteenth Infantry—what's left of it. That's what he asked for. But he would not have known that Omaha was reestablishing the Mountain District with Wessells to command it at a lower rank."

The long line of slow-moving freight wagons had taken some time to enter the fort. Their movement had blocked my view of the hospital, but when the last wagon passed, I stood up in the well of the driver's seat. Katy stood in front of the hospital. I yanked off my slouch hat and waved it overhead. She waved back.

"I think you have something more important to do than watch these officers transfer command," Major Bonnet said.

We exchanged grins.

"We'll secure the pay chests in the guardhouse," the major said. "I'll get the sergeant of the guard to have his men unload them."

"Thank you, sir. I'll come back shortly to move the ambulances into the quartermaster yard and take care of the mules."

"Get me down off this seat," he said. "Then you can go."

I helped him descend and settle his arms on the crutches. Then, I took off at a trot toward the hospital.

The major yelled after me, "Remember, you have to help with pay call tomorrow!"

Without looking, I raised a hand to acknowledge his shouted reminder.

As I approached Katy, I slowed to a walk. "I . . ." My grin spread from ear to ear. I could feel it.

"You don't have to say any more." Her equally broad smile made her dimples radiate. "You came back . . . safely."

I wanted to kiss her, but the stewards, patients, and surgeons also stood in front of the hospital to watch the procession.

"All right, men," Doctor Horton proclaimed. "Inside before we freeze."

He winked at me, and I blushed.

"Your shawl's in the ambulance," I told Katy. "It's not in the condition it was when you tied it around my ears."

I described our battle with the Arapahos. "I think I killed Duggan Maguire."

"I hope you did," Katy said. "That's not a proper Christian attitude, I know, but he and Running Bear have caused too much trouble."

I tucked my slouch hat between my knees, lifted the chain and shamrock pendant from around my neck, and lowered it around hers. "I'm sure it brought me luck. Thank you."

My hands came to rest on her shoulders, and I did not remove them.

Her face was inches from mine. She tilted her head up and pecked a kiss onto my chin.

"Zach, your whiskers scratch." She giggled.

"I'll shave."

"No, don't. It's scraggly right now. You'll have a nice beard after it's properly trimmed."

She stared at me with her mesmerizing smile. My desires overwhelmed my inhibitions, and I dropped my lips onto hers. She did not pull away. I slipped my hands to her waist and drew her close. I had never kissed a girl before. What a marvelous sensation.

I reluctantly broke the kiss. "Katy, I have to go. I'll be back later. And . . . Katy . . . I love you."

Before she could reply, I jammed my hat on and raced to the guardhouse. If I could have jumped and kicked my heels together, I would have. I glanced back in her direction and waved.

From the guardhouse, I drove the lead ambulance into the

quartermaster yard with the soldier driving the second one following. We groomed, fed, and watered the mules. The feed wasn't much—a forkful of hay. The wooden stalls of the stables revealed where the mules had chewed chunks out of the rails. Tails and manes were ragged where the hungry animals had dined on one another.

I offered a mental apology to Luke for bringing him to a place with no feed. Matt, Mark, and Moses had all lost weight. The ribs on the three Bible mules revealed their plight.

Captain Dandy, the new Mountain District Quartermaster, who'd been busy directing the unloading of the fifty freight wagons, approached while I was inspecting my mules.

"Mr. Wakefield," he said, "I have a proposition."

"Sir?"

"After you help Major Bonnet tomorrow, he will not need a clerk for awhile."

"I should go with him to Fort C. F. Smith, Captain . . . I mean, General?"

"Captain will do. As for traveling to Fort Smith—no one's been able to get north of here because of the snow. It's even worse than what's between Fort Reno and here. When the road's clear, and Major Bonnet feels it's safe to go, you can go with him. In the meantime, I'd like you to return to your duties as quartermaster clerk. I'll dock your pay for the time you were absent, of course, and I won't pay you when you're on the paymaster's payroll. What do you say?"

"I accept, Captain." I wasted no time making that decision.

"I've got others working in the warehouse trying to straighten out Captain Brown's paperwork. I hope you can help us get everything in order."

Captain Dandy apparently wasn't blaming me for the poor record keeping. I decided to remain silent.

A warehouseman who'd been unloading the freight wagons

interrupted us. "Captain, there isn't any grain in any of these wagons."

"None?" the captain asked.

"Whatever they had," the warehouseman said, "they consumed on the trail."

The captain pointed at the fenced hay enclosure. "That dwindling pile isn't going to last much longer. All these new cavalry horses and mules are going to starve right alongside our existing animals. General Wessells isn't going to like to hear this."

When I finished in the quartermaster yard, I took my saddlebags and bedroll to my old quarters. I wanted to reclaim my bunk before any of the newly arrived teamsters landed on it.

After I'd grabbed a bite to eat in the teamsters' mess, I went in search of Katy. She and Major Bonnet were sitting at the hospital's kitchen table drinking coffee and comparing notes on their respective arrow wounds. Katy offered me a cup of coffee, but I declined.

"Did you see Doctor Horton?" I asked the major.

"Yes. He said it was fortunate the arrowhead passed through without breaking a bone, like it did in Miss O'Toole's case. My recovery time will be shorter than hers."

I told Major Bonnet about my agreement with Captain Dandy.

"That's fine," the major said. "Pay call tomorrow will take most of the day. We'll get an early start. So, don't stay up too late." He looked from Katy to me with a big grin.

"No, sir," I said. "I'll be there on time."

The major stood and tucked his crutches under his arms. "If you two will excuse me, I'm going to go rest this leg."

After he left, Katy trimmed my beard with a pair of surgical scissors. She held a mirror up when she'd finished. I was glad I'd kept the beard.

"Well, handsome," she said, "let's not just sit here. Let's go see Fannie Grummond, and you can tell us about Portugee."

A few minutes later, Mrs. Carrington escorted us into her sitting room, where Mrs. Grummond sat on a sofa with her hands lying across her expanded abdomen.

"Sit down, Mr. Wakefield," Mrs. Carrington said, indicating a straight-backed chair opposite the couch. From her sleeve, she withdrew a lacy handkerchief and held it to her lips. She turned her head to the side and coughed more harshly than I'd heard before. She noticed my concerned look. "It's just the weather." She slipped the pink-tinged handkerchief into her sleeve.

Mrs. Carrington sat to one side of Mrs. Grummond, and Katy sat on the other.

I described my troubles in catching up to Portugee and how he had probably experienced similar ones. I told them how Portugee had disrupted the Fort Laramie officers and wives engaged in a Christmas ball. I also told them about Portugee's frostbitten fingers and toes.

"And how is Mr. Phillips now?" Fannie asked.

"When I left Fort Laramie, he'd been discharged from the hospital, but he was not in any condition to travel with us. He was fortunate he didn't lose any fingers or toes. My guess is he will return here with the next supply train."

"I'd hoped to thank him personally for what he did, but we may not be here that long." Fannie looked at Mrs. Carrington.

"Probably not," Mrs. Carrington said. "The colonel informed me earlier this evening to start packing. We are transferring to Fort Caspar, as you may know."

"Yes, ma'am," I said. "I heard that."

"Mr. Wakefield," Mrs. Carrington asked, "I assume you read the newspapers while you were at Fort Laramie?"

"Yes, ma'am. I did."

"What do the folks there think of the stories we are reading today for the first time?"

She was referring to the mail we'd brought that included several Eastern newspapers containing fallacious stories about the Fetterman fight. One article quoted the Commissioner of Indian Affairs, located in Washington, D.C., as stating the number of Indians engaged was greatly exaggerated. Another article claimed the inhabitants of Fort Phil Kearny were at fault because the ladies were in the habit of throwing packages of sugar over the stockade walls to appease the squaws. The most far-fetched account claimed Fetterman's men were slaughtered outside the walls of the fort when the commanding officer refused to open the gate to let them in.

"I told anybody who would listen that the articles were false," I said. "I don't understand why reporters and officials who were not present make up such tales."

We sat quietly for a moment. The only sound came from the ticking of a clock perched on the mantle above the brick fireplace.

"It's time we go, Zach." Katy stood quickly. "These ladies have to prepare for their travel."

After leaving the Carringtons' residence, we'd only taken two steps when Katy abruptly stopped. "I'm going with them," she said.

"What? What about us?"

"Well," she said. "What *about* us?"

"I thought we loved each other."

"Just because we love each other doesn't mean I have to stay here."

"Well . . . no, but what about us?" I repeated.

"That's what I asked you," she countered.

"I thought we might get married."

"Is that a proposal?"

"Well . . . I reckon."

"You reckon? Is that the best you can do?"

Conflicting thoughts swirled through my mind. Married? Yes, I'd been thinking about it.

"I'm waiting!" She uttered the statement as a command.

"Oh . . . will you marry me, Kathleen O'Toole?" I blurted out.

"Aye!" She threw her arms around me and planted her lips firmly against mine.

My God! Kissing her was great! She had my arms pinned against my sides for a second, but I slipped them free and gathered her against me. I'd done it! I'd asked her to marry me. So—there had been a good reason for me staying at Fort Phil Kearny instead of going to the Montana goldfields.

We walked arm in arm to the hospital. She made a fresh pot of coffee. We sat across the table from each other, fingers entwined with one hand and cups held with the other. We talked late into the night.

I asked Katy when she'd determined she loved me.

"When you decided to go help Portugee," Katy said, "my thoughts coalesced. Brandon Hollister abandoned me for a squaw. Duggan Maguire lied to me about who he was. Captain Fetterman never really showed any interest in me. He was consumed with his own self importance. I know I told you I considered you to be like a brother. It didn't occur to me that the way I expressed it might offend you or hurt you. I was trying to convey my respect for your honesty and judgment. You have never lied to me. You always supported me. I guess I had been thinking of you as more than a *brother* for quite some time . . . yet not realizing it. It was when you opened the water gate, and I knew you were really going, I realized I would be devastated if I lost you."

"I've been in love with you since the first time I saw you at Fort Laramie," I said.

"I know." Her dimples were teasing and beguiling. It was well after midnight and much discussion that I accepted her decision to accompany Fannie Grummond on what would undoubtedly be an arduous journey.

CHAPTER 53

The next morning, Friday, January 18, I helped Major Bonnet prepare for pay call. I told him I'd visited the Carringtons' residence the evening before and learned they planned to leave soon.

"I saw General Cooke's order transferring Colonel Carrington," the major said. "I see Captain Bisbee's hand in drafting it. The wording makes it sound like the colonel's reassignment is punishment for the Fetterman fight."

Because of the freezing weather, Major Bonnet forwent the regimental parade formation. The band did not play. The companies assembled one at a time in front of the guardhouse. After the company commander presented his muster roll, the men entered singly to collect their pay. Even though a potbellied stove heated the guardhouse, with the number of times the door opened and closed, we might as well have been outside.

That day, the military payroll totaled over eight hundred personnel, counting officers, enlisted men, and the laundresses. Major Bonnet advanced funds to Captain Dandy to pay one hundred seventy civilian quartermaster employees, including the fifty teamsters who had just arrived. The major also reimbursed Captain Dandy for outstanding vouchers to pay the contractors, who in turn would pay their fifty employees. A dozen sutler employees would be paid after the soldiers settled their IOUs at the store.

Over a thousand people now jammed the confines of Fort

Phil Kearny. Since I did double duty as commissary clerk, I had first-hand knowledge of the lack of food supplies. The garrison's beef herd had numbered seven hundred when we'd arrived in July. Now, partly through consumption, but mainly due to losses from repeated Indian raids, the herd was less than one hundred. The commissary warehouse had no potatoes, no cabbages, no desiccated vegetables. Soldiers were sent into the woods to scrounge for wild onions to help fend off scurvy. Additional cases of that disease showed up at the hospital daily.

At payday's end, I helped Major Bonnet close out the muster rolls. Most of the pay chests were empty. A couple still contained enough cash to pay the troops at Fort C. F. Smith. When we would travel there remained anybody's guess.

Katy joined me that evening for a meager supper at the teamsters' mess. I had to pay the cook extra for her meal, but I didn't mind. I had received my pay earlier in the day. After eating, we returned to the hospital and sat at the kitchen table. This was the most private place out of the weather we had found.

"Shall I ask Chaplain White to perform a wedding ceremony for us?" I'd pondered that question all day and finally drummed up enough courage to pose it.

"No," Katy replied.

"You've changed your mind about getting married?"

"No."

"You don't like Chaplain White?"

"No. I don't want to get married in this sad place. I want my mother and father to be in attendance. I want to go back to Pennsylvania."

"*Pennsylvania?* What about your plans to go to Montana? What about *my* plans to go to Montana?"

"Zach, Montana will be there after we're married. I'm not suggesting we live in Pennsylvania. I've grown fond of the West.

But we don't know how far Red Cloud has taken this war into Montana. We've had no communication from north of here for weeks. I don't consider any place on the Bozeman Trail a safe place to live right now."

On Saturday, January 19, the weather, which had remained clear since General Wessells led the relief column into Fort Phil Kearny, turned ugly again. The Big Horn Mountains existed, but they rose invisibly to the west. The Montana Road remained deserted. No signal flags waved from Pilot Hill. Timber cutting at the pineries was reduced to felling enough trees to provide firewood. No Indian signal mirrors flashed from the Sullivant Hills. No wood train had to fight off savages. The inhabitants of the garrison slowly starved on half rations. The mules and horses suffered even more.

Each evening, over the next few days, the musicians gathered in the bandstand at the flagpole and entertained the garrison. Soldiers swept snow off the road in front of the officers' quarters and invited the ladies to dance. Of necessity, some men wore a kerchief tied to their bicep to indicate they were substitutes for females. Katy did better dancing with capable soldiers than with me. Had she planned to remain at the fort, I might become jealous.

Katy and I spent as much time together as we could. Most of that time was in the evenings after work. She kept busy as a hospital matron. I tried to help Captain Dandy make sense of the incomplete quartermaster and jumbled commissary records.

Colonel Carrington selected January 23, 1867, as his departure date. Katy had been with Fannie Grummond and Mrs. Carrington when the colonel told them that, despite the cold weather, he had received orders for immediate transfer, and he could no longer stay at Fort Phil Kearny.

Captain Dandy asked me to coordinate the preparation of wagons to transport the families to Fort Caspar. In addition to the Carringtons and Mrs. Grummond, there were Lieutenant Wands's wife and son, and three families of band members. The band was attached to the Eighteenth Infantry and would transfer to the new headquarters.

Officers were entitled to an ambulance for transporting their families, but Captain Dandy decided that, like the earlier departure of the Bisbees, the army blue freight wagon was more suitable. Despite being un-sprung, the wagon was larger and more solidly built. The fort's carpenters doubled the canvas covers and boarded up the sides and ends. They installed a window at the front and a door with a window at the rear. The blacksmiths fashioned small sheet-iron stoves with a vent pipe that extended through the canvas roof. As fuel for the stoves, pine knots and pre-cut wood blocks were loaded into each wagon. A separate wagon was filled with additional firewood. In each family wagon, a straw mattress was laid on the floor and topped with a regulation hospital mattress. Buffalo rugs were scattered on the floor boards. A chair was placed in each wagon for the lady. Portugee Phillips's wolf robe graced the chair in Fannie Grummond's wagon.

The morning of January 23 came too soon. Following two days of clear weather, snow started falling at sunrise that Wednesday morning. The temperature plunged to thirty-eight below zero. After breakfast, I turned the collar up on my jacket and trudged from the teamsters' mess to the hospital. The weather was the least thing depressing about the day. Katy was departing.

I was surprised to see Major Bonnet hobbling on his crutches toward the hospital.

"Are you ill, Major?" I asked.

"No, Zach, I'm not ill. Just coming to say goodbye to Katy."

He and I entered the hospital and found Katy finishing her breakfast of hardtack and coffee in the kitchen area. She offered us coffee, but we refused. She cleaned her cup and plate and returned them to the cupboard.

"Kathleen O'Toole and Zachary Wakefield," Major Bonnet said. "I'm glad to have found you together in a private place. I am pleased you are betrothed. I've watched you both mature under difficult circumstances. You will make a fine couple. Katy, do you still have the shamrock pendant?"

"Aye, Major." Katy lifted it on the chain from beneath her dress. "Do you want it back?"

"Oh, no. It's your shamrock now. I know you will cherish it." The major took Katy's hand and laid a double eagle gold coin in her palm. "This is my wedding gift to you both. Take this and have a jeweler change the initials on the reverse to yours."

Katy closed her fingers over the coin, leaned forward, and placed a kiss on the major's cheek. "Thank you, Major Bonnet. Zach and I will honor the shamrock forever."

"Thank you, also, Katy," the major said, "for letting Zach stay with me to finish my job."

Katy laughed. "He didn't exactly volunteer to go with me." Her dimples accented her teasing remark when she glanced at me.

I'd hoped to spend the morning with Katy, but that was not to be. She kept busy helping Fannie Grummond get settled in her wagon, assisting Mrs. Carrington hustle Harry and Jimmy into their wagon, and aiding Jenny Wands in getting little Bobby loaded into theirs. Katy also lent a hand to bandmember Sergeant Fessenden's wife in settling baby Sedgwick into a nest of blankets in a cradle in their wagon.

William Bailey, who'd ridden with Portugee to Horseshoe Station and who regularly traveled the mail route to Fort Caspar, had been designated as guide. At 1:30 p.m., Colonel

Carrington exchanged salutes with Lieutenant Colonel Wessells, and the procession headed out the main gate.

Bailey led while Colonel Carrington rode beside First Lieutenant Wilbur Arnold, the Eighteenth's adjutant. Second Lieutenant Alpheus Bowman followed at the head of a detachment of twenty cavalrymen. Then came forty infantrymen, of whom twenty-five were members of the band, all under the command of Lieutenant Wands. The soldiers marched with Springfield rifle-muskets at right-shoulder arms.

The first wagon through the gate was loaded with axes, shovels, and picks. Men would rotate through the thankless task of serving in a pioneer corps to clear snow off the road. Assistant Surgeon C. M. Hines rode a horse alongside this wagon.

Next came Mrs. Carrington sequestered within her enclosed wagon. I could not see her or her boys. George, the Carringtons' servant, walked beside the wagon. His final duty at Fort Phil Kearny had been to cook Mrs. Carrington's last live turkey.

Mrs. Wands's wagon followed next. Laura, that family's black servant, walked alongside it. Surely, she would eventually be invited to ride inside.

When the wagon bearing Fannie Grummond and Katy rolled past, I stepped in behind it and followed along as they approached the gate. Katy was looking out through the frosted pane of the rear door's window. She laid a hand against the glass. Lengths of chain were wound around her fingers, and the shamrock pendant nestled in her palm. I touched my lips with my fingers and blew her a kiss. I stepped aside when the wagon passed through the gate.

Trailing Fannie's wagon rolled a freight wagon carrying the frozen body of her husband. Brevet Lieutenant Colonel George Washington Grummond's corpse had been exhumed the day before, and his pine-board coffin now commenced its journey toward reburial in Tennessee. Fannie had written to her family in Franklin asking her brother to come to Dakota Territory to help her get back to the States. The weather had abated enough on January 4 that a mail courier had been sent to Fort Laramie. Fannie could only hope her letter would be delivered and her brother would meet her somewhere along the way.

After the remaining family wagons and the wagon transporting the spare firewood passed, two dozen empty wagons rumbled by. The empties would go only as far as Ft. Reno, from where they would return with desperately needed food and forage.

Katy had neither complained nor objected when I made the decision not to go with her. I felt I owed Major Bonnet the courtesy of serving as his clerk when the weather permitted us to travel to Fort C. F. Smith. No word had been received from that isolated post on the Big Horn River since before the Fetterman affair. Perhaps the Indians had turned their vengeance on that tiny garrison and wiped it out. Jim Bridger had not returned from Montana, or if he had tried, perhaps he lay scalped somewhere along the way.

I climbed onto the empty southeast bastion. Pilot Hill hid its summit in the low clouds. The caravan bearing my love disappeared into the snow falling on the Bozeman Trail.

"God speed, Kathleen. When will I see you again?"

HISTORICAL AFTERWORD

Upon arriving at Fort Caspar on January 27, 1867, Colonel Henry Carrington received orders to relocate headquarters to Fort McPherson, Nebraska. While fending off an Indian attack during the journey taking his command from Fort Caspar to Fort Laramie, Carrington accidentally shot himself in the thigh. The colonel recuperated at Fort Laramie for two weeks before proceeding to Fort McPherson.

Frances Grummond reburied her husband in Franklin, Tennessee, in March 1867. On April 14, she gave birth to a son, William Wands Grummond. Soon after, she discovered her husband had been a bigamist. The first wife had already been awarded George's pension, but Fannie eventually got the courts to award her one, also.

In March 1867, a commission investigated the Fetterman massacre. The *Sanborn Report*, named for the chairman, found ". . . the commanding officer [Carrington] of the district was furnished no more troops or supplies for this state of war than had been provided and furnished him in a state of profound peace. In regions where all was peace, as at Laramie in November, twelve companies were stationed, while in regions where all was war, as at Phil Kearny, there were only five companies allowed."

The Department of the Interior's Bureau of Indian Affairs, always at odds with the War Department on how to treat the Indians in Dakota Territory, mysteriously filed the *Sanborn*

Report away. Colonel Carrington struggled for twenty years to get the report published to clear his name.

Throughout 1867, freighters refused to haul supplies to Fort Phil Kearny at any price. Because of forage shortage, Lieutenant Colonel Wessells sent the Second Cavalry back to Fort Laramie early in the winter of 1867. The troopers made it, but all one hundred fifty horses died on the march.

Jim Bridger returned to Fort Phil Kearny from Fort C. F. Smith in the spring of 1867. He published a lengthy statement in the *Army and Navy Journal* in June 1867 supporting Carrington's policies. He stated: "The only way to settle the question is to send out a sufficient number of troops to completely whip the hostile Sioux, Cheyennes, and Arapahos and make them sue for peace."

Two battles occurred in August 1867 that removed some stain from the Fetterman incident. The Hayfield Fight occurred on August 1 near Fort C. F. Smith, and the Wagon-Box Fight took place west of Fort Phil Kearny on August 2. In both cases, a small army force using newly issued breech-loading Springfield rifles defeated larger Indian forces. The rapidity with which the soldiers could load and fire the new weapons surprised their attackers.

In April 1868, another peace commission convened at Fort Laramie. Many chiefs agreed to the new treaty, but Red Cloud refused to sign until the Montana Road was closed. On May 19, 1868, Major General Christopher Augur, who had replaced Major General Phillip St. George Cooke as commander of the Department of the Platte, ordered the "Powder River" posts closed. In August 1868, the Indians burned the abandoned forts to the ground. Red Cloud signed the treaty at Fort Laramie on November 6, 1868. The only war in which the Indians defeated the army was over.

In 1868, Margaret Carrington published *Absaraka: Home of*

the Crows. Her memoir, written at the suggestion of Lieutenant General William T. Sherman, provides a first-hand account of life at Fort Phil Kearny.

In 1870, Carrington retired from the army. That same year, Margaret Carrington, 39 years old, died from tuberculosis. Frances Grummond wrote a letter of condolence to the colonel, and their continued correspondence led to her marrying Henry Carrington in 1871.

In 1888, the remains of soldiers originally buried at Fort Phil Kearny were reburied at the Custer National Cemetery at Little Bighorn Battlefield National Monument, Montana. Some believe the bodies of civilians, like photographer Ridgway Glover, were not included in the transfer. No photographs Glover took in the Powder River region have been found.

John "Portugee" Phillips returned to Fort Phil Kearny in early 1867 and worked as a mail carrier. He later married Hattie Buck in 1870. They named one of their children Paul Revere Phillips. Portugee died in 1881 at age 51. In 1930, at the site of Fort Phil Kearny, the Historical Landmark Commission of Wyoming erected a monument commemorating Phillips's ride.

The real, German-born, paymaster for the Mountain District, Henry Almstedt, had served with various Missouri units during the Civil War. Following the war, as an Additional Paymaster with the rank of major, he served along the Bozeman Trail. The National Archives cannot locate a copy of his retirement records, and little is known about his life after leaving the army in 1868. He died in 1884.

On July 3, 1908, several survivors of the Fort Phil Kearny garrison attended a memorial celebration in Sheridan, Wyoming, a town that had grown up near the old haying fields along Goose Creek. The entourage traveled to "Massacre Hill" to dedicate a monument at the scene of the Fetterman fight. Henry Carrington, accompanied by wife Frances, gave a speech exonerating his actions while commanding officer. The monument contains the statement: "There Were No Survivors." An Indian participant in the battle, viewing the monument in later years, wondered why he was still standing there.

Red Cloud outlived all major Sioux leaders. He died at age 87 at Pine Ridge Reservation in South Dakota in 1909.

In 1910, Frances C. Carrington published *My Army Life and the Fort Phil Kearney Massacre*. The title inexplicably adds an *e* to the fort's name. The book describes her experiences at the fort and the struggles her second husband underwent to reclaim his reputation.

Frances Carrington died, probably of tuberculosis, at age 66 in 1911. Henry Beebe Carrington died in 1912 at the age of 88.

Native Americans call the battle "Hundred in the Hand." The chiefs finally decided to execute their ambush plan only after a Hee-man-eh (transgender) clairvoyant predicted he had "a hundred men" in his hands.

Some sources claim Crazy Horse was among the decoys who enticed Fetterman to cross Lodge Trail Ridge. This famous warrior's name does not appear in the contemporary accounts of the battle, because at that time he was unknown to the military.

Fort Phil Kearny is a National Historic Landmark. One stockade wall has been partially reconstructed and plaques placed to identify where structures stood. A museum and bookstore are operated by the Fort Phil Kearny/Bozeman Trail Association. Nothing remains of Fort Reno or Fort C. F. Smith except for small location monuments at the sites.

Modern-day historians prefer to call the battle the "Fetterman Fight" or the "Fetterman Disaster." At the time it occurred, the press, the army, and even the United States Congress referred to it as the "Fetterman Massacre."

ABOUT THE AUTHOR

Robert Lee Murphy was a paymaster himself. In 1961–1964, he was an army finance captain responsible for paying troops stationed in northern France.

Murphy's *The Iron Horse Chronicles* trilogy received one bronze and two silver Will Rogers Medallions. The second book was awarded first place in fiction by the Wyoming State Historical Society.

As a civilian, Murphy worked for over thirty years on all seven continents. Murphy Peak in Antarctica is named in recognition of his work supporting polar science. Murphy is a member of Western Writers of America, the Fort Phil Kearny/ Bozeman Trail Association, the Wyoming State Historical Society, the Society of Children's Book Writers & Illustrators, the Railway & Locomotive Historical Society, and Anthem Authors.

Visit the author at his website: https://robertleemurphy.net.

The employees of Five Star Publishing hope you have enjoyed this book.

Our Five Star novels explore little-known chapters from America's history, stories told from unique perspectives that will entertain a broad range of readers.

Other Five Star books are available at your local library, bookstore, all major book distributors, and directly from Five Star/Gale.

Connect with Five Star Publishing

Website:
gale.com/five-star

Facebook:
facebook.com/FiveStarCengage

Twitter:
twitter.com/FiveStarCengage

Email:
FiveStar@cengage.com

For information about titles and placing orders:
(800) 223-1244
gale.orders@cengage.com

To share your comments, write to us:
Five Star Publishing
Attn: Publisher
10 Water St., Suite 310
Waterville, ME 04901

.